## Praise for Edith Layton's
## *The Cad*

"The very best romance novels are almost like an adrenaline rush: there's the excitement of realizing that you are hooked, the intense focus that comes with being totally engrossed and the sweet, oh-so-satisfied letdown when the last page is turned. *The Cad* gave me all of this and more. . . . **THIS ONE GOES STRAIGHT TO THE KEEPER SHELF. . . . WONDERFUL.**"
—*Romance Reader*

**"A REAL TREASURE."**
—*Romantic Times*

**"TITILLATING, DANGEROUS, AND IRRESISTIBLE** . . . full of passion and plot twists that I could never have imagined. **BRAVA, MS. LAYTON!"**
—*Under the Covers*

ALSO BY EDITH LAYTON

*The Cad*

# The Choice

## Edith Layton

HarperPaperbacks
*A Division of* HarperCollins*Publishers*

📖 HarperPaperbacks
*A Division of* HarperCollins*Publishers*
10 East 53rd Street, New York, NY 10022-5299

ISBN 0-06-101392-7

HarperCollins®, 📖®, and HarperPaperbacks™ are
trademarks of HarperCollins Publishers Inc.

Cover illustration © 1999 by Jim Griffin
Cover design © 1999 by Saksa Art & Design

First printing: August 1999

Printed in the United States of America

Visit HarperPaperbacks on the World Wide Web at
http://www.harpercollins.com

❖ 10 9 8 7 6 5 4 3 2 1

For Norbert, of course.
Now, as then, and always.

# 1

It was mild, but cool in contrast to the ballroom. The trees above him were in full green leaf, the music from the ball seemed faint and faraway, and somewhere a nightingale did scales.

It was a small walled garden, cleverly designed, Damon thought. London had built itself up at an incredible pace since he'd gone abroad, but the best townhouses still had gardens. Damon was grateful for it. He stood alone in the shadows, near a stone cherub tipping his pitcher of water so it spilled into a small pool. The tumbling water sounded better to Damon's ears than the music of the waltz he heard faintly from afar. There was a bench, but he stood, his back against a tree, one ankle crossed over the other, relaxing, smoking his thin cheroot. His friends thought it was a filthy habit he'd picked up on his travels. It was. But he thought it better than shoveling snuff up his nose, the way they did. And it had gotten him outside now. He stared up at a camellia-colored moon and decided the fashionable world of London was much better seen through a thin blue smoky haze.

He soon saw it much more clearly.

"*Here!*" a male voice called excitedly. It was so close, Damon's pulse raced. He dropped his cheroot, grinding the glowing ash beneath his heel. From force of habit, his hand snaked into an inner waistcoat pocket, closing around the small pistol he always carried there.

There was a patter of footsteps on the shell path as a gentleman and a lady suddenly exploded from the shadows into the moonlight in front of the cherub. Damon's shoulders relaxed. They were unaware of him.

The moon lit them theatrically. He had to think fast. An assignation, probably. Why else would a man and a maid stray from a ball, and go off alone into the moonlight? A married or engaged couple wouldn't have to, a proper couple wouldn't dare. It would be awkward for all of them if they noticed him. Maybe they'd move on. He hoped so. From where he stood it was better than a front row at the theater. And just as bad. Because a man leaving a front row seat before the act was over made himself noticed by everyone in the audience, and was an insult to the actors, too.

But there was no place Damon could go without being seen. There was nothing but bushes at his back, and the garden wall behind those. He was a captive unless they left. Even if he stepped lightly he'd set the shrubbery to rattling. He sighed and resigned himself to being uncomfortable—bored, at best. Or so he thought until he saw the lady clear.

"Where is the poor thing?" she asked worriedly, looking into the shadows.

Damon shrank back. The sprite! Unmistakable. He'd noticed her earlier, inside, at the ball. He'd noticed little else after that. She wore a pale gauzy green gown that showed a small, delicately curved figure to perfection. She was so lithe, it had taken him a moment to realize she had all those curves when she'd first danced into his view. Because, for once, it hadn't been the first thing he'd seen.

Hair pale as moonlight, little animated oval of a face glowing bright as sunlight. Her small, even features made a man look twice at that pretty pink mouth. He couldn't see the color of her eyes from where he'd stood. She was the most enchanting female he'd seen since he'd come to London. She'd looked ethereal as she'd stepped through the intricate paces of the country dance.

He'd forgotten what he was about to say.

"Even you?" His friend laughed when he saw it. "Even such a rebellious jaded rogue as you, Damon, find her delectable? Well, but she *is* something, isn't she? Utterly ineligible, of course. At least for you and me. Too well-connected to sport with. Not half enough to wed. But something to look at, isn't she?"

"Ineligible? How so?" he asked, his eyes never leaving her.

"A ward, merely, of the Viscount Sinclair's. But there's

no birth there at all. No money neither, except for whatever Sinclair decides to settle on her. She and her sister are orphans. Their parents were great friends of the family or somesuch, who knows? There it is. Obscure or nonexistent family, parents complete unknowns. Lovely piece though, ain't she? Why can't I find needy orphans like that? If Sinclair wasn't . . . the man defends her like she *was* his daughter. And he, the greatest rake in London Town after his wife died, until he wed again. Still—who better than he to know a fellow's evil intentions? He's a devil with the sword and a demon with pistols. Yet there's that wretched Dearborne prancing with her. He'd better watch his step in more than the dance. So should she. A rake's one thing. But there's no greater cad in London than Dearborne."

Damon had watched, waiting for the music to stop. But when it did, the sprite immediately waltzed off with another gentleman.

"Fortune or no, her dance card's probably filled," his friend said with a smug smile. "Serves you right for coming so late. Don't worry, you won't be alone long. Most of the females in the room are watching you, hoping you'll claim their next waltz. Daresay not a few would burn their dance cards for the chance."

He had been noticed, Damon knew that. Not only by eager mamas and their wallflowers. Many of the dancers were looking at him, too, even as they whirled around the floor with other men. He'd been told he was attractive, and had used that information to his benefit many times. He also had funds now, and supposedly everyone knew that, too. But that wasn't the reason for the fascinated stares he was attracting.

But he was not as interested in them. Apart from the sprite, the young women at the ball all looked alike to him tonight. Most were dressed in the height of fashion, in simple white Grecian-style gowns that made them look like garden statues. They all sounded alike, too, and were about as animated as what they resembled.

He'd been to one ball already this week, and had passed an interminable hour at Almack's just last night. He suddenly discovered he couldn't stand another round of flirtation. Not another forced giggle, flippant answer, or ripple of artificial laughter.

"You're as much hunter as prey now," his friend had said before chortling, echoing his own thoughts. "Bad enough you're so eligible and came here at the end of the Season when they're the most desperate. You let it get out that you're shopping for a wife. A mistake."

"I don't think so," Damon said. "A man in the market for a bargain is better off being honest about it. That's how he learns about all the available merchandise."

"Trade's one thing, the marriage mart is another. Well, even if you *do* have a point, you'll soon get tired of being hounded. Some of these mamas are like bloodhounds. You'll find yourself treed if you don't watch out."

"But that's exactly what I want," Damon said.

"Ho! Then you haven't seen how a good man can be trapped by circumstances. Mind you don't end up married to a Gorgon with a clever mama. London's a dangerous place for a bachelor."

"The danger," Damon said, "is sometimes the best part of the hunt."

"You've just got back from abroad, and savage regions at that. You're only used to being hunted by red Indians and wolves and such. You haven't gone up against a desperate society mama yet. Watch your step!"

Damon laughed. He knew he was being tracked, but reckoned he'd get used to it. He had to. He was serious about finding a suitable bride and this was the best way to go about it. Newly returned to England, he wanted to settle, refurnish his home, and that included producing children to fill it. He needed someone of breeding to help him achieve that.

But he wanted someone he could talk with, too. Passion and pleasure were easy. Love, obviously, was not. One would have to come after the other in his case, no matter what the poets said. He didn't put much stock in what they said anyway. None of them were that successful at love or marriage, at least judging from all the longing and disappointment in their work.

Damon was not a romantic. He expected to find love in marriage—if he chose right. He would. He had access to the cream of London society, young women whose birth and fortune was the highest in the land.

But not tonight. He'd find a likely female in time, but now he was suddenly restless and out of patience. He'd eyed the sprite. It turned out she was ineligible, and otherwise engaged, as well. He found himself curiously reluctant to pursue his quest further now.

He looked toward the windows. "I'm off to blow a cloud," he'd told his friend and stalked out of the ball-room. He went down the long marble hall, out on the terrace, stepped down a fan of shallow stairs, and walked out into the peace of the garden.

Which had just been disrupted by the fairy-like vision he'd seen at the ball. He recognized her before she turned that flaxen head. He needed no more than a glimpse. She was radiant, her skin luminous in the pale light. Even her slender arms were shapely, he thought, entranced. But she was here with young Dearborne?

A young lady could dally with a gentleman, he supposed. But not when the gentleman had such a bad reputation that even he, so lately arrived in London, had heard about it. Lord Dearborne didn't have a decent bone in his whole long, comely body. He was more than a rake. Handsome as sin, they all said, and just as virtuous. He was famous for his folly and for leading females into it. And then abandoning them.

So what in God's name was the chit doing romping out into the garden with him? Unless she wanted to entrap him? But what woman with half a brain would want such a rogue? Unless she was lost to shame—or could she be a fool? Or an innocent beguiled?

He was a captive audience, but the drama was suddenly riveting. And potentially disturbing. The last thing he needed to see tonight was this lovely creature locked in another man's arms. He wondered whether to step out of the shadow, or stay. Until Dearborne spoke. Then Damon's eyes narrowed.

"But it was here just two minutes ago," Dearborne said. "It can't have got far. I told you its paw was bleeding. Poor little creature. I ought to have brought it into the house, but you know old Merriman, he'd cut up stiff if I brought an animal into the house the night of his daughter's ball."

"But if it was bleeding! Were you afraid to get your fine feathers dirty?" she asked, with a hint of a sneer.

Nothing short of cannon fire would dislodge Damon now.

"Well, I certainly wasn't going to carry a sick puppy into the house," Dearborne said. "Can you imagine the screech the ladies would set up? But *you* said you liked dogs and it was such a charming pup. And you've got such pluck, everyone says so. . . . Wait—I think I heard something."

She stopped, tilting her head to listen. *Adorable*, Damon thought. She was so slender and fine-boned she looked like a creature out of a story he'd heard in the nursery. He almost expected to see gossamer wings on her back when she spun on her heel, turning her head to hear more than the nightingale.

"Well, I guess we'll have to go look," she said with an audible sigh. "Can't leave it suffering alone in the dark." She gathered her skirt in two hands, lifting the hem from her slippers so it wouldn't be wet by the dew, preparing to step into the shrubbery in search of whatever it was she thought was hiding there.

Damon drew in a breath and tried to think of a plausible reason explaining his presence, should she happen to bump into him. At the same time he couldn't help hoping she'd do just that.

He could have saved himself the bother. Because a second later, young Dearborne's arms wrapped around the sprite. She froze and looked up at him. Their faces were close. Damon's own face was a study in annoyance and frustration. The last thing he wanted to watch was an expert seduction. Or was it an attempted assault? Would it turn into a seduction? He held his breath.

"Let me go," she said in flat, cold tones.

"Why should I?" Dearborne asked smoothly, gathering her even closer, tipping her face up to his with one hand. "You danced with me with every evidence of delight. You liked my jests, my style, my wit. Now we'll see if you like my kisses. I'm willing to wager you will."

"Let me go," she said firmly.

"Oh, I think not," Dearborne chuckled, and lowered his head to hers.

Damon readied himself to spring from the shadows. If she seemed to want him to. Because although he hated to admit it, this might have been exactly what she'd asked for.

She turned her head away and said, "No!"

Dearborne laughed and forced her face back toward his own. She grimaced and struggled, pushing at his shoulders, angling away from him as Dearborne chuckled, pressing in closer.

Damon burst from the bushes. He heard a high-pitched cry of agony. He rushed forward—and paused, astonished, realizing whose cry he heard.

The first thing she did was bring up her knee in a flash, hard and accurately. Damon couldn't help wincing at her precision and timing, even as young Dearborne shrieked and doubled over, clutching his groin. Once Dearborne folded, the sprite raised linked hands high over her head and slammed them down on the back of his neck. As he fell, she slammed the heel of her hand up against his nose. He lay writhing at her feet, bleeding, groaning, and trying to protect first one part and then another as she kicked him again and again.

Damon had to subdue the attacker just as he'd planned. But not the attacker he'd anticipated. He wrapped two arms around her middle and dragged her, spitting and kicking, from the man on the ground.

"Have done!" Damon shouted in her ear, because she was so determined to slay the man at her feet, it seemed she was trying to kill Damon for stopping her. It was lucky he'd had to fight even more savage opponents in the regions he'd just returned from. They didn't fight fair either.

"He's done, take a look," he panted in her ear, trying to catch her flailing hands in his as she tried to remove his nose. "Finished. Bloody and bowed. You won, call in the mortician. Ouch! Damnation!" He side-stepped another lethal knee. "He's done for, I said. Have done!"

"I'll kill him," she said through clenched teeth. "The damned lying rogue, the villain, the bloody, dismal, rot-gutted whoreson of a . . . Oh."

She stopped struggling when she finally realized Damon's intent was only to calm her. She stood still, breathing hard. He dared release one of her hands. She raised it to brush back a bit of bright hair that had fallen over her eyes. She stared up at him. They were very close. He looked down, warily, into that enchanting face.

"Thank you," she said, keeping her eyes riveted on his, "I—I believe I was extremely vexed and seem to have lost my head."

"No," he said, fascinated, "actually, you almost removed his."

She glanced down at the man on the ground at their feet. So did Damon. Dearborne was laying still enough to alarm him. But after a second Damon was relieved to note one of the man's hands starting to claw feebly at the ground, and he heard him finally utter a muffled groan. He turned his attention back to the sprite. Her lovely mouth twisted.

"Remove his head? I wish you'd let me! He's not really damaged. It's just blood," she said with a sneer. "Huh! Although he's willing to try to maul a woman, he's just a dainty flower himself. After a week or two he'll be mended and up to his foul tricks again. His face is still pretty enough. Too bad a man's character don't show in his face."

"Nor does a woman's," Damon said, with a hint of laughter in his voice. "I thought I was going to have to rescue you. I didn't know there was an avenging angel hidden behind that innocent face of yours."

He could feel her shoulders stiffen and realized he was still holding her. He dropped his hands at once. "Were you following me?" she asked suddenly, her eyes widening.

"I might ask that of you," he said reasonably. "I was here first, having a nice, quiet smoke, when you decided to cut up my peace and go a few rounds with that cad."

"Oh. Well, I didn't see you. He told me there was a puppy in trouble out here."

Now Damon groaned. "And you believed him?"

"I'm not such a flat," she said, her chin coming up.

"Well, I *almost* believed him. He sounded convincing. But I knew his reputation. I decided to have a look anyway. I wasn't worried," she said to his expression of astonishment, "because I knew that if he was lying I could take care of myself."

"Indeed," Damon said with wonder, "and so you did. But what if. . . ."

"If he'd had a pistol? Or a knife?" She gurgled with laughter. "I doubted it. Not that I couldn't deal with that if I had to."

"You astonish me," Damon said honestly.

Long lashes dropped down over her eyes, and for the first time, she looked disconcerted. "Well, I'd just as soon you didn't tell anyone about it. Not that *they'll* be vexed with me . . . for *they'll* know I'd no choice. *They'd* approve of me defending myself, too. But it isn't the sort of thing one wants bruited about, you see."

"They?"

"My friends. I don't care for my own sake, but I'd hate to make them the subject of gossip." She raised her eyes to his and now the moonlight struck deep gold in her eyes. It took Damon a moment to answer because he had to catch his breath.

"No, of course not," he said, "I won't say a word, but—what about Dearborne?"

"You think *he'll* tell folks I beat him to bits?" she asked with a grin.

Damon smiled, too. "Hardly. Well, then. I think the first thing we have to do is get him up and back to the ball. Or failing that, into a hackney and on his way home. We can't just leave him here. Not that he doesn't deserve it, but if you want to avoid gossip. . . ."

"Right, right!" she said eagerly.

"You go back, I'll take care of it," Damon said.

She put her hands on her slim hips. "What sort of a female do you take me for?" she asked angrily. "Leaving you with my messes? I'll help. More than that, I'll leave him with a flea in his ear in case he thinks of saying anything to anyone."

"The man would be a fool to try," Damon said, and meant it.

Damon went to the stricken young lord and raised him to a sitting position, propping him up against his own leg to steady him. The sprite snatched a handkerchief from Dearborne's pocket and, grumbling, went to the fountain to wet it down. She returned and briskly and none too tenderly wiped the blood from the young man's face. Making a terrible face herself, she went back to the fountain and rinsed out the handkerchief. Then she silently handed it to Damon and stood looking down at her erstwhile attacker. He was sitting on his own now, with his eyes closed, and not just because one of them was swelling shut.

"He'll have to turn his neckcloth inside out if he wants to wear it again tonight," Damon said, mopping up a blotch of blood on Dearborne's chin and eyeing his patient consideringly. "It will feel terrible, but he can't go into public with a naked neck or looking as though he was almost decapitated. It's getting late. We have to dispose of him one way or the other. And I don't mean finally," he said to the sprite's hopeful expression. Sighing, Damon began to unwind the bloody cloth from around the young man's neck.

Between them, working silently and in concert, they

got the fallen man cleaned up. He sat slumped when they were done, his face ghastly gray in the moonlight, his neckcloth crushed and rumpled, his jacket stained, his face mottled and bruised.

"Still . . . I've seen drunken bucks look worse," the sprite announced critically after circling him a time or two.

"Not much," Damon said, "but it will have to do. Here," he said, squatting Indian-style to speak to the man. "Dearborne—you want us to put you into a hackney cab? You can't spend the night here, much as you might feel you want to right now."

One eye opened and looked at him balefully. "Ah'll be aright," Dearborne said through swollen lips, "Jus' gimme a moment to get mah wits togetheh, eh? Ah'll go home—but through the house. Doan wanna jus' disappear. Not done. Jus' a moment—and keep that witch away from me!"

"Huh!" the sprite said in disgust, and moved away toward the house.

Damon rose to his feet. "You might as well go back in now," he told her. "I'll see him in and then enter the house again after he's there."

"What, do you think me such a poor piece? I'll wait with you in case you need me. I'll nip in after he goes back. You can come in after that. No one will notice. If anyone does, and asks, you can always say you saw me getting a breath of air and had a word with me. I'll say we knew each other because we met before tonight."

"But *did* we meet?" Damon mused.

"Oh." She paused, then laughed. Not a giggle, he was pleased to note, but honest full-bodied laughter.

"No, we haven't actually, have we? But I'll change that right now. Allow me to present Miss Gillian Giles," she said formally, making a deep curtsey. "'Gilly' to her friends. And you certainly are that, sir."

Damon bowed. "Damon Ryder, at your service my lady. 'Damon' to my friends, because 'Da' would be too familiar, I fear."

She laughed again. "No, not a *lady*, Mr. Ryder. Which is just as well because I never act like one, I fear."

He smiled. She paused, really looking at him for the first time. Such a handsome fellow, she thought fleetingly. Even the wan light couldn't leech the gold from his thick brown hair. Though he dressed and spoke like one, that smooth handsome face didn't have a gentleman's pallor. It was vivid, lightly kissed by the sun. Thin straight brows highlighted the way long eyes, graced with starry lashes, turned down at their corners. And such a perfectly formed, suggestively kissable mouth! Any woman would have envied it; it was only saved from looking feminine by that straight narrow nose and the rest of that virile face. Gilly was shocked at herself.

But he *was* a pretty fellow. Not too tall, not short at all, lean but well built. The man probably could handle himself against all comers, she thought with admiration. And a charmer, too.

Too bad, she thought, because it couldn't matter to her. She shrugged, and said, "I'm in your debt, Mr. Ryder, and don't think I'll forget it. If you're ever in need of a friend, please count me as one."

Damon blinked, surprised and enchanted by the comment. It was a thing a young man might have said to another, but charming to hear from the lips of a such a lovely young female. He bowed. "I'd hoped we might meet again even if I'm not in need, because I can always use a new friend."

She laughed. "Yes, who can't? But the polite world don't think men and women can be just friends, and that is all I can be to you, Mr. Ryder. In case the gossips haven't bent your ear, I'm hopelessly ineligible for such as you, because even a blind man can see you're a gentleman. And I'm a female with no noble connections of blood, only those of friendship. Though that suits me to a nicety, it don't impress the matchmakers, and certainly not noble mamas. That's why Dearborne attempted me. There are prettier ladies here tonight. But they *are* ladies, you see."

"Why, even that blind man of yours could tell you your mistake, Miss Giles. As you said, a man's character doesn't show in his face, and Dearborne's a famously successful rogue because of his. I've just returned to England after two years abroad and even I've heard of his exploits. He doesn't attempt any females but diamonds of the first water, my dear. You sparkle so, it's no wonder he was taken with you."

She grinned. "Nicely said. And thank you for it. Ah, look, he rises. Want to escort him back in to the ball? Or do you think he can make it under his own sail? I'd offer to help, but the temptation to trip him would be too much for me."

"Allow me to do the honors," Damon said.

He helped the taller man to stand and make his way across the garden again. Dearborne staggered slightly, but shook off Damon's helping hand once he got to the bottom of the terrace. Damon stood in the shadows as Dearborne lurched up the steps. As the beaten lord emerged from the darkness of the garden he surprised two gentlemen who were standing, smoking there. He made a wobbly bow to them, then stepped to the long French doors, flung them open, and walked into the blare of light and music that was the ballroom. The doors closed and the garden was cast into silence again.

Damon heard a light sigh behind him. He turned. The brightness from the house had temporarily blinded him. But he couldn't mistake the sweet scent of freesias surrounding the figure standing beside him.

"Well, then," Gilly said lightly, "over and done. Thank you again for your part in it."

"I wasn't joking," Damon said. "I'd like to see you again."

"Nor was I," she replied. "Believe me, there's no future in it. You can ask anyone. But thanks for that as well."

"At least allow me to see you in," Damon said, offering her his arm.

"What? And have the scandalmongers link you with me? Poor payment for such a good deed." She laughed. "I'll slip in by the side door, thank you. There's one to the left, see? That's how that wretch led me out." She snorted. "While the other gents are checking their coats and hats at a ball, I expect he checks all the exits and entrances."

"Then I'll go in by the terrace doors," he said. "But wait! I don't give up that easily. You *are* staying with the Sinclairs?"

Gilly hesitated a moment. Her voice was low and sad when she spoke again. "The gossips got to you already, I see. Well, they're right. But so was I. Adieu, my newfound friend. As I said, I don't think I should see you again—except in passing."

There was a blur of movement and she was gone. Damon strained his eyes but only saw her in the brief stab of a sliver of light, quickly doused when she slipped in the hidden entrance at the side of the house.

He would see her again, though, and talk with her, too, he decided as he strolled up the steps, nodded to the two smokers, and entered the ballroom.

But he didn't expect it to be so soon.

Because although the music was still playing, no one was dancing now. Instead, the glittering company was stopped in place, looking to the side of him at one slender figure standing facing them, alone. She was pinned by their stares, looking like a woman facing a firing squad.

"Yes, an' now there *he* is," Dearborne said triumphantly, his slurred voice strong with indignation. "See what happens to a fellow who only tries to help a lady in distress? But she wasn't—'til I came along. I saw her locked in his arms and knowing she was a single chit, and he a stranger to us all, thought she was being attacked by him. Attacked? H*ah*! They turned the tables on me, all right. I tried to rescue her from an ardent embrace. He pounded me for it. *She* kicked me. My friends, it's a scandal, is what it is."

It was. Undeniably and damnably. Gilly refused to cringe. But she turned her head and stared at Damon, too. They exchanged a long look. Her eyes, he realized, were golden as amber, bright now with distress.

He wouldn't have it.

Damon laughed and walked to her side. He put his hand on her shoulder. "Ditched, my dear," he whispered, and said, loudly to the gaping company, "So much for keeping secrets, eh? Well," he told the fascinated onlookers, "what would you have done? There you are, newly returned to civilization. And after months of letter-writing, you finally have your lady close at last. More than that, she's just said yes—she'll marry you! You clasp her to your bosom, give her an exultant kiss—and then some strange man comes boiling up out of the shadows, snatches her away, and tries to plant you a facer. I ask you, wouldn't I have been justified in murdering the wretch?"

Gilly turned an astonished face to his. Damon dropped a kiss on the tip of her nose and said, smiling hugely, "The secret's out, puss." And remembering her quick reflexes, quickly clipped her close to his side and turned her to face the delighted company, just in case she disagreed.

But she didn't even raise a finger. She just stared up at him, looking as amazed as he was by what he'd just said.

# 2

Dancing and chatting stopped as everyone at the ball goggled at the young couple. Here was scandal, romance, and mystery, all unexpected and all in a night. The Merrimans' ball was fashionable, but not exclusive enough to be thrilling, if only because poor old Merriman had so many daughters to marry off that there was almost always some kind of "do" going on at his house of an evening. But this! That young cad Dearborne staggering into the ballroom, pounded to mincemeat! And then claiming to have been attacked because he tried to rescue Viscount Sinclair's beautiful but ineligible young ward when he found her locked in a passionate embrace with London's newest rich, handsome, and eligible stranger! Then to have that selfsame stranger stroll into the room and announce the affair was a secret of long standing suddenly resolved? *Wonderful*, the assembled guests whispered to each other—whether they believed it or not.

The couple was besieged as young Dearborne slunk out into the night. Well-wishers and gossips converged on them. They were such a pretty pair, and so everyone exclaimed. Some of the young ladies might have been envious, not a few of the gentlemen were chagrined. But they were social animals to their bones. They offered congratulations, they were full of questions. This was delicious stuff.

Gilly wasn't a timid person but she was an astonished one, so she stood silent at Damon's side, letting him answer everyone. He did it with ease. He was as calm and merry as a host at an afternoon tea. Even she almost believed he'd just attained his heart's desire.

"No, no," Damon said to the first questions. "We met years ago. Yes, in fact, that *was* why I left England. There's only so much disappointment a man can take. Well, this man, anyway. It was a wrench to leave, but I was desperate. It was only a glimpse and a passing meeting or two, but that was enough for me. I was done for. Yet she wouldn't even walk out with me because she refused to let me so much as dream! She was too young, I was too smitten, I don't know. I thought maybe absence might make her heart grow fonder. I don't know whether that did it or if it was all those letters we kept writing." He bent a fond look at his new fiancée, who gazed back at him in wonder. "It doesn't matter. At last, she said *yes*."

But then the happy babble of voices fell still. A tall, broad-shouldered gentleman parted the crowd. He strode forward, the well-wishers instantly giving him leeway, as though the force of his personality alone scattered them. That, and his thunderous expression. He was a darkly attractive man some ten years Damon's senior. He strode up to the pair, but had eyes only for Gilly—and the arm around her waist.

"Are you all right?" he asked Gilly. "What's this I heard?"

"I'm fine, Ewen. Oh, where's my head? I mean, my lord Ewen, may I present Mr. Ryder? Mr. Ryder, here is the Viscount Sinclair."

As the men measured each other with their eyes and then bowed, Gilly saw the lovely woman at the viscount's side. She sighed with relief. "My lady! All's well, don't fret. Just a misunderstanding. No one's the worse for it—except maybe Lord Dearborne." She laughed. "And that's all right, too!"

"But they say you're engaged to this—to Mr. Ryder!" the woman said anxiously, eyeing Damon.

"Well, they say a lot of things. . . ." Gilly began.

"And most of them true," Damon interrupted with an easy smile. "Viscountess," he said, bowing again, "Gilly wrote of your kindness and your beauty so often I feel I know you well, although I've only seen you from afar. You're even lovelier than I remembered. I'm very glad to meet you at last, my lady."

The viscount and his lady did make a striking couple. He was not so much handsome as devilishly attractive. She was unique, too, with sable hair and fine features, lovely even with the scar that marred her cheek—or perhaps because of it, since it made a viewer look twice and become even more impressed with her quiet beauty the second time. Now they were matched in their expressions of surprise and suspicion.

The viscount looked at Gilly, and then more pointedly at Damon's arm, which was again around her waist. "You *are* engaged to marry this man?" he asked with incredulity.

"She is," Damon said promptly, drawing her even closer to his side. "I regret you had to find out in this fashion, my lord. I'd planned to call on you and ask you for her hand, in the time-honored fashion. But events moved before I could. We can discuss it further, if you wish. But the thing is done."

"Indeed, so I see," the viscount said, his dark head snapping up as he stared into Damon's eyes. Damon didn't so much as blink. Sinclair nodded. "But since this is neither the time or place for discussion, I fear we must delay that happy moment. Tomorrow morning at my house?" he asked. "Say, ten o'clock?"

"Say it and it shall be so," Damon said easily.

"I hate to interrupt such a tender reunion," the viscount said without a trace of regret, "but my lady grows weary. I thought we should leave soon, Gilly."

Gilly's eyes flew wide. "I'll come right now!"

"No need, she's not ill, just tiring. We'll have the coach brought 'round, that will take some time. Meet us in the outer hall in fifteen minutes, that will do. Good evening to you, Mr. Ryder. Tomorrow, then. Come along, my dear." The viscount inclined his head, offered his arm to his lady and led her out of the ballroom. She glanced back over her shoulder, looking more confused and dismayed than weary.

"You will forgive us?" Damon asked the guests as

soon as the viscount left. "But since I've only just found *my* lady again after so long and have to be parted from her so soon, if only temporarily—I'd like a few minutes alone with her before I face the thought of her being gone from me for—" He took out his pocket watch and groaned. "Twelve entire hours!"

The company laughed. Damon smiled but began steering Gilly from the ballroom in the viscount's wake. The guests good-naturedly gave them a path through the throng, some slapping Damon on the back, all adding congratulations.

"We've got to talk!" Gilly whispered as they walked from the room. "And the sooner the better."

"Absolutely," he agreed, "that's vital. Let me see . . . the Sinclairs will be in the hall waiting for their carriage . . . aha! The secret door Dearborne used. Let's inch around, duck in back of that pillar, wait a few seconds behind that bank of ferns, and then make for the door and have a moment in the garden again."

It didn't take long. The music struck up and the guests began dancing, so they made their escape unseen. The terrace was empty, the garden dim and silent below them. Gilly swung around to Damon the minute she was sure they were alone.

Lord! He was a handsome man, she thought again, the sight of him causing her to pause before she spoke. The bright candlelight at the ball had shown it to her clear. That glowing image of him was burned into her mind's eye, she could still see it in the muted moonlight.

He was dressed in black and white. Black fitted jacket, high white neckcloth, black silk breeches. She couldn't see the color or design of his waistcoat. But he didn't need more color. There were golden streaks in his brown hair, that amazingly shapely mouth of his was a dusky blush, his gray eyes held sparks of blue and silver, and his teeth were a flash of white when he smiled.

It was somehow even worse that he was so good-looking. This was a man to whom all things must have always come easily, and she found she resented it. But she was glad of it, too. It fueled her anger now and helped dim her heart's mutinous response to reason.

"What the devil did you think you were doing back there?" she demanded in a fierce whisper. "I know you think you were helping me, and I suppose you did, but now look at the trouble we're in!"

It took a moment for her words to register. Damon was too busily noting how her hair had glowed gilt in the lamplight indoors, and yet became silver floss in moonlight. In the blanched light she looked ethereal. Yet no man could see that figure and think she wasn't mortal. He watched, enchanted, as her every indignant huff made her lovely breasts rise and fall. "What trouble?" he asked absently. "You think Sinclair will object to my suit?"

She shook her head in disgust, her hands clenched. "We're *engaged*!" she whispered. "At least in the eyes of society. Do you remember what that means here in England? Have your travels to pagan places made you forget? It's good as married! Ewen will understand, I suppose he'll even thank you for your quick thinking, and for saving my reputation. But now what? Have you thought of that? I mean, even if we say it was a jest, I'm still in the soup because Dearborne said you kissed me. What's to do?"

"This, I think," Damon said, and reached out, drew her close, bent his head, and kissed her.

She froze in surprise, then astonishment. His lips were warm and firm, his breath fragrant with wine, his scent like warm spices. He didn't embrace her. She felt only a fleeting pressure on her mouth. But the merest touch of his lips made her traitorous mouth tingle in response. It was dizzying, exhilarating, fascinating. She leaned forward, without thinking . . . then realized what she was doing and stepped back, appalled. Her hand flew to her mouth. She was even more astonished that it hadn't flown to his, to slap him silly. *That* shocked her.

He watched her closely. "You asked and I answered," he said softly. "And we are engaged, after all."

"No, we're not and you know it," she said seriously, her brows lowering, her eyes troubled.

"No," he said, seeing she was honestly upset and honestly sorry for it. "I apologize."

"Why did you do it?" she asked, her eyes searching his. "Because you thought I was the sort of girl who would welcome it?"

"Some women do. I misjudged. Again, I apologize. It was just a whim based on an excellent opportunity. I've rag manners from being abroad so long, I suppose."

"Because I'm not a lady?" she persisted, as though she hadn't heard him.

"No!" he said angrily. He scowled, as vexed with himself as he was with her. Because it had been a delicious kiss and he didn't know when or if he'd have another.

And because it had obviously startled and displeased her. But he never thought she'd take it as an insult. "Because I find you stunningly beautiful, and I thought it would be—no. Because I didn't think at all, I only acted. It won't happen again. If I kiss you again, be sure, I'll get your full permission first. Am I forgiven?"

She nodded, becoming brusque to cover her confusion. "All right. But we have to talk this thing out. I can't be known as a flirt! It's all very well for young ladies of fashion to step over the line. They can cuddle in the shrubbery all night and everyone looks the other way. They've got pedigrees to back them up. I've only myself. I don't want to bring gossip down on the Sinclairs and my sister."

"It's absurd," Damon muttered. "It was only a kiss."

"I don't mean yours!" she said angrily. "I mean what Dearborne said. All they have to do is start thinking I'm ready for a bit of pinch and tickle in the shadows and it's all over for me!"

He laughed. "Don't worry. We made Dearborne look like the cad he is."

"By saying we're engaged," she said through gritted teeth. "By lying about those letters. By—"

"By acting as though we *are* engaged. I won't find it a hardship, if you won't."

She eyed him suspiciously. "But you're looking for a wife, or so they all say."

He raised an eyebrow.

"Well, a person hears gossip even if she don't add to it," she said hurriedly, "but if that is true, being tied up with me won't help you much."

"We can untie when the Season is over," he said reasonably. "There's always another. I'm not exactly ancient, you know. There are other Seasons left for me. I may act old and wise," he added, grinning, "but, in fact, I have only eight and twenty years to my name. And you?"

"Oh. I'm just turned twenty."

"Congratulations. Now, I suggest we carry on as though we had something to carry on about. I'll take you for drives in my carriage—which reminds me, I'd better buy one. What colors do you like? We can discuss that later. Any rate, I'll escort you to balls, the opera, the theater, anyplace you'd like to go. I'm newly returned, newly retired from my work, there are many things here in London I want to do. You'll see. This will be a pleasure if we play it right."

She stared at him, stricken. "You're newly retired from work? But I don't even know what you did—or where you come from, apart from having just returned, as they all said. Don't you see? I don't know a thing about you."

"Easy enough to remedy. For a start, I originally come from near Dover, but I've just returned from America. I went to make my fortune. I did. I traded English goods, chinaware and silver, for American furs and sugar . . . there's too much to tell in a stolen moment on a terrace. But see? Don't be afraid we won't have conversation. There's so much we can talk about. I spent two years abroad and saw a whole new world filled with wondrous things, but nothing prettier than you."

She scowled. "Well, if we're going to get along I have to tell you right off I don't want compliments. Unless saying them gives *you* pleasure, you might as well cut line. Because they don't do anything for me. I don't believe them, nor trust them neither. No reason a man has to keep pouring butter over a person just because she's a female. It's annoying, to tell the truth. Well, you're a handsome sprig. How would you feel if I kept telling you how beautiful you were instead of talking sense?"

"*Would* you?" he asked, entranced, "Oh, wonderful. It's been so long since anyone composed a sonnet to my eyes. And I can't tell you how long it's been since anyone even spoke of how pure my skin is, not to mention how they've neglected commenting on my hair!"

She couldn't help it, she laughed. He was very pleased. "Now, I return you to the viscount," he said, offering her his arm. "Then I'll see you tomorrow morning. Don't worry. We'll stay engaged until the need for it is gone, and it doesn't trouble me, nor should it bother you. Unless," he said on a sudden thought, his face suddenly serious, "I hadn't considered . . . what a clunch I am. Is there someone you're attached to? Do you think this fiction of ours will spoil things?"

She laughed again. "Little fear of that. I intend to get leg-shackled one day. But not that soon. And the men I'm considering won't be any the worse for a few weeks of worry about my availability. Might raise their interest in me, at that."

He looked at her curiously. There was much he didn't know about his pretend fiancée. Why would such a lovely young woman put such a low value on herself? How had she learned to defend herself so successfully? Had Sinclair taught her? It was useful, but even so, few females showed such gusto for the art of self-defense. And while she wasn't vulgar or brash, why—charming though it was—did she lapse every so often and speak as a young man might, and not like any well-born maid he'd ever met, here or abroad?

The Viscount Sinclair was pacing when they entered the hall. His lady's worried expression vanished when she saw them.

"Oh! I'm so sorry," Gilly said. "Did I keep you waiting? Are you tired?" She hurriedly wrapped herself into the coat a footman held out for her and went to the viscountess's side. "I told you not to go out so soon," she said fretfully, "but you wouldn't listen to me, would you? A woman who had a babe not three months past ought not to be out to all hours. Let's go home right now! Oh, bother! I told you this ball meant nothing to me!"

Damon watched with interest. Were all wards so familiar with their benefactors?

"It meant *nothing to you*?" Sinclair asked silkily, glancing at Damon. "Odd. I wonder how that can be when your long-lost love was here waiting for you?"

"Don't tease the girl," the viscountess told her husband. She dropped her voice. "I'm not ill, Gilly. I just wanted to get you out of here."

"Oh. Well, thank you for that," Gilly said. "Wait until you hear the whole!"

"I can hardly contain my curiosity," Sinclair said dryly. He offered one arm to his wife, another to his ward. He turned his head to Damon. "Her version tonight. I'll see *you* tomorrow—at ten."

"Ten," Damon agreed, and watched the trio walk out to their waiting carriage.

*     *     *

Damon wanted to leave the ball the moment Gilly Giles and the Sinclairs did. Not only had all his interest in the affair left with them, but the townhouse itself was hot and crowded. The ballroom smelled of melting tallow, perspiration, and too many warring perfumes. But there were things he had to know before morning, and this was the best place to learn them. He turned back to the ball.

"Sly dog!" his friend said, appearing at his side before he could take another step. "You let me blather on about her, and didn't breathe a word to me. No, no, I'm not offended in the least. I understand, you're a gentleman and couldn't speak until you knew her mind. But it's a lucky thing I didn't say a word against the lady, isn't it? Um, I didn't, did I?"

"You'd have known if you had, Charles, that I promise you," Damon said good-naturedly.

Charles turned pale. Damon wondered if his old friend was appalled at the thought of having said anything rude. But watching him more narrowly, Damon realized Charles might actually be worried that he'd made a remark that could result in a challenge. With good reason. They'd been old school chums, but time had changed them both.

Like many of his London cronies, Charles avoided any play that involved much more than his wrists. Holding cards, throwing dice, hefting glasses of wine, and placing bets were his only recreations since he'd left school. Sporting with wenches involved more muscles, but was acceptable because there was all that bed rest afterward. Damon had done much more.

He looked as rudely healthy as a savage from the land he'd just returned from.

Damon had been glad to see his old school friend at the ball, because though his figure had certainly changed, he was at least a familiar face. They hadn't exchanged three words in as many years until tonight. But now he judged it was time for them to pass some more, while Charles obviously still feel uneasy.

"You didn't say anything wrong, but now you can tell me more," Damon said mildly. "I'd heard about the Viscount Sinclair in my lady's letters, of course. Tell me what you know about him."

"Oh," Charles said, vastly relieved. "Well, that's simple enough. The man is much discussed, or was. Before he met his lady he was wild to a fault—or so all said. He lost his first wife and the shock of it sent him to the Continent, where he became a rake. When he came back he met his Lady Bridget and turned meek as a lamb—staid as a parson, in fact. He's got eyes for no lady but his own now, and God help other men who look at her the way he still does." Charles shuddered. "He was a dangerous fellow, too, famous for his skill with his fists, pistols, and sabers. He uses his tongue and his wit to slay his foes these days. They're just as lethal. I tell you, few dare his wrath.

"Some say he was working for the Crown as some sort of spy when he was abroad." Charles leaned close to whisper, "Who knows? Napoleon's gone, he's home, and it's all done. But he's a powerful fellow in society, with connections in the government, too. You've aligned yourself well, Damon, and that's a fact!"

"But I thought you said his ward was ineligible,"

Damon drawled. "You were warning me away from her, weren't you?"

"No, no," Charles said nervously. "Of course not! I only meant she had no fortune. A nice competence, to be sure, I don't doubt. No one thinks Sinclair will be a skint when it comes to her dowry. But no estate. Well, you know what frippery fellows we London bachelors are! Why else would we be here at such tame pleasures as this ball? Looking for wives to settle our futures, of course. Most fortunes are made and estates settled by wedlock, just like in olden days, for most of us. You made your own fortune and can look wherever you choose for a wife. Even marry for love! Few of us have such freedom."

"Only that?"

"No 'only' about it," Charles said indignantly. "Many's the fellow wed to a dragon only because she's sitting on a pile of gold. You think there'd be half as many married men playing fast and loose if they'd been able to wed where they would? Just look into the ballroom. There's Jessup, dancing with that Turner woman, and he with five children at home with his wife. There's Johnston trying to pretend Lady Johnston don't know why he's avoiding Lady August's eye. Ho! All know that affair's exploded even if she don't. There's Lord Wycoff on the prowl again, as is his wife. Don't you see how she's watching you? As if you'd have any truck with her, when you've the pick of the crop. That's only what I can see from here!

"Half the married men have their little *cher amis* from the ranks of the impure, ladybirds who amuse them under the sheets but who can never appear at a respectable ball like this. Love don't come into it either way. Getting children's one thing. Finding pleasure with a female is another. Love is something else altogether, I suppose. No 'only' about it, my friend!" Charles said, so worked up he forgot to worry about Damon's temper. "You went out and made your fortune. But the rest of us? There's those who sneer at the word *trade* and act like you've dirtied your hands. But we have to dirty far more. Marriage is the best chance most of us have of making or keeping our fortunes."

"So that's the only reason you said she was ineligible?" Damon persisted.

Charles showed the first trace of color in his cheeks Damon had seen since they were boys at school, coming in from a rough game of ball. "Well, but there's no family there either," Charles mumbled, "and there's them that sets store by old names and such, y'see."

"I see," Damon said, content. No scandal then. Nothing against the sprite herself. Only that she had nothing these London fools needed. Not enough money nor worthy enough ancestors. Neither meant much to Damon. If he'd been firstborn, maybe they would have. Or even second-, or thirdborn, for that matter. But he was the baby of the family and had more nephews and nieces than he could count. No, he thought with a smile, he did keep count, and rejoiced in each new addition. Since he'd left England he'd gained four more he hadn't met. Apart from the fact that it was a joy to welcome new members of his clan, with so many worthy heirs in his family he was obviously free to wed where he would.

And so he would. It *might even be* Miss Giles, he thought with pleasure.

"Coming back to the dance?" Charles asked.

"Why? I got what I came for," Damon said. He looked around the crowded ballroom. "I'll never find old Merriman in this crush. I'll say my farewells to you instead. We'll share a dinner one of these nights—if I can tear myself away from my fiancée, that is to say. Good night, Charles."

Damon called for his coat and hat and walked out into the night. He stood on the front step gazing up at the sky. He was used to more stars and less smoke. Rawer streets, with dust instead of cobbles. But the earth under his feet held centuries of his history. He was home, and very glad of it.

He shook his head when a footman offered to call a hackney for him, even though the street was crammed with waiting coaches and cabs. One thing his adventures in the new world had given him was a taste for walking or riding horseback instead of riding locked inside a coach. It gave him time to think.

Damon strolled to his hotel, still humming the waltz he'd heard as he'd left the ball. He was very pleased with himself. She was a beauty, rare and unique. Just the sort of prize a man looked for in a wife. This man, at any rate. Her hair, those eyes, that figure. . . . Still, a man ought not be ruled by his organs—his heart or his masculine ones. Because there was often little difference between them where women were concerned.

But there was a clever brain ticking away in that lovely head, and a backbone of steel, too. She'd courage and a lively sense of humor, and a fresh and breezy manner that was a relief from the coy young women of quality on both sides of the Atlantic. There was also a delicacy of mind . . . or so it seemed. Marriage was a lifetime affair, a man had to be sure.

Now a trick of fate had given him time to evaluate the lady who claimed she wasn't one. Time to spend in her company, hear her thoughts, and see her reactions to his. Few men were lucky enough to do that without committing themselves for eternity. But she was willing—eager—to set him free. He knew people well enough to know it was no trap. She honestly hadn't wanted him from the first. Not because she didn't like him. He knew women well enough to know that kiss had shocked her with the intensity of its pleasure, too.

But she said she wasn't good enough for him. Why? She said she wanted a husband one day. She only accepted his mock courtship to save her reputation, and said she couldn't wait to free him from his obligation. A mystery. An enthralling one.

Still, a courtship meant intimacy. Not the kind of intimacy he most wanted, of course. He could wait for that. He'd had as active a sensual life in the New World as he'd had in the old one. Women liked him. He genuinely liked them and always was able to find one he wanted who was willing to take what he offered. Which was sometimes money, often affection, usually both. All he asked in return was an eager partner in bed as well as an amusing companion at dinner. If there was the possibility of love, even better. There was almost always that. For a while at least. He couldn't imagine making love to someone without the thought that he might love them . . . but he'd never known the real thing. Miss Gilly Giles had possibilities he'd never found before.

He'd come to London to find a mate. He'd never seriously looked for one until tonight—and there she'd been. Fate had favored him again. Not only had he found her, but as the hapless Charles had said, he was lucky enough to name his own destiny. Though luck wasn't all it took.

Damon would have been comfortable if he'd stayed at home these past years. His oldest brother got the estate, those next in line got acreage, funds, and professions suitable to gentlemen. But his father had a nice amount settled on him, too, and he'd a fine education. He'd only begun to wonder about how he'd spend his life when a great uncle had obliging shuffled off his mortal coil and left him the lot of his worldly goods. He'd inherited a tidy manor house and a neat little fortune. It was actually the inheritance that decided him. It had all been so easy.

His family and friends congratulated him. But one friend said one word too many. "Your life falls so neatly, Damon," the fellow said enviously, "I think if you walked off a cliff the earth would rise up to meet your feet. You never have to ask for anything. It all falls to you."

That stung. Everyone in the family had petted and cosseted him since birth. The thought of being on his own, rebuilding and refurbishing his great uncle's house for himself, had given him pleasure—until then. Because he wouldn't be on his own, would he? It would only be more of the same. Another gift. He had to prove he could earn his future for himself, if only to himself.

His mother wept, his father thundered. Go to America and establish himself in trade? Some families might have been appalled at the word *trade*. They weren't. They were horrified at the word *go*. Whatever for? Didn't he have everything? When he told them what he didn't have—a chance to discover his own abilities, to make a life with his own brain and two hands—they fell still. Until they marshaled new arguments. They loved him so, they couldn't bear to let him go. Which was why he knew he must.

His brothers warned him, his sisters begged him to change his mind. But his family had loved him too well. All that unrestricted love had also made him a man with a strong sense of self-worth and amazing tenacity. He could have become a lap dog, pettish, snappish, and selfish. But even as a boy he'd rejected that. Because it hadn't been unconditional love—they had set standards and lived them themselves. He refused to be less than they were.

Fortune kept smiling on him. He thought he was lucky. That his family had also created a man with a sunny, even disposition who liked his fellow man and woman and showed it, and so got back from the world just what he put into it, never occurred to him. In his travels he made friends it was as much of a wrench for him to leave as those he'd left at home. He was lucky to find such good men and women, he thought, never knowing he worked, knowingly or not, for every bit of luck he found.

He'd missed his family in that alien land. But he did

find himself. And found to his surprise that fellow wasn't much different from the Damon Ryder he'd known at home in England. Except eventually much richer.

Only back in England for two weeks, and he'd found himself a gem of a girl to wed, he mused now. But he'd have to work for that, too. He had to get to know her, discover if this love at first sight would turn out like all the others had. If his luck held, she'd be as perfect for him as he imagined and he'd make this mockery of an engagement a reality. If she wasn't, he'd played the hero and saved her reputation.

Either way, he didn't see how he could lose. He picked up his pace. He couldn't wait until morning to see her again, and try his amazing luck once more.

"I don't want her hurt," the gentleman said as he paced.

"Nor do I," Damon agreed, "which is why I said what I did."

The Viscount Sinclair paused and gazed at Damon, taking complete measure of the man who sat before him in his study. His dark face was intent as he tried to stare down his visitor.

Damon looked back, humor in his steady gray gaze. Other men might have squirmed under that fixed regard. Damon relaxed. He had a clear conscience.

"You told society you were going to marry Gilly," Sinclair finally said. "She told me why, and I thank you for it. I'd have Dearborne meet me for what he did, with his choice of weapons. But it would only fuel more gossip. It's how he gets away with such outrageous behavior. But I won't forget," he added in a way that made Damon almost pity Dearborne. "Still," Sinclair said, frowning, "a declaration of love and marriage before all of London society? Rash. You went so far to protect a stranger?"

"I've hopes she'll become less of one," Damon said mildly.

Sinclair's thin eyebrows shot up. "You're prepared to actually go through with it?" he asked incredulously.

"I am . . . although she says she'd have to be two weeks dead before she'd do it. An impediment to my plans, you'll agree." His fierce host couldn't suppress a sudden grin as Damon went on serenely, "I had no choice, my lord. Not after what that bastard said. It was my reputation as well as hers. Still, all's well that ends well, and I have great hopes this will. Now she's got her reputation back and fashion smiles on her. Dearborne looks like an idiot, which is the least he deserves. What he really needs is to let Gilly have at him again. But I'm not that cruel."

His host grinned wide at the thought as Damon added, "And whether or not you believe it, the idea of marrying Miss Giles grows more pleasing to me by the hour."

Now the viscount looked thunderous again. "You don't know what you're suggesting. No—hear me out." He sat, at last, perching on the edge of his desk. Though he faced Damon, now he fidgeted with a pen he'd picked up instead of looking at him. His voice grew troubled as he tried to explain. "There's no finer young woman in London for a man to marry, in my opinion. But there are few as ineligible. Oh, I'll dower her well. I made her and her sister my wards almost five years ago. I've seen to their education and upbringing since. I did the best I could for them, and it was the least I could do. I owe them much. I like them, too.

"Gilly is bright, brave, and beautiful. But it's no secret she has no family but her sister. She's not common in any sense but birth . . . but the truth is she has no claim to being anything but a child of commoners, London born and bred. That's not all. . . ." He saw the sudden alarm in his guest's eyes and added quickly, "There's no murder or insanity being hidden, I assure you. But the rest of her history is hers to tell, if she chooses."

He levered himself up from the edge of the desk and began pacing again. "I'll only say that whatever I did for her, she's a remarkable young woman to have raised herself to what you see now. Her history doesn't impel her to wedlock, nor do we blame her, nor will we urge it on her. Though," he added in a softer voice, "we do hope she'll find the happiness we have."

"I understand your wishes for her happiness, though not her history, of course," Damon said.

"It's not mine to say more," Sinclair said abruptly.

"Well, then," Damon said amiably, "I'll wait to see if she confides in me. In the meanwhile no harm can come of my courtship. I promise you that."

"But it might, there's the point," Sinclair said in annoyance. "What if she grows fond of you? It isn't impossible. She said she might marry one day, in spite of everything. You're considered a catch on the marriage mart. But what could be more futile for her than to form an attachment to you?"

"I beg your pardon?" Damon said. He rose to his feet, his face set and cold. "You're telling me that I'm ineligible?"

"Of course not! Just the reverse. What would your family say about such a liaison?"

"Oh, my family." Damon laughed and sat again. "My lord, I'm the strayed lamb, or rather, the prodigal son returned—which is why I went away in the first place. I'm the baby of my family," he said to the Sinclair's puzzled expression. "I've four older brothers, each more handsome and clever than any man has a right to be. And three beautiful older sisters, each as opinionated and stubborn as any man I've ever met. And a doting mama and a fond papa. For as long as I remember I've delighted them by simply *being*. When I inhaled, I was applauded for remembering to take the next breath. No one expected anything of me but smiles, no one ever frowned at me except for not smiling. I left England because of a surfeit of love! And to prove I was as much of a man as any of my brothers—or sisters."

Damon smiled nostalgically. "I had to show them—and myself—that I could make my own way in the world. I did, and spectacularly. That's not bragging, but you ought to know that I'm wealthy in my own right now. I did it myself. I may not have a title, but I'm well to grass, my lord. There's the reason for me being a 'catch.' As for Gilly, it's not just that she doesn't want to fish for me, although I'll admit I find that refreshing. It's that I've traveled to America and traded with French, Indians, and Dutchmen, and never met anyone like her. She has the heart of a lion in that pretty little body of hers."

Damon saw the Viscount's sudden glare, and said peacefully, "Glower as much as you like, my lord, I'm not a eunuch and won't pretend I am. She *is* a beauty and no mistake. But I won't do more than appreciate that fact in a philosophical kind of way—until she agrees to make our charade the truth. I'm hoping she will."

"Hold that thought," Sinclair said with a frown. "You don't know her yet, nor all about her. She's clear as spring water. If she trusts you, you'll know more. Then we'll see. But in the meantime, well then, so be it. Let the courtship commence, but only a courtship, mind you. If she still agrees."

"She saw the necessity because of my announcement last night. I see more, of course. We'll see."

"And I begin to see what made you so successful," the older man said with a wry smile. "Do you ever take no for an answer?"

"Of course," Damon said. "It's just that I have a terrible memory and that's one of the words I tend to forget."

"And the other words?"

"'Never.' 'Impossible.' And 'You can't,'" Damon said promptly.

"Damn!" Sinclair said on a broad white smile. "My Bridget was right! A catch, indeed. You almost make me wish our little Margaret was twenty years instead of not yet twelve weeks old."

"There are some things even I can't change," Damon said with a great deal of mock sorrow.

*      *      *

He'd never taken a living statue driving in the park before. It was an interesting experience, with such a very lovely statue, but devilish dull. He told her so.

Gilly turned her head so quickly she didn't even blink against the blinding sunlight that made Damon seem only a dark shape where he sat on the high driver's seat next to her.

"What?"

"You haven't said a word since we left your house," Damon remarked, regretfully leaving off looking into those shocked, sun-drenched amber eyes so he could guide his horses again.

"Yes, I did. I said the weather was fine and that you had a handsome carriage."

"Oh, is that what you mumbled a while back? Thank you, so it is, and yes, it is very fine. The rig is rented, I took it out for your approval. I thought you'd like the gold and brown colors. I was trying to match your hair and eyes. You nod? That means yes? You know, when I first saw you I was reminded of some sort of elfin person, but now I wonder if I was more right than I knew. Does daylight deprive you of speech? You seemed so witty and spirited in the night. Or is it just that you were up celebrating so late last night after you landed my declaration that you've no voice left now?"

"Well!" she said, sarcastically, "I like that!"

So did he. He stole a quick glance. Her cheeks were blushed with indignation. It suited her dusky rose carriage dress very well. He'd been disappointed to see her flaxen hair tucked up under a charming straw bonnet. But that did show the purity of her bone structure clear, and pointed out the fact that her face didn't need even such glorious embellishment. He was glad the bonnet had a brim to shade that translucent skin from the light. Although, he mused, it might be good to see a few freckles marching across the bridge of that straight little nose. It would make her seem a little less perfect, a little more warm and human. Lord! She was a lovely creature. It made a man yearn to see just how human she was.

"I didn't say anything because I was just enjoying the ride," Gilly lied. "It's a nice carriage, and I haven't been driving in the park for a while."

She turned her head so he wouldn't see the truth in her eyes. The truth was it was hard to look at him even now. This morning he'd looked so fine, the sight of him when he'd called had robbed her of conversation. She'd gaped at him, then stood mute, which must have shocked Bridget and Ewen, too. She winced now, remembering the viscount's quick question when he saw her face as she walked to the front door with Damon. "Are you sure you want to go, Gilly? You don't have to if you don't want to, you know."

Even then she couldn't do more than mumble, "Oh no, I do." When she heard that and realized how matrimonial it sounded, she blushed and added, "I do want to go, that is."

Which made Bridget grin and surreptitiously poke her husband in the ribs with an elbow to silence him. Their son, little Maxmilian, grew narrow-eyed and spoke up jealously. "You don't have to go, Gilly, if you don't want to. Papa said so."

"Oh, but it will be fun, Max. I'll be back soon," she

said to reassure him. Max was three, going on thirty, and possessive as an old bear because his friend Gilly was going out without him. So she'd pasted on a serene smile and stepped out for her drive with her false fiancé.

Now she realized she was more nervous with him than she'd been with a man since she'd been a child. Not because he threatened her . . . although she supposed he did, in a different way.

The dratted fellow had got himself up all in tones of gold today. Exactly like the glowing image she'd held of him through all those restless hours when she couldn't sleep last night, pondering her rash decision to playact an engagement with him. He wore a dark gold jacket, buff pantaloons, dark brown boots, even his caped driving coat was brown. The matched team pulling the phaeton were bays. He glowed in the setting. Or at least he did when she could bear to look at him.

Gilly turned her head, pretending the sun was still in her eyes. But he was the dazzling image she couldn't look directly at. In fact, he was just about the most handsome man she'd ever seen, outside of the ones she'd admired in their frames at the Royal Academy, or the marble ones standing in the corridors there. Only he was fully dressed. Which also made him the first man she'd ever mused about seeing without clothes.

"But if you want to chat, I'm very willing," she said quickly, turning her head so he wouldn't see how pink her cheeks must be from her treacherous thoughts. He made her feel like a girl again. The girl she'd never been.

"We could talk about London," he suggested. "I've only been back two weeks. And so you'll have to tell me where you'd like to go after this. We're here now because Sinclair told me this is the place to be seen in the morning. We're establishing ourselves today. So when we turn into the park and go down the main drive I expect to see you simpering as I gaze at you adoringly, to put the icing on our arrangement in the eyes of the world."

"I don't think I can simper," Gilly snapped. "How about laughing? If you keep saying such ridiculous things I should have no trouble with that."

"Laughing is good . . . but simpering would be better," he said wistfully. "Tittering might do, too. No? Then do you think you could manage a fit of giggles? What will all the other fellows think of my courting if you don't?" he asked mournfully. He glanced at her outraged expression and burst out laughing himself.

She liked the sound, and cocked her head to hear it. It must be the result of his travels, she decided. English gentlemen seldom laughed aloud, at least when they were with ladies. They smiled or grinned or chuckled, sometimes even coughed to cover their laughter if they couldn't restrain it. It was rare for them to so much as show their teeth. They only let loose and guffawed when they were with other men. She hadn't noticed that before. She did now because it was so pleasant to be treated like a companion by a man other than Ewen and his oldest friends.

She smiled back at him and relaxed. "They're bound to think a lot of your courting because they think it was successful. Wouldn't I just like to see that devil Dearborne's expression when he hears!" she added with relish. "Now he's got the name *liar* to add to *vermin*, which he is. Oh, I hope he shrivels at how he'll be treated now!"

"Remind me never to anger you," Damon said seriously, "because if you don't floor me immediately, you'll ill-wish me into eternity."

"I believe in repayment, ounce for ounce," she said as seriously. "It isn't right for people who hurt others to get off with less suffering than their victims."

"An eye for an eye?"

"Payment in kind," she said, nodding, "or worse, especially if the ones they hurt weren't looking for troubles."

"And that bothersome bit about turning the other cheek?"

"I'm no saint, Mr. Ryder," she said, looking off in the distance. "I wouldn't want to be one even if I could. It's my experience that turning the other cheek only gets you slapped harder. Evildoers look for weaknesses and they don't think forbearance is strength. But retribution, dealt swift and direct? Oh, that will do for me, thank you very much!"

Damon was so startled, he couldn't answer. He used the moment to guide his horses through the park gates. Why was she so bitter? Who had treated her so harshly? Who had dared? Had Sinclair been such a stern taskmaster? Or was this part of the mystery the viscount warned him about?

"But then, I have no patience," she admitted. "It's a terrible fault, and well I know it," she went on chattily, turning to face him because now the sun was to the side, and he was concentrating too hard on driving to see how hard she was concentrating on him. "You know? I always wondered why impatience wasn't one of the seven deadly sins, because it's clear it leads to all the others, or at least it always has in my case."

"*All* the others?" Damon asked in shock, only half-joking.

"Oh, no! What must you think of me? I haven't committed all the seven deadly sins. That's not what I meant." Gilly thought about what she'd said, and then because it was irresistible, added with a glint in her eye, "Not *all* by any means . . . just . . . most!" She gurgled with laughter before dissolving into something very much like giggles. Just in time, because now they were on the main drive through the park, and so were many of the most fashionable people in London.

Their carriage had to crawl because of the congestion. There were fine private coaches, phaetons, and other elegant rigs touring through the park today. The other carriages rolled by slowly, their occupants nodding to each other as they passed, or to the groups of horsemen also riding along the paths. There was no way to stop and really chat, only a chance to see and be seen.

"It's slow going," Damon commented, lowering his hands so the reins rested on his knee, "but a healthier way to catch up on gossip and be in fashion than suffering at a ball. At least there's fresh air. All right, no need to drive now, we just follow. Let the play begin!"

He turned to her. "Now, give me a glowing smile. No. That looks like you've got a cramp. Now you look like you want to remove my scalp, and I didn't come home to England for that treat. Now you look insulted. My dear beloved long-lost love, didn't you ever act in a Christmas pantomime? Or tell a fairy story to a child? Just start acting. You can do it. Look into my eyes and imagine I'm the best thing you've ever seen. Think of me as a tasty ice, a cake, a biscuit—Ah, good. You're hungry."

She couldn't help it, he was outrageous. She laughed aloud. It was a rich, full-bodied sound and made heads turn. Damon noted it and smiled. "Good. Romeo and Juliet in the park, act one, scene one."

They inched along the road, joking, laughing, looking like a young couple enjoying each other's company. They were. But there were huge differences between like and love and lust. Those who had a reason to look hard at them saw the couple didn't exchange long heated glances, or color up as they gazed into each other's eyes, or fidget and look down when one stared too long at the other. Those who knew desire didn't see it. Damon knew, but suppressed it. Gilly knew, but didn't feel it, or at least, not the kind she knew best.

A lone horseman came up alongside their carriage. The gentleman removed his hat and held it over his heart as he gazed at Gilly. "My dear Miss Giles, allow me to offer my best wishes," he said with an obviously insincere smile. "There must be dozens of broken hearts in London today. You deceived us all. Congratulations Mr. . . . . Ryder, is it? You've caught the toast of London. And done it all from a distance, at that. My hat's off to you."

But it looked like he wanted his head off, for all his

smiles, Damon thought. Smiling himself, he said, "Damon Ryder, at your service, sir. And you are . . . ?"

"Wycoff," the horseman said, inclining his head in a brief bow, "an old friend of Miss Giles."

"Obviously," Damon drawled, his tone of voice giving the word *old* two meanings as his gaze ranged up and down the other man. Though slender and fit, he was obviously middle-aged. The older man stiffened; the sudden coolness in his eyes showed he knew exactly what Damon meant.

"Thank you, my lord," Gilly spoke up, feeling the tension between the two. "I'm sorry we couldn't stay longer at the ball last night to receive the good wishes of you and your lady. But I see your lady isn't with you this morning either."

Lord Wycoff bowed his head again, this time acknowledging a hit. He was married in the way of some of London's most fashionable gentlemen, in name only. Gilly had let her new fiancé know that immediately, and had reminded him of it at the same time. Lord Wycoff's eyes sparkled with amusement and obvious approval. She was as straightforward as any man he knew. It was only one of the reasons she fascinated him so.

"Much too early for my lady to be up and about, or so I'm told," Wycoff said calmly. "I'm sure she'll regret not seeing you today, but doubtless we'll soon meet again. London's a very small place for such as we, after all. Servant," he said. He clapped his hat back on, bobbed a slight bow, turned his horse, and rode away.

"He acts like a disappointed suitor," Damon remarked, watching him leave.

"Well, I suppose in a way, he is," Gilly said, hating the heat she felt rising in her cheeks. "He isn't very married, after all. And he has his hopes. Well, he as much as told you so just now, didn't he? That's what I like about him. He's honest enough, in his way. I don't like his morals. But they're not my concern. I do like him otherwise," she said, her chin rising. "I mean, to joke and talk with. Because he's clever. But he never oversteps himself if you don't want to play a deeper game. And be sure, I let him know I didn't."

"Hence, his disappointment? Oh, I see."

Gilly lowered her eyes. She didn't know how he managed to make his disapproval felt without one accusation or harsh word. Or how he made her feel so guilty for no reason, either.

"Well, but most London parties and balls are dull, and he amuses me. Oh, blast," she went on as his bland expression didn't change. "The thing is, we live deep in the countryside. We're only here now because my Lord Sinclair had business in town and he and his lady hadn't been in London for years. They decided to take me along because I suppose they wanted to make a push to get me popped off. There aren't that many eligible men in our district. I have no name or estate, so they can't arrange a suitable match. I think they brought me here to see what they could see in the future for me. I'm twenty now. That's not very old, but let three or four more years roll by . . . well, they worry. They always try to do the best for me—no matter what I say. But aside from the theater, which I love, and the museums and such, there isn't much here for me. *Especially* at the kind of party where we met."

"Not much here for you?" Damon echoed in astonishment. "With all the bachelors in London?"

"No, not much at all. Except for the likes of Dearborne and Wycoff. Or knights in shining armor, like you. Confess," she said impishly, "the gents you asked about me last night praised my face and form all right, I suppose. But then they said I was ineligible, right? Well, by their standards, that's true. So, being gentlemen, they can't raise my expectations by spending time with me. Being admired from afar is dull stuff and so are most parties I go to. The unmarried girls don't want to sit with someone who isn't the thing. The married ones wonder why I want to hang about with them. The companions are too afraid to squeak, and the mamas have each other to gossip with. So, a fellow like Wycoff livens up things for me, is all I meant to say."

"He'd liven things more if your name was linked to his more often," Damon mused. "Now. Back to being adored and adoring, if you please. But do you think you could take a minute to tell me more about yourself? Without skimping on the sighing and mooning over the complete magnificence of me, of course. You live in the countryside. Where? What do you do when you're there? What do you want to do? What's your favorite food? What perfume are you wearing? But first," he said, suddenly serious, "I have to tell you one very important thing because I find I absolutely must, and bedamned the consequences!"

"What?" she asked, half afraid to hear it.

"Did anyone ever mention that the sunlight turns your eyes to gleaming gold?" he said in a rush. He raised his hands in surrender. "I had to say it, it was overwhelming me. I knew you don't like flattery. But this was an emergency. I ask you to bear with me when I'm overcome like that," he said gravely. "Suppressing compliments is very bad for my health. Makes me break out in spots, and then see them before my eyes. All that pressure builds up, you see."

The fashionable of London noted they'd never seen Miss Giles in better spirits; she was laughing so hard, it brought tears to her eyes. And her fiancé was grinning in sheer delight at the sight.

They drove the main path and eventually emerged from the park. He took her for ices at Gunters, the most fashionable place for it. They sat in the window, where anyone might see she had no chaperone. It was something only an engaged couple could do without scandal. He said it helped firm their arrangement in everyone's eyes. Then he drove her back. They laughed, talked, and measured each other so much that by the time they returned to the Sinclairs' townhouse, they were both pleased with the progress they'd made convincing everyone they were lovers reunited.

"The opera tonight, then," Damon said as he left her.

"Tonight," Gilly said happily.

"We'll have a wonderful time," he promised. He gazed at her for one long last time and nodded, looking smug. He wasn't just thinking about their appointment. He tipped his hat, and drove off, humming to himself.

Gilly watched Damon and his carriage go round the corner and was surprised to discover herself regretting it.

*      *      *

"You know, it does feel as though I've known him for a long time," she confided to the viscountess a short while later. "I suppose it's because he's so good with people. He is, you know. That's how he made his fortune."

"And will make yours!" Bridget, Viscountess Sinclair, said gleefully. They sat in her bedchamber as she fed her infant daughter. She refused a wetnurse for the baby. She hired a nurse for her and a nanny for her son so she wouldn't scandalize her husband's friends, but preferred to pass her time with the children herself. Lady Sinclair was a noblewoman, but she didn't behave like one in private. That was only one of the reasons her elegant husband adored her even more than he had when they'd wed.

"Make *my* fortune? Not hardly!" Gilly yipped as she plopped down full-length on the bed. She leaned on her elbows and grinned at the baby. "He's above my touch, my lady, and we both know it."

"He has no title," the viscountess said.

"What's in a name?" Gilly asked saucily. "He's handsome as he can hold together, smart and very, very rich. He can have anyone in London. He's nice, too. Imagine! Risking marriage with a stranger just to save her good name."

"But knowing you—and knowing you two spoke together alone before he did make that offer—I think he knew it wasn't much of a risk. We're not pushing you, Gilly," Bridget said seriously, shifting the baby away from her breast, putting her up on her shoulder, and patting her back. "You know that. But you did say you might like to marry one day. That's why we thought this trip would be good for you. And so it was. Who could be better for you than a fellow like Ryder? Clever, and so handsome. You know Ewen has my heart entirely, but even I looked at him twice."

Gilly reached out and gently stroked the silken fuzz on the baby's head. "Marry?" she said softly. "Aye, so I will, I think. So I must if only so I can get one of these. . . . But Damon Ryder? Please. He deserves much more, and he'll come to know it in time. I wouldn't want to be Mistress Ryder when he does. No," she said, flopping back on the bed, staring up at the ornate ceiling, "Mr. Matthew Harding or Mr. Fleming. They're more in my style."

Now it was the viscountess's turn to yip. "Harding? But he's twice your age! A widower, and only a gentleman farmer."

"But a proven breeder," Gilly said mischievously. "He's already got three kiddies, hasn't he? And a neat little farm at that."

"And Fleming!" the other woman said heatedly, patting the baby's back with a fluttering hand. "Yes, he's got a nice house and a snug living, but he's bookish and a bore and still his mama's pet, for all he's a grown man. And a vicar? For you, Gilly?"

"For me. Because he needs a wife. As does Harding," Gilly said softly, "and neither will ask much of me."

"Gilly, you want a husband who asks much of you. And you need much more of him than a roof over your head and a baby at your breast."

"No, I don't, my lady. The truth is I do not."

The viscountess's lovely face grew sad. She rubbed

her cheek against her baby's downy head. "I'll never tell you what to do, my dear," she whispered, "because I never had to lead your life. But I will tell you that there's nothing like love, and that if you find it, it will heal as well as nourish you."

"I'll love my babies, if I'm lucky enough to have them," Gilly said briskly, sitting up.

But her friend and mentor didn't laugh. Instead she gazed at her thoughtfully. "You feel you can never love a man, Gilly?"

A brief look of sorrow came into Gilly's eyes, and she shrugged. "I feel it isn't likely, but I don't let it bother me so it shouldn't bother you. Enough talk about men and marriage. We're going to the theater tonight. Let's discuss more important things. Like gowns and gloves."

They both laughed.

And so the viscountess never knew that Gilly's fleeting sorrow was because she'd thought of the man she did love. The one man she could never have, except in her wildest dreams—the ones she always tried to forget when she awoke. Because though he was available, he wasn't for her, and life had taught her how to put futile longing away and get on with other things. She'd never had gotten as far as she already had otherwise. That was far enough to see the necessity of making a marriage for herself without love.

Damon Ryder was too nice a man to offer false coin. And she had nothing else to offer any man but one— and that one would never know of it so long as she lived. That, she vowed. And she always kept her word.

# 4

"**P**ink," Gilly said with loathing.

"*Apricot*," Bridget, Viscountess Sinclair, corrected her.

She and her maid stood watching the younger girl staring at herself in the long looking glass in her room. They were admiring her new gown. It was beautifully cut, simple and elegant, high at the waist, low at the neck, with long sleeves and slim, shimmering side panels of apple green. The gown drifted over Gilly's slender form, showing off her small high breasts, caressing every curve, making her skin look luminous in the reflected glow of the apricot silk. Her hair was drawn up, bound with a ribbon and allowed to tumble down in random slips that resembled flaxen silk. Gilly was disgusted.

"Oh, Gilly." Bridget sighed. "You can't automatically rule out a color that does so much for you just because you think it's too . . ."

"Girlish, missish, insipid," Gilly sneered.

"Feminine," Bridget said flatly. "Well, so it is, and so you are, and you must overcome your prejudice against delicate trappings. You've come so far. But for you not to see that it's perfect for your coloring! Please wear it tonight . . . unless it makes you feel uncomfortable, of course. Because I've found that feeling well-dressed is the greatest cosmetic, and if you feel insipid, trust me, you will be. I once wore a gown Ewen thought looked fine, but I thought it made me look stout and wouldn't budge from behind a potted palm all night, no matter what he said. It's what's in the mind's eye that counts, and *how* I wish you could see yourself in my eyes, because you look lovely in it."

"Oh, bother," Gilly said gracelessly, turning from the mirror. "If you think so, I'll wear it. Your eye's better than mine when it comes to fripperies. Had I my own way though, I'd dress more like your lord than you." She gave the viscountess a crooked grin. "Well, admit it, my lady, men have the best of it in fashion as well as everything else, don't they? Just look at the men in London! Some dandies wear puce and canary and fret over every stitch in their waistcoats, true. But a *real* man don't care so long as it fits and is clean. If he's a gentleman, add the fact that he wants them to know it costs the earth. But that's it. If females could only wear pantaloons and jackets, too."

The viscountess and the maid wore matching expressions of dismay. Gilly laughed. "Don't look so horrified! Just think about it. Skirts are ridiculous. If they're long, they sweep the floor and collect dust. If they're short, you may be sure you'd be clapped into Bedlam for wearing them—unless you're a man, and then you're a Scot, and that's different and not something I understand. Apart from Scots, the Romans were the last men to be comfortable in them. Still, it's warmer in Rome, isn't it? But pantaloons and boots? Very sensible, and comfortable in most weather.

"Men don't expose their chests to every breeze," she added, glowering down at the exposed tops of her white breasts. "This gown isn't cut to cover me decently. If I tug it up, it will make me look a dowd—I know, I know, don't tell me again. But I don't have to approve it, do I? A gentleman doesn't have to bare his chest to attract attention, does he? Huh!

"Look at what we have to wear!" Gilly picked up her skirt, frowned, and let it flutter down again. "No more weight than a handkerchief, thin enough to court pleurisy if the wind changes, transparent enough to shock a sultan if you don't wear an underdress, and nothing to hide a bulge anywhere. Only the dowagers can afford not to care. Younger females have to watch what they eat or they'll look like you did the day before little Margaret was born," she told Bridget with a fierce frown. "It's so easy to resemble an overstuffed sofa when you're wearing next to nothing at all."

"As if you had to worry about that!" Bridget scoffed.

"But men never do," Gilly protested. "A fat woman is a joke, but a fat fellow's considered 'well-breached' or 'successful.' They can eat like hogs and if their clothes don't fit, they don't mourn. Those that do can strap themselves into corsets until they creak, and look respectable no matter what their size."

"That's not true," Bridget said. "A man's admired if he has a good form and you know it. Their limbs are more on display than ours are. A good leg and a broad pair of shoulders has turned many a girl's eyes *and* heart."

"Aye!" the maid, carried away, put in fervently. "Some of the finest gents pad out their shoulders and some even stuff their pantaloons to fill out their calves! S'truth! They pop in bags of sawdust or bits of wood carved to look like muscles, so they won't look like they're standing on a pair of noodles. Or so they say in the servant's hall," she added, and fell still, blushing.

"I wish you'd tell me which ones do it!" Gilly said, fascinated. "Or what else they pad, for that matter!"

"*Gilly!*" Bridget squeaked.

The maid ducked her head. But her mistress urged her to speak. "Yes, which ones do add a little something? I mean," Bridget added, looking self-conscious, "it would only be fair to Miss Gilly to say, Annie. She has to pick a husband from them, after all."

The maid lifted her head, confused. "But she's already nabbed the best of 'em! Mister Ryder, why, he's the best-looking thing come to town in many a year. Not a pad on him, nor do he need any, no, not nowhere, nor is there another young gent in town who's got a patch on his looks, and so say all."

"Oh. Yes," Bridget said guiltily, remembering the falsity of the engagement. "Just so."

"What my lady means is we'd like to know anyway,"

Gilly said quickly. "Well, who wouldn't? Come on, Annie. Who? And what is he padding?"

But the maid only blushed redder. Gilly laughed and said lightly, "Well, I suppose I'll have to find out for myself!"

Which set them all to blushing and laughing.

Gilly gave herself a last glance. "At least the thing has a green overskirt," she muttered. "All right. I'm ready to face the audience at the theater now. Since I've got engaged to Damon Ryder I've been goggled at by everyone. I suppose there will be as many eyes on us as on Mr. Keane tonight. So be it. I'm ready." She plucked up a shawl and marched to her door, ready to go to the theater and be gaped at.

But she didn't expect Damon to be the one who stared.

"Lord!" he finally said, when he realized he'd stopped talking to the viscount and instead had been standing stock still looking at Gilly as she descended the stair. "You take my breath away, Miss Giles."

"Yes, well, I do clean up a treat," Gilly said gruffly.

"*Gilly*," Ewen Sinclair said with a shake of his head and a reluctant grin.

Damon laughed. She really did dislike compliments. He had forgotten. He'd have to try harder to remember. He knew she'd dislike an adoring beau as well. Odd that she disdained what most young women enjoyed. But so she was singular, and so she was fascinating. He tried to play her game so he could win his own.

"A pity we'll have to sit in the dark most of the time," was all he finally said. When he saw the slight sneer on her lovely face, which showed she anticipated another compliment, he only added, "We'll have to wait for intermissions to make our point. So when the lamps are lit, remember to dote on me, if you please. May I have a sample of some superior doting? No!" He laughed. "That's superior bellyache." He turned to Bridget, imploring, "Now, I ask you, my lady. Is that the look of love?"

Bridget turned to her husband to see his reaction to the question. But before he could speak, Damon did. "Yes, *exactly* like that," he breathed, watching the viscountess. "Miss Giles, just look at your lady's face and you'll know exactly the look to imitate."

"I am not such a good actress," Gilly snapped.

"Oh. So you want the world to think we cooked up the whole thing to avoid scandal?" Damon asked placidly.

The viscount and his lady exchanged a quick glance, stifling their grins at the look on Gilly's face.

"Of course not. Oh, bother!" Gilly said crossly. "I'll slaver all over you if you like. But *not* until we have an audience."

"Behold me wild with anticipation," Damon said.

"He may well do," the viscount whispered in his wife's ear, as he tenderly enfolded her in her cloak in the hallway.

"Oh, Ewen, I pray so!" she whispered back.

"Do you want to stay for the farce? Or do you think we've seen enough of that tonight?" Damon asked Gilly, laughter in his voice.

"You'd think they'd pay *some* attention to the play," Gilly grumbled, looking down from their high box at the audience milling below. "I mean, it's one thing to gape at everyone else at intermission, like now. I suppose it's even fun. Oh—there's Lord Wycoff again. Standing there talking with that Turner woman as though they'd just met? Rash of him, I must say!"

"You take special note of his activities?" Damon asked mildly, but his eyes were fixed on Gilly, not the lord in the crowded box across from them.

"Yes. How can I not? He smiles and bows whenever he sees me," Gilly answered absently, still avidly studying the audience. But then she frowned. She turned to Damon. "It's fine for everyone to gossip together now. But they talk all through the play," she complained. "The audience is only still when Mr. Keane's speaking. No wonder the actors have to shout! They have to make themselves heard, if only to each other. It would be lovely to hear an actor actually speaking as though he was just talking to another character, instead of bellowing at him," she added wistfully. "I'm sure that's not what Shakespeare meant them to do."

"Don't bet on it," Damon said, laughter in his voice. "From what I've read his audiences were even louder. They ate and drank and brawled, flirted and gossiped, not to mention hawking oranges and prostitu—er, other things during the plays then."

Her eyes widened. "The lightskirts did their business *inside* the theaters then?"

Damon bit back his smile. "So they did, but say I told you and I'll strangle you—Gads! Gilly, how do you get me to say one wrong thing in order to correct another?"

She grinned. She liked him best when he forgot he was dealing with a female and talked to her straight from his shoulder. It made her feel easy with him. Sometimes when he looked at her she could see desire lurking in the back of those beautiful eyes of his and it made her uncomfortable. Yet that wasn't as bad as the times when she saw his expression soften, becoming tender as he gazed at her. That troubled her.

But so did her own reaction to him these days. She genuinely liked him. It had been two weeks since their false engagement had been announced, and now she'd discovered that without being aware of it, she'd begun to enjoy their charade and looked forward to seeing him. It didn't matter if she was going to accompany him to a party or the theater or just going for a walk with him. He made each occasion a delight. He always entertained her, whether he was talking about something they'd just seen or telling her of his travels.

He was a good storyteller. He never told the same one twice, and never forgot to gauge her mood so he could change the subject along with her changing responses. He got a joke when he was told one, and saw more humor in everyday life than she'd ever done. And she could enjoy his company with a light heart, because he never tried to presume on their arrangement, not once since that first night when he'd kissed her. He sometimes looked as though he might . . . but he never did.

Once he'd left off flattering her she'd dropped her guard against him altogether. And so it was peculiar, she thought uneasily, that after having trusted him, she began to distrust herself. She gazed at him now, so correct in his black and white evening clothes, so attractive as he grinned back at her. She'd felt the warmth of him at her side all through the play, the clean scent of his soap and linen and self, the solid presence of him there. His personality was so vital, he could project it even when he didn't speak.

"You're sure you don't want to go for a stroll?" he asked her now, seeing how she gazed at him with a troubled expression.

They were alone in their box. The viscount and his lady had gone out to mingle with the other theatergoers in what many of them felt was the most important part of an evening of playgoing.

She shook her head. "No, thank you very much. The way people stare and watch my lips as if they expected me to say something they could rush out and quote to the world? Huh! I'm not such a wit as that. They make me feel like they're trying to trap me into saying something indiscreet or scandalous."

"They are," Damon said placidly. "That's the whole point of this kind of evening out on the town."

"Well, I doubt that's how it is in the clubs and gaming hells, taverns and bawd—um, I mean, the places you gentlemen frequent!"

"Thank you," Damon said, "for editing your views on how I spend my evenings. But you're wrong. Gossip is king in London. It's exactly the same in those places you almost mentioned. Not that I know them much better than you do. I've only been back a little more than a month and you've claimed half of it, you know."

She looked stricken. "I'm sorry, I hadn't realized. Our fiction is really cutting into your pleasure, isn't it?"

"My dear Miss Giles," Damon said, reaching out and taking her hand, "I don't regret a minute I've spent with you—and no, don't bristle. I'm not pouring the butter boat over you. I mean it. If you take it as a compliment, I'm sorry. But it's only truth. Would you rather I lied?"

She shook her head again. She was doing it a lot this evening, she thought, that must be why she felt so light-headed. "So. Tell me," she said in a struggle to recover her equilibrium. "Do they chatter through plays in America as well?"

"Oh, no," he said serenely. But Gilly wasn't as calm, because Damon didn't release her hand. He absently stroked his thumb over the smooth back of it as he spoke, as though he'd forgotten he still held. it. She'd taken off her gloves, and he seldom wore his. *It's only a light touch, and only a hand, you goose*, she scolded herself, wondering why she felt her breath shorten and her whole being focus on such a simple thing.

"They hardly breathe during a play," Damon said. "If someone coughs, he's glowered at. Because they don't get much in the way of theater, although the larger cities have some fine ones. But they're as riotous during musical reviews and comedies as you would wish."

"You look so far away when you speak of the way things were there. Do you miss them?"

"No. I'm very happy to be home again. Because this *is* my home. Most of the people I met in America went there because they had no home, or the home they had was no longer good for them. If I had to make a new start, there'd be no better place on earth for it, I think. You see," he said, his voice growing reflective, "if you went to the Continent, or any settled country in the world, for that matter, you'd arrive an immigrant, an outsider, an alien. It would take time to be absorbed into the life of the country because you'd be so different. Like many of the French, here in London.

"They escaped the Terror a generation ago and yet they still live apart in many ways, speaking their own language, eating in their own restaurants, shopping in their own markets, staying with each other for friendship. I suppose some of it's because we were at war with France so long, they may have felt unwelcome whether they were oppressed or oppressors. It's too bad, but many were under suspicion, some for good reason. But much of it was for their own comfort then, and now. They band together, strangers in a strange land.

"But that's my point," he said. "Almost everyone in America is a stranger. There's some whose parents were born there, some even have grandparents who lived there, and some of those aren't even Indians." He grinned. "But they aren't a majority, and it doesn't make much difference. Everyone speaks with an accent of one kind or another; everyone's trying to build a new life or rebuild an old one. They're escaping from broken homes and hearts, shedding lost dreams and old loves. They're creating a new world as well as living in one. That's why I say that if I had to begin my life over again, it would be there. Some are doing that exactly. They've left not only the Old World behind, but their real names and memories, too. Sometimes even their real husbands and wives," he said with a reminiscent grin. "But my name, my family, and my memories are good ones, and so I had to return."

Gilly slowly withdrew her hand from his. He let it go

at once. She smiled at him, easily. It was an easy thing to do. She liked him very well, she'd love to have him as a friend. But he'd reminded her that she knew too well she could never have him as a husband. His name *was* a good one, and his family obviously doted on him.

Again, she realized how wrong she was for him. Once again, she vowed to end their charade. Surely it was too soon? But a few weeks weren't enough time to reclaim her good name. Or, she corrected herself, at least the good name Ewen and Bridget had given her.

She'd take a little more time with him, she decided. Just a little. Because apart from needing society to see that their liaison hadn't been just what it was—a sham to save her reputation—she was enjoying herself enormously. And maybe they could remain friends after all. After all, she was friends with the one and only man she'd ever wanted to marry—if the world and time were altered. If she could bear that, she could bear this new male friend, couldn't she? *What a lucky girl I am*, she thought wryly. *So many dear friends and no lovers to complicate my life.*

"So, you like this gown?" she asked suddenly, to change her thoughts.

He paused. "I thought you hated compliments."

"I do," she said gruffly, "but haven't you ever asked a friend what he thought of how you were dressed?"

"I may have . . ." he said slowly, suspecting a trap.

"Well, I usually hate pink," she said, plucking at a fold of her skirt. "But Bridget said this gown isn't. It's apricot or some such fruit or other," she added quickly, vexed with herself for not finding a less foolish topic to turn her thoughts.

"No, not pink," he agreed thoughtfully, gazing at how she glowed in the reflected light of the theater's blazing torches. She saw his intent concentration and was glad she couldn't see the expression in the glittering depths of his eyes now, because his voice was intimate and tender. Or so it seemed in the fading light in the recesses of their extravagantly carpeted and padded exclusive box. The theater's noises were a low babble since most of the audience was promenading in the corridors. It was warm, it was cozy, they were alone together. Now, suddenly, they were very aware of it.

"Nor apricot neither," he drawled, studying the lovely form he was not allowed to touch, the lovely face, suddenly shy, turned to his—not for a kiss, but only waiting for his answer.

"Peach?" he murmured, considering it. "No. It makes me think of succulent things. But not fruit. It's a rarer shade, I think. That's it exactly," he said, struck by the elusive thought that had been haunting him. "It's the color of secret, hidden, blushing things. It reminds me of the innermost lip of a seashell. You know, the faint color on the smooth shiny part inside, in the inner whorls of it? Like the inside of a woman's ear, right under that little curled up part of the rim," he mused. "Or the color of her lips . . . or the slowly unfurling petals of her—like a rose," he said abruptly, as Gilly's face became almost the color he described, and he realized how far his thoughts had strayed from convention.

He hesitated, appalled—and then amused. He smiled, crocodile tender as he looked at her heightened color, the result of his musings. Not much embarrassed Gilly. He was almost ashamed, but her blush was too rare and charming a thing to see to regret it. "No," he said gently, "though it makes me think of delicious things, I don't think of fruit."

"Well!" Gilly said, struggling with her answer so he wouldn't think she guessed what sort of shocking things he was hinting at—if he even was and it wasn't her evil mind at work. "I don't think you'd answer another fellow that way!"

"No, but you aren't another fellow, are you?"

"Couldn't you just pretend?" she asked, almost despairing.

"No, Gilly," he said seriously. "And I'm very good at pretending things. I had to be, to be a good merchant. But some things are beyond my abilities."

Gilly was glad Ewen and Bridget chose that moment to return. She turned her flushed face to the stage again, unfurling her fan as though it was the overheated theater and not Damon's words that had warmed her cheeks to match her gown. She'd end the engagement before it became too painful to end, she decided. The world might allow her to remain his friend, but she didn't think he would. Still, given how she felt about her other dearest male friend, maybe it was just as well. She waited for the farce to begin. And hoped it would be more amusing than the one she was living now.

Gilly said good night to Damon at the door, and then turned to go up the stairs to bed.

"A good night." Ewen yawned, as he and his wife paused at the foot of the stair for a last word with Gilly. "Don't you think? Ryder is indeed a catch, Gilly. At first,

I'd my doubts. But he's a man I'd be proud to call friend. Don't make such faces. They'll stick and then where will you be?" he added, as though he were talking to Max. "And don't doubt me. I have very good taste in friends—and women," he added, bending to drop a kiss on Bridget's nose. "Never met a friend of mine you didn't like, did you? Oh—and on that head, I wrote to Drum the other day and told him your happy news."

"How is he?" Gilly said at once.

"Fine, as ever. The rogue writes reams about his travels but doesn't even mention returning to England yet."

Gilly nodded. "Looking for trouble, most like. He and Rafe seem to be the only living things in the world to regret the end of the wars. So, what has he to say about the 'happy' news?"

"We'll know when his reply gets here," Ewen said. "Though I doubt he'll be as thrilled as Betsy," he added with a grin.

Gilly sighed. Her sister, Betsy, had been ecstatic when she heard about the engagement, even though Gilly tried to make the thing sound as temporary as it was without actually putting it in so many words.

"Yes, it's true, I am engaged," she'd carefully written, "but I am not yet wed. So don't build any air castles. For one, I'm not ready to move into one yet. And two," she'd added, keeping to the agreed story until she could speak to Betsy directly and explain the whole of it, "Damon and I know each other on paper, but not so well in person. Writing to a person is never the same as keeping company with them. Which is exactly why I'll have more to tell you when I see you."

Betsy was twelve, and Gilly's responsibility since she herself had been a girl. She took that duty seriously, and so Betsy had grown to be as trusting as she was pretty, and that was saying a lot. She was also bright as a new penny. Gilly would gladly die before she'd let a bad thing happen to her sister. Which was why Betsy still believed the best of everyone. Dangerous as that was, Gilly supposed it was better than being a realist, as she'd had to be.

"Still, however he feels, I believe Drum may be able to control his ecstasy a bit better than our Betsy has," Ewen said on a half-covered yawn as he gazed at his wife.

"You told him all?" Gilly asked.

"Of course," Ewen answered, on another monstrous yawn, though he secretly winked at Bridget.

"Don't let me keep you from bed," Gilly said innocently. Bridget blushed, showing she understood that Gilly knew just what Ewen was so eager to get to, and it wasn't his rest.

"Wild horses couldn't," Ewen agreed.

*Well, well*, Gilly congratulated herself as she went up the stairs alone a few minutes later. *No need to worry after all*. Once Drum got word of the nonsense, he would put an end to it. He might think of her only as a sister, but he was too goodhearted and too clever a man to let a sister go to ruin, or into the arms of a fellow she'd just met. A gent who was only being kind to a chance-met female. And a gent that Drum didn't know, at that.

The Earl of Drummond might be careless in some ways, but he took good care of those he loved. Gilly never doubted he loved her—if not in the way she tried not to dream about anymore. Hadn't he taken pains to teach her the right things to say and do those years ago when they'd first met? Mentor, tutor, and indulgent friend, hadn't he always shown her easy affection and care? For no reward but that of friendship? Didn't he visit her every time he returned to England and write back to her every letter when he left again?

But she hadn't sent him so much as a line since she'd become engaged to Damon. She found she couldn't write to tell him the news. It would have been too much like begging, even if he never realized just exactly what she was begging for. But now Ewen had told him that she had got herself in a scrape, and then in an even deeper one trying to free herself from scandal.

Gilly fairly danced up the stair. Damon Ryder was a good man and a fine friend. In fact, she thought, Drum and Damon would get on wonderfully well if and when they finally did meet. But Drum was more than a good man and a friend to her. He was more to her than her life itself, though he didn't know it and never would. He'd find a way to disentangle her, cleanly and cleverly. She grinned, thinking of his sly sense of humor, wondering how he'd express his outrage at how she'd been coerced into a false engagement.

She felt infinitely lighter. And why not? A weight had been lifted from her shoulders, a difficult decision taken out of her hands. It was what Drum had always done for her. With any luck the two men could become friends and remain her friends, too.

But what of herself, and any possibility of a lover?

She didn't need one. She needed love, but not a lover. Because she knew she couldn't love him back. Her heart was already taken. Her body would be. But with luck, that would only bring her babies to love. She was sad for a moment—but then, content—because she was a realist. But even realists have fantasies. She was to discover she had dreams she hadn't yet given up, though she thought she'd relinquished them all.

She was at breakfast a week later when she found out.

"This just came in the post for you, Miss Gilly," the butler said, bringing in the mail to her at the table himself. He knew how eagerly she waited for the Earl of Drummond's letters. It made her wonder, sometimes, how much the servants knew. But she didn't care now. It was a letter from Drum!

Ewen grinned as he saw how eagerly Gilly plucked the letter up from the silver tray and how her hands trembled slightly as she unfolded the page. But Bridget frowned.

Gilly's face was alight as her eyes skimmed over the boldly scrawled words. Then, slowly, her eyes lost their luster. She blinked. And then her face went white.

"What's amiss!" Ewen demanded sharply.

"Oh. What? Amiss?" Gilly said, returning to the room and the present and herself. "Nothing. He's fine, or at least, he says he is. No, nothing at all. It's just that the silly clunch understands nothing! *Men!*" she said, turning to Bridget. She smiled widely, but unconvincingly, because her lips were quavering, and not with laughter. "What did you tell him, my lord?" she asked Ewen. "For I vow he doesn't understand a thing. He congratulates me on my good fortune at finding such a match! He is in alt about it, in fact. Men!" she said again, shaking her head.

But it didn't shake as much as her hands did. And she spoke in high, artificial tones. She sounded like a fashionable, frivolous young woman, and not at all like Gilly Giles. Now Ewen frowned, too.

His eyes narrowed. "I simply told him Damon Ryder was a good man, one who seemed to me capable of being a good husband, too. Why?" he asked, his voice becoming suspicious and hostile. "Do you know otherwise?"

"Then you spoke truth," Gilly said airily, "but the silly creature forgot the how and why of it. Bother! He writes that his only regret is that he's not sure he can come to the wedding——but note, he don't ask when it will be! Huh! Some friend! Well, I won't let that vex me. Is there anymore of that delicious ham, I wonder?"

No urging, however subtle, would lure her to discuss the matter again that morning, and her eyes began to glitter when the subject was mentioned. But they weren't glittering with tears, the viscount and viscountess, knowing Gilly all too well, noted uneasily.

It had all been a pipe dream, Gilly thought as she chewed and swallowed whatever was on her fork, and then stabbed something else from her plate. She was too blinded by her thoughts to see what it was, too busy holding her tongue to keep from spitting out her pain and shock to taste her food. And too wildly angry to do more than sit and pretend she was eating her breakfast.

Because that was so much better than being hurt.

Tears had been vanquished by rage. *He had discarded her that easily!* Given his blessings to her marrying a man he didn't even know—had never set eyes on! She knew he didn't think of her as a woman, so of course the idea of her in another man's arms wouldn't trouble him— although it near killed her. But she'd thought, felt, dreamed he valued her as a friend at least. To discover she meant so little to him that he could let her go, dismiss her from his life that effortlessly! The words so smoothly written stabbed her to the heart. She read the letter again.

> *Congratulations, you clever puss! I know it's the lucky fellow I ought to be congratulating. But you see, I know you, too. And knew I could count on you to set Society on its ear. Nabbing yourself a gent with a handsome face and a handsome fortune? No less than The Catch of the Season, Ewen says. I expected no less of you. Bravo! You've done well for yourself, child!*

Gilly ducked her head over her plate. She knew Ewen and Bridget were worrying and wondering what to do. She knew it from their silence and the troubled looks they'd exchanged. But she couldn't say anything. Not now, not yet. First she had to conquer her disappointment and all the grief of it.

Then, she knew she had to do something. And soon.

Before anyone could feel sorry for her. Or at least, as sorry as she felt for herself.

# 5

There was no one to talk to. Gilly paced her room, muttering to herself because she couldn't think of a single person she could discuss her problem with now. Not even Bridget, who was her best friend in the world. She had few other friends. Few real ones, at any rate. But that was because she didn't make any other kind. It may have been because her standards were too high, as Bridget chided her—but not too often. Bridget knew it was the singular circumstances of Gilly's life that made it hard for her to find friends of the heart.

The ladies of the *ton* were utterly alien to her. She could imitate them because she was an excellent mimic, but she didn't know any of them well. Nor had she tried. They terrified her. She was afraid of few things, and wouldn't back down from any of those things, even so. But she avoided the company of fashionable ladies. Bridget had only married into the aristocracy and so wasn't like the rest of them. But the others, with their heads filled with gossip, clothes, and beaux! What did she have in common with them?

Gilly was a fair-minded person, and she admitted some fashionable young ladies did worthwhile things. Some did charity work. Others were musical, singing or playing pianoforte for more than fashion's sake; still others painted or wrote poems. The most daring ones spoke out for social reform, risking being known as bluestockings. But no matter how much they cared about the downtrodden, they'd never been trodden upon. They might have soft hearts, but they also had soft beds and ate regularly. They'd no real idea of what they were trying to remedy. Gilly did, and also knew she was an interloper in their privileged world. She knew how she'd be treated if they knew the whole. The kindly ones might pity her. That would be worse than the outright horror the others would feel.

The friends of her childhood were either dead, gone, or best forgotten. The working-class girls, town or country, that she met since she'd gone to live with the Sinclairs, held her too high for their company. The minor aristocracy in the countryside were wary of the stranger, the new girl without a history suddenly come into their midst. That didn't bother her. She was more comfortable in men's company than women's anyway. Until recently. She still couldn't understand that. If she liked a man, she was only too happy to treat him as an equal. Just because a person found another attractive was no reason to change toward them, was it?

She paused in her pacing. *Liar*, she told herself, remembering Drum and the artificial way she'd behaved with him after she'd finally seen what was really in her heart. . . .

*But I kept that to myself, didn't I?* she asked herself. Because she had to for everyone's sake. This was different. She'd made up her mind, but for the first time in long years she wasn't entirely sure of her course of action. She went over the list of people she might consult. She had friends, as many as could be counted on one hand. But how many more could anyone have? The heart had only so much room, Gilly reasoned, and she couldn't see the point of having half-friends; everything she did was absolute, or not at all. She sighed. She couldn't speak to any of her heart's friends now.

Her sister, Betsy, was her delight. But at twelve, only a child. Still, it would have been good to speak with her; Gilly didn't need advice so much as a sympathetic ear. But Betsy hated London and had remained in the countryside, still reveling in being allowed to be a child.

Bridget was Gilly's best friend. But Gilly knew where Bridget stood on the matter of her false fiancé. And the truth was, she didn't want to hurt and disappoint Bridget for any reason, and what she was about to do would do both.

Gilly counted Ewen Sinclair as a good friend and a reasonable man. Clever and worldly-wise too . . . but with a habit of being managing. She couldn't tell him what she was about to do. He might try to talk her out of it; he'd surely think she'd run mad. Perhaps she had.

She liked Ewen's friend, that redheaded rascal, Rafe, and called him friend, too. A soldier of fortune, easy to talk to, easier to tease, yet with a sound mind in that sound body of his. But he was presently roving the globe with his friend the Earl of Drummond.

And then there was Drum himself.

She would *not* think of him.

So who could she talk with? Who could listen, then tell her that whatever she did, if it made her feel better and hurt no one else, it was for the best? That was her personal code, after all. She needed only to hear it from a friend. But she feared there wasn't a soul in the world who would tell her that now.

Even little Maxmilian had come over to Damon's side. Literally as well as emotionally. Like when Damon happened to sneeze—which he always did, theatrically, when he saw Max.

"Oh no!" Damon would exclaim, putting a finger under his nose. "Here I go again! It seems your hair tonic makes a fellow sneeze!"

And Max, in a fit of giggles, would reply, "But Damon! I don't wear any!"

With a great show of trying to hold in that sneeze, Damon would reach into his jacket to get a hand-kerchief—and instead there was always something that just happened to be there for a sharp-eyed little boy to discover. Damon would slowly take the mysterious thing from his pocket, scratching his head, wondering how it got there. Little things: sweets, toy soldiers, whistles, colorful strings of what he called genuine Indian beads. And somewhere in his travels he'd learned to pluck coins out from behind a boy's ears.

Gilly found herself smiling at the memory, and froze. *No.* That way lay hurt and disaster. *No.* When the time was ripe, it was best to act quickly, before everything good turned rotten. She took a deep breath. *Today, then.*

"What's happened!" Damon demanded the moment he saw her face.

Gilly blinked. He'd come into the morning room to fetch her for their carriage ride. But the moment he laid eyes on her, his own had widened. Then his face went cold and hard, and he strode up to her and took her hand.

"What is it, Gilly?" he asked in a softer voice.

Little Max cut off his glad cry of greeting, looking from Damon to Gilly. His mother stared. Then they both turned to look at Gilly. Bridget hadn't noticed anything but a vague uneasiness on Gilly's part this morning. Damon had taken one look and read her heart. Gilly swallowed hard. He was making this much more difficult.

"I've been thinking—I have to speak with you, that's all," she said. But she could hear Bridget's sharply indrawn breath.

"About something dire, I think," Damon said, his eyes searching hers.

"Not *dire*. No need to upset my lady, she'll think I'm dying," Gilly said on a forced laugh. She saw how intent his gaze was, and shrugged. "I'm not ill or upset . . . well, I suppose I am upset, but not about anything dire." She made a face she hoped looked comical and added uneasily, "Well, the truth will be out by this afternoon, so I might as well come right out with it. I was thinking it was time we ended our charade, is all. I can't say more right here and now," she added with a quick look to Max. "But it's been on my mind, and you know very well that what's on my mind finds it way to my tongue. We'll talk about it later."

Gilly hated the silence that fell over the room, and hated the look in Damon's eyes even more. She sought a diversion. "Ah—how is your nose today?" she asked him.

"What?" he said, still holding her hand, still looking at her with deep concern.

"Has your allergy to hair tonic cleared up?"

"Oh, that," he said, obviously trying to force his mind back to the present.

But before he could say more, Max spoke up. "It's all right. I don't need a sweet. You go talk to Gilly, Damon. Then come back. When you come back, we'll play the sneeze game, all right, Damon?"

Damon sank to one knee. He put his hands on Max's shoulders and looked him in the eye. "A sweet? I don't think so. Not today. Today you proved you are a true friend. That means that when I come back I have to present you with something more important. An eagle feather or some other special talisman for you to keep to show that we are true friends forever."

Max grinned. But Bridget cut a swift dismayed look at Gilly. Damon saw it. He rose to his feet and bowed to Bridget. "We'll talk about it," he told her. "We *both* will," he added with more force, as he escorted Gilly to the door.

They got into his carriage. But Damon didn't pick up

his whip right away. "Now," he said after Gilly was seated next to him on the high driver's seat. "I'll head toward the park, where there's some quiet. But you may start talking. I'm listening."

She looked out at the street, at the other horsemen, carriages, a passerby, at anything but him. She shook her head. "There's nothing really to say. I just think it's time we ended it."

"Why?" he asked. He held the reins still, his team stood waiting for his command. But he didn't move them. He was staring at Gilly.

She shrugged her shoulders again, still avoiding his eye. "Well, it's been several weeks, and how long should we go on, after all? I mean to say, the longer we do, the harder it will be to explain the breakup."

"Why?" he asked again. "What happened? Don't gammon me. Something happened. I think you owe me the truth."

"The truth? Well, the truth is I'm grateful for what you did that night when Dearborne threatened to ruin my name, but—"

"No," he said, cutting her off. "That's over. I thought we'd become friends since then."

She was silent a moment. "You're right." She squared her shoulders. "I won't tell you tales. Excuse me for trying, you deserve better of me. But what I have to say needs concentration. Let's talk about the weather till we get to the park."

But they didn't speak about anything as they drove toward the park. Gilly stole a glance at his profile and saw he'd set his jaw tight. He didn't look at her. He didn't dare. He'd seen her clear when he'd stepped into the morning room, all in yellow, her flaxen hair picking up color from her vibrant gown until she glowed like a jonquil in the muted light. But the look on her face cut him to the quick.

It wasn't a bright day, but it wasn't raining, and the streets were full. London was bathed in that special kind of watercolor light that meant rain would fall before night did. Since there was no sunshine, there were no shadows anywhere but in her lovely face. She looked beset. He would know why. She suddenly wanted to end their engagement? Something had happened to force her hand. Whatever it was, he believed in himself enough to think he could change her mind. He had to.

The weeks they'd passed together had turned his impulsive act into firm resolve. She wasn't like any other woman he'd ever met. Lovely, with a bright, inquiring mind and a lively sense of humor, she was as exotic as a courtesan, but with a sense of honor steadfast as any man's he'd ever admired. She looked like a lily, but was tough as a thistle, and yet, curiously vulnerable, as he witnessed today. He wanted her body, heart, and mind, in whichever order they came to him. But he wanted them all, and for all of his life. He hadn't sought her, but now he had no doubt she was the woman he'd sought all his life. He'd fight for her, even if it meant he had to fight against her. In his experience what he fought for, he would win.

They passed through the gates of the park and, still without speaking, drove toward its center. At a grassy verge beneath towering trees, Damon slowed. He edged the horses to a stand well off the road, and flipped a coin to a grinning youth who came bustling up to them.

"We'll be back within the hour," he told the youth, handing him the reins. Then he helped Gilly dismount, took her hand, put it on his arm, and strolled with her on a winding path in the dappled light. She walked head down so the brim of her bonnet hid her face.

"I wonder if I should hire on a boy to act as tiger for me, to hold my horses whenever I stop," he remarked after they'd walked a few minutes, "though most places have likely lads eager to earn a few coins by watching a gent's cattle for him. Still, a boy in livery helps a fellow cut a dash. I never cared about that. I didn't think you did either. I could go on jabbering, you know, but I thought you were going to tell me something. So tell me, whenever you're ready—this year or next."

"Trying to find the right way to put this," she muttered.

"Put it any way, I'll sort it out."

She turned her face to his, and he was blinded for a moment. Her eyes made her remarkable instead of simply lovely. Sometimes, when light filled them as it did now, they glowed tigress amber and took his breath away.

"The thing is, Damon, that you don't know the whole truth about me," she said without preamble, getting over rough ground as fast as she could. "I mean, you know me—but not my history, and it's fairly terrible, and not at all what you need in a wife. I won't be coy. You seem to like me. You've hinted we could make this thing reality, if I wished." She stopped walking and faced him squarely. "If I'm off there, tell me, and don't worry about my feelings."

"You're right," he said, keeping his voice slow and steady, watching her carefully.

Gilly nodded solemnly. "So I thought. And so I suppose if the world were different—but it isn't and I'm not, and you deserve better. The thing is . . . oh, blast! I want to tell you, and think I can, but you know? I think it would be better if I showed you. Will you come back to the rig with me? And then drive me where I tell you? Now? That's the best way to get it over and done. Because just words just won't do it. They couldn't."

He looked at her gravely. Then nodded. "If it's what you need, then yes."

"Good."

They went back to the carriage. Damon gave the puzzled boy another coin, and after helping Gilly up to the seat, turned to her. "Where?" he said simply.

"After we leave the park, go toward Picadilly and then to Thames Street and then keep heading east."

He looked his question at her.

She nodded. "Just east. And keep going, a long way. Don't worry, I'll tell you when to stop—if you don't decide to turn 'round and come back first."

He looked at her for another moment, then picked up the reins. They drove in silence. Soon the noise of the streets made that seem necessary, since the roads were so crowded, they'd have had to shout to be heard. As they went on past the fashionable districts to those of shops and craftsmen, they came to streets that were even more crowded and with people who were less well dressed. Damon looked at Gilly.

"Go on," she said. "We aren't halfway there yet."

He frowned, but drove on.

The streets became dirtier, noisier. The houses at the sides of the road were older, increasingly less cared for, and there were obviously more people living in them. The vendors crying their wares became louder, more poorly dressed. The traffic changed as much as the surroundings did. Lone horsemen and carriages became scarce, carts, wagons, and barrows common. The horses they saw were heavy cart animals, and there were as many carts propelled by humans as horses. There were more dogs and children in the streets, and fewer of them under anyone's control. And the streets themselves were filthy, and reeked.

Damon was frowning fiercely now, his face set in an unaccustomed scowl. "Is this some sort of a joke?" he finally asked after he had to pull his team to a sudden stand because of a wave of ragged, screeching children who came pouring across his path.

"I wish it were," she murmured. "No. It's a thing words can't tell as well as eyes can." She didn't speak again until they'd gone a few cluttered, noisy streets farther. "Here!" she called. "Pull over to the curbside now. No one will harm the carriage, it looks too fine. They don't court troubles with the gentry, and besides, it's broad daylight. No—don't give them a penny!" she cried, shaking her head at the small crowd of urchins who had stopped to goggle at their carriage. "Be off!" she told them, brandishing her parasol. "No coins, nothing for you here. Maybe you have something for him, though? This bloke I'm with? Like information? He's with the Redbreasts, looking for the wretches who stole my . . . There, that's done it. No one will bother us now," she said with satisfaction as the crowd, child and man, scattered at the mention of the Bow Street Runners.

"Well," Gilly said, looking around, "I suppose this will do."

They'd pulled to the side of the road just off a busy intersection. The shops and houses that lined the streets here were so close together that if they didn't have signs with garish pictures of the goods for sale, it would have been hard to tell which were homes and which were not. Laundry hanging from windows competed with clothing hanging for sale, and all the goods were equally shabby. The streets leading from the intersection were narrow, dark, and winding. Some had arches over them; others had drunken-looking buildings that leaned toward each other over the cobbles so sunlight seldom reached them even on the brightest days. This wasn't one of them.

Gilly glanced around through narrowed eyes. "Yes," she said. "At least this way you can see what I'm saying. So, what do you think of this place, eh? Ever seen the like?"

Damon gave the street a brief glance, but his gaze was keener when he turned it back to her. "Of course. Here, on the Continent, and in America. The poor have to live somewhere."

"Have you ever lived in such?"

He was taken aback. "No. But I've visited such. When I was at university it was considered fashionable to mingle with the lower depths and come down here at night to go to taverns and . . . such. When I took a

Grand Tour, dropping in on this kind of district was as important as seeing landmarks. When I went to America, I went to slums on business many times. They were different there, rawer, newer, with mud instead of cobbles on the ground, and makeshift tents or wooden hovels instead of tenements. But poverty's the same everywhere."

Gilly's bonnet bobbed as she nodded. "As I thought. You came to such places for sport or business. If we went a few streets farther you'd see much worse, places no one in their right mind would go to for fun or profit."

"I don't doubt it," he said calmly, though his eyes were dark as slate, troubled as they searched her face. "I've seen worse, too," he added, and waited for her response.

At last she looked full at him. He hoped he'd never see such despair in her face again.

"I come from here. I'm not an impostor, I never pretended to be something I'm not," she said in a rush, trying to get the whole story out and over, like plucking out a splinter so the hurt would come before her brain could register it, before her own hand wavered at its task. "Everyone knows I'm Sinclair's ward, and they assume my parents were old friends of his, but he never knew them. We met just four years past.

"My sister, Betsy, sold flowers in the park. I worked at what I could turn my hand to and took care of us both, though the money she brought in helped. Any money did," she said bitterly. "We were alone. My father was a merchant seaman, but after he married he lost the taste for long sea voyages. Maybe he knew how hard it would be for our mother to live alone and raise us by herself. So he worked loading cargo on the docks. He dropped one day. His heart just gave out. Betsy don't remember him, she was only a babe. My mother was too proud to crawl to her family for charity. Well, I don't blame her. She'd gone to London to make her fortune against their advice, and with a sailor, at that. So she didn't ask them for help. But our dad didn't leave us a cent, and she'd no trade to turn to, except for being a wife and mother, and there's too many of them down here.

"She didn't have to starve, though. She was pretty enough to make her fortune on her back. But she was too proud for that, too. She took in washing—until she took a chill one day, and sickened and died soon after. So I turned my hand to what I could to keep Betsy and me from the poorhouse, or worse.

"I kept us together for eight years, but it was getting harder by the time we met Sinclair. I was nearly sixteen and Betsy eight. He hired her to come to his wedding as a flower girl as a surprise for his lady. They'd bought flowers from her when they were courting, you see, and he thought it would warm his lady's heart to see the little flower girl all cleaned up, carrying the flowers for their wedding. It certainly warmed our pockets. Well, no harm in it for one day, I thought when I got wind of it," Gilly said, her accent becoming gruffer, rougher, as she traveled back in her thoughts. "A viscount and a lady, after all.

"But then I saw them, and got to thinking. Then I heard they were bound for the countryside after their wedding and I thought some more. So I came to them the very next morning and asked if they'd take Betsy with them. I hated to part from her. But this is no place to raise a girl, and there were those who had their eyes on her for blanket work and I couldn't be everywhere at once, could I?"

Damon didn't breathe a word. He was astonished and dismayed. She was talking rapidly, changing before his eyes from a delicate lady of fashion to a rough and grieved child.

"They were good enough to take her. But then I heard there might be . . . some irregularity in their marriage. It was a hum, nothing but a lie, but I didn't know that. But Sinclair had gone back to London, and Betsy was alone with Bridget in the countryside. That I did know. So I went to bring Betsy back. Once there, I stayed on with Bridget. After Lord Sinclair returned from London and cleared up the matter, they persuaded me to stay on with them forever. So, here I am. And there you are."

"Am I?" Damon asked, watching her closely. "There's a lot you haven't said. Left alone to cope at such a young age? How did you earn money?"

She laughed harshly. "Think I was petticoat goods? Think again. Never. I wouldn't sell myself. I learned from my mother, and from watching the streets, too. There's money in the flesh trade, to be sure. But it goes as fast as a girl's looks do. There's a deal you don't know, true," she said, avoiding his eyes, "but I didn't sell my body for anything but hard labor."

She glowered at him, as though he'd said something insulting rather than just watching her so closely. She lifted her head, her eyes demon gold. "I gleaned nails from the streets and resold them; I picked coals that hadn't burned from the slag heap to resell, too. Odd bits of bottles, rags, string—there's nothing that can't be used again. And kids are closer to the ground and can find things faster than older gleaners. Then I learned that a quick mind beats a strong back. I ran with a pack of other children who taught me how to turn my hand to profitable work—selling off things the peddlers don't want to throw away at the end of the day. Then selling better things, because the faster you get rid of their stock the more they trust you with new goods.

"I learned a line of patter," she said proudly. "I learned who the laziest and simplest vendors were. I learned how to patch up old goods to look like new. I even did street labor when the money pinched."

"They hire females for street labor? You amaze me. The rest, I can see," Damon said softly, warily. "But Gilly, that tries even my credulity."

"You're right. They don't hire females for that kind of work," Gilly said proudly, raising her chin. "And they didn't. This part of London isn't a safe place for a girl alone. So I wasn't one after . . . after Mama died. I dressed as a lad. I carried a knife. Everyone knew it, because I had to use it now and then. So those who knew the truth didn't say. Those who didn't never got a chance to find out."

"As a *boy*?" he asked.

She moved restlessly. "Why not? No one notices a street rat. And the other rats are too smart to care."

He sat and studied her. The delicate line of her clenched jaw, the slender arch of her eyebrows, the small fine-boned hands. He shook his head. "No, even before you became a woman, I can't see it. They had to know."

"Hah!" she said with the ghost of a real laugh. "Easy to say *now*. The quality never looked beneath the dirt. Only Ewen knew. He knew right off. Bridget didn't. Ewen's friend Rafe didn't know, neither. Even Drum didn't guess until he was told!"

"Even the great Earl of Drummond?" Damon said, with the first smile he'd shown since she began talking. "Good to know his halo slipped, if only once."

She flushed. "Well, but he's a downy one in the normal way of things," she said defensively. "Though I still tease him about it now, he didn't have an inkling when we met. But once he found out he did all he could to turn me into a proper female. He taught me to speak more correctly. He helped with my manners and deportment, too. He's no saint but he was good to me, and if I go on about it, it's because I'm grateful. I never forget a friend."

"Don't apologize, I have older brothers," Damon said gently, "and I think the sun rises and sets on them, too."

She plucked at the folds of her parasol instead of looking at him. "But there it is. I was a slum child, and I masqueraded as a lad until I met up with the Sinclairs. It's time I told you. I feel badly about it—but in a strange way, better now." She met his eyes again. "It's right that you should know. No one else outside our circle does . . . or so I think. But sometimes I think that somehow Lord Wycoff does, which is why he pursues me—me, of all the other young unmarried females in the *ton*. He usually only hunts married women. But he met up with me when I first came to the Sinclairs. And I was so awkward with being a proper female then and he's so clever. I think he guesses more than most people. But you know? That may be why I feel more comfortable with him than I ought. Because I don't like to live a lie."

Gilly faced Damon squarely. "This one's gone on long enough. I like you too well to keep up the pretense. Now, tell me you could seriously consider taking this false engagement of ours one day further!"

He was silent. She put out a hand and laid it on his sleeve. "Please understand that I understand," she said. "No one will think the worse of you when we break it off. Not Bridget, Ewen, or anyone. That's why I didn't even want to start this thing and why I think it's time to end it now. Imagine if others found out! If people knew, they'd think I played a vile trick on you. A no one, a less-than-that, a slum brat dressed up in lady's clothing, trying to snare herself a gentleman! Not just society. What would your family think? And who could blame them?

"I didn't mean to deceive you, Damon," she said when he didn't speak, just stared at her, his eyes gone stormy and still. "But it's better to end this before it begins to hurt anyone."

He nodded. Her heart broke from its steady beat, just once. But then she nodded, too. "Well, and so," she said, swallowing hard, trying to think what to say next.

"It would hurt," he said. "I think it might just about kill me. But tell me, Gilly, would it hurt you?"

"Of course," she said, only talking to drown out her unruly thoughts. "Of course, we're friends . . ."

"I don't see how what you've told me changes that."

"Don't you?" she asked, her voice growing thin. "Listen carefully, then. I was like any of the children you see running through the streets here, a mongrel, a castoff, a homeless thing fighting to stay alive. Clever, I grant, for here I am as you see me now. But in your world, Damon . . ." She shook her head, biting her lower lip to keep it from showing all the self-pity and loathing she felt. "I'm . . . i am not at all 'the thing'!"

She laughed. "That's an expression Drum taught me. Much better than the one I was going to use. The one I was born and bred to use. As you were born and bred to better than me."

Now Damon moved. He broke from his rigidity. He grasped both her hands hard, his eyes blazing, his voice angry. "There's none better! You're worthy of better than me, Gilly Giles. You're brave and honest, and good to the bone. That you survived is a miracle, that you grew to be so honorable and fine is not a surprise. Because goodness and valor is in the bone, not in the name. Never—*never* apologize to me!"

Her eyes widened. He loosened his tight clasp on her hands but didn't let them go. "Yes," he added after a long indrawn breath, "you're right. Now is as good a time as any to end our charade."

"Well," she said, so buffeted by emotion she couldn't find another thing to say.

"Let's make it real," he said fiercely. "Marry me, Gilly Giles. We'll put the past where it belongs. It only matters to me because it helped forge you into the woman you are—the one I want to marry and raise my family with. You may not be as convinced of it as I am—at least, not now, not yet. But you can't deny you feel something toward me. I'm not being a peacock. We've gotten to know each other more in these past weeks than most couples do before they marry. But it's not a thing we can debate. I was going to wait for the right time—and I think it's come. Deny you feel anything, and we'll end it here and now. Admit even a little—and marry me in truth."

"*Truth*? Oh, God!" Gilly said in anger and vexation, pulling her hands from his, beating one small fist on the seat, clenching the other tight. "Pardon my blasphemy, but damn and blast and . . ." She came to a decision. He saw it in her face, and flinched at the fury and pain he saw. "There's more. And it's worse."

"Worse?" he asked.

"No." She corrected herself. "The worst. I wasn't going to tell you. But you force me . . ." She stood in one jerky movement and gazed down at where he was still sitting, noting his surprise. She tossed her parasol aside, her hands fisted at her sides. "Let's have it over with and done," she said, as a man might when he challenged another to a duel. "Get down from your high seat, Damon. Come with me. This is a thing I have to face, too. It *is* time. Find another eager lad to watch your carriage. The street's too narrow for it where we're going. It's just a little way—there—in an alley down that street. It's where Gilly Giles was *really* born. It's a place I think we both have to see now."

# 6

They made a handsome couple, the slight young woman all in jonquil yellow, with her jaunty straw bonnet, moving like a lost ray of sunlight ready to illuminate the cramped and dingy side street. The gentleman in his fawn jacket, buckskins, and high shining boots, walking at her side. They'd have been remarked upon anywhere. They were gaped at here, where they looked like visitors from a foreign land.

Gilly held her breath as they entered the side street, and not just because of the stench from rotting rubbish in the gutters. She hadn't come down this street in over a decade. When she'd lived in the district she'd gone blocks out of her way to avoid it. She couldn't believe she dared come here again. But it was right for Damon to see and she was never a girl to shrink from duty, however loathsome it might be. He said nothing, only looked around, and at her from time to time. His grim expression matched her own.

He didn't know what she was doing, or why. But he knew it hurt her. And so it hurt him because he couldn't protect her from whatever it was. The atmosphere was stultifying. It was a filthy byway in a sullen slum, the decaying houses around them huddled together, frowning down at them, blocking air and light. Not so very far from the traffic at the intersection, this street was leagues away from it in character. Narrow and crooked, it seemed deserted except for whatever ghosts Gilly was pursuing.

She finally paused midway down the street at the entrance to a dim alleyway between houses. It seemed to Damon that Gilly shuddered. She turned an ashen face up to his.

"Well. Here we are," she said in an artificially bright voice. "I don't know why I'm surprised it hasn't changed. Nothing here changes but the people. I suppose I thought there ought to be a plaque or something." She laughed unconvincingly as she glanced down the alley. Her eyes went flat and dark. "Well," she said, "I'll tell you what's what. But first, I think we ought to go in there. You have to see what I have to say. I have to go, because I see now that if I don't, I'll never be able to get out of there—at least in my mind. I know it don't make sense to you now. It will.

"Come with me, please. Mind your boots, though. Around here, good garbage is gleaned and sold. Only the worst kind remains. That's what's here. In every way," she muttered. She braced her shoulders and stepped into the dim passage.

It was wider than it had looked from the outside. At one time there might have been two fine houses here, with room between for privacy. But everything fine had left centuries ago. Now it was clotted with debris, muck heaped in the corners. The facing windows in each neighboring house were either boarded over, overlaid by dirt or decades of pigeon droppings.

But Damon wasn't looking at his surroundings now. He was watching Gilly. She stopped halfway down the alley and stared at something near a wall, something he couldn't see. When she spoke, her voice was low and rushed, gruff with suppressed emotion.

"Well, and there we are," she said to the air. "Nothing much to see. I didn't see much then, neither. See, I was only seven or so, and he was so big. Aye, Old Rot Guts was a fat man. See, we all knew to stay away from him, because he fancied kiddies. But one day I was thinking too hard to pay attention, and I ran past here on my own, a mistake, and he grabbed me. Well, he did me. Fast and hard, and he laughed all the while. And so that's what it is."

There was a silence as he tried not to understand what she meant, every particle of his being rejecting the terrible thought. She took a long shuddery sigh, and turned her eyes to him at last. Her voice was cool and contained now, though he could hear the pain beneath. "See, it isn't just that I am no one, Damon," she said in her usual accent, "or that I grew up here. I could deal with that—you say you could, too. So that may be a problem, but it isn't the biggest one. It's that

I'm not a virgin. A gentleman has a right to expect that of his bride."

"What did you do? What happened to him?" Damon demanded, ignoring the rest.

"Oh, well, who could I tell? My ma? I told her I fell and hurt myself badly. But she called in a quack, and he rumbled it. I had to lay abed a week but I didn't need stitching, so I was glad. But what could she do but cry? My word against his? And who's to care? Just another slum brat despoiled, and so what? They sell girls cheaply down here. Unless they work at it, then it costs the gentlemen good coin to get themselves one at a brothel. But those girls have protectors. I had no one to fight for me. If I'd a father, or brothers, or a family, though . . ."

She shook her head. "But I did have friends, and they kept watch on him for me. Soon as I was up and around again, I got word. And for the first and last time in my life I went to the Runners and laid evidence against a man. He swung for it. Not for doing that to me, you understand. The law doesn't work that way for those down here. But for nabbing a purse. I went to his hanging. I cheered so much, I tickled some young gentleman and he threw me a coin for it. I spent it on the best dinner I ever had. And threw it up right after, of course. A waste, all 'round. Then I got myself up as a boy, and never looked back."

She seemed to recall herself. "But you must! Oh, look at me, Damon," she cried. "*Really* look at me! I'm like a bad apple, all polished on the outside, but rotten to the core inside. Not a fit wife for you."

"Then for who?" he asked, deadly calm.

"For someone who doesn't deserve the truth, I suppose."

"But you will marry? This didn't turn you against all men?"

She frowned, puzzled. "Why should it? What sense would it make for you to hate all women if one hurt you? Oh, at first, of course I was afraid and angry and I hated all men. But my mother talked to me. She wasn't educated, but she was wise. She talked and talked, and I thought on it. My father had been a good man, hadn't he? she said. The world was filled with good men. Old Rot Guts wasn't a man, he was a beast. And didn't I want children, and a home of my own one day? It made sense. It still does.

"If that didn't do the trick of convincing me altogether, Ewen Sinclair did. He didn't have to take us in, but he cared too much to fob us off on anyone else. He made me and Betsy his wards for no other reason but kindness. He and his father, Drum and Rafe, they taught me men are capable of great goodness as well as wickedness. I'd be a fool to let what happened to me at the hands of one madman rule me forever. And I'm not a fool. I intend to wed. But the thing of it is, Damon, that I have nothing to offer you. Because you deserve the very best."

"Gilly," Damon said urgently, "you are that. If I could I'd render time itself to change things . . ." He clenched his hands in impotent rage. "But I can't. I can only deal with it, as you have. No—don't speak now, only listen. A child was violated here. That child is gone as surely as that time itself is. You've changed inside and out. You're a woman now. And what a woman doesn't give can't be taken, not her virtue, not her heart. Not fit for me? When you match me heart and soul? Just because of one terrible moment in an alley a generation ago? Because you're not a virgin? Oh Gilly, you're more of one than many I've met!"

She frowned in incomprehension. He touched a hand to her cheek. "Yes, proper young maidens are supposed to be virgins," he said, "but I assure you there are virginal young women in the highest reaches of society who are much more experienced at lovemaking than you are, Gilly Giles. You'll understand one day," he said, unable to restrain a crooked smile for her confusion, "but for now, trust me on that. You're innocent in all that matters, visited only by violence.

"Hear me, Gilly," he said, looking down into her eyes. "That man's actions didn't mark you, your triumph over it did. He didn't desire a woman. Your lovely body takes my breath away, but it isn't the one he wanted. That one vanished with the years. You're no longer the child he violated, either. You're a woman, untouched. I might not deserve you. But I promise you, I'll try to."

And there, in the filthy alley, he tenderly cupped her face in his two hands. Slowly, watching her carefully all the while—so as not to miss it if she drew away—he lowered his head and brought his lips to hers. He was thrilled at how that tentative touch bloomed into a real kiss, at how the warmth of her mouth slowly answered his, and touched beyond his experience at how she crowded into his welcoming arms. Until he tasted tears between their lips. Then he stepped back.

He smiled at her. "Will you marry me, Gilly Giles? Mind, it's the second time I've asked."

She smiled back at him. "I think," she said mistily, "that we ought to wait another day or two, at least, so you can think it through."

"Not so *you* can think it through?" he asked, locking his hands around her waist, pulling her up close to him.

He didn't hear her answer if she gave one.

"Oh, lovely!" a rough voice hooted. "Look what we got, lads! Lovers snogging in the alley. *Rich* lovers, too! Well, boyos, what say we takes the gold, and then the blonde, eh?"

There were four of them. Four ragged men. The alleyway wasn't wide enough to hold them side by side, so they stood in pairs. The two in front were leering at the couple they'd surprised, boldly assessing them. One held a length of lumber to use as a cudgel, the other a knife. The two behind them fanned out as much as they were able so they could watch, and so no one else could get in or out of the alley no matter how much noise was made.

Damon put Gilly away from him, refusing to think about how white-faced she'd gone. He stepped in front of her. He knew how it must look to the intruders. A fragile girl, a useless fancy gent. The men wouldn't wonder at why they were there, they themselves were there to take everything they could. First money, and then whatever finery they could rip from their victims' bodies. Then, the body of the lovely young woman. Damon would not allow it, he'd die first. But he knew his death would be of no use to her now.

He didn't intend to die. He only wished he could assure her of that. But he had neither time or opportunity.

He faced them. Four against one. Not bad odds. He only needed luck, and skill. He had the skill. He had no time to pray for the luck. He carried a pocket pistol as many gentlemen in London did, and a knife in an inside sheath in his boot, from force of habit. But he wouldn't be able to go for his pistol or stoop and flick out his knife fast enough to prevent them from charging him in a wild melee. He didn't want that. Their careful formation was his best ally now. He put his legs apart and waited. Let them be on the move. The two in front were very sure of themselves. Good. The two behind were watchfully waiting; they weren't leaders.

The two men in front looked at each other, grinned, and began to edge forward. The one with the knife half crouched, moving crab-like toward Damon's right. The one with the club was swaggering toward him to his left, beating the weapon against his palm, to show his power. Good. Damon waited. They took it for terror and moved more confidently.

When the man with the knife was almost abreast of him, Damon moved. A gentleman fought with his hands. But Damon had fought with few gentlemen, at least not for his life. He ducked and swerved, kicking out strong with his high hard boot, catching the wrist of the hand that held the knife. As the knife went flying in a shining spiral, he spun, jabbing an elbow into the surprised man's jaw, using his momentum to drive his arm forward as he spun round again and crashed his fist into the astonished cudgel-bearer's face.

When Damon straightened from his crouch a second later he had his own knife in his hand and was slashing at the arm that held the club. He kicked the wavering cudgel loose from its now bloody grip, and turned round again to throw all his weight behind his fist as he floored the teetering man on his left.

It was all done in three heartbeats. On the fourth, Damon narrowed his eyes to turn his attention to the men who'd hesitated, lagging behind their leaders.

One was open-mouthed with agony, holding a bleeding arm to his chest. The other was running back down the alley. And Gilly Giles was standing by Damon's side now, a bloody knife in one hand, the cudgel in the other.

The men on the ground lay still before them, feigning unconsciousness.

"You!" Damon shouted to the bleeding man, brandishing his pistol. "Go now!" The man lurched away, vanishing down the alley.

Damon turned his attention to the men at his feet. He toed them with his boot tip. "Crawl away," he snarled, "then, when you're three body lengths away from us—and *only then*—run. Fast. I'll give you to the count of five. At six, I fire. Turn back to look at us only if you want to look your last. One . . . two . . ."

They were gone, sobbing and panting, within moments. Only then did Damon look at Gilly again. He caught her around the waist. "Come. Keep the weapons, but let's go."

They didn't speak again until they were in the carriage and heading west at a trot. "Are you all right?" he asked when the horses were well away.

"I'm fine," she said, as she caught her breath. "I wasn't in any danger. See, I grabbed the knife when it landed, and while those two fools were watching you, I

stabbed one and went at the other, and he broke and
ran. I would have been in trouble if you weren't so fine!
You were wonderful!"

"I was not!" he growled, concentrating on steering
around a barrow in his path.

"But four to one!"

"Those are no odds with such men," he said, almost
angrily. "I had every advantage over them. I eat good
nourishing food. I sleep in a soft bed. I have no dis-
eases I know of, because I can afford the finest doctors
if I'm sick. They have none of those advantages. And
I've fought with worse, at worse odds but with better
tactics. It was the Americans who showed me the
advantages of ignoring custom. Men in a row go down
in a row. Surprise is everything. I was taught that a gentleman doesn't use anything but his fists, a whip, a pistol, or a sword. They taught me a man uses his brains,
hands, feet, and anything else he can find if he wants
to live to be a gentleman again."

"Well, however you did it, you did it!" she crowed.
"And I only had to go after the one, because when the
other saw what you did, he couldn't run fast enough."

Now Damon turned his head to look at her. She
was glowing bright. Her bonnet was gone, her wind-
whipped hair was flying like streaming pennants of
sunshine around her flushed face, her eyes shone
tiger bright, and she was grinning widely. He began
laughing.

"Look at you!" he managed to say when she
frowned. "I'd have needed salts, at the least a physician, for any other female in that situation, gently bred
or otherwise. She'd be trembling still. If she was even

conscious. I'd have had to lug her back to the carriage at the very least, instead of racing back to it side by side with her. But you! You protected me, and did it well, and reveled in it, too!"

Her animation vanished. She swept the hair back from her eyes. "Yes," she said sadly. "So now you see what my answer to you must be."

"Exactly! You were made for me. We're two of a kind. Oh, Lord, Gilly!" he exulted. "You're perfect!"

"You've lost your mind," she said.

"My heart, alone. My mind is firmly made up."

"You want a street urchin, a hurly burly female? And a ruined one, at that, as a wife?"

"I want you, Gilly Giles, a woman who's a lady when she wants to be, brave as a lioness when she has to be, and with a heart that's whole, whatever happened to her in the past." She began smiling tremulously until he added, "And with a heart that's wholly mine."

And then she looked away.

"Or is that you think you can never care for me?" he asked quickly, seeing her sudden disquiet.

"Not that, never that," she answered as quickly, because she did care for him, and knew she could learn to care more. It was just that she didn't know if her heart could ever be wholly his, since she'd given it away so long ago to someone else. But that wasn't what he asked, so she only said again, "No, not that, never that."

"Whatever possessed you?" Bridget cried, after she heard the whole story when they returned.

"My fault entirely," Damon told Ewen Sinclair. "I

should have thought. I never should have driven there with her."

"A lot you had to say about it," Ewen growled, glowering at Gilly. "She probably cloaked the thing in mystery and pleaded with you prettily, and you were in trouble before you knew it."

"He had to know the truth," Gilly said defensively.

"That," Ewen said, glaring at her, "is why they invented language. It's not your fault, Ryder. I'll allow it mightn't be Gilly's either. She's always believed she can handle any situation by herself. Indeed, as she just so graphically showed you, she had to for a very long time and didn't do too badly at it either. She's as impulsive as a spring breeze. But her heart's as sound as any man's, and as you saw, she has more courage than most of them."

"Thank you," Gilly said, exchanging relieved looks with Bridget.

"I'd want her at my side in a fight, but now you can see why we wouldn't mind getting her off our hands," Ewen teased, with a sidewise glance to see Gilly's reaction.

"Wouldn't mind taking her off them," Damon said, "but that isn't in my power. It's for the lady herself to say now."

"Indeed?" Bridget asked with bright-eyed interest, looking from Damon's amused expression to Gilly's suddenly flustered one.

"Yes, and I wish she would, and soon," Damon said, watching Gilly, too. "Since we put the notice of our engagement in the Times I've been getting letters from my family asking for the date of the happy occasion so they can make travel plans. There are a lot of them, and they live far from here."

"But we wouldn't have the ceremony in London," Bridget said. "Our church at home would be so much nicer, wouldn't it, Ewen?"

"Well, if it's to be soon it would have to be," he answered. "We leave for home in a week. We never intended to spend the summer in London. Of course, if it's to be later, it doesn't matter."

"What *matters*," Gilly said, goaded, "is if it's to *be*!"

"Yes, of course," Damon said. But they all looked at her as though waiting for an immediate answer.

When none was given, Damon shrugged. "I think I'd better be going now. We're promised to the Wentworths this evening? I have to change, I'll be back here at seven."

"Need a compress for that hand?" Ewen asked, noting how Damon favored it.

"Let me see!" Gilly said, rushing to Damon's side. She snatched up his hand to look at it. It was obviously too swollen for him to put his glove on. "It's bleeding!" she cried. She held his hand, turning it over, absently noting its width, how long his fingers were, the strength and warmth . . . and suddenly let go, clasping her own hands hard together, shocked at how she'd reacted to him.

"It's scraped," Damon said, flexing his swollen knuckles, "nothing more. I should have had my gloves on."

"But you wouldn't have had the flexibility," Gilly said seriously. "Can't handle a knife so well with a mitt." She was frowning, but then had to grin because everyone else was laughing so hard at her.

*          *          *

They sat in the Sinclairs' salon, alone together, as was the prerogative of an engaged couple, discussing the evening they'd just passed. There was a footman in the hall and the door was only half closed, but they could sit side by side on a sofa, and since they'd just got there he could stay another fifteen minutes.

"I tell you, I don't know where you get the control," Gilly said in wonder. "I'm glad I don't carry a pistol, because I'd have shot the woman myself."

"It was a temptation," Damon said, his voice shaking with withheld laughter.

"A soprano? And supposed to be singing opera? Huh," Gilly huffed. "She sounded like she was being forced to sit on spikes—slowly."

"I do appreciate music," Gilly added seriously, "and regret that by the time I could take music lessons it was too late for me to learn to really play well. It's all I can do to pick out a tune on a piano, much less a harp. But I wouldn't ask everyone to sit and listen to me try. And to think they paid her to sound like a sack of strangled cats! I'm so glad Bridget said she was feeling faint, and then gave me *that* look, so I knew she was shamming it. Speaking of strangling, I was ready to throttle that soprano, I really was."

Her murderous declaration only made him look at her more fondly, if that was possible. She wore green and pink again tonight, but this gown was leaf green, decorated with tiny embroidered rosebuds. She was scented with white freesia, and wore one in her high-dressed hair. It was all he could do to keep his hands idle on his knees and not touch the tiny pulse he could see beating at the base of her neck. He didn't dare look anywhere else. Her gown was low enough to make him yearn to know how the skin on her smooth white breasts would feel against his palms. She spoke about his control? She didn't know the half of it.

He yearned for her. But knew he had to be cool and collected. She was a fiery creature, but that sort of fire would alarm her. Especially because of her early experience. She said she'd got over it, but he didn't want to rush things or risk shocking her. He shocked himself, though. He'd never wanted any woman so much.

He had to be very careful. But he'd learned to be a careful man. You couldn't buy or sell for any profit if you let those you were dealing with know how much you needed to make the bargain. This bargain meant the course of his entire future. He shifted in his seat; there were things that had to be said.

"So," he said idly, as though he'd just remembered. "Have you given it any more thought? I wasn't joking before. My family does want to know when the date will be. I think everyone in society must be wondering, too. But they've seen you. My family hasn't. They're desperate to get a look at you. For that matter, they're anxious to get a look at me, too. I arrived in London only planning to rest a little while before heading home. I'm a good traveler but weeks at sea make a man long for a quiet bed, and the trip from here to my home is a long one. Weeks don't matter much in the usual way of things, but they haven't seen me for years."

"That's terrible!" Gilly cried, eyes widened. "Why did you linger so long here?"

"You know the answer to that, Gilly."

She toyed with a fold of her skirt.

"I don't want to press you," he said, and though he wanted her so badly he dared not say it, that much at least was true. "But I won't leave London till I have an answer. We did this as a temporary ruse. I want it to be permanent. If I'm expecting the impossible, then yes, let's end it here and now, before expectations grow too high." And that, too, he found was true. He wouldn't linger where he wasn't wanted. He was besotted with her, but never a fool, and he refused to play one. There was nothing so pathetic as a deluded lover. "So. Do we end it? Or go on to a wedding?"

She hesitated. It was the same question she'd been asking herself all day. And answering all day, as well, differently every hour. She could do far worse. He could do much better. She liked him very much. She gazed at him, thinking of the children this man could beget, strong and handsome, clever and charming. A girl with that shapely mouth, a boy with those hands . . . and so sunny-natured. She remembered how he'd delighted in her fighting at his side, how he laughed with her so often, how he'd taken the news of her ruin and somehow made it sound like triumph.

She remembered her two suitors at home in the countryside, too. They couldn't compare to this man. Only one man she knew did, and he was the only man who surpassed Damon in her heart. But she also remembered the letter lying on the desk upstairs in her room, the one she no longer had to read, she knew it so well.

. . . *Nabbing yourself a gent with a handsome face and a handsome fortune? No less than The Catch of the Season, Ewen says. I expected no less of you.* Bravo! *You've done well for your-self, child!*

But not only did Damon Ryder want her, he had no title, so society couldn't be *that* shocked if she married him. He wouldn't be ostracized or cut by his friends and acquaintances. He said his family wouldn't mind. He said he wanted her . . .

"But I don't love you," she blurted. "I mean to say, I like you very well, but I told you I won't lie to you."

"Have you heard any declarations of love from me?"

"No," she said, much struck, "but then why would you want to marry me?"

*Because,* he thought, *I think you'll someday come to love me as much as I do you.* But instead he said, as truthfully, if less accurately, "I've never been in love, Gilly. Not in all this time. But I think we'll grow to it together, in time."

She nodded, thinking about who and what he was, of chances lost and gained, and those invisible unborn children who seemed to be waiting breathlessly for her answer, too. And of the letter upstairs in her room.

"I think I will," she said, "if you're still sure."

"When?" he asked lazily, putting an arm on the edge of the sofa's back to keep himself from catching her up in his arms.

"When would you like?" she asked, hardly believing she'd actually agreed.

"Soon. I'd like to see my parents again. I'd like you to meet them, too. Even if we marry from the Sinclairs' country estate, it takes three weeks for the banns to be read, a week on either side to travel to and from . . . in six weeks?"

"Six weeks?" she gasped.

He raised an eyebrow. "You think double that—or triple—will make a difference in your decision?"

"I only meant, won't people think we're too hasty? Dearborne will probably spread stories, his evil tongue is probably itching to do it. I mean, they might think we *had* to rush to the altar. . . . Will I never learn to mind my own tongue?" she said in chagrin, her cheeks turning pink.

"No," he laughed, "it's not your tongue that's at fault, it's your math. We announced our engagement four weeks ago, add six weeks to that. Our wedding guests will be eyeing your waistline, but if you don't stuff yourself with cream puffs every hour from now to then, I don't think we'll have a problem with gossip."

"Are you sure?" she asked, "I mean to say . . . well, you're very trusting. I told you I wasn't . . . pure. I agree to a hasty wedding. How do you know I'm not bamming you?" she challenged him, because right now argument seemed the best way to stave off the nervousness she was beginning to feel about her decision. "How can you tell? I mean, how do you know I won't present you with something unexpected, after all?"

"Because I believe in your honor," he said seriously. "And," he added, too nonchalantly, "because I've kissed you."

"*What*?" she asked, sitting up straight and staring at him.

"You don't kiss like a woman who's in the habit of kissing, you see."

"No, I don't see," she said in a fierce whisper, looking toward the doorway to be sure no one heard. "You don't think I *kiss* right? I've had no complaints . . . that is, I mean to say . . . Well, bother! I have kissed a fellow or two. When I grew up, I mean, and dressed as a girl at last." She tilted her head, considering it. "It was to see if it would make me ill. It didn't."

"Gratified to hear that," he said.

"Well, it was a consideration," she explained seriously. "It didn't want to make me do more, but it was all right. Since then, I let one or two others try it, for the same reason, of course." *Two*, she thought, thinking of the hasty attempts she'd allowed her two suitors at home. "And you, of course, and you didn't complain, as I recall."

"No, certainly not," he said reasonably, "but I could tell your experience was limited to those experiments of yours."

"How?" She looked chagrined.

"Simple," he said, suddenly so close he had to lower his voice. "Here, I'll show you. Look at me. Now say, 'Oh!' as though you're surprised."

"Oh," she echoed doubtfully.

"No, as though you're *really* surprised. Yes, just so. But no! Don't close your lips again. You see, dear Gilly, that kiss we shared was very pleasant . . . but you didn't let me taste it, and you didn't sample mine. Kisses are delicious. You really do have to taste them to know how much they are."

"Oh," she said, surprised.

"Yes," he said, and angled his mouth over hers to kiss her parted lips. And then drew her into his arms and deepened the kiss.

She was shocked, then staggered. Then she stopped

thinking as sensations coursed through her. His mouth was warm, he tasted of sweet and tangy liquors, he made her stop thinking of anything at all—until she felt the rough tip of his tongue trace her own, and went stone still—and then leaned toward him to experience it again, because it was so strange. He must have a reason to do such a bizarre thing. She would know why. It was challenging. And she could never resist a challenge. She had to see if it was merely shocking, or delicious, as he'd said. She gave it a moment. It was delicious. Dark and deep and intriguing.

"So," he said, when he finally drew away, his voice a little shaken. "So, very good. It will be a real marriage after all."

"I *said* I wanted children, I don't know how else to get them," she said without thinking because she was so bemused. "Oh!" Her hand flew to her mouth.

"*Oh* indeed, my dear Gilly," he laughed, and drew her back into his embrace.

He mightn't be what she wanted, she thought as she went willingly back into the warm shelter of his arms and offered up her mouth to his again. But the man she did want was right again, as usual. Because she had done well for herself, and had gotten more than she'd expected, or deserved.

But she'd be good to Damon, and for him. And if he was second best, she vowed he'd never know it or have cause to feel in second place . . . and then stopped thinking of anything but his embrace.

# 7

Damon idly shuffled through the cards of invitation to his wedding. "You aren't inviting Lord Wycoff?" he asked with interest. He became even more interested in the way the color rushed to his fiancée's face at his words. "I thought he was a friend of yours. An odd choice for a friend, but if he is one I wonder why I don't see his name here. I don't mind his being there. Do you?"

"Why should I?" Gilly asked, surprised.

"There are those who might wonder at your friendship."

"Oh, as if I give a fig for that!" Gilly said irritably. "I met him a long time ago at a weekend we spent at someone's house, when I was still new at being a girl. I made *so* many mistakes," she said with a shake of her head. "But he, of all people, covered up for me and tried to set me at my ease. And he was *not* trying to seduce me then . . . I don't think. Well, I don't guess, not with Drum there! And Ewen and Rafe, to boot. As I said, he's guessed my beginnings, I suppose, and takes an interest in me. He's wise in the ways of the *ton*. Very amusing, too. Don't worry, I can take care of myself."

"I don't doubt you can, although I'd hope you'd let me do that now. But if that's all true, then I don't know why you haven't included him," Damon said, too carelessly.

She glanced down at the blank invitation under her hand. "I didn't think he'd want to travel so far," she invented quickly, "he's got so much town bronze, it might rust in the country dew."

"Mmm," Damon hummed. "A lovely analogy," he said, taking a seat beside her. "Now, myself, I find it's interesting to see people out of their usual surroundings. It's almost always depressing, though. So I don't blame you for not asking him. If he's a friend of yours, I suppose it would be embarrassing for you to see him in an awkward position, not to mention putting him in one."

Gilly laid down her pen and looked directly at him, trying to assess his mood and exact meaning. But when she did she found it was hard to get past the actual appearance of the man. He always looked handsome, but now some wicked thought was tilting his mouth and his eyebrows, making him even more attractive. Which was difficult, she thought, because he filled the eye just sitting there. He wore casual morning clothes, a dun jacket, buckskins, and boots.

His hair glowed tobacco gold in the morning light. His eyes sparkled with laughter.

She sighed. Constant exposure to him ought to have made her accustomed, not more susceptible, to him. She couldn't understand it. She saw him every day, they'd kissed over a dozen times since they'd decided to actually marry. And yet . . . instead of his attraction fading with familiarity, it was growing. When he kissed her, her wits fled and she didn't miss them while she stayed, stunned, in his embrace. When he touched her, it seemed he touched more than her body, and she found to her shock that she wanted to offer him ever more body to touch.

She went into his arms with wonder and utter trust. It scarcely mattered if it was the base of her neck or the curve of her breast he caressed—his touch made her senses thrum. She'd feel the warmth and strength of him and yet relax, secure in the knowledge that his ardor was matched by his control. Because he was the one who always ended it, even though he said it was becoming difficult to do so. Just last night he'd drawn back murmuring something ruefully humorous about men's fashions and how he had to leave her soon, with his dignity, at least—if not his mind—intact.

Just last night, she'd surprised them both. He'd held her close and she'd felt his urgency, that foreign shape suddenly risen hard against her body. He was right, their clothing was too thin for her not to notice. With all his control, there were some manifestations of his desire he couldn't conceal. No more than she could hide the sudden rush of sensation that caused the tips of her breasts to rise and tighten, pebbling against his shirtfront. He reacted to it, and it made his other problem worsen—"Or better, as the case may be," he said on a rusty chuckle as he drew away from her.

"I'm sorry," he'd said, sitting back.

"For what?" she asked, still dazed with pleasure. She, of all women, expected men to be easily aroused. That didn't surprise her. The amazing thing was her own response, how often lately she longed to touch more than his jacket when she put her arms around his neck.

"I didn't want to worry you, just remind you," he said to her bewilderment. "I am in control, Gilly. I'll always be with you. For you."

"Remind me?" she asked in pretty puzzlement. "About what . . . Oh! *That*? I mean, what happened to me?" It had been late and she was tired, off balance, and utterly honest, as always. She said it as she thought it. "But how could you? You're . . . Damon. You're you, young and strong and clean. You smell good and are good. You're nothing like that blubbery piece of garbage. *That* wasn't this. I don't remember much but anger and pain, darkness over me, and the fact that he was suffocating me and I wanted to kill him. Oh, Damon, this is nothing like."

"And there's no one in the world like you, is there?" he said tenderly, taking her hand. "You're right. But so am I. I'd never do anything you didn't want, or like. Remember that. My job, of course," he said on a laugh, "is to make you want and like everything I do."

"I don't?" she asked, honestly confused.

His laughter chased her doubts. Her slowly rising grin banished his fears.

Well, *good for the future, and we shall see*, was the only thing she allowed herself to think, refusing to dwell on it. She turned her thoughts to his sly grin instead. "Wycoff in an awkward position?" she mused. "A fish out of water? Lord Wycoff? No, I don't think he'd ever be at a loss."

"High praise," Damon murmured. "Then why not invite him?"

"Hmm," she said, and wondered why herself.

He said, too casually, "But you're right not to. It might be embarrassing for him in a different way. He pretended to be your friend. A friend would rejoice at your marriage. I wonder if he will. Or would it present a conflict? To go and pretend? Or find an excuse to refuse? Hard for him to admit by not coming that he had an altogether different kind of relationship in mind from the first."

"You think that's why I hesitated?" she asked, genuinely surprised at herself. "Because it would be a test? You know? It may be so! Only I didn't think I was such a hen heart. Well, so be it," she said, picking up her pen, "I'll send him one. If he doesn't come, I'll know, won't I?"

"Or maybe you didn't want him at your wedding because you want to keep him from remembering it? Because you want to keep him as a beau?" Damon asked. He drummed his fingers on the arm of his chair, his mood turning serious. "Many married women like to have a string of flirts. But Gilly—I wouldn't like that. I'm not that fashionable. I want a real marriage, and there'd be no room for even the most innocent flirtations in ours. At least, that's how I see it. If you don't, I suppose we'd better have that out now. I'm an easy-going man. But not about that."

But he hadn't known that until he heard himself say it. He frowned at the sudden knowledge.

She sat up straight and looked him in the eye, her own becoming molten gold. "If I didn't know you so well, I'd . . . well, you don't want to know what I would do! Look you, Damon Ryder, I'm an honest woman— honest to a fault, I think. If I marry you, and mind, I say '*if*' now, I'd be as true to you as I tell the vicar I will be. Which also means," she added, pointing her pen at his heart, "that if I find you've been grazing in other pastures, I pity you—and whatever trull you take up with! I don't hold with infidelity. I'm a woman of my word."

He took the pen from her fingers because it was dripping ink on the invitation it was poised over. And because it would have prevented him from taking her into his arms.

"Gilly," he said, his lips against her hair as he tried to cradle her stiffened body in his arms, "I know it. Your word is as good as gold. As you are. Forgive me. I surprise myself. But you see, I never knew I was a jealous man before. Maybe because I never cared enough about anything to be jealous of it. I'm known as a man who'd give the shirt off his back to another who needed it, and I have. Now I find I resent your giving the smallest smile to any other fellow. It's not right, I know. Don't worry. I think I'll get over it once I know I have your heart. I'm still not sure of that. Because I know you're not sure either. But don't change. Be as jealous of me as you want—I love it!"

"Huh!" she said in a little gust of breath. "Cockscomb! As if I'm jealous! This is practicality, not jealousy. It's as well you spoke of it now. Because some gents like to trifle once they get bored with their wives. I'm telling you right off that I won't have that."

"I won't get bored with my wives," he promised. And was delighted when she pretended to swat his shoulder, and giggled. Even more so when she offered him a simple kiss of peace before she left his embrace.

"Now, then," she said, flustered by how quickly that kiss began to distract her, "let me get back to the invitations. Bother! I've ruined this one, haven't I? Run your eyes down the rest and see if we've forgot anyone else, will you? These must be sent out today or we'll have only crickets and moths at our wedding supper."

"We'll light our brightest lamps and serve them nectar," he said, "and dance the night away anyway. We don't need guests, nothing will ruin our wedding day."

She flashed him a quick grin and bent her head to begin writing carefully again.

"Why don't you have Ewen's secretary do that?" Damon asked curiously.

She looked up quickly, her pen arrested, her eyes wary. "Why do you say that? Don't you think I can do it well enough? Is there something wrong with my writing? I thought it looked neat, elegant almost, I thought—"

"Hold! Hold!" He laughed. "I wasn't criticizing. It looks fine. But it's a fine day, too, and I was hoping you could go riding with me instead of spending the day copying out names and addresses."

"Oh. But . . . you see, I wanted that personal touch, and . . . no," she said resolutely. "The thing of it is that it's a promise I made to myself long ago . . . I suppose you ought to know it wasn't *that* long ago."

She faced him squarely. "I could write my name when I met the Sinclairs. Only that. I could read a few words. It served me, then. They told me I must learn more, but I didn't like the idea of taking lessons with a schoolmaster at my age. But Drum told me there was more to being Ewen's ward than living off him, that I ought to repay him by becoming educated to better fit in his world. I was so insulted at the thought of him thinking of me as a sponge, I vowed to be the most educated female on the planet after he said that. He knew I would.

"I paid attention to my lessons. The reading came easily. The writing was harder. But I kept at it. I had to be better than adequate, just to show him I could be. I picked the hardest scripts to master and practiced hours on end. I showed Drum my copybook every time I saw him. Eventually even *he* said I could find work as a secretary—if they ever decided to hire females as such. I suppose I ought to have mentioned that before. Damon—are you still sure you want to go through with this?"

"Surer than ever. What is it now?"

"You ought to be marrying someone who could write from the cradle!" she said in frustration. "Not someone who had to be taught exactly how to cross her Ts when she was all grown up!"

"An infant prodigy? Who'd know what a dunce I am? I doubt I'd want that kind of wife," he said in mock alarm. Then his voice softened. "Dear dunderhead. I want a wife who has grit and determination, a woman who can learn something later than others and yet learn to do it better than they can. Life's a learning process, and marriage, I hear, one of it's hardest schools. You've shown you're qualified for any lesson life throws at you. Wait! I see your game! You *pretend* you're ashamed. I think you only told me this to show me how gifted a pupil you are. Clever puss. Don't worry, I won't change my mind, you don't have to brag about your brains. Next thing I know the woman will be sewing and baking for me to prove her worth," he commented to the air.

Gilly made a face at him.

He laughed, but rose from his seat. "Now, I'll leave you to your invitations, because no one can do them better. But hurry, I'll be back for tea and nothing will prevent me from dragging you out of here if you aren't finished by then."

He dropped a light kiss on the nape of her neck, catching the scent of freesia there, and left with a sigh of sorrow that was only half feigned. Not only because he wanted to take her into his arms and pursue that elusive scent to where her pulses warmed it. But also because although she kept objecting to their marriage on his behalf, he knew it was because of her own doubts. He had none.

Gilly waved an absent good-bye to him, bowed her head, and set to work again. Until she heard him say good-bye to the butler and the sound of the front door closing. Then she put down her pen and dropped her head in her hands.

Talking about those lessons from Drum had brought him back to her so clearly, it was as if she'd suddenly seen him there before them. She'd seen him clear—

lounging in the shadows of the room, a tall, slender gentleman, his straight raven hair brushed back from his high forehead, his thin sensitive mouth wearing that faint mocking smile he always wore when he teased her.

A few years younger than his cousin Ewen, the Earl of Drummond looked vaguely like him, but he couldn't be called remotely handsome. Drum was better than that, she'd always thought, staring at the image of him she'd etched in her mind. He was distinctive. His face was hard, with a narrow nose and high cheekbones. Some said it was almost homely. She didn't. She couldn't see how anyone could, not with those unusually beautiful azure eyes of his. Not with the intelligence burning bright in them. He had the same height and width of shoulder as Ewen, but was built on leaner lines. He was darker in every way, too, from his slightly swarthy complexion to his cast of mind and ironic sense of humor.

*Drum!* She almost reached out to touch him. But didn't, not only because he wasn't there, but because she'd never dared touch him except by accident.

There couldn't be two more different men in shape and appearance than Damon and Drum. Damon was classically handsome, disarmingly so. Drum had character and intelligence alone to recommend his face. Drum was lanky, Damon had the sort of body men ought to have, at least if the ancient Greeks were to be believed. But the thought of Drum was enough to set her heart fluttering. And yet Damon's touch made her pulses race.

*What's the matter with me?* she groaned. Was she no better than the easy females she'd always disdained?

But she cared for them both, too. They both made her laugh. Both made her feel better about herself than she'd any right to, Damon by telling her how good she was, Drum by mocking her fears and doubts. But who could calm them now?

Not Damon. And Drum had been only too glad to hand her over to another man. A tear fell on her painstakingly written invitation to Lord Wycoff. That, too, she thought miserably, hurrying to pick up a blotter to save the Y in his name from becoming a blurred X. Was her forgetting to invite that adulterous nobleman a more sinister thing than she knew? Was she divided against herself as well as divided in her emotions?

Because she oughtn't to have forgotten him. Whatever his state of grace, she genuinely liked Lord Wycoff and the game they always played when they met. She'd thought it was only a game of wits. But was Damon right? Was it really the pleasure of playing with fire? Was she just a flirt? She grimaced at the thought. She thought she was above that kind of thing.

She admired Wycoff, too, in a grudging way. He was a wily creature, as all hunters had to be. He knew women and the darker side of their hearts and minds. A confessed unhappily married man, he was always seeking diversions—and finding them. He never stayed with any of his women long. But he was never alone long either. Gilly liked his wry humor, but also had an almost supernatural respect for him. Had she purposely left him off the wedding invitation list because she was afraid he'd see the truth in her not-so-pure heart when she turned her eyes to her new husband?

Oh, *damn, damn, damn,* she thought, holding her

aching head. Drum always told her to beware her impulsive starts. And look what happened the moment he left her!

She'd agreed to marry Damon because of his impulsive attempt to save her reputation. She'd agreed on an impulse, too. But what else could she do? Wait for Drum until he married someone else? Which he would—which he had to do. Take a lesser man than Damon to wed instead? But maybe it *wasn't* fair to Damon, no matter her determination to be a good wife to him. How could a wife who only gave half a heart be good? What if it was not only selfish of her, but cruel to him? It wasn't too late. . . .

"Miss Gilly? Are you all right?" the butler asked from the doorway.

"Oh." She lifted her head. "Yes, Wilkins, I am. It's just these dratted invitations. See? I smudged another. And I know they cost the earth to print. I'm a frugal creature, it goes against the grain to see waste. But how can I send out a card that looks like it was in a hurricane?" She laughed and tore up the innocent card.

He smiled at her. Miss Gilly was a favorite of the servants. A charming young woman, agreeable enough with them to put them at their ease, just lofty enough to show she was well bred.

"The others look very well, miss. Are they ready for me to send out?"

"Not yet. I have to write some more." *And think some more*, she thought. "And I want to show them to my lady to see if there's anyone we've forgotten. What's that you have there?"

"A letter for you, miss. It just came and I know how

you like for me to bring them soon as they arrive."

A *letter from* Drum! Gilly jumped from her chair and took the letter off the silver tray the butler offered.

"Thank you! The very thing, I was getting tired of scribbling, to tell the truth," she said, blushing with excitement.

A *letter from* Drum! She held it tight as she sank back in her chair and Wilkins, smiling, left her to her treat.

*Now here's an end to the nonsense at last! He's thought about it and come to his senses*, she thought with relief. She carefully unfolded the letter, trying not to tear it in her haste. He'd tell her to postpone the thing until he returned, she thought excitedly. He couldn't offer her more than advice, of course, and wouldn't think to. But he'd want to look Damon over. That would buy her time. Of course she shouldn't wed at a moment's notice! Of course that was why the thing never felt quite right, no matter how charming Damon was. The world seemed to be spinning back to normal again for her. Drum wouldn't let her take such a rash step for the sake of propriety. Not Drum.

The letter *was* an apology! Her hands shook.

*Dear Gilly, my friend,*

*Wrong of me to send such a hasty, careless note last week. You of all people deserve better of me. The news of your coming marriage rocked me to my toes, but you must know that.*

She did, but now so did he, and so everything would be all right. She might as well tear up *all* the invitations

now! Or put them aside until he returned to give her
his good counsel. She ran a hand under her eye to
catch a foolish tear that blurred her vision for a
moment, and then read on, smiling tremulously.

*My dear little friend getting married! It didn't seem possi-
ble. Not only did it make me feel ancient, but I had this
instantaneous vision of you as you looked when I first met
you—as you'll always look in my mind's eye. A starveling
whey-faced youth wearing a ghastly old oversized jacket,
scarred thick-soled boots, and those breeches! So clever to
wear mud-colored ones so no one knew if they were clean or
not. A length of rope as a belt around nonexistent hips and
a drooping, slouched, and totally disreputable hat almost
but not quite hiding those glowering yellow eyes of yours.*

*Thus my sudden vision of you, dressed the same, in the
same dirt and with the same swagger—strolling up the
aisle in front of all the ton to join hands with the Catch of
the Season, standing beaming at you like a mooncalf. It
was so vivid and so ludicrous. Thank you, my child, for
providing me with the best laugh I've had all month!*

She read on, too impatient to be amused at his recollections.

*And I needed some humor, let me tell you.*

Her heart raced. Was he ill?

*Cupid hasn't been idle here either, my friend. I've met a
charming young woman. She's from London, here visiting
an aunt. A lovely creature of the kind that always caught*

*my eye, buxom, with dark eyes and inky curls—but respectable, I assure you, you wretch! A widow whose gallant husband fell at Waterloo. We walked out together. I had the highest expectations. But we quarreled over a trifle. I've been sulking, at least until I got your good news. It made me try my luck again. And so now my dark lady and I speak again, at least. The rest? We shall see.*

Gilly stopped breathing. She didn't realize it. Her eyes raced down the page.

*So I won't be able to be back in time for your wedding, Chick, and I'm sorry for it. But I can't leave until I know my fate. I know it's Ewen who should give you away, but I'd have liked being part of the wedding party, too. I'll make it up to you, I promise. Perhaps you can be part of mine when I return.*

*Until then, my duck, be good, be kind, and pray manage not to slay anyone . . . But I don't have to say that anymore, do I? Now you've got your Catch of a groom to tell you that. I wanted to send a gift with this letter but am still searching for the exact one. Something rare and memorable as yourself is not easy to find. Wish me well and wish me luck, and know I wish the same for you.*

*Your devoted friend,*
*Drum*

Gilly put the letter down. Then raised it up and read it once more. Then she put it down precisely on the desk, and didn't look at it again. Instead, she picked up an invitation and dipped her pen in ink. What an idiot she'd been. She began writing so she wouldn't keep thinking, because otherwise at the rate those infuriating tears were falling, she'd waste every last one of the invitations.

"Wilkins said there'd been a letter from Drum," Bridget said at tea that afternoon. "What does he say?"

"That he wishes me well," Gilly said, trying to sound bored and amused as she hid her expression behind a raised teacup, "and that there's a certain female who's caught his eye. She's his usual type, plush and dark. But he's having unusual problems. She's giving him difficulties. He says he's serious about her. A worthy widow, he says, so this time it might be true."

"Indeed?" Ewen said. "That *is* news. When is he coming back to show her to us?"

"He didn't say. It sounds like she's hard to persuade."

"Then he's serious about something else and isn't asking the question you thought he was, depend on it," Ewen said. "And if she is worthy, the difficulties probably have more to do with her good sense about her good name than with his offer. Which while undoubtedly generous, probably doesn't include a wedding ring.

"My cousin the Earl of Drummond is prime marriage goods," he told Damon. "Rich, titled, and charming. Silver-tongued, too. But elusive. Almost my age, and yet he hasn't married. But he's seldom alone long enough to attach a decent woman. All the other kind flock to him and he welcomes them with open arms— literally. But that and his purse is all that's open to them. Not his heart, or his house. Rogue he may be, but he knows what's due his name."

"You're too hard on him," Bridget chided.

"You see?" Ewen laughed. "Otherwise sensible females dote on him. God knows why. The rascal's not an oil painting by a long shot."

"He's not handsome, but he's attractive, very much so," Bridget said. "He's got the most astonishing eyes. Blue as the summer sky, startling in such a harsh face. He dresses elegantly and looks regal. And unlike *some* persons I could name, he always pays attention to a person. When he stares down that long nose at you, you feel you're the center of his universe. You don't know whether to be flattered or run away. Why, when I first saw him I thought he was the most arrogant care-for-nothing. But within minutes I liked him."

"Just as well he came straight to me afterward with news of meeting you that day, instead of staying to dally. Or we wouldn't be here together right now, my dear," Ewen said ruefully. "Lucky thing for me the rogue has a rudimentary sense of honor, at least."

"And you think *this* rogue doesn't?" Bridget asked with mock insult.

"All this because I forgot to pick up a packet of her favorite sweets at Gunters this morning. Beware," he told Damon, "courtship doesn't end at the altar. It never ends, it seems."

"Which is how it should be," Bridget said with satisfaction, "and I want two packets when you go there tomorrow."

"I've heard so much about him from Gilly," Damon said, "I'd like to meet him. Will he be home in time for the wedding, at least?"

"No," Gilly said in a stifled voice, "it appears not."

"That might not be so, after all. I got a letter today, too," Ewen said, scowling. "I was just going to tell you all about it. I'm glad the invitations weren't sent yet. We have to change the date again."

"No!" Bridget said.

Gilly looked up. Damon frowned.

"The vicar wrote three sheets pleading for my understanding," Ewen said in disgust. "What can we do but agree? It seems a certain female from the parish, of good family but bad judgment, needs her wedding day moved up—precipitously. The sooner the better for her eventual offspring. Bad enough it will be a six-month wonder, every week makes a difference at this point. The silly wench was afraid to tell anyone sooner. But her mama's a seamstress and noticed that after all the fittings, suddenly the new dress the bride was going to wear for her wedding didn't fit. At all. And likely won't, at least not until after she whelps."

"Not Sally Hedges!" Bridget gasped. "Well, I'm not surprised, we've had geese that were more clever. Poor Mrs. Hedges, so embarrassing. You were right, Gilly, it's hard to hide anything in these styles."

Damon looked at Gilly with interest. "I was only saying that men have an easier time of it in the fashions they can wear," Gilly said defensively. "So, when is my wedding to be?"

"Set back yet another week," Ewen said, "I know it's hard. First a delay because of a death in the vicar's family put his schedule back two weeks. Now this. We wanted a summer wedding, but that's impossible now. It will have be early autumn. Unless, of course," he told Damon, "you wish to marry here instead. We can send for Betsy," he told Gilly. "We'd have to. If we didn't, she'd walk all the way."

Damon gazed at Gilly. She didn't say anything.

"For my part, no," Damon said slowly. "I think we'd look like Sally Hedges and her beau if we did that at this point. I've told everyone where it will be—the when of it will just have to be changed. I'm disappointed, of course." He paused. When Gilly didn't speak to agree, he added slowly, "So be it. Maybe your cousin Drummond can return in time for the wedding, after all."

"That doesn't matter," Gilly said.

"And so, what does matter to you?" Damon asked Gilly when she walked him to the door later.

He'd waited until the footman left them alone in the hall. Damon's face was grim. Gilly was confused at his dark mood.

"I mean, Gilly," he said, "I don't mind marrying a girl who has reservations. It only means she's a thinking creature. But I won't marry one who has serious doubts. I begin to think you do. I can't spend my life convincing you. Maybe I can. But I don't want to. Because I begin to suspect those doubts are about me, not you or our suitability. So?"

"I'll be a good wife to you, Damon, or at least, I'll try," Gilly said, saying what she'd been thinking since she'd read Drum's letter. "I don't react like other women because I haven't lived like them and don't know how. But believe this if nothing else—I want to marry you. I want to be good for you. I'm nervous about it. But never doubt my intentions now."

He wasn't sure. Her voice trembled with too much

suppressed emotion, there was still too much he didn't understand.

But when he took her in his arms and she gave him her lips, shuddering under the lightest touch of his hands, he knew it wasn't from distaste or fear. Of that, he had no doubt. And with all his cleverness and perception, he was still only a man. With a willing, warm woman in his arms, pressed against his heart. The woman he desired with all his heart.

"Oh, Gilly," he breathed into her hair at last. "Damn and blast that wretched Sally Hedges anyhow!"

In that moment, she agreed, and silently damned poor Sally's soul to hell.

# 8

He usually wondered where he would find the will-power to let her go when he kissed her good night during those scant treasured private moments they were allowed each evening. But this afternoon they'd talked about doubts, and tonight Damon was bedeviled by them. Now something was niggling at the edges of his delight at having this lovely, vital creature so warm and willing in his arms. He left off kissing Gilly and gazed at her, trying to read her mood. She was everything acquiescent, her eyes closed, unreadable. But when he'd caressed her breast she'd caught her breath. He'd moved his hand to her back and she relaxed. Her breathless reaction had happened before when his caresses grew bolder. Tonight, in his uneasy mood, he wondered. Was it a gasp of fear or pleasure? And so he experimented with her senses, and sacrificed his own.

He took her back into his arms, kissed her, and gently cupped her breast again. She gasped again, and shivered. He removed his hand. "Gilly?" he asked quietly. "Do you dislike it when I touch you?"

Her eyes flew wide. "How can you ask such a thing?"

"Because just now, when I touched you, you didn't seem so much thrilled as chilled. A fine distinction, but one I worry about. Was it a shiver of anticipation—or a shudder?" He wished they could talk about this somewhere intimate and dark, where they could be alone for hours. Like in his bed, he thought, and smiled at the ridiculous thought as he waited for her answer.

"I like your touching me," she said. "It just makes me nervous. I mean, *that* kind of touching. I expect I'll get used to it."

"I'd rather you didn't—get used to it, that is. It's supposed to always be thrilling. Gilly?" His voice became softer, "Is it because of what happened to you when you were young? I know thinking and feeling are two different things, but you yourself said you didn't blame all men . . ."

"I don't! It's just that *serious* touching isn't the same as the other kind. You know, it isn't just touching . . . it's *fondling*," she said, triumphant at finding the right word. She squirmed. "I suppose it does make me a bit nervous. I know what's to come, is all. I'll get over it."

He was appalled. "No, you won't! Gilly, oh Gilly, that's not what's to come. You know about violence. You don't know about the way of a man with a woman."

"Do I not?" she asked, her head to the side, grinning cheekily as the boy she once pretended to be. "Damon, oh Damon," she mocked him, reaching up and stroking back a curl from his forehead, "I told you I'm no sheltered miss. I know about men and women. Plenty. I lived in cellars, I shared rooms with dozens of people—when I was lucky enough to find one to share. You close your eyes and ears. But not before you find out what you're closing them to.

"Where I lived before? Huh," she said scornfully, "not much room for ignorance about 'the way of a man with a maid' there, I can tell you. Not just in sleeping quarters! Bad enough in the rookery, when I was on my own. But even before, I saw things done in doorways and alleyways, against fences and walls, all kinds of things—for sport or coin—since I was little. My mother walked me past, fast, and I learned to look the other way. But I saw enough to know what's what, I assure you!"

"That's not what I mean, either," he said. "Fences and walls? Gads! I think you've seen more that I've done!" He laughed, but shook his head, his eyes somber. *There it is, the riddle, the lure of Gilly Giles*, he thought. Such an angelic face, so lovely, more so because it was so honest and unguarded. She'd seen and done more than any female ought to have, and yet remained untouched in the soul of her.

"Gilly, I'm not saying I've been celibate. But I haven't been rakish, either. The truth is that though I've had affairs of the heart and body, I've never actually bought a woman, in so many words—or deeds. Gifts are one thing—commerce another. I never enjoyed visiting fashionable brothels, like so many. . . . Good God!" he shook his head, astonished. "What a thing to tell you!

I wouldn't discuss this with any other woman, but that's the point, you're *not* any other woman, so I have to tell you. There's a world of difference between love, or even fondness, and sex as commerce. Giving pleasure is as important as taking it. At least for me, and for most decent men, and any man honestly in love. It's more than your body I want. I'm trying to tell you it's *you* I want to reach when I touch your body.

"Can you understand that?" he asked, watching the sudden doubt and wariness in her eyes. "I don't want you enduring me. I won't have you accepting me. Can you trust me enough to let yourself be loved by me?"

She thought about it. "And if I can't?"

"Well, then," he said, his heart growing heavy, "I don't know what to say. But I'm being foolish. How can you promise a thing you can't try?"

"You want me to share your bed before we marry?" she asked, obviously considering it. "Well, I don't know. . . ."

"I *do*!" he said, shocked. "No, and no again! Because good as it might be, it's the opposite of what I mean." He sighed. "I don't mean just bodily love. I meant love in all it's dimensions. I won't ask you for the one without I give you the other. I just wondered if you thought you could trust me enough to enjoy my lovemaking. It's important, Gilly," he added when she didn't speak.

"I think," she said carefully, "I could learn to enjoy your lovemaking. But Damon," she added, troubled. "What if I don't? B*last*! You see? A nice well brought up young thing wouldn't worry about that, would she?"

"Exactly," he said, drawing her back. "Precisely why you're the only young thing for me."

They shared a long deep kiss. This time she didn't gasp when he touched her. But when he put his lips to her throat, she did. And when he put his whole palm over the tightened bud of her breast, she froze, but then wriggled, and it was finally Damon who had to gasp. They looked at each other. Gilly giggled.

Damon grinned. "Now that," he said as he reluctantly rose to leave, "was just what I had in mind."

"Only that?" she asked pertly.

He left in laughter. Which was as well, he thought as he strolled back to his hotel. Because the longing was too painful without laughter to relieve it. It was a physical ache as well as a longing for her love.

But his mind was made up. It would take time, it would test his endurance, but he had time and endurance. The day would come when she'd want him as much as he wanted her. He had her memories to overcome. But other men had their brides' shyness or ignorance or rigid upbringings to deal with. She, at least, was braver and willing to talk about things other girls might faint at.

Damon was resolved. He may not have been a rake, but he'd been a lover. He'd do what he could. And there was much he could do. He'd tempt and tease her and show her her own desires. Good things had always come easily to him, but he knew the best things took time and cunning. Gilly Giles, the singular girl who had pretended to be a boy, and now waited to be a woman? She was the best thing he'd found in his lifetime, and he was greedy enough to want her the best she could be. She'd lived through an experience that could have soured another woman, angered her against all men for all time, even driven her mad. She'd triumphed over it. More than that, he knew she'd only denied the passions she had in her. Passions he could tap for both of them.

A *campaign, then*, Damon told himself. A war waged with kisses, caresses, soft breaths, and light touches, promising delight, just avoiding ecstasy. *By the time we're wed*, he promised himself, *she'll be breathless with eagerness to be in my bed. A wonderful scheme, if I can survive the campaign*, he thought, and laughed aloud, causing other strollers to give him a wide berth.

Gilly was still chuckling as she went to her room. *Well, well, well*, she thought contentedly. *Who'd have imagined I'd feel such pleasure—at that?* But she had, when she'd let herself. Shocking, slightly frightening, and so awfully exciting.

She was a practical soul. She didn't forget Drum. She could never do that. But Drum was a dream. Damon was her new reality. A potent one. His face was a treat, his body very fine, and his gentle persuasion caused her to feel inchoate longings she'd never believed she could. So, she thought contentedly, she well might be able to give him what he wanted and deserved, and there might be more in it for her than she'd thought.

Damon didn't touch more than Gilly's hand when he called on her the next morning. But she felt the warmth of it right through her gloves. Something had changed. He'd brought another open carriage for their drive in the park. They didn't speak much, but exchanged long measuring glances before she had to look away. There was definitely something new between them. Something that made her senses tingle and turned his smile slow and knowing. This morning, they were chaperoned by legions of nannies, children, milkmaids, and strollers. But they remembered what had been said and those nighttime thoughts pervaded these daylight moments. She was bemused. He was aware of it, and enchanted.

Until they got back. They stepped in the door, and found the Sinclair's townhouse under siege, Ewen and Bridget doing their best to cope with a throng of eager visitors awaiting Damon's return.

Damon's family had arrived. Or, more accurately, invaded. But it was a merry, handsome horde that had descended on the Sinclairs. So many tall, laughing, good-looking men and women converged on Damon when he entered the front door that Gilly stepped back, amazed and dismayed. He'd mentioned his brothers and sisters, but she wasn't prepared for the effect of them all together.

They were a handsome family and bore marked resemblance to each other. Gilly thought none of their features as finely chiseled as Damon's, and none had his body's perfect proportions. But they weren't the only ones there. There were others who were obviously in-laws, and their children, too, for all Gilly knew.

They pounced on Damon, overjoyed to see him again. They couldn't wait for the wedding, one said. It was time for a trip to London to get ready for the wedding anyway, another said. And "Botheration!" one exclaimed, if he wouldn't come to them, they'd come to him, their Damon was in England at last, and bedamned to waiting until autumn to see him.

"And where's the enchanting Miss Giles?" one of the men demanded when the first flurry of back-slapping and bear-hugging was over.

"Yes, from your letters we're expecting Aphrodite!" another called.

"Aphrodite and Circe and Venus all in one," a man laughed.

"Dolt!" another man sang out. "Aphrodite *is* Venus, what will she think of you?"

"She'll think you hated school as much as you did, Alfred," Damon said, drawing back, coming to Gilly and taking her icy hand in his. He squeezed it as he faced his family.

"Mother, Father," he said formally. "Sisters, brothers, and brothers and sisters-in-law, nephews, nieces . . . Lord! No wonder she's trembling. What a multitude to present her to! But she's a brave lass. After all, she's agreed to marry me. May I present Miss Gilly Giles, my promised—and now obviously petrified—bride? With cause. Wolves have looked at lambs less eagerly. Gilly—this disorderly crew is my family."

Gilly nodded. Her mouth was too dry to speak. She could only curtsy to them all, her heart beating too fast to do more than hold Damon's hand for support as she rose.

They were too quiet, she thought in a panic, looking up to see their appraising eyes on her. Did they see beneath her facade already? Were they looking at a young woman in a fine walking dress? Or a ragged street urchin dressed as a boy? Were they wondering what they could say to their poor deluded Damon?

"Good Lord!" one of the men said in shock, and Gilly's heart squeezed tight. Ewen grew a scowl. Bridget held her breath.

"Damon, what could you have been thinking of?" the man continued, clearly amazed, "You wrote and said *'lovely.'* You did *not* say *'divine.'* Miss Giles," he said fervently, one hand on his heart. "Why, oh why, did I not see you first?"

"Because you're already married, you idiot!" one of the other men said, giving him a mock swat with his glove as they all began laughing, Ewen and Bridget as well.

By the time dinner was served for the guests, Gilly began to see the differences in them, and it made her anxious. Although no one made a point of it beyond introductions, too many of Damon's siblings had married nobility for her comfort—there were ladies and lords aplenty. Gilly had thought titles meant nothing to his family, it was one of the reasons she'd accepted him. Now she began to wonder how his clan would accept a woman out of nowhere. The thought made her quiet. They were such a lively group, no one noticed. Or else they were used to overwhelming strangers. But at least Gilly was able to sit back and observe them, and slowly began to see personalities emerging.

Brother Alfred, the middle child, was the jester of the family. Arthur had a sense of humor but took himself more seriously, maybe because he was the heir. Thomas, the second son, was a bit vain; his plain little dab of a wife made him more so because she was in such awe of him. Francis, a few years older than

Damon, was the watchful one. His twin sister, Margaret, was athletic. Younger sister Mary brought three lapdogs with her and constantly worried aloud about the dogs, cats, horses, and birds she'd left at home. Bethany, the oldest, had seven children of her own, and yet still mothered her sisters and brothers.

They were a family who laughed often and touched each other frequently. Gilly had seen such in the slums where she'd been raised. She didn't see it often in society. Bridget and Ewen exchanged secret smiles and sly caresses, but the easy familiarity the Ryders shared had nothing to do with sensual thoughts. This clan clapped each other on the back, caught at an arm to get attention, gave easy hugs, even exchanged frequent pinches in fun. It made Gilly realize how often Damon brushed her cheek, touched her shoulder, or took her hand. And how good that felt.

Damon's parents had raised an impressive family, but they were an impressive couple. Arthur Ryder was tall, lean, and distinguished. Elizabeth Ryder was still a handsome woman, his partner in elegance. That wasn't surprising; they were distant cousins. Their eyes filled with tears of gladness whenever they looked at Damon, and they couldn't stop doing that; it was clear they'd starved for the sight of him. From time to time they dragged their gaze from him and looked at his fiancée, and then their eyes grew shadowed. Or so Gilly thought, guiltily.

They sat at the Sinclairs' dining table and the uproar was hilarious. Until Damon's mother tapped a spoon on her glass for silence. "Children!" she chided, as though even the middle-aged men and women were really children. "What sort of impression are we making? What a clamor! Thank you," she said into the sudden hush. "I've a notion to talk to Miss Giles, and I don't wish to shout, she'll think I'm ferocious."

"But you are, Mama!" Alfred shouted.

"I wish I could be—to you!" she answered, as they all laughed. She leaned forward. "Now, Miss Giles, don't let my disastrous brood discourage you. I promise you Damon was ever his own man. So, having shown you the best and worst we can do, what I wish to know is when we are to meet your family? At the wedding? Or are they in town?"

"You have," Gilly blurted. "Or at least, all except for my sister."

"Indeed, there is only my Gilly and her sister, Betsy," Damon drawled, putting his arm round the back of her chair, his eyes daring criticism. He was usually so charming and friendly that his sudden frostiness was even more threatening.

His implied protection was noted. No one spoke for a moment.

"But how sad," his sister Mary called from down the table. "Miss Giles, you've no other relatives at all?"

"She has us," Ewen said quickly. "Both Gilly and Betsy are my wards. I know we can't make up for the tragic loss of their parents, but we do our humble best." He sat straight in his chair at the head of the table, his gaze sweeping over each of his guests in turn.

There were few people, even among the jolly Ryder clan, who would question the haughty Viscount Sinclair when he looked his most imperious, as he did now. But Damon's mother didn't. She kept her attention on Gilly.

"You're from London?" she persisted. "Your family as well? Any connection to the Giles of Stratford, by chance? A delightful family. Francis went to school with Herbert Giles, clever boy, and they're all fair as Vikings, like you."

"No," Gilly said, "or if they are, I haven't heard of it. There was only my mother and father."

"You've no cousins, aunts, uncles or such?" Damon's mother persisted, as though amazed.

"I might," Gilly said, raising her chin. "I never met them, though." She wouldn't lie. It was what and who she was. Well, and if they disapproved, she thought defiantly, though her face flushed and her stomach grew cold, they'd see the thing ended before it began, and so be it. Maybe it would be best. His family meant a lot to Damon. She wouldn't stand between them. She'd never really understood his desire to marry her and always wondered if he'd one day regret it. Maybe today was to be that day.

"Well, then!" Damon's mother said, sitting back with an expression of surprise. Gilly looked down at her plate. But her gaze flew up again at the next comment. "All the better for us," Elizabeth Ryder pronounced. "We'll be family enough for you. This way I won't have to compete with other grandmothers for my grandchildren's attention on holidays, as I do with *some* of my ungrateful brood!" She glanced around the table, as the culprits she was talking about either laughed or grew red-faced.

Gilly blinked. Damon smiled and bent his head to

whisper, "Not what you expected? There's a reason I love them. Now you know."

"But, surely they must wish you'd found a girl who had at least some kind of family," she murmured.

"Wrong, wrong, wrong," he whispered, his breath tickling her ear, "No one cares. You'll find out."

"Ho! Leave off that snuggling, Damon!" Alfred roared. "You've got to wait until you're married, and wait you shall!"

Gilly tried to believe what Damon said as the conversation picked up to a roar again. He'd said she was "wrong, wrong, wrong." But she'd lived by her wits for too long to doubt her instincts, and wasn't consoled.

Gilly finally found herself alone for the first time in over a week. For the first time, in fact, since the gregarious Ryders had come to visit. His parents and his sisters Mary and Margaret and their husbands were staying at the Sinclair townhouse; the rest had taken rooms at hotels, or with friends. But they congregated together from the moment they woke in the morning, and the place they met was always the Sinclairs' house.

This morning, though, the men and many of the women, bored with being pent in town, went out riding to the nearby countryside with Ewen and Damon. The other woman had gone on a shopping tour, taken in a convoy of carriages. Bridget was in her rooms, feeding the baby. The other children were on a long ramble in the park with a crew of visiting nannies.

When Gilly poked her head into the morning room, she found it blessedly empty. She stole in and sank into a chair with a sigh, reveling in the time alone.

Lately her days and evenings had been so busy she hadn't had time to think. There were so many new people to be charming to, so many stories of Damon's childhood and youth to hear again and again. Gilly was so busy being civil and fond, she was too weary when she found her bed at night to do more than fret for a few minutes until exhaustion claimed her.

It was good, because she hadn't had time to panic. It was bad, because she wondered if she should. Now, at last, through some quirk of fate, she was alone.

"There you are! What good fortune!" Damon's mother cried as she peeked in the room. Gilly leapt to her feet. "No, no, sit down. We finally have time for a good long cozy chat! Don't mind Cousin Felicity," she added, motioning to the white-haired woman with her, "she knows me better than I do myself." Gilly nodded at the sweet-faced elderly female who always trailed after Damon's mother.

"And not a moment too soon!" Elizabeth said, taking a chair next to Gilly. "Because in a matter of weeks you'll become my daughter!"

There was nothing to say to that. Gilly only nodded again.

Elizabeth laughed. "Don't worry, it won't be that bad! After all, after the wedding, you'll be on the Western border and we're on the Channel, as far east as you can go without speaking French. We'll have half a country between us!"

Gilly smiled weakly. Was she joking? Or was she relieved because this cuckoo's egg of a girl, this stranger found in a noble nest, wasn't going to be on her doorstep?

"It's as well," Cousin Felicity said. "Can't think of what Lady Annabelle would do if she had to see her every day."

"Felicity!" Damon's mother said, looking shocked . . . and amused. "Oh," she said to Gilly's confused expression. "You see, Lady Annabelle is . . . well, the thing of it is that she. . . ."

"Expected to be in your shoes," Felicity said with relish.

Elizabeth shot her companion a strange look. "Not really. Well . . . yes, really, I suppose," she sighed. She turned to Gilly, her face pink. "Annabelle's a near neighbor and a dear one. She's known Damon since she first opened her eyes, and doted on him since then. We all felt she never married because she was expecting him to . . . Not that she's that old. Only a few years older than you, in fact. But he was always so charming to her, we all thought. . . . But who knows what's in a young man's mind? And just look at the lovely bride he found! But Felicity's right. Just as well you don't have to cope with Annabelle every day of your life from now on."

"A good family and thirty thousand a year," Felicity said.

Gilly knew old people were often outspoken, but she felt implied criticism. She didn't know what to think. But she knew how to defend herself. If she'd thought about it she wouldn't have found the courage, but defense was automatic with her. "Perhaps you ought to remind him of it, then," she said sweetly. "Maybe he forgot. I have a dowry, but it isn't anywhere near thirty thousand a year. Yes, better tell him quickly.

There's still time for him to change his mind. No sense whistling a fortune down the wind. I suppose Lady Annabelle is beautiful, too? Sunny-natured and kind to animals?"

"Yes," Felicity said, "and she's a raven-haired beauty and—"

"*Felicity*!" Elizabeth gasped. "Gillian was funning you—at least, I hope she was. My dear," she told Gilly. "We never meant to imply he'd be better off with Annabelle! After all, we only want what he wants, and he never offered her anything but kindness in all these years."

"I see," Gilly said. "Well, you know Damon! Did I tell you what he said about that time you sent him dancing slippers when he was in America?" She deftly changed the subject, and soon they were talking about the subject nearest to Elizabeth's heart—Damon. But though Gilly laughed at the anecdotes about him, she was hardly listening. She was too busy reviewing what had been said. She couldn't forget that Damon's mother hadn't said *she* didn't think he'd be better off with Annabelle . . . *Lady* Annabelle, which was worse.

So that was the first thing she resolved to ask Damon as soon as she could get him alone. The only problem was she didn't know when that would be. The way things were going, it mightn't be until her wedding night.

"The only way I can talk to you is while we're dancing," Gilly told Damon the moment she stepped into his arms for a polka at the ball Ewen and Bridget were giving for her, "and I can't tell you what I want to because half the world's listening. Except for you! Are you *listening* to me?" she hissed, as he grinned in answer to a jest one of his cousins called to him as they whirled around the ballroom floor.

"Yes, she has a terrible temper," he told the air over her left ear, and then grinned down at her. "You want to get me alone? Now we're getting somewhere."

"Nowhere!" Gilly said through gritted teeth. "Can we slip out or sneak away behind a pillar? Don't leer. I have to talk to you! You found a way to sneak away at the ball the night we met. Why not here?"

"Because here, my sweet, we have as much privacy as a pair of elephants in the Tower zoo. We're the main attraction. But I'll find a way. Ah, here's your next partner, right on time, or even earlier. Interesting. He's so eager to claim his dance, he hardly waited for the music to stop. Good evening, my lord," Damon said louder, turning to bow to Lord Wycoff as he came up to them.

"Ryder," Lord Wycoff said, inclining his head. "My dance, my dear Miss Giles?"

The waltz began. Gilly flashed Damon a look of annoyance. She was frustrated and angry at his making a joke of something so important to her . . . and then as she stepped into the dance with Lord Wycoff, she forgot her problems, and became suddenly aware of her partner. Aware of the intense scrutiny in those dark eyes, aware of the way he held her so gently, yet firmly, aware of the tension radiating from the long body so close to her own.

"I wanted your last dance as a dewy maiden," he said in his dark velvet voice, "so I can see what it will be like when I claim the first one after you are wedded."

Her gaze shot up toward his. "Then you'll be disappointed," she said gruffly. Because what he'd said was innocent on the surface, but suggestive. And she knew he meant it to be. "I'm not being married for a month. And when I am, I'll dance with Damon first, Ewen next, and probably Damon's papa after that, *and* his gang of relatives after. You'll have to wait your turn."

She frowned. What she'd said seemed even less respectable. She gave herself a mental shake for her nonsense. They were only talking about dancing, no matter what his tone implied.

He smiled at her predicament, but there was such tender pain in his expression she missed a step. "Careful," he said, as he held her up and turned her 'round again. "It's too easy to make a misstep here. And don't I know that!"

"You don't find it hard to make one anywhere," she said angrily.

"But you do, which is my problem . . . or was."

"You think things will change after I'm married?" she asked, amazed.

"Things generally do," he said mildly.

They were talking so normally, about such normal things. He hadn't said one word out of line. But everything he said was double-edged, and she knew—or would swear—they were both talking about something else. "I don't change," she told him.

"You are changing," he said sadly, his eyes devouring her face. "You will again. This is difficult for me, but why I came tonight. I had to tell you, before the fact, that marriage is a final step, one that oughtn't be taken unless you're sure of the path ahead. There's marriage for expedience, which was my fate." He turned her in the dance and she moved with him as one, unwilling to miss a word.

"There's marriage for love," he continued without missing a breath, "which is rare as unicorns in Picadilly. But the most foolish is marriage for gossip's sake. Dearborne wouldn't have been believed beyond an hour. Difficult to think that hour could define all the hours of the rest of your life. Be advised from one who knows too well, if love isn't found within marriage, it will be discovered without."

"It's not that!" Gilly said.

"Indeed? So it's a love match?" He was a subtle man who seldom showed any emotion but desire or amusement, but his eyes were pained and oddly tender. So she said nothing. She wouldn't lie, and found she couldn't to him.

"I see," he said. "But about those changes. . . . Although I regret some that will happen shortly, I cannot regret the fact that it might put you more easily within my reach. By which I mean to say," he said when she gasped, "now that you're going to be a married woman it will mean you'll be able to visit us. You know, of course, I could never have invited a respectable single female to my house for even the most innocent of reasons. Not with my reputation."

"You have no innocent reasons," Gilly said flatly.

He laughed. "That, my dear Miss Giles, apart from your beauty, is what I most like about you. There is no nonsense about you."

"Do remember that," she said fiercely.

"But I am not talking about nonsense," he told her

gently and whirled her away across the floor too fast for her to find the breath to answer him.

He left her with a bow, and another of those strangely sad smiles that troubled her so much that for a few minutes she forgot her burning desire to talk with Damon. He didn't, however.

"Come with me," Damon said, catching up her hand. "We've got an excuse. Lady Sinclair needs your help with Max."

"*Max*? Is he all right?" Gilly exclaimed. She left the ballroom with him at a trot. "It's his stomach!" she muttered as she pattered up the stair by his side. "I knew it. He was in the kitchens watching them prepare. They must have stuffed him with so many sweets that . . . oh!"

Because no sooner had he got her up the long stair then he pulled her into a darkened niche in the hallway and spun her into his arms. His kiss was just as sudden, wild, and impassioned, his mouth hot and sweet as it stole all sense from her.

He dragged his mouth from hers and stood locked tightly to her, his hands on her bottom holding her, his lips against her hair. She could feel his risen passion, she could scarcely believe her own. "Gilly," he muttered, "if our wedding day doesn't come soon . . ."

"It will come soon as it always does," she said shakily.

"What is it you wanted to say to me?" he asked, his mouth on her brow, his lips soft against her cheek, and then demanding against her mouth again.

She couldn't remember. But when he finally let her go, she did. "The lady . . . Annabelle," she breathed.

"What?" he asked, confused.

"Your mother and Felicity told me about Annabelle," she said, tilting her head back, trying to read his expression in the dim light.

"Annabelle who?" he said.

She laughed and flung her arms around his neck. With his lips on hers, that was enough answer for her. For now.

# 9

Gilly sat on the quilt they'd spread on the grass and watched the sun strive to make Damon even more radiant. It seemed impossible. He reclined on his side, head propped on one arm, watching her, his expression mischievous. Or so she thought. She couldn't be sure, because she couldn't look at him too long. He dazzled and daunted her. Damon Ryder, the Catch of the Season, and looking every languid inch of it this long, late summer afternoon.

He wore form-fitting fawn breeches, a brown-and-gold waistcoat, and high brown boots with golden tassels. He'd taken off his tightly fitted jacket, and lay there in his shirtsleeves, the white of his linen making his smile even more dazzling as he grinned at her. His skin was so clear and smooth, but now she could see the tiny laugh lines that radiated from those sun-filled eyes. She longed to move even closer to him, to touch the soft hair that gleamed in the sunlight, to see from up close what exactly to make of that new light dancing in his silvery eyes.

Such a handsome fellow! But she'd always known that; she'd just never felt it before. These past few days had changed something subtle between them. She'd never been so aware of him. Or of her own reactions to him. And of her growing uneasiness about it and their situation. He wasn't making it any easier for her today.

They'd found a grassy spot of lawn near a small fountain, behind a flowering hedge. The age of pleasure gardens might be over, but Vauxhall Gardens was still a summertime haven for those elegant persons who stayed in London, as well as those who couldn't afford to leave it. It had huge pavilions and galleries, and spectacular spaces where hordes of patrons could listen to music and dine, dance, or watch staged tableaux and spectacles, and fireworks in the evenings. But it also had dark walks through heavily treed lanes, dozens of hidden grottoes, as well as unexpected little garden spots everywhere for the adventurous, or scandalous, to discover.

This was a little bower tucked behind a flowering wall of roses and honeysuckle. The fragrance, borne by a soft breeze, drifted over them. A bronze Triton and his adoring nymphs poured spouts of tumbling water into a tiny rock-lined pool. It reminded Gilly of the night they met, though it was brilliant daylight now. Birds sang to the accompanying sound of the gushing waters, the light wind riffled the leaves in the towering trees overhead. As soon as Bridget and Damon's sisters had gone strolling, Damon had taken Gilly to the hidden garden he'd discovered and spread out one of the quilts Bridget had supplied.

The only concession Gilly could make to the warmth of the afternoon was to take off her bonnet and let the breeze have its way with her hair. She wore a charming round gown of buttercup yellow, but she desperately missed her boy's garb. She had to sit up straight. It was hard for a lady of fashion to sit any other way without having more joints than an acrobat, impossible to lie down the way Damon was doing without looking positively sluttish. Most of her bosom might be exposed to the air, but not her ankles—her arms, but not her legs. It was a rarely lovely day; morning mists had cleared to a radiant afternoon. Which Gilly couldn't appreciate, sitting up like a stuffed duck. Ridiculous, she fumed, just another thing to unsettle her today.

He saw her uneasiness. "Relax," he commented lazily. "It's all perfectly proper. We look like we're alone, but it's only Vauxhall Gardens, where the world and its uncle comes to play. Well, we are alone in a bower, I grant you, yes. But my mama is patrolling the gardens, my sisters and all their noisy offspring are within shouting distance. Look at me. I'm not worried at all. If you try to compromise me, they'll get you."

She smiled, but kept fidgeting.

His expression softened. "Gilly? They are nearby, that's true. But so are you, and we *are* sheltered from prying eyes by all the shrubs. Do you think . . . ? Could you sit a little closer? There's nothing to worry about. It's broad daylight, you know."

"Huh," she said, flustered. "As if that makes a difference. Half the bastards in London town were made in the daylight . . . oh! Oh, Damon," she cried, agonized. "Just listen to me! You don't deserve that. Not the thought, not the kind of female who'd even think it, much less say it!"

She didn't know a man could move that quickly. "No," he whispered in her ear, one arm going around her, the other on her flushed cheek, tilting her head up. "Look at me, Gilly girl. Not such a bad thing to say, or to think. Especially since it's true. Not the sort of thing to say in polite company, but since when am I polite company? Come, this isn't like you."

"You know what I found out just today?" she asked, laying her cheek against his, glad she couldn't look in his eyes, sorry she breathed in the scent of him now. Because she needed a clear head to say such an important thing to him, and the attar of sun-warmed clean linen and spice and Damon was intoxicating.

She drew a shuddering breath when she felt his steady heartbeat against her own breast. And because of what she had to say.

"I heard your sisters wanted to go to Almack's," she said in a rush, "but your mama said they shouldn't because I couldn't go with them. Because I was never given vouchers to go there. Much I care! Or cared, that is, when I heard that even with all of Ewen's influence, those old crows wouldn't give me permission to enter what they consider their sacred halls. It is just a drafty hall, whatever society thinks. And it *is* for society misses, not for the likes of me. But who cares? It's a paltry place for dancing, worse for eating and drinking, or so Ewen said. I didn't mind, really. But I do now. I mean, your sisters should go. How often do they come to London, anyway?"

She felt his body tense as she spoke. His hand slowed as he stroked her hair. "It don't mean a fig to me," she explained, still not looking up, "but they'll miss their old friends and a chance to hear new gossip. Because of me. And as for that, what about our children—if we have any. Who can say what they might have to miss? This is all because of me. It makes me think, and so should you. It's a problem, Damon, we can't ignore it."

His voice was deceptively calm when he spoke again. "Almack's?" he said. "I see. And how did you hear this today?"

"Well, I came down to breakfast and your cousin Felicity was telling your mother about it. They hushed as I came in and changed the subject. But I'd heard enough to know the way of it."

"Have to rise before dawn to fool you," Damon muttered, "but I don't think the old wretch was trying to. Gilly," he said, drawing back, holding her shoulders as he tried to catch her gaze directly, "Cousin Felicity's a scandalmonger. If she can't find scandal, she invents it. She looks like the dear old auntie everyone wishes they had, but she's a harpy in disguise. Mama puts up with her because no one else will. She's always saying Felicity isn't so bad, but we all know she is. She's not a favorite of mine. I'm not one of hers, either, though she'd cut her throat before she'd admit it. She knows how her bread is buttered and knows there are some things Mama will not stand for. It isn't that Felicity prefers Annabelle, it's that she knows I don't."

But now Gilly stiffened. She flung back her head to clear her eyes of the errant strands the breeze had slipped from her topknot. She stared at him. "You *do* know who Annabelle is!" she breathed.

"Well . . . of course," he said, taken aback. "We grew up together."

"But the other night!"

"Oh," he said, with the flicker of a smile that faded when he saw her eyes were glowing bright, smoldering with repressed emotion. "That. The other night when you were in my arms?"

He paused, running a hand through his hair, wishing she was in his arms now, where he could speak to her with his heart as well as his lips. "I didn't lie," he told her in all honesty. "It's just that I can't think when you're that close. Gilly, I could've asked Annabelle to be my wife any time this past decade. But I didn't want her. I want you."

"Why? No!" She put up one hand. "Don't go on about my eyes or nose or any of my body parts. Or give me that nonsense about how unique I am. That's the point. I am. And not at all acceptable, either, in spite of Bridget and Ewen and all the king's horses and all the king's men. Or all the viscount's men," she muttered.

"Your sisters have every right to go to Almack's. I don't belong, and everyone knows it. I'm a slum brat jumped up to a nobleman's ward, but I am who I am. Damon . . ." Her voice was almost pleading. "I didn't know how highly placed your family was. I didn't realize how they all adore you. I *am* 'not quite the thing' and well I know it. Think long and hard about the future, will you? I *do* know more about life than most girls. And what I know too well is that men—even the best of them—often think with their . . . um, that is to say . . ." She paused, lowering her lashes over her eyes to hide her dismay. She'd almost said the common vulgar expression right out loud. It was one thing to admit her low origins, even to try to discourage him from a misalliance. But she couldn't bring herself to give him a disgust of her.

"They often think with their . . . impulses," she concluded weakly.

"*Impulses*? Interesting," Damon said. He spoke soberly, but he was grinning like a boy, though Gilly was too embarrassed to look up and see it. "What an inventive euphemism," he mused. "But one that would get a gent in trouble, I'd think. Consider if he has to go to a physician for an annoying malady he contracted from a lady—say, one who shared her favors too generously? 'Doctor, I seem to be having some trouble with my impulses.' 'Hmmm, indeed?' the good physician says. 'You mean you wish to do things you ought not?' 'Oh no,' the unfortunate fellow says, 'I mean my impulse is doing things it ought not.' 'Like making you act out things you should only think about?' 'Good heavens, no! I never think about such painful things as my impulse is feeling now!' Oh?" Damon asked, seeing Gilly's bent head and shaking shoulders. "You're weeping for the poor man?

"And why not?" he asked pleasantly, tickled at her response to his nonsense. "Who knows what the doctor will treat given such a complaint? The fellow might end up in Bedlam instead of being given mercury for the pox. But it's you who used the word. Surely a lady can mention a gent's 'member'? Or 'attachment'? No? Maybe 'appurtenance'? Too loose an interpretation?"

He heard Gilly make a stifled sound, and encouraged, went on. "Hmm. 'Organ of generation' is scientifically correct. But too medical, we don't want you getting the reputation of being a bluestocking. 'Sex organ' is correct, but never correct, if you know what I mean. I suppose 'member' is the most acceptable. But not *impulse*, please."

He heard another muffled noise, and tilted her head up with one finger. When Gilly peeped up at him from under a curtain of spilled flax, he saw her face was rosy with suppressed laughter.

"But whatever you call them, we don't think with them," he said seriously. "They try to think for us, and if we act on it, then we *are* fools. Truly, those are impulses. A grown man learns to think with his brain. I'm thinking and speaking from that, as well as a much more important member—my heart. And yes, absolutely," he whispered, as he looked at her lips and lowered his mouth to hers, "with that other as well, because I love you with every part of me, even that important *impulse* of mine."

Damon's marvelous mouth was warm and soft and beguiling. Gilly relaxed and let herself lose herself in his kiss. Such a wonderful thing, she thought muzzily, the way he kissed. The way she'd learned to tolerate, then like, and then need the feel of his tongue against her own. The way she'd learned to accept the little jolt of shock when his smooth hands touched her smoothest skin, and then to look forward to it. The way she allowed herself to touch him with her hands, and then with her lips—his cheek, the delicious places where his neck wasn't covered by his neckcloth . . .

She discovered it was possible to lay back against the quilt after all, because a lady's ankles and legs weren't exposed to the day if a gentleman was laying over her. If his big warm hands covered over her thighs, then they weren't exposed either. And if his hand then concealed even that most intimate part of her, who was there to see or complain? Not her. Because the feelings he provoked robbed her of speech. They were warmer than the sun, more secret than this hidden place they lay in.

Gilly was lost. They'd caressed, but never like this. She'd never been touched like this, she'd never been touched much at all. Ewen and Bridget and Betsy hugged her now and again, but she'd never known such intimacy. The sensations he was arousing were stupefying, but that wasn't all. She reveled in the very closeness of his embrace.

The feel of the man, the gentle strength that held her so tight, yet so lightly. The way he seemed to encompass her, his wide shoulders blocking out the sunlight, his soft words she didn't hear but felt in the marrow of her bones as he breathed them against her neck, her breasts. It made her feel whole and necessary, cherished and good. So good that her lack of control over herself didn't frighten her.

She wasn't aware of it, only of him. The spiraling feelings he touched off in her. The look of him whenever her eyes fluttered open to see. How starry his lashes were over his closed eyes when she opened her own, how hot his mouth—so hot it made her close her eyes again to see what was inside herself, to feel how good his touch was, how—

Then she was alone. Damon murmured something and drew away, rising to his knees, and she blindly reached for him to come back. But then with a sudden oath, he was entirely gone, and she'd only the sun to cover her.

Gilly blinked. She opened her eyes to see herself as good as naked, her gown off at the top and up at the bottom until it was only like a bright band of sunlight around her waist. She sat bolt upright. All she saw of Damon was his broad back; he was sitting up next to her, turned from her, his head bowed.

"Damn, damn, damn," he muttered.

Gilly scrambled to cover herself. She'd never seen herself look so naked, she'd never felt so exposed. She looked and felt positively *raw*! she thought in horror. There was so much white and pink. Her bare breasts were poking up, rising from her gown, and that hair *there*! She gasped. How shocking, how out of place in the broad light of day! In an agony of embarrassment she fumbled, trying to pull her skirts down and her top up. His hands stopped hers.

"Here, let me help," he murmured, kneeling at her side. "Stop struggling, it's the work of a moment—and don't I know it?" he added ruefully. "There. You're covered. Now if you stand, it'll all fall into place. I wish my head would. *Damnation*! Forgive me, Gilly. But for a girl who swore she knows all there is to know, you certainly seemed to forget."

"I!" she gasped, in shock.

"No, you're right," he said. "That's not fair. I was supposed to remember, you only trusted me. Well, so did I, until I touched you. Easy to say you're so tempting a man can't help losing control. But not fair. I ought to have stopped, I should have known. Damnation!"

"But I . . ."

"No!" he said, rising, walking a pace away and then one back. He looked down at her and his gaze softened. Her gown was proper again, but everything else was not. Her silken hair floated over her flushed face, she was rumpled, disheveled, and unutterably desirable. Now she was covered, but he remembered how easy it had been to expose the treasures of her body. He remembered those small but perfect breasts, so white, tipped with rose, tasting like flowers and honey, just the right size, and the exact shape of all his desires. And that tiny pink birthmark high on her thigh, rosy as what lay so near to it, beneath that golden thatch. . . . He remembered too much. He had to fight the urge to sink to his knees and then to her again. As it was, his voice was hoarse when he finally spoke.

"Gilly Giles, we—you and me—almost made a scandal of ourselves that Felicity could have dined out on for years." He shook his head as he gave her his hand so she could stand. "Three buttons! I only knew what I was about on the third one!"

She looked confused. "But I've no buttons on this gown. It's all drawn together with a ribbon . . ."

"On m'britches, my dear," he said with regret, "on the fall that covers my . . . impulses." He gave a bark of laughter. "Oh gods! Autumn *can't* come soon enough!"

He gazed at her and all laughter fled. She didn't look amused. She looked upset, embarrassed, wary.

"Gilly Giles, you part my hair with the nearest article of furniture you can grab if I forget myself like that again, before we marry. Yes, I deserve that look. I make fine speeches, and the taste of you drives them from my head. Things got out of hand—well, at least not literally, thank God." He started to smile, but seeing no response, said soberly, "I won't let it happen again. I promise. Not until you're ready."

She didn't look any happier with that promise. Because she had been ready. And he knew it. But she, at least, wasn't ready for that knowledge.

She was neater and very much quieter when Bridget and Damon's sisters came back. Nor did she touch Damon except when she had to as he helped her into the carriage again.

"I'm sorry, again I say I'm sorry," Damon told Gilly softly when he left her that afternoon. He took her hand, captured her other one, and held them both as he spoke. He didn't like how subdued she was, he hated how out of control he'd been.

"If you'd said one word, even hesitated in any way, I'd have remembered," he said. "I should have, even so. But I'm not insensible. Just too human. I went too fast. I'll remember in future. I'm not ruled by my passions, I promise you."

They stood in the hall, face to face, linked only by their hands. Their thoughts couldn't be further apart. He was deeply worried, wondering if she was remembering that other man, the one who'd been more like an animal. The one who'd hurt her with his lust. Worrying she might make that connection, too, and put

him in the same class. His loss of control had surprised him and now he damned himself, fearing he
might have alienated her with his passion.

She gazed at him with new eyes, never thinking of
that brutality in her youth. But he was right about one
thing. She was worrying about passion. Her own. She
knew so much about men and women. She hadn't
known that about her own femininity, and didn't know
what to think of it just yet.

"Gilly?"

"Don't apologize," she said. "It was my fault as much
as yours. And I'm not sure it was even a fault," she
added, as always, honest with him. "Just a surprise. I
didn't know it would be like that."

"Oh, it can be better. But as everything, it's best in
it's right place and time."

She nodded. He'd showed her a new Damon. But
now she was a new Gilly, and she wasn't sure she liked
it. All these years she'd been strong, sure, in control of
herself. He'd showed her that she'd been foolish to
think that could go on. She'd be his wife, and had
planned to be a good one for him, never knowing it
would change her life in ways she'd never been able to
guess at. She'd reckoned on a marriage of expedience,
maybe pleasure, too. Now Damon showed her passion. She needed time to think on that! But she was
fair.

"You didn't do anything wrong," she told him. "You
just showed me the way of things."

"Too much," he said, kissing her hand. "Too little,
too," he said with a grin as he raised the other and
brought it to his lips.

\*      \*      \*

Gilly was packing by the following morning.

"No," Bridget said again, watching her. "Put everything back, if you please. There's no point to it, and no need for it either. The doctor said the infection's in London. Margaret doesn't have it, thank goodness, it was only teething that shot her temperature up last night. Max is perfectly fine. But if any infection *is* here in town, we won't be. You know how Ewen worries. If there's typhus in the East End, he wants the children in the countryside. Adults aren't in such danger. So it doesn't and shouldn't concern you."

Gilly swung around, her hands on her hips. "Not concern me?" she cried. "Oho! Then you don't consider me a member of the family anymore?"

"More than ever," Bridget said calmly, "and forever, too, and well you know it, so don't give me such sauce, thank you very much. But adults aren't so susceptible, and you have things that must get done here. Mind, it isn't such a bad idea, at that, since me being at home will help me get things done there. There's Betsy's gown to fit, and speaking of Betsy, the flowers for the ceremony, of course. How charming if she carried a basket of violets, for old times' sake. And the catering and provisions and lodgings for all the guests to see to. There's so much to do. Weddings don't arrange themselves, at least not magnificent ones, and we'll have no less than that for you."

"Well, I don't need to be here then, either," Gilly said, turning and flinging a chemise into her traveling case with such violence Bridget winced.

"Annie can pack for you," Bridget said, and then

added, "when it's time for you to leave. Which it is not now. You have a raft of gowns still being fitted, a trunkful of bonnets, and robes and slippers and fans—Lord! Gilly, you can't leave now! Unless . . . I've noticed . . . Is there a problem, Gilly?"

"Problem with what?" Gilly said too quickly, turning to stare. "What have you noticed?"

Bridget perched on the edge of the bed, folded her hands, and looked at Gilly. Her eyes were troubled, because she saw the shadows in Gilly's eyes. "There is such a thing as wedding nerves and that's perfectly natural. But if it's more than that, I wish you'd tell me."

"Why should you think that?" Gilly asked, her cheeks growing pink.

"Because I'm not deaf or blind. After we left Vauxhall yesterday you hardly said two words to Damon. He was quiet, too. I know we made a noisy party at the theater, but at dinner? And later? Come, what's toward? Have you two quarreled? Is it serious? Or only pre-bridal nerves?"

"Ho!" Gilly said hollowly. "I don't have a nerve in my body, and you know it."

"There's a mare's nest! But I'll let it go. Did you fight?"

Gilly shook her head.

"I see. Then what could it be? Every girl is a little nervous before her wedding . . . Lud! Could it be?" The viscountess seemed to ask herself, her eyes wide. "I just realized! Gilly! Do you know? With all the things we've talked about through the years, we never talked about . . . you know, things to do with your wedding night."

"Of course we did," Gilly said with a forced laugh.

"Don't we gossip about every lecher and loose lady in the *ton*, and every affair we hear about in the countryside, too?"

"Yes, but that's not what I mean. That's in general. I meant specifics, this time. We never talked about that. You know? I suppose I was a coward, because I didn't want to bring it up because of your early experience. And so if you think . . . But this would never be the same, and you ought to know that."

Bridget's eyes widened on another sudden thought. She ducked her head and stammered, "Unless, of course, it's a thing that you and he have already . . . ! Not that it matters. Unless it was uncomfortable or such and then we ought to talk about it, because . . . because it might be a thing that can be remedied by knowledge of how such things go. But even if not, it wouldn't be the first time such a thing happened before the wedding night, and I'd have no business knowing if it did, I'm not prying or . . ."

"Don't get into such a dither," Gilly said with a sweet smile, plunking down on the bed beside her friend and mentor. "Of course you're prying. I'm glad of it, because you're my friend and friends are supposed to pry. But I haven't, we didn't, and there's an end to it. I expect you're right; it's just that I've lived with you gentry coves too long."

Gilly wore a cocky smile that reminded Bridget of the girl she'd been as she went on. "I'm getting missish. Me! But marriage is a big step and I think my feet were getting too cold to take it, is all. I owe Damon an apology. I suppose I am on edge. The thing is, I hate to stay here without you here with me."

"But it's only for a few weeks, and Damon's mama and papa are perfect chaperones."

"Aye, perfect. Them and sweet old Aunt Felicity," Gilly grumbled. "There's one who'd like to dance around my head in a basket."

"Gilly," Bridget said in exasperation, "they all adore you, because he adores you. Don't invent problems."

"No fear of that," Gilly said, as she rose and began pulling things out of her traveling case.

Because, she thought, she didn't have to invent them. She'd be left in London, alone with a family that regretted her lack of family. Alone with a man who had surprised and confused her. She'd thought he'd be a comfortable husband. She'd never imagined anything else in marriage, except with her secret imaginary lover, her phantom husband, the Earl of Drummond. She'd always known that was only a fantasy, but such a delicious one that she'd never wanted to replace him, only to find someone to build a real life with.

Her response to Damon had been profound, and it had also been profoundly unsettling. She should be glad. Instead, she was uneasy and off-balance. She'd lost herself in his arms, completely. But for all it had been, and with all she now realized it could be with Damon, she couldn't quite dismiss that old, essential dream. She loved Drum and always would. She was cursed with honesty; she neither gave nor gave up her fidelity easily. She knew it was folly, but still the stunning passion she'd shared with Damon was tinged with regret and guilt, because with all she'd felt, it still seemed like a betrayal.

Her dreams and her reality were colliding. She'd

thought Damon a common man. Not such a com-
moner as herself, but certainly not from such an
exalted family as she now knew he had.

Last time she'd been alone in this city she'd known
it from the bottom. Now she suddenly found she was
to be alone at the top—without Bridget and Ewen, for
the first time since they'd met. Back then, in those
fearful days before she'd met them, she'd worried
about how she'd be able to eat the next day. That was,
if she'd be alive in order to eat. Even so, on balance,
Gilly thought sadly, remembering her past as she half-
listened to Bridget giving instructions on how she was
to hold her head high and never worry about Damon's
family in future, in many ways it had been so much
simpler then.

# 10

"I shall write," Max said grumpily, drawing a small circle on the marble tiles in the hall with the toe of his boot. "It would be nice if you'd write to me, too."

"I will," Gilly promised, "but there's no reason for us to be sad. I'll be coming home in a month's time."

"But then you'll be getting married," he said, still looking down and not at Gilly.

"And then she'll live not one hour's ride away from us, remember, gudgeon?" Ewen said, reaching down to ruffle his son's downcast head. "At first we'll have to visit by carriage but before you know it you'll be able to take a horse and go galloping off to visit her all by yourself. Now, make your bows, it's getting late, we have to go galloping off ourselves."

Gilly felt as glum as Max looked. It was true she'd see

him soon. But right now that seemed as far away to her as commandeering his own horse did to him. A lump rose in her throat as she took his hand and slowly walked out to the waiting carriage with him. But she knew he was better off away from contagion, safe in the countryside. For herself, she'd never felt less safe.

Which was nonsense, she told herself sharply. Because if anyone knew the face of danger, she did. And it certainly was not the calm, handsome face of her betrothed, standing at her side as she made her good-byes to the dearest, truest friends she'd ever known. She sniffled. Max ran a finger under his nose and scowled horribly. They stood by the carriage looking as though he was going to be carried away to the scaffold, before she was to be sent to the Tower.

"Max," Damon said, bending to one knee beside the boy, ignoring the risk to the close-knit fabric of his breeches, "what your father said reminded me of something. Could you do me a favor? I got a letter this morning. From my house, The Lindens. Topsy is a yellow dog that lives with the gatekeeper there, but she used to be my uncle's favorite. Half spaniel, half terrier, I think, but all heart. Or so they say. But now? Well, it seems she's pining. She's been lonely since my uncle left. She could do with a friend. It'll be a while until I get there. The servants like her, but they have so many duties now, preparing for the wedding, you see. So, I was thinking—if your father could take you over to The Lindens, do you think you could throw a stick or two for her? For me?"

Max thought about it. "I'll do it. But don't she need more?"

"A pat or two would help, too," Damon said, considering it. "A scratch on the tum? Maybe a long amble through the gardens? I don't know. What do you think?"

"I think maybe I should take her home with me."

"Well, maybe," Damon said, not daring to look up at the viscountess. If they had any more dogs, Bridget groaned, they'd be a kennel. "But The Lindens is her home. You know how it is. Maybe if you just visited her often? And told her we're coming soon?"

"I could do that!" Max said, brightening.

"You might tell the barn cat and her new kittens, too," Damon mused.

"Kittens?" Max asked.

"Six. Ginger ones, I suspect, like their mother," Damon said. "I'm not sure. Maybe you could tell me?"

So Max was smiling as he got into the coach. No one else was. Bridget blotted her eyes after she hugged Gilly good-bye. A muscle in the side of the viscount's hard jaw knotted after he kissed her cheek in farewell. "Take care of our Gilly girl," he told Damon curtly, as he stepped into the carriage after his wife.

Damon's father answered for him. "Of course! Never fear," Arthur assured him. Damon's mama added, "As though she were our own."

Damon put his arm around Gilly. And frowned to himself at how stiffly she held herself and how grieved she looked even after the coach went out of sight. "It's not forever," he told her, as they turned to go back in the house. When she didn't answer, he added, "Maybe you'd like me to bring Topsy here so you can play with her?"

She gave him a weak smile. "Thank you," she said

mistily, "but leave that to Max. I know I'm being foolish. It's just that I haven't been on my own in a while, and I'm a little anxious about it."

Now he frowned. "On your own? With my parents and ten thousand relatives of mine living in your pocket?"

"Yes, but that's it. They're yours," she said simply. "I know they'll be mine. But they're still strangers to me. I've no one of my own here with me now."

"You have me," he said seriously.

She gazed at that grave, handsome face. "I know. Thank you."

"I'll be here with you every minute," he promised.

"Even I feel glum!" his mother said, as she bustled up to them. "Partings can certainly put you in the sullens. But I've a cure. Get your bonnet, Gillian. My husband's off to keep Damon's brothers entertained, but you're promised to me this morning, remember? We've more shopping to do. I don't know anything that can cheer a girl more."

A *hanging might*, Damon thought, with a look at Gilly's expression. "So much for my promise," he said with regret, "but I'll make it up to you. Be back on time," he told his mother. "I'll be here for luncheon, and I've promised Gilly a drive right after."

"After it is then," his mother said. "Now, we must get some more gowns made! Come along, Gillian."

Gilly ducked her head. "I'll just get that bonnet," she said hollowly, and with only one backward glance at Damon, went up the stairs to her room. Damon put a hand on his mother's sleeve as she began to follow. "Wait," he said softly. Elizabeth looked at him in surprise. "Felicity going with you?" he asked.

"Of course. Try discouraging her from such a treat! Why do you ask?"

His eyes were troubled. In immediate reaction, she reached up to touch his cheek, only realizing he was a grown man at the last and touching his neckcloth as though to straighten it instead.

"Gilly isn't used to family," he said, taking her hand. "Bear with her, please."

"Why, but I'm doing just that!"

"Yes, but . . ." He sighed, and lowered his voice. "If you tell Gilly this, I'm afraid I'm going to have to remove your scalp, the way I wrote and told you they do in the wilderness, remember? In the nicest way possible, of course. But I'll do it. Listen, Mama. I'm afraid your dear Cousin Felicity's given Gilly the feeling you'd have preferred Annabelle as a daughter-in-law." He wasn't pleased to see her face turning pink.

"Oh my! Has she? Well, but Damon, you can hardly blame her for that. We all cherished hopes . . . that is to say . . ." She saw his eyes change to slate and added petulantly, "Well, but that's of no account now, is it?"

"It is," he said through clenched teeth.

She stepped back in alarm.

He took a deep breath. "I suppose I understand it even if I regret it, so I don't blame anyone," he said with thin patience. "But I will if it doesn't change. I'd like it if you could pretend you never felt that way. Not so much for Gilly's sake as mine. Gilly doesn't know you. I do. I wouldn't want to feel that wasn't true. Nor would I want any part of our affection for each other to change."

His mother's eyes widened.

"I think if you pretend, it'll be truth in no time," he said a little more gently. "She's wonderful, Mama. Give her a chance to show you. She can't if she thinks you resent her or wish her half a world away."

"I don't! What a thing to say! I suppose it's because she doesn't know me. Well, but how can she? It's difficult to know what to say to someone who's a complete stranger," she said defensively, "and one who knows no one you know . . . and who doesn't even know how to behave in our boisterous family." She saw his face, and winced. "I mean to say, how to fit in, for she behaves very prettily, to be sure. Oh drat, Damon! It's just hard to know how to approach her. I'm sure you know what you're about, but it would have been—if nothing else—just so much easier with Annabelle!"

"Going by that reasoning, it would be even easier if I offered for Felicity, wouldn't it?" he asked wryly. "England's full of girls who grew up exactly as I did and who know everyone I do. I waited this long because I was looking for something else. And *that* someone is Gilly. Mama, if you want to make me happy, make her happy. That's all I'll say."

"Oh," she said, affronted, but afraid to show it. "Well, I can only try."

"Don't try as hard, it will be easier," he said, smiling at her in the way that always melted her anger.

So his mother was careful to be on her best behavior as she, Felicity, and Gilly visited the dressmaker. Maybe too careful. So Gilly was subdued and quietly polite, too. Felicity was the only one free to chatter, and she did. And so she was the only one to enjoy the morning.

*    *    *

Damon saw that the moment the trio got home. He saw Gilly get out of the coach and straggle up the front steps after his mama and Felicity. He went quickly to meet her. Gilly was silent. Pale to begin with, she looked drawn and exhausted.

"Had a good time?" he asked.

"Delightful," Gilly lied.

"Oh, yes," his mother echoed with false sincerity.

"Excellent!" Felicity said, and meant it.

Gilly told him why on their drive in the park after lunch.

"Lady Annabelle's a complete lady," Gilly reported with bitter spirit, "but she knows how to ride to an inch, follows the hunt as well as the latest fashions, and has more beaux than most girls have hair on their heads. As to that—her hair's lustrous and black, with hints of blue in the sunlight, and so she has, as a matter of fact, even been called the 'Black Rose of Surrey' in a poem or two dozen, one actually printed in the *Gentleman's Magazine*. But I suppose you know that, and all the other wonderful things about her."

"Yes, I read the poem. They sent it to me," Damon said carefully. "The rhymes were terrible, the meter off, and the whole thing sludge, as another matter of fact. But the poet's father's an old school chum of the editor's. What else did you talk about this morning? I mean, apart from Annabelle's perfection?"

"Is she really that good?" Gilly asked.

He owed her honesty, and nodded, not looking at her, glad the horses required his attention. "She is. Very good, mind and heart, and yes, pretty, too. But though I've said I think green suits you, I have to add that she's good for someone else. Not me. I like her. I never loved her or wanted her for a wife. There's no explaining these things. So don't go looking for deeper meanings. She's a wonderful girl—woman, now. But not for me. Want to go into who is, chapter and verse? Or will you accept that?"

"Fine," she said, but she looked like she'd bitten something sour.

"So what else did you talk about? Annabelle's charming, but surely not a whole morning's worth of conversation."

"We talked about the same things we talked about at dinner last night," she said crankily. "And at luncheon today, as well as at breakfast. Old friends at home, old friends in London. And I do mean *old*. Doesn't your family know anyone whose great grandparents didn't know each other? Or did they all meet at Hastings at that battle when you were trying to repel the invaders?"

"No, you've got it wrong," he said mildly. "Most of them were those invaders. A lot of Normans, a few Saxons, and a Viking here or there, and there we are."

"Aye," she spat. "There *you* are! As for me? I'm an Englishwoman, but I don't know a thing past that! Damon, don't you see how ridiculous this is getting to be?"

"Yes," he said, turning his head. "Don't you?"

"I see. You're still certain of this marriage of ours?" she asked, but it was more of a statement.

"Still," he said. But didn't ask her the same.

*     *     *

There was more reminiscence at the dinner table that night. Every time Mary told a story about a neighbor, or Alfred joked about a cousin, or anyone told an anecdote about someone Gilly didn't know—and that was everyone they talked about—she looked at Damon with something like triumph. And something like despair.

"Now at least they understand why I picked you for my bride," Damon said idly, hours later, when they finally were able to sit alone in the drawing room for their last half hour of the night. "They know I'm softhearted. And they think you're a mute."

"Well, what was I supposed to say?" Gilly demanded, anger banishing her melancholy.

"Nothing," he laughed, happy to see her eyes sparkling and the color flashing into her face. "Gilly, my silly, that's what families do when they get together. Did you notice all your counterparts yawning? Mary's husband practically dozed off in his soup while she told about the time I ran away from home to escape punishment for shaving the dog. And I heard Thomas's wife groan when he told that frog in my pocket story again. But she was polite and did it as she bit into her pastry, so it would sound like 'Oh, yum' and not 'Ho hum.'"

Gilly grinned.

Such a cocky, arrogant, little boy grin, he thought tenderly. Not at all what you'd expect from such a wholly feminine face. She ought to lower her long lashes over those remarkable yellow eyes of hers, smiling the slow languorous smile of a woman with a wonderful secret, the way the acknowledged beauties did. But instead she grinned and tugged at his heart as no other woman had ever done. His heart and other impulses, he thought, catching himself beginning to bend toward her. She saw the motion, and leaned forward slightly, her eyelids drifting closed. Her lips parted, her breath came more quickly. He reached to touch the satin softness of her cheek . . . and snatched back his hand to sit up straight again.

Her eyes flew open. She frowned. He smiled. "No," he said regretfully, though he was delighted by her surprised disappointment. "No kisses. No embraces. It's Father Damon the Pious you've got to yourself tonight, my dear Gilly. And every night until you're under Sinclair's protection again."

She looked confused. "It's nothing you said or did," he said. "In fact, I have the strongest desire to bolt the door and let the consequences fall where they may. Along with your pretty gown . . ." he added with a mock leer. Then he grew serious. "My desire for you hasn't changed. Our circumstances have. I could overstep myself when your protectors were here. It wasn't right, but at least understandable. I won't when you're under my protection. I can't. They trust me. I gave my word. Do you see?"

She nodded, unsure. He was unsure himself. The desire to take her into his arms was a powerful goad. But the knowledge that there was no one for her to depend on but himself now was a more powerful deterrent. He'd wait. Even if the sight and softly floral scent of her was tempting him badly. He thought of other negatives in order to quell the powerful urge to ignore his conscience. He thought of one of the worst.

"Apart from that, what if Felicity came in?" he asked,

half joking. "She's probably just outside the door. As soon as she doesn't hear voices, she'll burst in. I refuse to entertain her, much as I yearn to entertain myself and you. So," he said, clearing his throat and looking away from temptation, "since my family bored you to bits with stories about my youth, your turn. Tell me some silly ones about yours. You never have, you know."

"I do know," she said sadly, "because I haven't any. Or at least, the silly ones aren't the kind anyone else would understand or enjoy. At least, anyone else of breeding."

"Let me judge that."

"Well, your family talked about your frogs and ponies and puppies and such. And your governesses and tutors and—"

"I know what they talked about," he groaned. "Enough! Tell me about your childhood."

"The pranks I played?" She considered it. Then she grinned hugely. "All right, my fine friend. We had games sometimes, too. See, there was this anvil outside of Higgin's tavern. Tavern? Huh. Blue Ruin was all he served, and in dirty earthen jars at that. But it was a busy place. It used to be a blacksmith's shop, way back, and when Higgins inherited the place, he left this huge anvil out front as a gesture, I suppose. Or maybe because it would be too much work to pick up and cart away. But strangers didn't know that.

"Well, the lads and me, we used to cover it over with a gunnysack sometimes, when we got bored and had nothing else to do. Which wasn't often, but even street rats play. They do," she said, diverted, "down to the oldest, scaliest of them, the real ones—rodents, I mean. You can see them frolicking in the gutters near the drains some spring nights. It's truth! Anyway . . ." She recalled herself.

"Sometimes, in the evenings, you'd see a sailor and his lass, or a poor working cully out to impress some mort, you know? Walking along, him trying to tell her how he's the best. Her, trying to pretend she believes it. So if we saw a couple like that, we'd send one of us over, the smallest, to say, all pathetic, 'Mister, could you give me a hand with my sack? I got to get it to the cart, and can't lift it, no way. So, I'm hoping maybe a fine, strong, flash cove like yourself could help me . . . ?'

"The cove would see this skinny little kid, and he'd puff out his chest, and say, 'Why sure!' And he'd bend over and start to lift like he thought he was picking up a gunny sack, only to find it was attached to the bottom of the world. . . . Oh lord!" she said, laughing to remember it. "Some did certain injury to themselves, and not just their pride, and that's sure. Ruptured six ways out of seven for all we knew, but they'd always let out a howl. We'd run like roaches when the lamp is lit, laughing all the way!"

But then she sobered. "*That*, Damon," she said seriously, "is one of my silly childhood stories. Cruel more than childish, not so much a prank as laughter for the misfortune of others. But I suppose we felt the world owed us a chance to deal pain, too. Sometimes, too, we'd pester some cully who was foxed. Just playing, mind, because otherwise, say if we turned out his pockets, then it was work. And that kind of work was best left to the dives anyway. . . ." She saw Damon's expression. "You know, the forks. Lud! I vow to give up the cant, and see how it creeps back! Drum would have my head! I mean pickpockets.

"The other games were tag and run, but it was from danger most of the time, and so where's the fun in that? Sport?" She sighed. "Not much of that. Or at least, not the kind I fancied. Want stories about particularly funny hangings at Newgate? That was considered fine sport for most street rats, though I never saw the joy in it—except for that once when I had a personal interest. And I wouldn't call that 'fun.'

"You want charming tales about animals? Puppies, maybe?" She scowled. "There were dog fights, but I hated them. Because I like dogs. And where I lived, dogs worked, or starved. No one was fed just to play with, except for pretty little girls, and that would be by—aye, not something I want to discuss, or you'd care to hear. Kittens? Try touching the kitties in my neighborhood, and a mother cat the size of a pony might remove your face for you. Let me see . . . birds? Yes. Cockfights. I know all about them. I didn't watch. But sometimes, if I was lucky, I got coin for caring for them between the fights, feeding and watering them and tending to their coops, because the best fighting cock is no more than poultry, after all.

"So, no frogs in my pockets, or pup at my heels, or ponies or cuddly kitties. But I did have the charge of fowl with sharp spurs at their heels. Those are my stories. Now, you still feel the same about me telling your family that?"

"Someday, you'll tell them. And they will laugh," he said, "and the sad stories will make them admire you even more." He wasn't lying. He meant her own family, her children and his.

"You know?" she said, cocking her head to the side. "You reminded me of the old earl when you said that." Her voice softened, as did her expression, thinking of the viscount's father. "So kind, so willing to accept me. When I first met him, I acted like I didn't care what he thought of me. I'd only been out of my boy's clothing for a week. That was after Ewen and Bridget's honeymoon, when we went to visit him. We weren't Ewen's wards then. Oh no. But even so, even then, Ewen didn't want to leave us on our own for fear we'd come to harm, or leg it back to London by ourselves, which would come to the same thing. So he took us along. The earl had been ill. Thank goodness, he was better by that time, and thank God he stays so! But back then, four years past, he was meeting Bridget for the first time, too. Well, there was nothing for him to find fault with in her!

"But me! I didn't know how to walk in a gown, or where to put my legs when I sat down. Drum and Rafe had already started to teach me, but it's not easy to get the hang of, you know. Well, you don't," she said on a giggle. "But I promise you, it is!"

Her expression grew faraway as she spoke, and Damon smiled, because this was a happy memory. "And what was I doing in an earl's home, after all? Not just a house, mind, but a castle! He must have wondered, I thought, and that was all right, for I was, too. Bridget insisted I come along, and I did for Betsy's sake.

"Oh, I swaggered," she said with a shake of her head

and a soft smile. "But I was in an agony of discomfort, missing my breeches, for I could be a passable boy. But I was miserably aware of what an inadequate female I was and looked, and defiant with it. And here he was an earl, no less, and see how he was staring at me. A slum brat in his house? Well, so I was, but I was no man's amusement, and would die before I let that happen again in any way, I can tell you. I was ready to leave if I had to.

"As it was, I saw his lips quirk as his son told him about me. I glowered at him, my worst face, ready for insult. But he heard my story, and must have heard it from Ewen in a letter before, I think.

"He saw my expression. Well, how could he miss it? I must have soured milk in the whole district. At least, I know I tried. 'Here's a firebrand,' he chuckled. 'Good for you. How dare I judge you, right? Know just how you feel. Put me in a gown and I'd snarl, too.'" Her voice grew low and gruff as she imitated the old man, and Damon grinned, hearing it. "'Want a sword or a dagger, my girl?' he asked me. 'I doubt poison's your way, is it? You're straight as a lathe, aren't you? Well, give me an honest enemy, though I'd rather stand as your friend, believe it or not.'

"I didn't, but he was my friend from that day forth," she said in amazement. "He agreed to me and Betsy staying on in the castle instead of being fostered out. No, in fact, he insisted on it. He said the place was too lonely, especially now with his only son married and occupied with his new wife. He taught me to be a lady as much as the governess he hired on did, even more than Drum could do. And with less teasing. Drum always made me mad as fire, and then I did things his way just to show him I could. But sometimes I did dreadful things to spite him, too. The earl only looked sad when I was bad. That worked better. I tried hard, for him.

"Why, the only reason he didn't take on legal responsibility for me and Betsy was because of his fears about his health. He'd been so ill that winter and the cold still affected him. That's why he spends so much time at his villa in southern Italy even now. He was—is—a real gentleman, blood and bone. Not high in the instep, and yet I know few men higher in morals and manner. I miss him," she sighed. "His wisdom, and his kindness."

"You haven't had enough of that in your life," Damon said.

"Oh, well," she said, embarrassed. "I've had more than my share since I met the Sinclairs, and there's truth."

"Now you have me, and I'll try to give you even more."

Her face grew sober. "I don't want you to want me for charity's sake, Damon. Good as it's been for me, I've had enough of that. Pity isn't a bad thing, but it rankles, after a while."

"Do you think what I feel for you is pity?"

"I don't know. That worries me, sometimes."

"Don't let it. I feel admiration. I feel a kinship, even though our cases couldn't be more different. And I feel desire. Too much of that right now, I think."

He bent toward her again, and this time brushed his lips across hers. They shared a long, sweet kiss. He was the one to end it.

"Enough excitement for Felicity," he said regretfully, putting her at arm's length. "I'd better go while I can. I'll be back at noon tomorrow and stay all day, and for as long as I can into the evening. You won't be on your own, Gilly," he said as he rose. "Not while I draw breath."

"I didn't mean you had to be my nursemaid!"

"You don't want me here?" he said, checking.

She stood up, and reached a hand to his cheek. "Vain creature. Want me to sing your praises, do you?" she asked on a crooked smile. "Too bad."

"Too good," he said, taking her hand and pressing a kiss into her palm.

Well, so she was alone again, Gilly thought after he left her, but it wouldn't be for too long, and then it wouldn't be so bad. It would be different than she'd thought, all right. And she still thought he was too good for her. But if he wanted her, so be it. Her feeling about being unfaithful to her dream lover was fading, as all dreams did, after a time. Damon was a solid reality. One she began to think she could maybe even learn to love. She certainly had learned to love his touch. She missed it. Damn the fellow for being such a gentleman, she thought tenderly, and bless him for it.

Still, she was nothing if not resilient. She'd make do, she thought on a grin, and went to bed smiling.

"Miss Gilly is in the morning room with your mother, Miss Felicity, and your sisters," the butler reported when Damon gave him his hat.

Miss Gilly was suffering in the morning room, along with his mother and his sisters, Damon thought when he came to the doorway and paused there. Gilly sat apart from the others, by a window, the sunlight making her hair gleam like a halo. That was the only radiant thing about her. She looked miserable. His mother didn't look happy either. Nor did his sisters. But he wasn't alarmed. Felicity was in full gabble, and so it only made sense.

But then a noise in the hall behind him made Gilly pick up her head. Her eyes widened. They filled with amber light, her expression changing from weary misery to full joy in a heartbeat. She stood, and he could literally see her spirit fly back into her slight frame. She fairly radiated rapture. He was touched, and gladdened, and very moved by her overwhelming reaction to him. He stepped forward, a smile on his lips.

But she kept staring—beyond him. Radiant, grinning ear to ear, she flew past him and fairly flung herself at the man who'd silently stepped into the house behind him. Damon turned to see.

Gilly pumped the tall, elegant stranger's hand, threw a mock punch at his lean middle, clapped him on the shoulder, and danced around him, beside herself with joy.

"Drum! Oh Drum, oh thank God, Drum!" she cried.

# 11

The new arrival was a tall, slender, exquisitely dressed gentleman, maybe a few years older than Damon himself, perhaps a few years younger than the Viscount Sinclair. It was hard to say, since the long face was so smooth and well schooled to a gentleman's amused composure. Straight jet hair, the kind Damon previously had seen most often on American Indians, was brushed back from a high forehead. His features were an inch from homely and a yard from handsome. But Damon didn't doubt women would consider that bony face attractive, if for no other reason than the intelligence and humor that animated from unexpectedly fine azure eyes.

Though he didn't look much like his cousin, Ewen Sinclair, there was nevertheless a reminder of the viscount in the man's expression and demeanor. This, then, was the redoubtable Drum, Earl of Drummond. Given his usually practical Gilly's boundless admiration for the man, Damon had expected no less. But he had no time to think about it.

Because Gilly gave out a yip that sounded like a dog being hit by a wagon. Startled, Damon wheeled to stare at her, ready to protect her. A second later, she sank into a deep, beautifully executed curtsey, and when she rose there were tears trembling at the tips of her lashes, though she was smiling tremulously.

"My lord," she said, offering her hand to the white-haired gentleman who had come into the room with the Earl of Drummond.

"Gilly, you were lovely when I left," the Earl of Kenton, the Viscount Sinclair's father, said, "but I vow something new has made rainbows in your eyes since we last met."

"My tears at seeing you again," she said simply, and came into his welcoming embrace, now weeping openly.

"Now, *he* is called 'my lord' and gets a curtsey deep enough to mine in," Drum commented dryly. "Yet I only get pummeled. Do you note the disparity, Rafe, old friend?"

"Note it?" a redheaded gentleman who had been standing in the shadows behind the earl complained. "I don't even get so much as a 'howjado!'"

"*Rafe!*" Gilly shrieked. The old earl, with a smile, released her. She hugged the harsh-faced, military-looking gentleman hard, and then stepped back and threw a mock punch at his shoulder. "Now," she exulted. "Oh, now my life's completely right again!"

There was a silence. Everyone stared at the new arrivals. The butler had come bustling up and stood looking flustered. But no more than Damon's mother and sisters did.

"Allow me to introduce myself," Damon said smoothly, stepping forward, "since Gilly obviously has her wits to let. But who could blame her? She's ecstatic at seeing you again. I'm Damon Ryder, at your service, my lords, and very pleased to meet you."

"The *Catch*!" Drum said, his eyes alight with mischief. He gave Damon a brief bow. "I give you good afternoon, sir. More than that, congratulations on nabbing our Gilly."

Damon's eyes narrowed at Drum's first words, but he inclined his head in a sketch of a bow. When he faced the new arrivals again his expression was as serene as theirs. "The Catch himself, my lord. May I present my mother, and my sisters Margaret, Mary, and Bethany? And our Cousin Felicity?"

"Delighted," the older gentleman said, bowing. "I'm Kenton, father to Sinclair." He hardly had to say it. Ewen Sinclair's eyes looked at them from a gentler face, and from less of a height, but the family resemblance was clear. If the earl had been ill, his years in Italy had mended him; all that remained of his story was in the deeply tanned lines in his face. "I'm also uncle to his cousin here, Drum, Earl of Drummond. I'm also happy to make you known to my close friend, this redheaded fury, Lord Dalton, best known to us as Rafe. And I'm most proud to declare myself friend for life and devoted servant of Miss Giles."

"Pardon our dropping in unannounced," Drum explained, "but then, we always do. We didn't expect company to be here at Sinclair's townhouse. We've just arrived in town, you see, and nothing would do but we hasten to see our Gilly immediately. Gilly, Ewen, and Bridget and that sly Max, too. And the baby we've never met. But it seems too placid here. No one's bawling except Gilly. Where is my cousin?"

"He took his family home to Shropshire," Damon said. "You missed them by a day. There's a contagion among children here in London and they didn't want to risk Max and the baby being infected. We'd have gone with them but Gilly's still waiting for the last of her new wardrobe to be finished."

"That I'm not!" Gilly sang out. "It's Bridget who insisted. I was ready to leave, too, but I'm *so* glad I didn't. I'd have missed you! I'd have killed myself!"

"Doubtless, and who could blame you?" Drum said sweetly. "But I prefer a wedding to a funeral. I'm delighted you listened to Lady Sinclair. Italy's a color-ful place, and I haven't a thing in black to wear that's decent, you see."

"Well, you've grown very niffy-naffy," Gilly said, her head to the side. "Continental airs, my dear Lord Drummond?"

Drum laughed. "Can't play any of my new tricks off on you, can I? I *have* missed you, my dear."

She linked her arm with Rafe's and turned a saucy grin on Drum. "My job, dear sir, is to keep your feet on firm ground, or so you always said."

"So you did, and so you do," he said, "and mine was to keep you out of scrapes."

"No," she giggled, "you were appointed to keep my feet out of boots—and into slippers, remember?"

He raised an eyebrow, looking over her head to Damon's relatives. She blushed and shot a guilty glance at the puzzlement on Damon's mama's face.

"But what tedious guests we are!" the Earl of Kenton exclaimed. "Ladies, my apologies. Barging in and boring you with our old jests, which are amusing only to ourselves. Forgive us."

"You're only paying us back in kind, my lord," Damon said. "Because if anyone's become the expert on suffering through old family jokes, it's poor Gilly here."

"No! I loved every word of them," Gilly exclaimed indignantly, and ruined it with an arch look and a cheeky grin at Drum. "Now it's my turn. We'll talk more later, when we're alone," she promised Drum. "Now, where are your traveling cases? You're staying here, of course."

There was a slight murmur from the ladies in the room as they looked at each other in sudden consternation. "Of course they are," Damon's mother said quickly. "There's no problem. I was just saying I'd love to stay at Grillion's, in Albermarle Street, because it's closer to the shops. My daughters and their husbands, too. In fact, Alfred's already staying there. He says he loves it, doesn't he, Damon?"

"Often," Damon agreed without missing a beat. "It's well recommended, especially its kitchens. No wonder you're envious."

"There you are!" his mother said almost gaily. "Bring your bags in, please, my lords, it will take us no time to make the change."

"Wouldn't think of it!" Ewen's father said, aghast.

"Don't stir yourselves. I've got my club to stay at. Been looking forward to seeing old friends, in fact, nothing could suit me better."

"I've got friends mad to put me up!" Rafe said immediately. "But I prefer Stevens' in Bond Street, like most old army men."

"But—but you *always* stay here!" Gilly cried.

"Ladies, do not so much as move a handkerchief from your rooms," Drum said, cutting her off. "I've old friends here in town, too, and clubs galore to choose from, as well. And Gilly," he said to her look of dismay, "think on. If we did stay here, you'd have to leave. Yes, that's right. Consider. Our arrival and Mr. Ryder's mama's departure would make it a bachelor household, and we can't play at that anymore."

She murmured something that looked like a *damn* on her lips, scuffed one little slipper on the floor and frowned. Damon's eyes narrowed. She wore a cherry red gown, her bright hair was twisted into ringlets and tied with a cerise ribbon, she looked charming as a springtime tulip in the park, but she'd suddenly become a swaggering boy again.

"You'll be back for dinner?" she asked Drum hopefully.

"Better," Drum said. "We'd like you all to be our guests for dinner tonight."

"At your club?" Gilly hooted. "Gammon! They'd tar and feather any female who dared set a toe over their doorstep."

"At one of the many London restaurants we've been missing," Drum said gently, "and since when did you start speaking cant again, my girl?"

She fell still, looking adorably grouchy and guilty at the same time.

"I enjoy Gilly's colorful speech," Damon said quickly, "so I'm afraid it's my fault. I encourage her."

"No one has to apologize for me," Gilly muttered.

"No, indeed," Drum said. "Forgive the presumptions of an old friend. So then, you'll be our guests for dinner tonight?"

"My dear Lord Drummond," Damon's mother laughed. "You can't have thought! There's my husband, and the girls' husbands, not to mention my other sons and their wives. We're a huge family. We can hardly fit around the table here. All told we'd make too big a handful for you to entertain."

"But not too big for the Clarendon, do you think?" Drum asked, naming one of London's most fashionable hotels.

Ewen's father made a face. "A fine French menu, to be sure, but I've had enough foreign food. Speaking of Grillion's, let's dine there. I remember their soup particularly, and their way with a joint of beef. I find I'm quite looking forward to it, in fact."

"Done," Drum said. "We'll expect you then, ma'am?"

"Why, that would be delightful," Elizabeth Ryder said. "What do you think, Damon?"

"I can see majority rules," he answered with a faint smile.

"Then excuse us while we go arrange accommodations and remove the dust of travel," Drum said, bowing again. "We did literally come here straight from the docks. But travel makes a man edgy, and it will be a while until we wind down. At Grillion's at nine, then."

He turned to go to the door, but then turned back again. "Now mind, Gilly," he said. "Put on your finest feathers."

"Oh pooh," she laughed, as she fairly skipped to his side and they began walking toward the hall. "As if you had to tell me. I've got town bronze by now. So much I feel positively weighed down. Oh, I'm *so* glad you've come back."

"Of course I came back. Miss your wedding, child? I think not!"

She blinked, then put up her chin. "I think not!" she echoed, but her own smile had slipped. Damon saw it. And he could see from the way Drum tilted his head and paused for a moment that he did, too. It seemed no one missed it.

"Such good friends they are," Cousin Felicity purred, watching them.

"Yes," Damon said, "Gilly's friends are her family, or at least, all she's known of one these past years."

"Indeed," Felicity said, "now they're reunited. How delightful."

"I hope it will be," Damon said, and meant it.

Grillion's dining room was crowded, but the waiters had cobbled together a great table for the Earl of Kenton, the Earl of Drummond, and their guests in the center of the room. They were the focus of all eyes. And no wonder. The party was jolly, even noisy, there were a great many noble persons, and many of those hadn't been seen in London for a long time.

All the diners in the room were dressed with care. But none caught the eye as much as the young woman in blue at the earls' table. She'd taken special pains with her appearance. It showed. Gilly sat near the head of the huge table, but she'd have been noticed wherever she was.

She wore an ice blue gown with a filmy gray overskirt, and an azure shawl covered her pale shoulders. The small gold locket at her throat reflected itself against her white skin, sitting in a buttercup halo, pointing up the way the candlelight made her odd eyes gleam gold. Her fair hair was pulled back from her face and dressed high with small blue flowers. But instead of looking like an ice queen, she bloomed like a rose. Her cheeks were pink with laughter, her face wreathed in smiles, and she never stopped laughing, unless it was to grin. She was everything ladylike, except that she bounced in her seat like a girl.

Damon was dressed with equal care, and by chance, in similar colors. But he looked more sober entirely, face and figure. He wore a dark blue jacket of superfine and storm gray breeches to match his eyes. The only other color was on his waistcoat, where tiny green and gold silken hummingbirds visited the dark blue morning glories embroidered there. Gilly didn't notice. She hung on the Earl of Kenton's every word, teased her old friend Rafe constantly, and never took her eyes from the Earl of Drummond.

It wasn't hard for her to do. Ewen's father had been given a place of honor at the head and she sat on his right, across from the Earl of Drummond, her friend Rafe nearby. Even if she didn't obviously adore them, she could hardly avoid chatting with them the way things were arranged. But she didn't address one word to Damon at her other side. Many noted it. His sister Mary, next to him, was worried.

"It's understandable," Mary murmured to Damon, uninvited, noting his silence and seeing the direction of his steady gray gaze. "A reunion, after all. After the way we were carrying on all week! It's only natural. Poor girl, no wonder she's so thrilled to see them again. And they *are* very nice, indeed."

"So they are," he laughed, patting her hand. "I don't mind, did you think I did?"

"Well, but . . ." she said, flustered.

"It's only that I just discovered I'm a selfish lump," he said seriously. "And I hate seeing my own faults. Part of it is your fault, you know, for making me the center of our family's little universe. And I'm so used to being the center of hers that I suppose I'm feeling a little left out. I'd better get over it, and fast. What about when our children come along? I have to accept Gilly has and will have other loves, and all of them important."

His sister looked up at Gilly, the men she was laughing with, and then down at her plate. She drew a little circle on the cloth with her spoon. "Damon . . ." she said hesitantly. She stopped and laughed, unconvincingly. "Well, that's good, then, isn't it? Why, when I remember how my George felt after our first was born . . ."

Damon covered his sister's hand with his. "You're so transparent, I wonder how the waiter saw you clear enough to serve you that soup you're ignoring. Don't worry. I'm not jealous for any other reason. I don't have to be." He looked rueful. "I'll know too soon if I ever have any cause for worry on that score. You don't know Gilly well yet, but when you do, you'll realize that whatever else you can say about her, the one thing you can depend on with Gilly Giles is complete honesty."

But he couldn't say that to all his relatives, and many of them were noticing the way Gilly seemed to have forgotten her fiancé. They could hardly not. The strangers in their company riveted their attention, too. The Earl of Kenton was not only charming, he was well known to society, even though he'd been absent from it for years. Lord Rafe Dalton was burdened with unfashionably fiery red hair. But the wars were not so long over that such an obvious military man didn't gain instant admiration.

The Earl of Drummond was the most commanding presence. Elegant, almost haughty, except for that infrequent slow and curling smile that saved him from arrogance. He wore a dark maroon jacket, and a small single ruby at his snowy cravat echoed the single ruby ring that graced one long hand. It was more than his faultless apparel, it was the man himself. He carried himself with quiet dignity, and while he never raised his voice, he acted as though he knew he would command complete attention and respect. He did.

Now he stopped smiling. So did Damon.

A sudden lull had made the discussion going on at the head of the table clear to everyone in the room. Too clear. "Come, come, my girl," Drum snapped, sharply cutting off Gilly mid-sentence, and halting all other talk in the room because of the exasperation in his voice. "Where are your manners? We've monopolized the conversation at the table long enough, I think."

No one spoke, least of all Gilly, who sat back, astonished.

Damon's lips thinned. Then he opened them to speak. "Her manners are good, maybe too good," he said firmly. "I think she's been trying to make up for our silence. Why don't you tell us something about your travels? Then we can let poor Gilly tend to her dinner instead of trying to cover our oversights."

Drum inclined his head. "An excellent idea. But hardly practical. I don't want to make a speech. It is, after all, dinnertime. Perhaps, later? Although, in Venice, you know, dinner might go on until midnight and beyond. Remember that night at the princess's palazzo, Rafe?"

"'Deed, I do," Rafe said hurriedly, putting down his glass of wine. "So dark and stormy, I didn't know whether we'd find our lodgings when we left. The tide was in and the water from the canal came to my ankles, and the fog was putting out the linkboy's torch. And we'd had a bottle or two of that excellent claret!" he said, warming to the subject. "Too excellent. Remember how you saved me from blundering into the canal?"

"But you swim like a fish, my friend," Drum said.

"Aye, but think of the indignity. I'm a soldier, not a sailor!"

That set everyone laughing. Except Gilly, who sat back, hollow-eyed with hurt. And Damon, who watched her narrowly.

But the dinner was almost over and the good food and plentiful wine made most of the guests sleepily content. Since they were at a hotel and not a private home, the gentlemen had to forego the usual after-dinner ritual of drinking and telling tales together while the ladies gossiped in another room, waiting for them to be done. So it wasn't much longer before the men finished the last of their port, and the women who had to visit the withdrawing room returned, ready to go home.

They stood in the hotel foyer, making their fare-wells. The Earl of Kenton said good night to his guests, took their thanks, and went off to his club. Damon's relatives peeled off in twos and fours and went into the night. The last of the party, Damon and Gilly, were about to climb into their carriage when Drum stopped them.

"I'd like a word with Gilly," he said, "alone."

"Alone? But I'd ask you to remember she's not alone anymore," Damon answered curtly.

"Either here, or at Sinclair's house, where we can be more private," Drum said to Gilly, as though Damon hadn't spoken.

"I'm sure I don't know why a fellow who wouldn't let me talk all night wants to talk to me now," Gilly said haughtily, flinging her shawl over her shoulder with a flourish.

This was so patently untrue that even Damon had to bite back a smile. She'd been prattling steadily all night, until her old friend Drum had been rude to her. But the meal had almost been at an end then anyhow.

"*Gilly*," Drum said threateningly, and took her arm to pull her into the anteroom.

He found his other arm taken in a strong hold. He checked.

"I'd ask you to remove your hand," Damon drawled, his voice at odds with the hard light in his eyes. "If she wanted to go with you, she would. I won't have her manhandled."

Drum shook his arm free, drew his head back, and looked down his long nose. "I wasn't. But you say you won't have it? And you laid hands on me? I see. You're adept with pistols? Or do you prefer swords?"

"My fists can do the job as well, or better," Damon said coldly, "since I've no intention of having to leave the country after I make my point!"

"Lord!" Gilly breathed looking from one man to the other, her eyes wide. "Don't fight! At least, not over me. Damon, it's just that he forgets I'm grown up. Drum—I am, you know, and Damon *is* my fiancé. He doesn't know our history."

"*Precisely*," Drum said impatiently. "My point exactly. Which is why I must speak with you, *alone*! Do you understand?" he asked with emphasis, and then looked around for the first time to see if anyone else was watching or listening to them. But only Rafe stood next to them, tense, alert, and unhappy.

"No," Gilly said simply.

Drum huffed a sigh of exasperation. "Listen," he said in a lower voice, "I cut you off, and shut you up rudely, and well I know it. I meant to. Because there are some things I thought ought not to be said in company. *This* company. Things you were about to say. So. Now. Will you come with me," he asked, biting off each word, "so we can discuss it? I don't want you angry with me. Call off the dogs. For his sake, if not mine. Precisely because your fiancé"—he shrugged one shoulder in Damon's direction—"does *not* know our history—and yours."

"Oh!" Gilly said, her expression clearing. "But he does! You mean how we met? What I was then?"

"My God, child," Drum said furiously, looking around again, "how that can be misconstrued! I don't even want to think about it. Grown up, are you? With as much discretion as a puppy. Have a care. We're in public!"

"I know everything," Damon said coldly. "If *you* knew Gilly, you'd know she'd never let things go this far with me if I didn't."

"Indeed?" Drum said, but he was silent as he thought that over.

"One thing is sure," Damon said in annoyance, noting a few guests were looking their way now, "you're right. This isn't the place to discuss it. If you have to have your say before you go to bed, come back with us. We can be alone in the front parlor, no one has to know." The parlor, Damon thought with regret, realizing the sacrifice he was making, the one place he and Gilly were granted the privacy to make a fonder farewell to each other each night. But not this night if her face were any indication. She was obviously upset.

"If," Gilly said, "I choose to let him speak to me!"

All three men looked at her. Drum's harsh words had transformed her as suddenly and utterly as a bright candle being blown out. Now, however, she smoldered.

"I think you'd better," Damon said. "If only for my sake."

Drum lifted an eyebrow in a gesture eerily reminis-

cent of his cousin Ewen. Gilly looked at Damon in surprise.

Damon shrugged. "If you're at war," he told Gilly,
lifting a shoulder in Drum's direction, "you need to
face the enemy right off, not run away and rehearse the
argument you're going to have with him all night
instead . . . or at least, I'd rather not be the one you
rehearse it on."

"You *do* know her!" Rafe laughed.

Even Gilly had to smile at that.

# 12

The hour was late. They sat in the Sinclairs' parlor, talking in low voices.

"You don't know what she was saying," Drum told Damon in annoyance. "That's the point. I had to stop her saying it. We were reminiscing—which we did all evening, granted. But Gilly's reminiscences are not like other women's. Though Lord knows I tried to make them so. I didn't know how much you knew, Ryder." He looked uncomfortable for the first time. "I'd no idea you knew the whole. Because, you'll grant, Gilly's history is unusual. And whatever you did or did not know, I doubted you'd want the scandalmongers to get their teeth into it. Ewen never did."

Damon nodded. Rafe, deep in a chair, was silent, watching them with troubled eyes. Drum was standing near the mantel, staring down into the banked fire in the hearth. Damon sat next to Gilly, on a sofa near the fireside.

"Of course not," Damon answered. "Gilly's life story is her own to tell."

"So I thought," Drum said, nodding. "After all, Ewen never lied about Gilly or Betsy. But he never told the exact truth. Because," he said, holding up one hand before Gilly could speak, "it's no one's business. Gilly *used* to understand that. But tonight?" He lifted a thin dark eyebrow and stared at Gilly.

Gilly bit back her retort and looked down at a thread on the lap of her gown.

"So, tonight," Drum went on, "whenever the subject got too dangerous for casual listeners, I tried to change it. It was like talking with a weathervane. I silenced her harshly, I admit—but just as she began telling an amusing story from our mutual past. About the time she refused to be plagued by French dressmaker I'd sent her to and flounced out of the establishment determined to have her own way. She was in raptures, giggling, as she started to remind me how she stole back her boy's jacket and britches and boots, and went tramping back toward the rookeries again to take up her old jobs of coal heaving or lading. Lovely anecdote, wouldn't you say?"

Gilly looked stricken. "I didn't think! I mean, we were talking, and I forgot about everyone else. *See*?" she said furiously, suddenly turning toward Damon, as though he'd been the one to do something wrong.

Drum raised an eyebrow again, this time in question.

But Damon thought he understood. "I do see. Your excitement at seeing your old friends made your tongue run away with you. Understandable. It's a good thing, I suppose, that the earl prevented you from going on with that particular story. One day, maybe . . . but as for now? Trouble was avoided. And we can assume he's sorry your feelings were hurt," he added with a too charming smile for Drum and his lack of apology. "So why are you still frowning? You look like a thundercloud. Where's the problem?"

"Bother!" Gilly swore, rising and pacing as though she wore brogues and not dancing slippers. "Well, there it is. Exactly. 'One day,' maybe? Which day? Tomorrow? Or the next? See? It's too hard. Damon, I am what I am, and I tell you, your fine family will never forgive you if you marry me! Or forgive me, I mean to say, because it's clear they'll forgive you anything."

"No," Damon said thoughtfully, "I'd be in trouble if I murdered Cousin Felicity. I asked."

Gilly almost smiled. But Drum spoke up. "She has a point, Ryder. That's why I tried to keep her recollections . . . *general*, shall we say?"

"But I don't want to forget who I was, because it makes me who I am!" Gilly cried.

"Laudable," Drum said, "but inadvisable. Child, Ewen said he was The Catch of the Season, and so he is. The Ryders are aristocracy as much as any titled family in England. They've been counselors to kings and cousins to queens since the invasion, and likely before. I thought you knew that."

"Well, I didn't," Gilly said, pacing. "I said yes to

Damon because I didn't," she muttered, "and now what's to do?"

"Only because of that?" Damon asked.

Drum looked interested, Rafe stifled a groan.

She stopped, abashed. "No, of course, no," she said, looking Damon full in the face. "But it was a consideration. How was I to know how famous your family is? Bad enough they might find out one day how common my family was. Worse, if they ever discover how infamous my history is.

"Oh, Damon, you see?" She looked grieved as she stopped before him. He stood and took her icy hands in his. His big hands covered them over and held them tight, trying to warm them, trying to banish that fear he saw in the back of her golden eyes.

"I never want to involve you in scandal," she blurted, "but I don't see how it can be prevented. I thought I might pull it off even after I found how highly placed your family is . . . but I *will* talk. You know that. I love to talk. I have memories. How can I deny them? Well, if you know me, you know I can't. So, perhaps—no, *more* than perhaps, I think our wedding can't be. It's not too late. I'll have Ewen send the notice to the *Times*, and no one will ever blame you."

"I will," Damon said, looking into her stricken face, forgetting there was anyone else in the room, and not caring when he remembered. "I want you as my wife, Gilly Giles. Not in spite of, but because of all the things you are, and were. Where else could I find a woman so filled with heart and high courage? Someday my family may find out what your history was. So what?"

"*So what*?" she gasped.

"Yes. So what? If you want to tell them now, you can. If you don't and they find out, we'll just say we thought they knew. It doesn't matter to me." He touched her cheek to emphasize the point. "It shouldn't matter to you. Your future's with me. Your past made you the woman I want to spend my future with. You see? Simple."

They stood in the center of the room gazing at each other. They made a handsome couple. She, delicate, shapely, graceful. He, vital, handsome, ardent. Since her old friends had returned to visit she'd been brash and jolly, exuberant as the boy she'd once pretended to be. Now she seemed utterly feminine. She held his hands as if for support, her eyes searched his and her own widened at something she saw there. He looked down at her as though he wanted only to gather her close in his arms, the kiss he longed for clear to see in his posture, easy to read in his devouring gaze.

Rafe nodded, pleased. Drum sat arrested, staring, his mask of imperturbability for once slipped and forgotten.

She nodded. "I see," she said slowly, a new emotion flooding into her face, something between shame and regret. "You're sure?"

He laughed. "Again? You'll say that at the altar if you aren't careful. 'Do you take this man to be your lawful wedded husband?' the vicar will ask, and you'll look at me, and in front of all the guests you'll ask, 'You're sure?' *That* would give the gossips something to chew! I don't mind you telling all the *ton* chapter and verse about your masquerading as a boy. But your lack of faith in me? Please get it through that lovely head of yours that I don't care about what was. Only what *is*! And what is—is that you're a find of a lifetime. Lovely. Clever. Brave. True. Resourceful. Where would any man ever find so much in a wife? Now, do you want me to keep saying it? I'll have to add *vain* if you do."

"No," she said. "That will do. In fact, it's too much. I'm promised to you, and I'll stay with you if you want me. But if you don't mind, I'd rather they didn't find out just yet. So, if you find me talking about such things in company again, don't even be as polite as Drum was. Just put a hand over my mouth."

"And get it bit off?" Damon chuckled, but his tender expression and the way he looked at her clearly showed what it was he wanted to put over her mouth just then.

Rafe cleared his throat and stood up. "Well, late's late, morning's coming, and I need sleep. Been traveling for days. Time to go. I said—time to leave, eh, Drum?"

"What?" Drum said. He looked like a man who had just woken. "Oh. Yes, very late in the day, indeed," he said musingly. He rose. "Well, child," he said, as Gilly became aware of everyone else in the room and stepped back from Damon, blushing. "Now that that's solved, you forgive me? I was only trying to protect you, as ever."

"I know," she said simply. "Thank you. But now you have to know, I'm no longer a child."

"That I do see," he said slowly.

"And now she has someone else to protect her," Damon said.

"Good. The more people we can muster to protect

our Gilly," Drum said lightly, "the better. She's a fierce little thing, you've no idea of the scrapes she can get into without trying. Did you tell him about the time you took it upon yourself to teach Squire Waring a lesson?" he asked Gilly suddenly.

"Oh, lud!" Gilly laughed. "I'd forgotten! What a set to that was! Remember, Rafe?"

"Who could forget?" he said with a grimace.

"See," Gilly told Damon excitedly, "the squire, he had this old carriage horse. Well, you know I don't have much to do with horses, but this Old Bess, she was a singular beast. Wasn't she, Drum? I liked her, and she'd worked hard for him. Well, I heard he was thinking of calling the knackers to take her and . . ."

Drum smiled, Rafe laughed, and before the story was half done, the three were sitting and talking animatedly again.

Or rather, Damon thought, watching them, Gilly was talking, and Drum was urging her on, watching her with a curious smile on his face. A new smile, fond as ever, but with something else in it, something assessing, the way a man might look at someone enchanting, some woman he'd just met. Or so Damon thought, and cursed himself for thinking.

Because he knew she was clear as rain, and he knew she'd missed her friends. Because he realized he himself could add nothing to the conversation except laughter or exclamations. Because he couldn't help but notice how her eyes were shining and how she hung on the earl's every laconic word whenever he offered a comment.

He knew it was innocent, knew he was being selfish.

He resented it, Damon told himself, because a glance at the mantel clock showed her guests were taking up what little was left of the night, and he wouldn't have time for more than a hasty caress before he left her.

He had less time than that. It was very late. He had to leave with Drum and Rafe, and so could only take her hand at the door. But Drum bent his head and gave her a kiss on her cheek. And then stepped back and stared down at her. Which was not as disturbing to Damon as the way her head shot up and she looked back at him.

Jealousy was a sick, sour feeling at the pit of Damon's stomach and had nothing to do with his brain. He hated it, and himself for feeling it. It was new to him. But then, he thought, as he went out the door with the other two men, so was everything he felt that had anything to do with Gilly Giles.

He was so troubled by his unworthy reaction to that simple cousinly kiss, he couldn't think of anything to say as they walked down the street together. Neither of his companions seemed to notice. Rafe gave a jaw-cracking yawn. The Earl of Drummond was lost in thought.

"I think we part here," Damon said after they'd walked another street in silence. "My lodgings are nearby. Do you need a hack?"

"A hack?" Drum said after a moment. "No, thank you. If I sit, I'm done for. Best we keep walking, it's not far. I'm famished for sleep. We only just arrived in England, hunted up Gilly, nothing would do but we go right to dinner, and now we've sat up half the night gabbling. Rafe, here, is asleep on his feet. He learned to do it in the army. I'll have to wake him when we get the hotel. I'm not so lucky. I need a bed—or at least, to sit down before I nod off. Nice meeting you, Ryder. We'll talk when I'm awake, I think. After about a year, or so I feel. Shall you be visiting Gilly tomorrow?"

"Yes," Damon said, trying to be polite in spite of his tangled emotions about Gilly's old friend. "I'll call around noon. My sisters keep fashionable hours when they're in London. Gilly doesn't. But I think she could probably use some sleep, too. I'm glad you came. She's overjoyed seeing you again."

"And I, her."

They bowed. Rafe bent only his head, and Damon smiled, wondering if the close-mouthed fellow had really learned to sleep with his eyes open. Damon left them and, still smiling, strolled on toward his hotel. But now he was thinking of her. Of her candor, her spirit, of her honesty, and lack of guile. And of her lips, and of her breasts and of her . . . *Any more such thoughts, my friend*, he told himself with a wide grin, *and you will never get to sleep tonight*.

But that was exactly what happened. He was humming with unfulfilled desires, and so even when he got to his bed it was hard to sleep, thinking of how long it would be until it was night again, when he could take her in his arms once more. It got more difficult when he started thinking of how many days and nights it would be until he could take her entirely, and never have to part from her again.

Sleepless, but jangling with energy at the thought of seeing her again, Damon bounded up the stairs to the

Sinclairs' townhouse the next day, a little before noon.

"Tell Miss Gilly I'm here," he told the footman blithely, as the door swung open. "If she's not ready, I'll wait."

"Can't do that, sir. She's not here."

"Not here?"

"Left with the Earl of Drummond over an hour past, sir."

"Good God!" Damon said, his mind racing. "Has the old . . . has the viscount's father taken ill?"

"Not that I know, sir. They was laughing to beat the band, so I don't guess. Mr. Wilkins," he said to the butler who had appeared at his side, "Mr. Ryder is wishful to know if the viscount's father was took ill?"

"Good heavens no, sir," the butler said in alarm. "Why? If I may ask, that is to say. Have you heard so?"

"No, but why did she leave so early? Why did he arrive so early? Where did they go?"

"Oh, as to that," the butler said, beaming, "the earl, he came for breakfast, and then took Miss Gilly to the park. They said they'd have a walk by the Serpentine, to shake off the cobwebs."

"*Really*," Damon said. But it wasn't a question. And he didn't wait for an answer.

Gilly walked at Drum's side, the place she'd longed to be. But now she kept her head bent to watch where she put her feet. There had been a time when she could look at him when she spoke to him. Now she was fine so long as she didn't. He saw too much. There was too much for him to see. But it felt so good, so right, so grand to be beside him again. To have him to talk with again. Even though he was talking about her, another thing that didn't used to be. In the past, it was only when he meant to criticize her. Now, she felt her breath catch at his praise.

"Amazing," Drum was musing. "I can't get used to the sight of you. Look at you in that walking dress! The latest shade of green, with a matching wisp of a bonnet, in the height of fashion. And walking demure as a little mandarin—no, wrong gender. Taking little steps, neat as a pin, charming as a geisha. Yes, that's it. But that's not the half of it. Your hair done up, your eyes cast down, the slightest blush on that silken cheek. . . . My girl, you look like a milk-and-water miss. And while we're on the subject of dairy, you look like butter wouldn't melt in your mouth. We're the cynosure of all eyes, and not just of the fashionable. You always had the face and figure, but now you've the *attitude*. You're a beauty now.

"And yet," he said, tilting his own head, "I keep seeing you as if in motion—one minute I get a glimpse of our Gilly of old, and then in the next, by a word or a gesture, I see this entirely new Gilly before me. Astonishing. One expression reminds me of the belligerent boy I met. Another, and you are become the toast of London."

She laughed. "Hardly that! Everyone stares at everyone else in London on a fine morning. And I am dressed well, thank you. But fashionable? Huh. I may be admired by park saunterers, but they know I'm beneath their touch. Because I'm not marriage material for anyone in the *ton*. And they all know Ewen would slay them if they tried anything else."

"Or you would," Drum commented dryly. "But wouldn't your Catch have something to say about that, too?"

"I wish you wouldn't call him that," she said with a frown. "It's demeaning, somehow. He's a very nice man, Drum, you'd like him if you knew him."

"Now there's the new Gilly, all demure and polite. But that's faint praise for a prospective husband, even for the new Gilly. 'Very nice'? You're all fire, my girl, or at least you were a fire-eater then. I can't believe you've doused it entirely. And yet you're ready to take a 'very nice' husband? Come, are you sure?"

"Ho," she said on a brittle laugh. "Just what Damon complains about. I keep asking him if he's sure. But I am," she lied. "Drum." She turned her face up to his, then looked down to her toes when the intent look in those knowing azure eyes made her feel shivers along her spine. Because it was a new kind of attention. Or her overheated imagination took it for such. But in either case, it troubled her, wondering if it might be something new, worrying that if it were not, he might know she thought it was. "Damon met me while I was trying to kill some miserable wretch who tried to take advantage of me at a party. And yet he found that admirable, or so he said."

"So Ewen wrote—obliquely. Did you use fists, fingers, feet, or steel?" Drum asked with interest.

"All," she said grumpily, "except for the knife. He was done for in a trice. I didn't need to draw steel on him."

"Who was this hen heart?"

"Well, he had *some* fight in him, but I soon took care

of that. I had the advantage of surprise. He was weak in the gut, too," she said moodily, "and I also got him with a knee, which few men can withstand, you know. But once I drew his cork it was all over. He was one of them what gets faint at the sight of his own blood."

"'One of those who,'" Drummond corrected automatically, as they slipped into their familiar roles. "A paltry fellow, in fact. But who was he? Ewen told me something of it, but not all."

"Dearborne," she said with a shrug. "Lord Dearborne. A pretty fellow who thought he was more clever than he is."

Drum whistled. "A bad fellow, from bad stock. They have old money and an evil history, the whole family. Can't see why you'd follow one of them out into a garden on your own, day or night. That certainly must have been the new Gilly."

"Too right," she said. "But the old Gilly fixed him proper, I can tell you. But the point is that Damon was going to rescue me and wound up rescuing Dearborne from me, and even so, he liked me. He did, Drum, right off." She dared a glance at him.

His face was inscrutable. "I can readily believe that."

"When we got back to the party, Dearborne was trying to spread filthy rumors to ruin my name, about me cuddling in the darkness with Damon. Me! He said he got mashed for trying to save me from Damon. But then up stepped Damon, and said we were going to be married, and that he was the one planted Dearborne a facer, since he thought he was an attacker. Ho! That made Dearborne look a fool!"

"And so you decided to actually marry him in gratitude? A considerable reward for him, I'd think. A generous, if foolhardy, gesture on your part, too, I'd say."

She stopped walking and looked at him directly. "I have to marry someday, Drum. I want a family and children. Damon's kind and good. And very smart. I don't think I can do better. In fact, I think I did more than better. I didn't want to marry someone whose family would be horrified at my lack of family, not to mention my past. I've not much to offer any man but myself and Ewen's generosity. I was willing to settle for much less. But I've got even more than I bargained for."

He stood very still. A scowl twisted his usually bland expression. "You have nothing to offer? You think that?"

Now she laughed. She threw back her head and guffawed. "Oh Drum," she chortled, "where have your wits gone? Everyone knows that! That's why . . ." She stopped whatever she was about to say, and looked away. "That's why I'm not married yet. It's hard to find a nice man of breeding and intelligence who don't mind marrying a wench out of nowhere. No, worse. Out of somewhere and something that polite young women don't even know about."

"A man who loved you wouldn't care about such nonsense."

"*You* can say that?" she asked, caught between shock and anger. "You know the value of a name, my dear Lord Drummond. Who better? Ewen's father might have been my champion from the start, but your own papa always looked at me like—like a *bug*. You apologized for it. But so it was, and so in a way, my dear sir, you are, too. You're from one of the oldest families in the land. My family might be, too, for all I know. But that's the point, I don't know. And don't I know how important such things are. E*specially* to you! Don't look at me like that, either, it's been ages since one of those icy looks frightened *me*.

"You've not married yet," she said, as he stood frowning, "and you could have anyone you wanted. You're seeking perfection . . . and as to that," she asked, diverted, "what happened to your dark-eyed beauty? I thought she'd appear on your arm with your ring on her finger, and hers in your nose, like any good husband. Yes! I'd forgotten. Where is she? It sounded very April and May to me in your letters."

"I haven't hid her in my trunks, you little baggage," he said lightly, though his eyes were still troubled, and still intent upon her. "It's only that I found the more there was to know of her, the less there was to care. Nothing wrong with the lady, mind. But nothing that was right for me."

"She was that bad at bedwork?" Gilly hooted.

He gripped her shoulder, hard, and gave her a little shake. "Hush! By God, Gilly, have you no discretion?"

She sobered. "Little, as I said," she replied with a show of bravado, her fair skin going from pale to ruddy, shrugging the shoulder he still held. "There was a time we used to jest, just so."

"Then I was a fool. You can't say such things. It's not true, for one. It's not proper, for two. And certainly not in public," he added, beginning to grin, in spite of himself.

"She truly broke your heart, then?" Gilly asked seriously.

"No fear of that, because I never gave it in her keeping." He stared down at her, his hand now gentle on her shoulder, his eyes veiled, intent. "My intentions were honorable this time, because she was an honorable woman. But I seem to have lost interest at the last minute. I found that what I looked for wasn't there. As it so often happens with me, whatever my interest in a woman, whether holy or unholy." He gazed at her as though trying to see her thoughts. "Perhaps I've been looking in the wrong places, do you think?"

Gilly hesitated, cursing her active imagination. She wondered if Damon's attentions hadn't changed her, if all his kisses and caresses hadn't primed her, sensitized her, making her see all men differently. Making her aware of men's eyes and mouths for more than the words they spoke. Because it seemed to her that Drum was looking at her differently now, asking her something altogether new, and watching her lips for more than her answer. She didn't know what to say. She was spared the effort.

"Well," Damon's voice caught them by surprise. "I see you weren't that tired after all, my lord."

Damon winced inwardly as they both startled and looked up to see him standing on the path right behind them. He hated the sound of the words the moment they left his mouth. Pompous. Foolish. A cuckold's entrance line. They both stared at him. But if he hadn't spoken, he didn't think they would have noticed he was there. Or if anyone else was, either.

He'd driven to Hyde Park, headed for the Serpentine. It wasn't hard to find them strolling on the path there. They looked too well together. She wore green, and he'd have known that lovely figure anywhere, that graceful gait, the proud tilt of her shapely little head. The tiny bonnet perched on that bright hair could never disguise its rare, white gold splendor. Nothing on earth could hide that pale and beautiful face from him; he saw its loveliness reflected in every passing man's appraising eyes. And the image of her tall, lean, broad-shouldered companion strolling close by her side, altogether attentive, was already etched into his future nightmares. Even now, confronted, the lanky earl still had his hand on her shoulder.

*What in God's name does a man say at a moment like this*? Damon wondered. How did he not make a fool of himself? How did he keep his pride, his countenance, and his heart from cracking, and all at the same time? Whatever he said would make him sound like the buffoon in a bad farce. He wasn't used to anything like this, it was entirely outside his experience. He wanted to turn on his heel and leave. But he couldn't with them watching. Certainly not with himself watching, appalled, from somewhere outside of his body. So he took in a breath and waited for one of them to say something, anything. They did worse.

The earl removed his hand from Gilly's shoulder. She blinked and bit her lip, looking upset.

There was a moment when no one spoke.

Gilly looked at the two men. They were staring at each other. She noted how different they were, the one tall, elegant, watchful, contained, powerful in his silence. The other, his usually laconic airs vanished, his handsome face showing silent fury, his immaculate clothes showing tensed muscles and readiness for action.

There was peril of so many kinds here that Gilly gasped. She could only confront it head-on, the way she faced all danger.

"Lud!" she said. "It looks like Drum and me are lovers met on the sly, don't it? But that's a laugh. He was about to drown me for defaming the name of his latest amour, is all. Good thing you came along when you did, Damon."

Drum broke from his silence. He shook his head, and smiled. "How do you do it, Gilly? One moment a guttersnipe, the next a lady, and now both at once? Amazing."

It was not a lover-like comment. Damon relaxed, but still felt sickly foolish. "That's Gilly, all right. But if you two aren't here for a bit of this and that, may one ask where her lady's maid is? You didn't come here alone, did you?"

"Of course not!" Drum said haughtily. "I'm delighted to see Gilly again, but hardly lost to civility. There she is." He gestured to a smiling little maidservant standing a few feet away. Damon, recognizing her, felt even more foolish. He'd had eyes for nothing but the pair of them.

"She's at a respectful distance," Drum went on, "but close enough to preserve Gilly's reputation. Gilly's like a sister to me, but believe me, I know—too well—that she is not."

But now again, no one could speak. Or would.

Gilly was wondering at Drum's choice of words. They were, like so much he'd said this morning, wry and ambiguous, and open to so much interpretation that a person could get dizzy trying to pin it down. He always liked to speak that way, sly and amusing. But he'd never looked at her that way before. Never. And what he'd said broadly hinted at something altogether new.

Drum looked amused now, and yet there was nothing remotely merry deep in his eyes.

And Damon was still angry, suspicious, and feeling sick, and furious at himself for it.

# 13

They sat in a sunny window alcove of the tea shop, their tea long gone, their conversation still absorbing them. Or at least three of them, Damon thought resignedly, watching them. There was little else for him to do. It was enlightening. Rafe's harsh face looked better with his frequent smiles, and those smiles, like the earl's, were bent on Gilly. They both were also bent on entertaining her, as she in turn was amusing them with her reactions. She blossomed under their attention, showing them a kaleidoscope of emotions, being charming and brash, adorable and impudent, boyish and womanly by turns.

Was she doing it to keep their attention? Damon wondered. Or was she really this confused about who she was now? She was changeable, but never so vivacious with him. Or so dramatic with it. It was almost as if she was on stage. They all looked like that to him; he had never been such an spectator as he was today. But what did he have to say that the others could remember and laugh with, the way they were doing with each other's memories?

Now they seemed to be done with her past, and were starting on the earl's. Damon sat back and watched, trying to keep his own emotions out of it. He had taken himself out of the equation. These were friends newly met after a long absence. She adored them. If he was going to make a life with her, he had to come to terms with that, and them.

But he hated sitting dumb as a stone while they chattered. He felt useless and foolish. And now, frustrated and angry by the earl's comments, his implication that all true Englishman had been soldiers in the late war. Probably Drummond didn't even remember he was there. He hadn't so much as looked at him, after all.

"One does what one can for one's country," Drum was saying, shrugging off Gilly's praise. "Rafe was a soldier, I did what I could to support him in my own way. I couldn't fight, not when I was the only heir. Wellington wouldn't have it. Nor would my father. But I could contribute my bit. What Englishman wouldn't?"

*This Englishman didn't*, Damon thought, as he held his tongue, gritting his teeth so hard a small muscle bunched in his jaw, *as you probably bloody well know, damn your so cool eyes*. But surely the earl hadn't meant to slight his patriotism? The comment was too carefully put to dispute, but Damon would have defended himself if he had to. And he could.

Damon hadn't gone to war as a soldier or a spy. Not because he wasn't patriotic, or because of fear, but because he'd had no desire for a career in the military. Gentlemen didn't buy commissions in the army or navy unless they, or their family, had a career in mind. Or unless they were second sons. His brother Alfred had that distinction and had been in the navy until he decided life with his Harriet was preferable to life at sea—no matter how he jested now that there was little to choose between living with a captain and trying to live with a wife.

When the little emperor went to Elba, Damon had gone to America, to make his fortune. But if he'd been called upon to act for his country, he would have done so. In fact, he thought, brightening, he *had* done. He'd often carried messages into the wilderness for his government in his years in the New World, but hadn't thought much about it then. Even now, he thought, his spirits falling, it didn't sound like much compared to what the Earl of Drummond had done. Or said he'd done. Those things that made Gilly sit enthralled now, listening to them again. Because from the way she reacted to each story it was clear they were as familiar to her as beloved fairy tales that had been told to a child each night.

"But now we're at peace. I suppose that's why I keep traveling so much," Drum went on. "It just might be that I'm looking for a fight!"

That made even Damon laugh.

"I never realized I was so warlike," Drum went on. "But most gentleman are, I suppose. Do you fence?" he asked suddenly.

It took the others swinging around to look at him to make Damon understand he was the one being asked. "Me? Yes," Damon said, "on occasion."

"Where? At Monsieur Marchand's? I understand he's the rage in London now. Myself, I'm currently looking for someone better, I studied under Antonio, in Italy. Do you have a academy here that you visit?"

"No, not in years," Damon said. "I came to London, met Gilly, and since that night seem to have devoted myself entirely to her."

"Where do the men in your clubs go then?" Drum asked curiously.

"They don't. I don't belong to any right now."

"No *clubs* either?" Drum asked, sitting back in surprise, just as he might have exclaimed, *"You can't read?"*

"Hadn't the time to join any when I got back to London," Damon said abruptly. "Haven't the interest now."

"You box, then? At Gentleman Jackson's? You look like you could strip to advantage and go a round or two."

"I suppose I could. I don't."

"Oh, how can you say that?" Gilly interrupted, "You should have seen him, Drum! It would have done your heart good. Did mine a treat. See, I took him down to my old haunts to see . . ." She paused when she saw how Drum grew still. She'd never taken him there, she remembered, and certainly would never take him to the street where . . .

"Well, I wanted him to see where I grew up," she said quickly, "if he actually meant to marry me, it was only fair. And we no sooner set foot in an alley when we were set upon by some scurvy coves! They had knives and cudgels, four of them to our two. But I didn't have to lift a finger! Damon knocked them flat! Oh, you should have seen! He fought like a fury! He gave one a perfect cross with his right hand, put an elbow in another's gut, and came up swinging to lay him out cold before you could spit. He bent noses and split lips and had them pretending to be dead where they lay at his feet, afraid to squeak! You've never seen the like!"

"Never saw the like," Drum said absently. "He had good science, did he?" he asked Gilly, not looking at Damon.

"No," Damon answered for her. "I brawled. I had no time for fancy footwork or to think of any sweet science. I had to get them before they could get me down and then get Gilly. That's all I cared about. Lucky for me I know street fighting. But I'm not sure I could come up to your standards of boxing by the Marquis's rules."

"You've never sparred here in London?" Drum asked.

"Not for a long time. I only got here at the start of the summer. Since then I've been too busy arranging my future to take care of the present."

"No sparring? Well then, do you go to Manton's gallery to shoot?"

"Not at present," Damon said tersely.

"What about horses? Cards? You must have some vices!" Rafe said on a snort. "Or maybe we should ask you that after we take Gilly home?"

"I ride, I drive, I play cards, and dice, too, if it comes to that," Damon said, sitting back and drawling his words, because he was getting angry and it was his way to slow down when his emotions sped up. "But not in any formal way, and not in London, lately."

"I see," Drum said slowly. "So then you weren't joking when you said you were pleased to devote yourself entirely to Gilly."

It was an innocuous statement, but said in a way that made Damon think he was being thought of as some kind of man-milliner, a foppish fellow who had nothing on his mind but women's skirts—and not even particularly in what was under them.

"I don't care for cockfights and bear baitings, true," Damon said through a tight smile. "Dog fights and ratting are not for me, either. Nor do I take snuff. But I fence—saber and foil. I drive, spar, shoot, fish and hunt, wager, play cards and dice, smoke cheroots, and drink, too. I have been known to pinch barmaids, but not since I met Gilly. I spit on the floor when the mood takes me, and can swagger and come up with an impressive belch if I try hard enough. Is that manly enough for you?"

Drum smiled with as much sincerity as Damon did. "My dear fellow! I was merely curious as to the sort of chap Gilly was marrying. I have a care for her, it sometimes gets out of hand. My apologies if I offended."

"No, please accept mine," Damon said curtly. "I mistook your intent."

"Well," Gilly said breathlessly, "good. Now we can all be comfortable again."

The two men didn't look it; they glared at each other, ignoring her comment. Even Rafe looked edgy.

"You might want to come along with me after we leave here, then," Drum told Damon sweetly. "That is, if you want to review your science. I'm off to Gentleman Jackson's and would love to oblige a new sparring partner. I'm up to all of Rafe's tricks by now."

But Rafe was up to Drum's tricks, too. "Let the fellow be," he said quickly. "He probably has promised himself to Gilly for some errand or other."

"No, matter of fact, I haven't," Damon said, ruthlessly ignoring his promise to stay to chat with his mother when he took Gilly home. "Delighted to oblige. I'm entirely at your disposal, my lord."

"I don't think that's a good idea," Gilly said, worrying her lower lip between her teeth.

"It's a fine idea," Damon said gently. "I have to get to know your friends, Gilly, and I can't do that hanging on to your skirts."

She knew it. That's why she thought it wasn't a good idea.

The two men were exhausted. They'd been at it a long time, and they were gentlemen, not really bruisers, in it for the cash. But they didn't want to stop until there was some kind of decision, and there wasn't one. As time went on, a crowd had collected around them, but the only one who looked worried was Rafe. The others were busily wagering. The two men were stripped to the waist and covered with sweat, blood, and rapidly darkening bruises. The Earl of Drummond was the taller and had a longer reach. He had no flab on that lean frame. He did have long, smooth muscles, and exquisite timing and grace. But he was beginning to stagger.

Damon Ryder could have posed for a Greek statue,

but that muscular golden body of his wasn't all just for show. He had power and agility, and cunning in that handsome head of his. Even if he kept shaking that head to clear his eyes and wits. The onlookers at Gentleman Jackson's exclusive sparring salon had even money on the pair of them as they danced and weaved and tried to remove each other's teeth. It had obviously gone beyond sparring.

Damon ducked a blow and swung 'round to land one flush on Drum's chest. Drum grunted and swung back, catching Damon's mouth, causing more blood to spurt. Then he crouched and started to move in. Damon shook his head and showed a bloody grin, swung hard, landing a clip flush on Drum's ear before he danced back out of the taller man's long reach.

Drum made a sound like a growl. "Gilly—said—you finished four men by yourself," he puffed. "She always did—have a gift—for exaggeration."

"No," Damon panted. "She told truth."

"Then I must be—extraordinary."

"No, I've been fighting by rules."

"Indeed? Then do your worst!"

"Not here! Enough, gentlemen!" Gentleman Jackson himself shouted, as he stepped between them and flung a towel on the floor. He held up his hands. "I call it a draw! And as it's my place, it's my call. If you've still got a grievance you'll have to take it outside to the street."

"No grievance," Damon puffed, bending to scoop up the towel and blotting his face. "I'm willing to call it a day—for today."

"Of course," Drum gasped, as he caught the towel

Rafe threw to him. "As you will—Mr. Jackson. Your will is—our command. Another day then, Mr. Ryder?"

"I'm at your disposal," Damon said, with a bow that caused him to grit his teeth at the pain in it before he turned his back and limped away.

"Lad's got science, and heart. Let him be," Rafe said, as he walked Drum back to the changing room. "Don't know what maggot you've got in your head anyway. He's a good sort."

"Is he?" Drum asked.

"Got money and breeding and courage. And Gilly likes him. How much better can she do, anyway?"

Drum stopped short. "You know," he said with ice in his words and his eyes, or rather, in one eye, because the other one was rapidly swelling closed, "I am *very* tired of hearing that."


"Good God!" Damon's father said, as his mother blanched.

"Good heavens!" Cousin Felicity said with eager delight, looking avidly from Damon's battered visage to the Earl of Drummond's painful-looking one. The look they both turned on her at her excited outcry silenced her immediately, and she took a prudent step backward, to stand with Damon's astonished sisters and bemused brothers as they gaped at the two men.

"Good grief!" Gilly said in disgust, her hands on her hips. She took off her shawl and threw it onto a chair. "Look at you! And *that* most likely is the best you can look after you've applied ice and leeches, isn't it? Huh! Well, I hope you two had a good afternoon, because you've ruined my night! How can I go to the theater now? Much less the Andersons' soiree afterward, eh? You might as well go home, gents, because I'd sooner be escorted by mad dogs as the pair of you! I don't know what you were trying to prove."

"We had a bet as to which of us could get you angrier," Damon said with a crooked smile. His mouth was too swollen to smile any other way. His lips were split, his mouth was bruised, his left cheek darkened, and he winced when he moved his right arm.

"Precisely," Drum said calmly, tilting his head to see Gilly's expression with his good eye. He held himself more stiffly than usual, had a black eye, a red ear, and kept one hand in his waistcoat, in the manner of the last Emperor of France. "And we are going to keep our appointment this evening. We'll say we were battling for your hand, it will do your reputation no end of good."

"That isn't funny," Gilly said, and it wasn't. Because for the tenth time since the two men had met that afternoon, she wondered if there was any truth in it. And was elated and terrified by turn at the thought and all its ramifications.

"We'll say the truth," Damon said. "That we met at Gentleman Jackson's, sparred for the fun of it, and got carried way. Enough people saw it to know it's true. It would look worse if we stayed home."

"There's truth in that, at least," his father told Gilly. "If they stayed home, people would think they were badly hurt. Or that there was bad blood between them."

"Instead of just spilled blood," Rafe said with a shake of his head. "This way, they can pass it off as a jest."

"Well, all right," Gilly grumbled. "But it's a good thing for you, Drum, that Ewen's papa had a card game with his old cronies tonight. He'd comb your hair if he saw you."

"My uncle saw, my dear," Drum said lightly, "and was as vexed with me as you might wish. But he is a man and so he understood."

"Well, then I'm glad I'm not one, after all," she retorted, "because I don't!" A look from Damon's sisters made her curse her hasty tongue. Her cheeks flamed as she realized that likely none of them had ever wished to be boys, nor known any females who had, either. She ducked her head. "I suppose we can muddle through. It's dark in the theater, and it's not like the Andersons' soiree is important, like Almack's."

"Here's a flight," Drum said. "Our Gilly concerned about Almack's?"

"Why, I'm not, of course," Gilly started to say, shot another quick look at Damon's sisters, and went on, "but people who can be admitted should be glad I can't be, tonight. Shall we go?"

"Can't be?" Drum asked.

"It's not important. I'll get invitations there one day, I suppose," she said, with a toss of her head. "If I don't, I won't languish. There's more important things to worry about. Like getting to the theater on time. Let's go. Looks like we've already seen the farce, but I don't want to miss the first act of the play."

"It is important," Damon said, "but not tonight."

But he was speaking to the air, because Gilly had stepped over to Drum and was standing in front of him, inspecting his bruised face, frowning fiercely.

*          *          *

"Why did you do it?" Gilly asked Damon, the first chance she got him alone. She leaned over to whisper to him. They sat in the Ryders' box at the theater, and she was sure there were more eyes on their party than on the stage.

He shrugged. Then chuckled. "For the life of me, I can't answer that," he said, because that, at least, was absolute truth. "It seemed the right thing at the time." He stared at her. "You look very lovely tonight."

Now she shrugged, a hasty twitch of her shoulders that drew his eyes to her breasts. He hadn't just said it to divert her attention. She was lovely. She wore a dark gold gown, a rich autumnal color to greet the coming season. It made her skin radiant and turned her hair to palest gold by contrast. She looked nothing less than divine, though the way the narrow gown fit made his thoughts much more earthy.

"I have to get you citrines to go with that," he mused. "Or topaz . . . no, something rarer, finer . . . Russian amber, I think, set in old gold."

"You'll have to live to do it!" she said acidly. "Why are you fighting with Drum?"

"You think he'll kill me? Or are you threatening to kill me if I dare to touch him again?" He heard her take in her breath, and wished he could call his words back.

"I'll kill you both if you do that again," she muttered, and he laughed and turned to the stage as though he'd forgot what he said.

But neither of them did, nor did Drum, sitting behind them, a slight smile on his lips.

They stayed until after the farce, because no one wanted to join the crush downstairs as the theatergoers filed out. Though it was the theatergoers, and not the crush, they wanted to avoid.

"I still say, let's go home," Gilly argued, as they waited for the theater to empty.

"And have them say we lack bottom as well as sense?" Drum asked, one eyebrow flying high, like a pennant over a bloody battlefield.

"You see the problem," Damon said, "we have to go to the party now."

Damon rose, stifling a groan at the effort, as well as a sigh when he thought about driving off to another entertainment tonight. In truth, he wanted to go home, badly. He ached in every part, including his heart when he saw how Gilly kept studying the earl's long face.

But he didn't have to worry about being ignored. Because when they arrived at the townhouse where the Andersons' party was in full cry, he met an old friend. Cousin Felicity noticed first. They had stopped at the entrance to the crowded salon, because Felicity planted herself there and refused to be budged forward.

"Oh my!" she trilled after they'd been announced, her voice trembling with suppressed delight. "Look who's here!"

"Oh my," Damon's mother echoed in faltering tones, as she too stared into the room.

"You knew of this?" Damon demanded.

"Well, she did write and say a visit was possible," his mother said, "but I thought she'd call on us first. . . ."

Gilly didn't have to ask who they were talking about.

Or who all the men with her were staring at. She knew at once. The lady was beautiful. She had raven hair. Gilly couldn't tell if she had a dowry of thirty thousand, or if she was kind to animals. But it could be no one else but Lady Annabelle, who had stopped talking and was staring at Damon, her face first registering shock at his wounds, then, clearly, embarrassment, and then tremulous joy at his presence.

Damon took Gilly over to her immediately.

"My lady," he said, taking Lady Annabelle's little white gloved hand. "It's been too many years, hasn't it? You've grown even lovelier. Now that," he said with a grin, as he turned to Gilly, "would have got me a giggle years ago. And she wouldn't have believed me either. But now she's so used to praise she doesn't even blink those long lashes. Gilly, here is Lady Annabelle Wylde, an old friend and neighbor you must have heard us talk about. Annabelle, I give you my fiancée, Miss Gilly Giles, and her friends, Lords Drummond and Dalton."

Drum bowed, but Rafe had to be nudged in his bow, because he was staring so hard at the lady. But she'd eyes for no one but Damon. Big dark eyes, Gilly noted nervously, before she realized Drum didn't even seem to notice.

There was dancing. It was a fashionable party in London, and even if it wasn't a ball, if it was evening, and if it wasn't a musicale or merely a *squeeze*, there had to be dancing.

"She's very lovely," Gilly told Damon's cravat as they danced.

He didn't ask who she meant. "And so you think I'm going to rush over and ask for her hand? A little late for that. Gilly, I can't keep telling you this. Sooner or later, you're going to have to believe in me."

"I believe in you, all right. Just not in me."

There was nothing to say to that, he knew it too well. "Rafe seems taken with her," he said, for something to say. He narrowed his eyes. The redhead had been gaping at Annabelle since he'd set eyes on her, and was still doing it. "Would that be a good match, do you think?"

"Rafe? Yes, whatever girl gets him would be lucky. He's gruff and forgets his manners sometimes. But there's no more honest man in London. Or a braver, truer friend."

"I saw your friend Drum eyeing her, too," Damon said too casually. "You said dark beauties were his style. She's that, and much more. What about him?"

She didn't answer. Her eyes widened and she quickly glanced over at Drum where he stood in the dim light at the sidelines. And felt her breath catch as she saw him watching her, just as he'd been doing all night, and not Lady Annabelle.

Damon saw Gilly's head turn, the direction of her glance, felt her sigh of gratification and saw her tuck in the edges of her pleased smile. He had his answer, no matter what she said.

"Oh, Drum would be perfect," she said too lightly. "But he's hard to predict."

"No doubt," he said, and turned the subject as they turned on the crowded floor. "You *will* understand that I do have to dance with her? You won't see high romance in a neighborly gesture?"

"I won't," she vowed. He'd have been content if he

didn't have the notion that it didn't matter to her.

Gilly danced with Damon, and then with some of Damon's brothers, almost as though it were the wedding day she'd told Lord Wycoff about, and not just another London affair. Then she danced with Drum. But that was a country dance, and she had no chance to do more than nod at him as they stepped through their paces.

At last, she pleaded exhaustion, sent Damon to get her something cold to drink, and retreated to a spot beside a pillar at the outskirts of the dance. But it was as if her idle thought of Lord Wycoff had conjured him.

"What am I to do with you?" Lord Wycoff asked, as he came up beside her. He leaned his shoulders against the pillar as though watching the dancers, too, but Gilly knew she had all his attention. "I become accustomed to the fact that you're lost to me, at least presently, and applaud you for it, even as I deplore it. And now, look at this."

"At what?" she asked.

"At the fact that you are still here in town, and still not yet wed. At the further fact that you can't take your eyes from your friend, the Earl of Drummond. That he and your fiancé look like they paid a visit to a sausage grinder, but everyone knows they had at each other today. And at the fact that your fiancé is dancing with a woman who looks at him as though he *were* a sausage, and she, starving. Though she's obviously not, as every man here tonight has noted."

"Been talking to the mamas here at the side of the dance?" she shot back. "I thought you'd be prowling, instead."

"I am," he said gently.

"Well, save yourself the trouble, for you'll get nothing but bad gossip," she said, deliberately misunderstanding him. "First off, the dark lady is Damon's neighbor, and he can't help the way she looks at him, can she? He's not looking at her that way, is he?"

He nodded. "Point taken. You astonish me, go on."

"Well, I don't know why sound reasoning should surprise you. What else is there to say?"

He chuckled. "Everything you didn't say." He turned serious. "Look you, Gilly. I find myself in an awkward position. I actually like you. I really respect you, and yes, I believe I have given up on getting you, just now. The way you're going, however, I will get you eventually. But it won't please me. No. Don't hit me, that would put paid to your reputation! Look back at the dance and listen, for I'm doing something extraordinary, and not for myself, for once. It shocks me as much as it will surprise you.

"Good," he said, as she turned her head resolutely from him and glowered at the dancers, so he could admire her perfect little profile. "Now then. Take note. I have an object lesson for you tonight. See my wife, there—the thin woman with the blade of a nose, short thin hair, in the red gown? The one dancing with the young captain of the guard?" he asked quietly. "Yes. There. An odd couple, surely, you'll agree. He's handsome, if a bit vacant. His mustaches are the most expressive thing on his face, but the ladies seem to like him. But notice. She's older than he by a decade and more. And married. And not, alas, it pains me to say, a very attractive female, in spite of her elegant gown and expensive hairdresser, is she? But she'll be in his bed tonight. Because he's the sort she always prefers—young, muscular, and dim. And many men don't care what's prime, so long as it's free."

"You don't object?"

"I don't. I did, once. Long, long ago. It didn't matter to her then. It doesn't matter to me now."

"Of course it does!" she breathed. "It pains you. It grieves you. Anyone can see it."

"No. Only you—and only because I tell you."

"Can't you do anything?"

"Short of murder?" he asked. "There's nothing to do. A divorce would be a scandal that would scar my children, my family, my name. And now I'd be a hypocrite if I objected. Because now I do the same. Whatever I am, whatever my catalogue of sins, acquit me of that. I am not a hypocrite."

"I'm sorry for you, I honestly am," Gilly said softly, "but I don't see what you hope to accomplish by telling me this."

"Don't be sorry for me, I brought it on myself, and no one could be sorrier than I am. The point, my dear Miss Giles, is that marriage without love is hell. Marriage without trust is worse. When I believed you chose young Ryder because you thought you could do no better, it wounded me—I couldn't offer better, after all. But I could see it, in a way. He has merit. I made it a point to ask about him, and then to speak with him. He's intelligent, humorous, has morals and manners, and drive. In time, I thought, perhaps it would work out for you. You clearly knew what you were doing, even if your heart clearly wasn't in it. That gave you hope.

Which is better than most of us can expect.

"But now!" He laughed bitterly. "My dear, do you know what your eyes are saying when you look at your friend, the earl? He's a good man, too, mind. I know him, and am pleased to say I do." His voice became harsh. "But I know your situation, too. Yours and his. Look you, my girl. I'll say it this once, and only because I'm in a strange mood tonight. But I warn you—if you languish now, if you yearn for something you can't have now, and take less because it's offered or expedient, you *will* burn for it later. In every way. And I don't mean just in an afterlife. Think on. And don't act until you know the consequence of your actions.

"I tell you this because you've touched me in ways I don't understand, and in too many that I do. You fascinate me," he murmured. "I'd love to be your lover someday. But in another way, I'd dislike it enormously." He levered his shoulders from the pillar and sauntered away.

Leaving Gilly alone, and wondering. She looked up at the dancers again—and saw Drum waltzing with some pretty miss. And saw he wasn't looking at his partner, but only over her head—at her. Gilly stood very still. Wycoff was right. He'd made his own life a misery. She'd had enough of misery. Now, too, longing wasn't an option for her anymore. She'd had too much of a taste of reality.

She'd vowed never to tell Drum about her feelings for him. What would be the point, except for embarrassment and shame? But if something had changed? It might only be herself and her perceptions of men.

But what if it was his perception of her? And what if he told her his feelings for her, first?

*If* was such a tempting, dangerous, daring word for such an unimaginable change. But Drum's azure gaze was clear and intent, and his eyes never left hers, and so she dared to imagine it.

Damon, the requested glass of lemonade in his hand, approached Gilly and then stopped where he stood, feeling foolish. Worse, feeling a sickness that had nothing to do with his bruises. Because he saw where she was looking, and recognized that look. And it wasn't at him. Or for him.

# 14

"Look!" Gilly cried in delight, rushing up to Drum the minute he set foot in the house the next morning, waving a card under his nose.

"Vouchers!" she cried. "For me! Which is only an elegant way to say 'invitation,' my dear sir, as you well know." She strutted in front of him, fluttering the card in front of her eyes in a parody of a lady with an ornate fan. She dropped the pose and looked up at him, her eyes shining. "But this is mine! For Almack's! Oh Drum, thank you *so* much! I know I'm a fool to care for such nonsense, but look! Now I'm as proper as a parson, welcome as sunshine *anywhere* I want to go in town. Even if I don't care to go, at least now I've a choice. I've been waiting and waiting to tell you. It came this morning but it seemed like a year till you came so I could thank you." She grabbed his hand. "Oh, thank you!"

Rafe smiled, but Drum looked blank. And Damon, lounging by the window, looked inscrutable. His mama, however, did not.

"But Gillian . . ." she began to say.

"'Miss Gillian Giles,'" Gilly read from the card with glee, "invited to that hallowed place. Hah! Now, that's put the icing on it!"

"I'm sure it has," Drum said, "but the thanks don't go to me. I intended to see to the matter, but between my bout with your fiancé yesterday, and then summoning enough energy to go to that party last night, I forgot to so much as make inquiries."

Gilly frowned. "But I was so sure! Wait! It must have been the earl! You probably mentioned it to him, and he acted. Of course! He has the influence, who else? What a dolt I am! So thank you anyway, and I have to give him more thanks soon as I see him again."

"I never said a word," Drum said. "I would have, but I confess I never thought it meant so much to you."

"But Damon knew," his mama said in exasperation. "He called in a few favors to get the thing done. I thought you knew, Gillian. He did some services for some people, and he . . ."

"And he is delighted you're happy, Gilly," Damon said quietly, "and there's an end to it."

"But you don't know anyone in London," Gilly blurted, swinging around to stare him.

"They weren't in London at the time," Damon said. "Or at least, not the people I did favors for. Neither was I. It happens Lady Sefton has a friend in America, the

Burrells have a cousin, that kind of thing. When I was there, the war between our countries was only over for a few years—there was still some suspicion of the British, they were uneasy. But I was well known and made all kinds of useful friends. I carried some messages, lent some aid." He shrugged. "I didn't do much, but when you're so far from home any help seems like a lot. You know I was a trader. Favors are as important as goods to a successful trader. Enough about that. When would you like to go?"

"I'm very sorry, Damon," Gilly said quietly. "It never occurred to me. You never said a word. Go? Oh, to Almack's? I don't know. When do you?"

"It's up to you."

"Well," Drum said, "if you're in such raptures about it I should think we should go as soon as may be, if only to show them what they were missing."

"Then we will!" Gilly said.

"Fine," Damon said. "It's not my idea of fun, but I'm at your command."

"Gallant," Drum commented dryly. "But we can't tonight, child," he told Gilly. "We're promised to the Richmonds, to go to their party at Vauxhall, remember? Any rate, the place is thin of company in summertime. Best leave it until autumn and make a grand entrance. But—I'm forgetting. You'll be married then, won't you?"

"Well, I don't see what difference that will make," Gilly said crossly.

"Don't you?" Drum murmured, looking at her for a long moment. "Well then, we'll plan to go this week, then, shall we?"

"Yes," Gilly said gaily.

"Friday night?"

"Absolutely," she replied with a delighted laugh.

They began talking about gossip then, and laughing together. But Damon didn't. His eyes were gray as sleet as he watched the pair. Nor was he the only one who realized he hadn't been asked what his plans for Friday night were.

They danced again that night. But this time, it was in the open air, beneath towering trees, under flowing torchlights that couldn't hide the fact of the endless night sky above them.

"Such fun!" Gilly laughed, as she caught her breath from the vigorous polka she'd just done with Drum.

Her heart was thumping, her breast rising and falling fast. She fanned herself, breathing hard; her hair had come loose and there were silvery spills of it everywhere around her flushed face. They stood by their table, waiting for Damon to bring his partner back to her own table and then rejoin them. In that moment they were alone, for all intents and purposes. Drum seized the moment.

"You've changed," he said, watching her closely.

"Have I?" She laughed. "How so?"

But he didn't laugh, and she paused to look up at him. He stood aloof, even though he was by her side. He seemed reserved suddenly, all laughter fled. His expression was thoughtful; the only thing moving in that long face was the reflected torchlight glittering in his eyes. He never took his gaze from her, her face, her breast, her eyes. She'd never commanded so much of his undivided attention, at least not this kind of attention. He was usually lazily amused with her. He was not amused now.

Her breath became shallow, not so much slower as withheld. She breathed through half-parted lips, silencing her heart as she waited for his answer.

"I didn't see it until now," he said quietly. "Or rather, I saw it at once but didn't know what I was seeing. You are changed. You used to pretend you were a woman, and it was charming, even engaging. But now—you *are* a woman, and it is so much more than that. Is it Ryder? Has he done it for you?"

Gilly grew still, lost in that so long wished for, intense regard. She'd dreamed about it but hadn't known how it would be, and it shook her. He'd changed, too. Too fast for her to comprehend. Or had he? Again, she wondered if it was her own perception that had changed their easy camaraderie to this thing she suddenly had such trouble managing. Or believing. She looked away and took a big gulp of breath.

"*Ryder*? You mean Damon? I haven't thought about it—but yes, probably." She met Drum's eyes frankly. "He treated me like a woman, you see."

"And I did not, did I? It was all a game to us, wasn't it? Do you love him, child?"

She laughed, but it was a shaken sound. "Well, there it is again, isn't it? He never calls me 'child.'"

Drum nodded, "Touché. But you didn't answer me. Do you love him?"

"I told you," she said with a trace of anger. "He rescued me. He is a 'Catch' for me in every way, just as you said. I'm grateful to him, and I like him very much. In fact, I never thought I'd like him so much as I do. What more do you want? What more could I want?"

He watched her with an unreadable expression. Then he nodded again. "You've answered me."

But he didn't seem pleased with her answer. So much so that Damon, returning, looked from one of them to the other and thought they'd quarreled. He was soon surer of it. Because they didn't speak much for the rest of the evening. But they stole glances at each other when they thought he wasn't looking. And since he was always looking, he soon grew as quiet as they were.

Gilly had survival skills she never had to think about, and would have been surprised to know she possessed. She'd learned to focus all her attention on one thing when there was something else bothering her she couldn't do anything about. It was an admirable skill and kept her on the job when there was something that might have aggravated and diverted her otherwise. It was how she managed to grow up and get on with her life. It served her well now.

She'd spent a whole day preparing for her evening. She wore a bright rose-colored gown, a string of pink coral at her neck, and a single rose in her hair. A simple costume that had taken her hours to decide on. She tried on every gown in her wardrobe, matched them with a dozen shawls, washed her hair and arranged it twice, and put on five different pairs of slippers before she was satisfied. In that way, she refused to think about why she was dressing up, who for, and whether or not she was mad to have seen such longing, love,

and frustration in Drum's eyes every time she looked—
which was as often as she could. And whether she was
wrong about seeing the quiet hurt slowly draining the
life from Damon's eyes.

But now she was ready, and so now she snatched up
a fan, gloves, and a shawl, and went downstairs to greet
her escorts. Because since Drum and Rafe had come
to town she had three escorts everywhere she went—
sometimes four, if Damon's father hadn't promised
himself to friends. She never saw Damon alone. Not
once since Drum and Rafe had arrived. His eyes told her
he knew that as well as her own in the mirror every time
she saw herself there.

His eyes, so filled with dancing light when they'd
first met, so dark and thoughtful these days when they
rested on her. Drum's eyes, so blue and watchful and
ever on her.

Which was why she'd never read the same book so
many times trying to make sense of it in the past
days. She couldn't make sense of herself, either, and
refused to try anymore. She wished Bridget were here.
And she was glad she wasn't. She went downstairs to
wait for Drum—*For Damon*, she corrected herself, *and
my other escorts this important night: Drum, Rafe, and the
Earl of Kenton*—as she fled the rest of the way down
the stair.

She was late because of her dithering. She heard
the voices as she crossed the hall to the drawing room.
The house was filled with people waiting for her.
Tonight, all four of her usual escorts would be there,
and Damon's father as well. Damon's sisters and
brothers and their spouses that hadn't left town yet

were at the ready, too. Tonight, all her forces were marshaled, because tonight they were going to invade Almack's. Gilly took a breath and entered the room.

She thought he'd like her outfit. She didn't realize he'd love it.

Drum's eyes widened when he saw her. He looked like he'd been dealt a body blow. Then delight leapt to his eyes, to be stilled there. He looked suddenly sad at the same time, and very guarded with it, the way he did these days and nights whenever he looked at her. "Lovely," he said.

"You look well, too," Gilly said, disconcerted. "All healed, or almost so. Well, so are we ready to go?"

But now the men looked at each other, and Damon's mama and sisters looked distressed.

"Though I deplore it," Ewen's father, the old earl, said slowly, "it may be better to postpone our visit to Almack's, my dear. I'm not feeling quite the thing this evening."

"What's the matter?" she cried, alarmed.

Damon frowned. "Nothing," he said. "Excuse me, my lord, but as I thought, that's not the thing to tell Gilly. Only truth will do for her. Gilly, listen. . . ." He sighed. "The thing is that a caricaturist featured you in a sketch this morning posted in a print shop window. I bought them all when I found out, but some had already been sold. I know you're courageous, and I never run from controversy myself. But some of us think that until the gossip wears off we ought to stay away from more. Almack's is where gossip lives."

Gilly back went straight. Her head snapped up. She stuck out a hand, and held it steady. "Show it to me.

No, don't look at each other. You think I won't see it? Or hear of it? I will. Might as well have done. Give it here, now."

Damon took a paper from his inner pocket and handed it to her. His mama actually winced as she heard Gilly unwrap the folded print, and her husband took her hand. The old Earl of Kenton went gray in the face as he saw the blood drain from Gilly's rosy cheeks. Drum's face grew tight, Rafe cursed beneath his breath. And Damon watched, very still.

It was a simple cartoon. Three men stood at the apexes of a triangle with a pretty blond female at the center. One of the men was tall and gaunt, one was ridiculously handsome with eyelashes like a girl's, one had a blunt haircut and a military air. The girl had a blindfold over her eyes and was pointing a finger.

She was labeled "MISS G— G—." A balloon coming from her lips said: "ENGAGED TO BE WED? I THINK I'LL PLAY INSTEAD! WHERE I COME FROM NO ONE CAN KNOW—BUT JUST WAIT UNTIL YOU SEE WHERE I GO!" The caption read: "THE QUEEN OF THE MAY? MAY I TAKE THIS ONE, OR THAT ONE, OR THE OTHER? WHY NOT ALL THREE? IT'S ALL THE SAME TO ME, NOW I'M LOOSED ON THE NOBILITY!"

Gilly looked up at them. "Well," she said in a stony little voice. "So, I have enemies. Who do you think had this bit of trash printed up?"

Damon smiled. "That's my Gilly. Attack first and feel badly later. You're allowed to be upset about it, you know."

"Much good that will do," she said with a trace of her usual jaunty spirit. "I know about these coves," she said, giving the paper a shake. "Seen them in enough taverns to know; they practically *grow* there. Caricaturists? Ho! Drunks, most—mad, some. Like that Mr. Gilray, they had to tie him down nights. Or that Rowlandson, drunk and disorderly with it, and wenching whenever he wasn't sketching. Aye, I know."

Drum winced, and she realized she'd said more than she ought in front of Damon's relatives. She went on, because it was too late to stop. "They make their money drawing scandal. That's why this doesn't make sense. Drum and Rafe have names, true. But there's not enough in this to sell enough to buy a pint. I'm not famous enough. I think someone paid for this to embarrass me."

"Yes," Damon said. "I'm making inquiries."

"Dearborne?" she asked, seeing the ominous expression he wore, her eyes widening.

"I think so, I'll know soon."

"But until we know more," Drum said, "the consensus is that you ought to stay home tonight."

"I'd never bring gossip on you," she said simply, "but were it left to me, I'd face it out. Can't hide this, trying will only make it worse."

"Just as I said," Damon told the others, "and as I said she'd say. What do you think? Shall we face it out? Mama? Father?"

"Well," his father said bracingly, "if Gilly can, why can't we?"

"Aye!" one of his brothers said. "Nothing spikes a rumor like staring it down. I'm for it!"

"All for one, then they won't dare say a word," another said.

"I suppose if the family is to be scandalized there's

no help for it either way," Cousin Felicity put in, "but we're just country mice, after all. What do you think, my lord?" she asked Drum with a sly smile.

"I think," he said, looking at her from a long way down his nose, "that no one had better gossip about Miss Giles tonight. Or any other night. At least, not in my hearing. And I have long ears."

Felicity busied herself with her fan.

Gilly grinned. "To war then!" And she laughed.

But she was apprehensive as she set toe over the threshold of Almack's. And sure she heard a sudden silence as she did. But it was hard to tell over the buzzing of her blood singing in her ears. By the time she rose from her curtsey to the hostesses present, she was the sinecure of all eyes. She raised her chin.

But there was no one to fight with, and nothing to object to. Either no one had seen the print, or no one dared say. Miss Gillian Giles came in with her army, and they stationed themselves around the room. Not a whisper would have gone unheard. And so Gilly didn't hear one.

She was introduced to the quality, and they bowed and curtsied to her. Lady Annabelle was there—but so was she. Tonight was extraordinary, because the sun triumphed over the moon in every way. Rafe was the only one of their party to care about Lady Annabelle's dark beauty. Because it was fair Gilly who was the evening star tonight. She danced every dance with every male who asked her—and they all did, except for Drum and Rafe, who stayed away from her as diligently as she did from them. Though she never stopped looking at Drum to see what he was doing. Nor he, looking at her to be sure she fared well. And Damon watched them both, silently.

"Well," she said, as they rode home a few hours later, "what a letdown! If there wasn't that bit of excitement about that wretched print before we left for me to think about, I think I'd have fallen asleep on my feet! What paltry food. What feeble drink! And the company? Why, if that's the cream of the cream, I think I'll take my tea straight from now on. I was never so disappointed!"

For once, Drum and Damon looked at each other straight on, as their gazes locked over her head. They smiled.

"Now get to sleep," Damon said, as he left her at the door.

"You're not coming in?" she asked, and he wondered if that was relief he heard in her voice.

"No, it's late. Sleep well. Good night." He took her hand, kissed it, and left her standing, staring after him.

Drum and Rafe said good night quickly, too. "Don't get into any trouble now," Rafe joked.

"At least, not until morning," Drum said.

Then they stood on the step and watched Damon's carriage roll off into the night.

"Didn't offer us a ride, did he?" Rafe grumbled.

"No," Drum said, raising a hand to call a hackney cab. "He was in a tearing hurry. And his eyes held enough veiled threats to cover half the females in Arabia. Now where do you think he's going?"

"Don't know," Rafe answered, "But we're following, aren't we?"

"Of course."

\*       \*       \*

It wasn't the lowest tavern in London.

"It looks it, I grant," Drum said with a sneer, as they stood outside the Bent Bough, the gin shop they'd seen Damon enter, "but it's too close to main streets and the district isn't that bad. I'll wager you'll find young gentlemen here, getting a thrill because it looks dangerous. But the kind of place they think it is would be one they wouldn't be able to leave easily—at least with their clothes on their backs, not to mention alive. This den of iniquity is no more or less than a stage set. For pretenders and the naive. So, that's the sort of fellow Ryder is. I wonder if Gilly has any idea?"

"Don't judge too fast," Rafe said.

"My dear boy," Drum said sweetly, "I am patience on a monument. We'll wait a bit, then go in and see what we can see. I'll also bet the place has nicely staged shadows we can lurk in."

It did. It was hot and dank and flyblown inside, and there were a score of gentlemen there, lounging at tables, or trying to belly up to the tap like so many of the other colorful patrons were doing. There was a sprinkling of rogues, a handful of beggars, some peddlers and street mongers, a merchant or three, sharpers galore, a pack of sots, and prostitutes of all conditions and descriptions. Drum's sneer was hidden by the shadows he and Rafe stood in. It became more pronounced as he saw Damon detach himself from the darkness and walk to a handsome young gentleman sitting at a table by a darkened dirty window.

The young gentleman looked up, visibly stiffened, and then made a theatrical show of relaxing again, though his hand remained clenched on his mug of gin.

"Good evening, my lord," Damon drawled. "May I join you?"

Lord Dearborne made a negligent gesture toward a chair. "Suit yourself."

"Oh, that would be difficult to do, since murder's punishable by death," Damon said easily, as he sat a bit away from the table. He leaned back and studied the young lord. "I spoke with Mr. Bishop, a caricaturist of some little note, you see. Very little note, actually. Yes, I see you *do* see. You're a little more pale now than you were when I came in. Would you like to open that window? No? Can't blame you, it overlooks an alley, and who knows what can crawl in? Or out? And I don't want you leaving just yet," Damon said abruptly, as he saw Dearborne tense.

Damon nodded. "See, Mr. Bishop, as he explained it to me, is a man with small talent and a big thirst. And some sense, I think, since he didn't want any trouble. But that's all he has, poor fool. So if he's offered money to draw a cartoon, and is given the idea for it besides, it's a windfall for him because he seldom sells any on his own merit. No, I said, I wouldn't leave if I were you," Damon added as Dearborne started to rise.

"It was merely a jest," Dearborne said weakly, falling back into his chair.

"Was it? I didn't think so." Damon leaned back, too, and studied the ashen gentleman. "I won't let Gilly have at you again, though you deserve it. Because I don't want her to dirty her hands. And I won't challenge you to swords or pistols at dawn, either. I don't want to have to leave the country just now. Yes, I'm *very* good at both. But I know some gentlemen who might want to challenge you because they're noblemen and men of fashion, and such gentlemen do such things. I'm not a nobleman, and don't care much for fashion. But I wouldn't want the scandal to touch the lady in question. Nor do I want to break her heart. She values her friends and I have this uneasy feeling that, good as they are at dueling, you'll find a way to cheat. Cheats do. So, what's to do, do you think?"

"I promise I—"

"I don't believe you," Damon said quietly, and reached inside his jacket.

Dearborne sprang to his feet, overturning his mug. He had a big, silver-handled knife in his hand in the next moment. "Threaten me, will you?" he snarled, brandishing the wicked blade at Damon.

"No," Damon said gently.

Drum and Rafe sprang from their corner, but had no time to get far. Because in that second Damon kicked out and rose in a blur of speed. The table was overturned and Damon had his hand over Dearborne's wrist before Rafe and Drum could take a step. A second later, and the knife clattered to the tabletop as Dearborne yelped with pain.

"Interesting," Damon said, picking up the knife and looking at it. Dearborne shrank back, nursing his wrist in his other hand, his eyes wide with terror. "But too big," Damon commented, turning it in his hand, "all show and no use. Too cumbersome, no balance to it. Good for making cutlets, not threats." He flung the knife at the overturned tabletop, and it sunk in deep. When Dearborne looked at Damon again, he gasped. Because in one smooth motion, Damon had reached down to his boot and came up with another knife in his hand. A thin, glinting one that looked like it could cut through shadows.

Damon smiled. "Now this is a good one. A skinner's knife, the riverman's wife, his weapon and friend. They have such a lot of interesting uses for these." He looked up at the far wall. A grimy poster hung there, another caricature, a memento of some long-dead scandal. Damon stared at it, nodded to himself, and with a lightning movement, sent the long knife spinning through the air to land on the poster with a sound that seemed to shiver through the suddenly spell-bound room.

The barkeep bustled over and stared at the print and the knife still vibrating there. He grinned. "There's a mug of mother's milk on me, m'lord! Y'got the fellow right on 'is nose, see if y'dint!"

Damon smiled. "Very nice, but that's not what I was after. Look and tell me, is there perhaps something else at the end of my knife? Something that was bothering me?"

The barkeep bent and stared, then whistled, low. He gingerly plucked the knife from the wall and held it up for all to see. "B'Gawd!" he cried. "Jest look! 'E's got 'isself a fly! Aye, the point went through it clean as can be, and the wings is still flutterin'!"

The patrons laughed, but then grew still. Dearborne had plucked his knife out of the tabletop, and stood crouched, facing Damon. "Brag, will you? Fool! There's better uses for a knife than a show, I think! As you'll soon see!"

"Really?" Damon said in bored tones. He reached

toward his vest pocket, and Dearborne's eyes followed the move. In another instant Damon surged forward so fast, neither Drum and Rafe had time to blink. Dearborne's big knife rose—and fell to the floor. Dearborne gave out another high-pitched cry of pain as Damon grabbed his downthrust arm and wrenched it aside with a snap, brought his knee up to the man's gut, then spun around, using an elbow to slap Dearborne's head back.

"It was over before you began," Damon said scornfully, as Dearborne writhed at his feet, gripping his broken arm, trying to bring his knees up to ease his stomach and get his breath back. Damon bent to speak to him. His voice was deadly dark and cold. "Now listen. I'll say it once, and only that. You are leaving England, for your health. Because you'll be dead if you don't. Remember, I'm not a nobleman. I don't think or fight like one. I always have a knife with me, and a pistol in my pocket. And I'm as good with one as with the other—better with a garrote. So, if you stay you'll have to remember to keep out of the streets, don't step into shadows, stay home in the dark—or even on a cloudy day. But if you leave England? You can come home in three years. No less. Not one day less. And then you are never to be in the same room as me, or mine, ever again. Am I understood? Am I?"

Dearborne nodded, and then more frantically. "Good," Damon said, rising. "No hard feelings, eh?"

He collected his knife from the barkeep and left the tavern to the sound of cheering.

"Nice work," Drum commented, falling into step with him.

"I thought you'd disapprove," Damon said, unsurprised, "seeing as what I did was not remotely noble. I brawled again, my lord."

"I'm lucky you didn't when you fought with me," Drum mused.

"Too right," Rafe commented, and when Drum glanced at him, wisely fell still.

"Oh, but when I fought with you, I did it by your rules," Damon said. "You're as good as I am on that kind of playing field."

"Thank you," Drum said, "but I'd like to know some of your tricks, too. I have some myself. I had to in the sort of work Rafe and I did in the past—during the war. But you've got some new ones, even for us."

"New world, new rules," Damon said with a shrug, never slowing as he walked along the dark, deserted street. "Times are changing, and they're changing there fastest. They don't dance around things as much as we do. It's startling at first, but then refreshing. What do you think of my match with Gilly, by the way?" he asked suddenly. "I feel you don't approve."

Rafe was startled; his head came up. Drum merely laughed. "Refreshing, indeed. Well, now you've brought it up—I don't. Approve, that is. It was gallant of you to offer for her. But I'm not convinced it will be best for her. Expedience seldom is."

Damon nodded, his face expressionless, as they passed under a flickering torchlight in front of a house. "I see. But can you see better for her? In the near future? Or in any future, for that matter?"

Now Drum was quiet as they stalked down the long street. When he spoke, his voice was wondering. "I think I begin to. More, I cannot say—now."

"I see," Damon said. Rafe's silence was one of shock.

"I go this way now," Damon said, as they came to a wide and lively avenue where he saw waiting hackney coaches. "Good night, my lords. It's been . . . edifying."

"Good night, Ryder," Drum said. "It has been that, indeed."

"What did you mean?" Rafe asked furiously, as soon as Damon was out of earshot. "I've put up with a lot from you, Drum, for more years than I can remember. But that lad is pluck to the bone. And he can offer her what you cannot. What you've never wanted to, by God, if it comes to that!"

"Have I not?" Drum mused. "Do I not? Shall I not?"

"No games! This is *Gilly* we're talking about, and her future. You have a name to consider. Despite all her charm, she has none."

"But the lad is right," Drum said thoughtfully. "Time and the world is changing. And a woman takes her name from her husband. Speaking of time, I need some. Leave off. Ryder and I understand each other very well, even if you don't. Even if I don't understand myself, not entirely, not yet. . . ."

"Bedamned to you, then," Rafe said and stalked away.

Drum was used to his temper, and only shrugged. He called a hackney, and was so busy thinking, he didn't miss company on his way home.

But when Damon got to his rented rooms a few moments later that night, he sank to a chair and put his head in his hands. And echoed Rafe, all unknowing.

"Damn, damn, *damn*," he said.

# 15

"What a risk you took! And without me? Of course I heard about it!" Gilly raged the next afternoon when Damon came to take her for their afternoon ride. "Did you think I wouldn't?"

Damon wasn't sure how much she'd heard. It tempered his answer. He watched her pacing and had to hide his smiles. She was all in yellow and white today, looking ethereal as a sunbeam. Lord, but she broke his heart! So fragile, so lovely, and pacing like a dock worker, grumping and waving her arms.

"He told me everything!"

"Did he?" Damon asked carefully.

"You can read the letter yourself," she said, thrusting a piece of paper at him, "I just got it an hour ago."

Damon took the paper and ran his eyes down it.

*My dear Miss Giles,*

*Please accept my most profound apology for a jest gone bad. Suffice it to say that your fiancé pointed out the error of my ways to me, and made me see that as penance, it would be best if I left the country for a while. Mr. Ryder suggests three years. I feel I must concur, indeed, I see no other course open to me. I will leave on the first fair tide, as soon as I am well enough to walk again. Which, I hasten to assure you and Mr. Ryder, will be within the week, or so my physician says.*

*Pray accept apologies and congratulations on your forthcoming marriage. You are well suited, I believe.*

*Yrs,*

*Dearborne.*

"I don't see what he's telling you except that he's sorry," Damon lied.

She didn't honor that with an answer. She just glowered at him with those tigress eyes.

"I convinced him the only way he understood," Damon admitted. "It was my honor as well as yours, Gilly."

"Oh, I suppose," she said, her shoulders slumping. "It's just that I was surprised. Drum said he'd take care of it. I wish I could have."

"But you wouldn't have left enough of him to leave on the next fair tide," Damon said with a tilted smile.

"True," she said, looking downcast. Then she looked up eagerly. "Tell me. How did you do it? Don't skint on details, if you please."

So Damon sat, and told his lady the particulars of

his encounter with Lord Dearborne. She hung on every word as if a few hundred years had rolled away and he was telling her about a dragon he'd slain for her. When he was done, she sighed with pleasure.

"Good," she said, "very good. And not just for me, mind. It may make him think harder next time he tries to hurt someone he thinks is weaker than he is."

Damon's smile faded. "I don't think so," he said, his drawl suddenly pronounced. "It's my experience that events don't alter people for the better or worse. People don't change from the outside. It's their realizing they have to change that does it. Dearborne's a bad lot, like his father and brother before him, or so everyone says. So I think it would take more than a beating or banishment to change a mind like that. In his case, nothing less than a holy annunciation would do it. He'll probably amuse himself being cruel wherever he goes. People have to change themselves because they themselves feel the need for it. It can't be imposed."

He looked troubled as he added, "On that score . . . Gilly, I have to talk with you. About just that kind of thing. About people, and changes of attitudes and minds . . . and things."

"What kind of things? What's the matter?"

"Everything, I think. And since I know my family's mousing around here, and it's of a personal nature, do you think we can take this talk outside? It's something we have to discuss alone. Are you willing to come with me now, so we can?"

"Yes, of course," she said, as her chest grew tight. She didn't say another word as she flung her shawl over her shoulders and went to the door with him.

They both knew that was odd. But she felt guilty and was hoping she was wrong about what he had to say. And he knew what she was thinking.

He waited until they got to the park. He left his carriage with a willing lad and, taking Gilly's hand, began to walk with her on the path that went round the Serpentine, where he'd met her with the Earl of Drummond the other day.

Gilly recognized the locale. It was too specific a place to take her just to walk and talk to be simply a coincidence. Her heart began to pick up its beat. She knew what he was going to talk about, and didn't dare speak.

Everything was different today. It wasn't gloriously sunny as it had been then. There were clouds, and a new autumnal chill in the air made the strollers walk more briskly. The leaves on the trees had grown dull edges, as if summer had given notice to quit.

"I was going to wait," Damon finally said quietly, when they'd paced along the path a few minutes. "I was going to keep watching. But I can't anymore. Gilly, I wasn't cut out to play the fool. I don't like myself this way. I've learned a lot about myself these past days. There are a lot of things not to like. I didn't know I was so full of myself, for example. I didn't know I was so complacent, so vain. I've always been loved, I once joked it made me a monster. But in truth, it may have." He paused for a moment, nodded, and then said in gentler tones, "We've come to know each other too well to lie to each other. Or at least, I've come to respect you too much to try."

He saw how white she'd grown, and it hurt him. But

now he knew he was doing the right thing. If he wasn't, she'd be jumping up and down, telling him to get on with what he meant, asking questions, blazing with curiosity. Instead, she paced meek and downcast at his side. The right thing to do was just about killing him, so he went on quickly.

"I offered for you. You accepted me. After you got to know me, I thought your only objection was that you felt your early life and experiences made you somehow ineligible. I thought I was well on the way to showing you that wasn't true. I even thought you'd learned to . . . But that doesn't matter. Gilly, the plain truth is I suspect your heart's otherwise engaged. And I cannot, *will not* try to fight that. There's that vanity I was just telling you about." He laughed, hollowly. "That—and the fact that I just don't think it's possible. You can win someone's love. But I don't think anyone can ever win someone's love *away* from someone they already love."

He hated to remember her this way, looking guilty and reserved and uncomfortable with him. But he knew what he had to say. He glanced down to see how she was taking it. She had her head bent. Her hair had been pinned up and the nape of her neck was exposed, pink and downy as a baby's crown. He longed to place his lips there and inhale the sweet fragrance of her sun-warmed skin and hair. He'd done that once. He knew he never would again, now. His heart was heavy, his voice dropped low.

"And so," he sighed, the harder because she still didn't speak, "let's have an end to it, then. Autumn's coming fast. Our wedding day's bearing down on us, we'll be run over if we don't get out of the way. The sooner we unhitch ourselves from this engagement, the better it will be for everyone. I can't pretend. And for all your charms, Gilly, you're a terrible actress. Honesty has its penalties," he tried to joke. But neither of them could laugh.

"So!" he said. "I can't send the notice to the *Times*. It would be considered vile of me. Gentlemen don't end engagements. And I'm not ending it, Gilly. I'm just letting you go your way, freeing you of a decision I can tell has been getting harder for you to live with every day. You can put in the announcement, or rather, you can have Sinclair do it. I'd like it if you could tell him the truth. But if you can't?" He shrugged. "That's all right, too. You can just say you changed your mind. They adore you. And it's your prerogative. I may be a monster of vanity but anyone can understand a woman may feel she was mistaken in the man she chose.

"Marriage is a long time," he said, "and I don't want to pass that time knowing I can never be what you want. I thought I could love you very well, and for all time. But it seems I was wrong. I find I'm not that gallant. I'm too human. I didn't realize love's a thing that changes, too, and your not being able to return my affection would surely poison my regard for you in time. No. Enough dancing around it. *Affection* is such a feeble word—like *regard*," he said with distaste. "It's become more than that on my part. I will not live with less from you. I cannot. I'm learning all kinds of bad things about myself, Gilly. Let me do something good, and release you before my hopes and your dreams bump heads and destroy even our friendship."

But now he saw her hand was pressed to her mouth.

He heard a strangled sob. He looked around. The path was busy with foot traffic, as always on a fine afternoon. Without speaking, he led her from it, onto the grass, past some shrubbery, into a clearing behind the trees. Then he stood looking at her while she fought for composure. It tore at his heart. Other women could weep like taps, and wail like banshees, but not his Gilly. She was trying to be manly about it, and it was almost tearing them both apart. But he also knew it was important to her, so he only stood by and handed her his handkerchief when she began scrabbling in her recticule for one.

"Gilly, Gilly," he asked softly, "was I wrong?"

"No," she said, and couldn't go on, and blew her nose, and tried again. "Damon," she said and choked, shook her head, and paused, while his heart just about broke for her. And himself. "Damon," she finally said. "Oh my, oh my. Look at me. About to blubber like a girl."

"But you aren't far from being one and there's nothing wrong with that," he said. "It's one of the advantages of your sex. Tears are a powerful weapon. They can stop any man in his tracks better than a knife or a gun. And wound him as much, too. They make a fellow feel guilty even if he hasn't done a thing, because he's always been warned not to make his sisters cry," he invented rapidly, giving her time to recover, trying to tease her from her tears even as he lauded them.

She lifted her head. Her eyes were pink, her nose was, too. She looked terrible, and he wanted to kiss her more than he wanted to breathe.

But he knew he couldn't, so he only went on, "And

since tears are a thing a man's not allowed to use, whenever a woman cries a fellow feels such a mixture of helplessness, guilt, and envy that he's immobilized. Then you can kill him at your leisure. Now, what we ought to have unleashed on Napoleon was a legion of weeping women—Oh, better now?"

"Oh Damon!" she wailed, and came into his arms and frankly wept.

He held her, his cheek against her hair, his arms 'round her tight. He tried to hold her close as a lover but with the passion of a brother, and could only curse himself and fate and the Earl of Drummond, and all in silence as she cried herself out.

"I don't want you to leave me," she finally muttered.

He saw how her hand was clenched in his jacket, and brought his lips to her forehead. It was warm and damp, and again his heart cracked. "But you don't want to marry me," he said gently, with a spurt of rising hope he tried to tamp down, "do you?"

"I don't know what I want!" she said in a blaze of anguish, lifting her tearstained face to his. She clutched the front of his jacket hard, as though trying to force him to understand. "I don't know, Damon, there's the *damnedest* thing of it. I—I am all at sixes and sevens. I had a dream, all my life, well, at least, since I came to the Sinclairs. But then because I couldn't have it, I was lucky enough to dream another, and it came out almost as well, maybe better. But nothing's like your first dream, is it? I don't know," she wailed, "too many of my dreams are coming true!"

He rocked her in his arms. "Oh Gilly, I can't say. I'm the last person to know about something like that. I've always been lucky enough to have all my dreams come true—until now. And see how badly I'm taking it? Don't vex yourself. I understand."

"That makes it worse," she wept. "Don't you see?"

"I do, and it makes it worse for me, too," he laughed, though it cost him to do it. "But I can't go on if you're not sure. You understand that?"

She nodded.

"I don't want to be a good loser or a good sport, either," he said, on a broken laugh. "I'd feel much better right now if I could go out and kill my rival. Bedamned to my wonderful upbringing, I'm being so nice about it, I could bawl myself!"

She giggled, and wept, and finally drew away from him. He let her go instantly.

"Your mama will be pleased, at least," she sniffled.

"No. You'll be surprised. But on that score . . . do you want to tell them or shall I?" She looked horrified. "All right, I'll do it," he sighed. "But I have to know. When? I mean, when will you return to the Sinclairs? When will they let the world know? I think it will be better for everyone if the thing's done quickly and quietly." *Like the best murders*, he thought bleakly.

"Not yet," she said. "Give me a little more time? Can we pretend for just another few days? I can't get used to it myself yet. It's wrong of me, I know. I don't want to give you up. But I don't want to . . ."

"Give up the dream. Yes, I know." He hesitated, and then spoke his mind to her, because he had to. "But there is one thing I don't know if you've thought through. I see—who better?—his obvious interest in you." He didn't have to say who he meant, she cast her eyes down as he said it. "And it doesn't look like a man's interest in a child. Or in a good friend, either. That's true. But there is the possibility he might not be more than *interested*. Have you thought of that? I'm not saying he'd ever trifle with you. But he hasn't actually come out and declared anything for you to pin your hopes on yet, has he?"

She shook her head.

"I thought not," he said. "You've burned your bridges behind you, haven't you? How like you. Oh Gilly, what am I to do with you? I mean that literally. Because I . . ." He tipped her chin up and looked into her eyes, his own fathoms sad. "I am yet enough of a man to have to tell you that even if he isn't interested—I couldn't be anymore. Not if I wanted to respect myself, or have you respect me. You do see?"

She nodded, swallowing hard. "Aye, and I don't blame you."

"But I'll always stand as your friend."

"I couldn't ask more," she said, and knew she lied. But she didn't know what more she could ask.

They still stood close, and she remembered his firm clasp, the security of his embrace, the excitement that was always to be found in his arms. She still felt a tug of attraction for him—more than that. She took another step backward, before she could think about it too much. He was, after all, as handsome as he was good, and good with his hands and that well-shaped mouth of his, and that warm strong body. . . .

But see what she'd done? He was kind, handsome, bright, and entirely worthy. And she'd just given him up for all time, for the sake of a dream that might not fade when she finally awoke. Or might, as it always had.

Lord Wycoff left the dance quietly and made his way swiftly and silently out the long doors to the garden, with an ease and stealth born of years of practice. He saw the woman who had requested his presence standing alone in the moonlight, the way he always wanted to meet her. But he didn't take her in his arms immediately, as he would any other lady who asked for such a clandestine rendezvous. He knew her too well—and not well enough. He was a man of discernment and patience but he had to search for the right thing to say to please her and yet not break the mood he hoped she was in.

"Don't ask," Gilly said, before he could say a word.

"Of course not," he said, resting his hands on the marble rim of the balcony she stood beside, gazing out into the darkened garden as she was doing. He couldn't see anything but the shapes of trees there. But he stared as though there was something to look at, too. "It's perfectly natural for an engaged woman not to speak to her fiancé all night," he commented mildly, "or even look at him. And for her not to spare a glance for her oldest friend so recently returned from abroad, either. And then for her to steal out of a party and into the garden—after giving the most vile reprobate in all of society enough signals to follow her to call in all the ships at sea."

"Not the most vile," she muttered. "There's worse."

"Thank you," he said pleasantly.

"Me," she said.

He looked at her. "I didn't think it was possible for you to interest me more tonight. You're a constant surprise. Am I to hope you've decided to throw over young Ryder, cast off the elegant earl, and run off with me?"

"No. But I wanted to talk with you. You make perfect sense when you care to."

"God!" he said, genuinely surprised. "Never say I've grown old and toothless enough to become the perfect confidante! I think it may be time for me to stir up some hemlock for myself."

"I like you, too," she said, as though she hadn't heard him. "And I've no one else who seems to care for me. At least, not here in London, right now. Well, no, that's not true either. There are other people who care for me. But I care too much for them to discuss this with them."

"Thank you," he said, turning his dark face toward the garden again. "Keep flattering me like that, and I'll use a pistol as well as the hemlock. What are you talking about, my dear?"

"You gave me advice the other night. I think I was thinking about it more than I knew. I acted on it. Now I don't know what to do."

There was a silence. He gave her a sidewise glance. She wore a pearl gray gown with a silver overskirt, and with her fair hair, she seemed to glow like a downed star in the deep night. But he knew the spirit that made her glow brighter. His hands clenched on the balcony rail and he felt his pulse beat heavy, like the thrum of the crickets in the late summer night. He couldn't touch her. It occurred to him that his courtship of her had worked. But not in the way it usually did with the females he pursued. Because she was not a usual female. He'd won perhaps more than the use of the body he'd lusted for. He'd won her trust. There was enough gallantry left in his soul for him not to abuse that trust, much as he wanted to. And he very much wanted to.

"What do you want to do?" he asked, keeping his voice level.

"I don't know," she said dully. "Not anymore. I think . . . do you know what I most want to do now?"

"I confess I have absolutely no idea," he said honestly.

"I'd like to sail away to the New World, like Damon did," she said dreamily. "Only not like he did, but in the way the others he told me about did. Right now, I'd like to take a new name and a new life for myself, too. He said there are people who leave here and leave their whole lives behind, even the memories of it. They go places like Boston, Philadelphia, Delaware. Such exotic names . . . places like here, only different. And they shed their lives and make themselves whatever they choose there. It's such a big place with so little history, it doesn't matter—a peddler's widow can say she was a lady. And who can know? No one cares, either, because so few had their beginnings there and everyone wants to start over again. They take you as you say you are there."

Her voice was earnest and full of longing as she tried to explain. "Damon says a wastrel lord can claim he got bored with his estates, and no one will know he lost them. A climbing boy can even say he was apprentice to a silversmith, if he wants to learn that trade.

Anything can be tried—you fail only if you can't carry it off. Why, a married man can be single, a woman with a bastard child can say she's a respectable widow. A bondsman can work back his freedom and become a master himself, and a gentleman, too, in time. The truth's an ocean away, and there's a whole new continent to lose themselves in. Anyone with the fare in his pocket to get there can say he's anything he can pretends to be. And *be* that. They go and become something fresh and clean and new, and no one knows or cares what they were—no more than they themselves ever look back."

They were both still then, each thinking about new beginnings with no memories to stain them.

He cleared his throat. "Yes, I see the lure. But I thought you had more than memories here."

"Oh, I do!" she cried in vexation. She lowered her voice. "That's it. I've got too many people here I love to ever leave. Well, only a handful, after all. Still, it would be like leaving my heart behind. But I've made such a muddle."

"It's over with Ryder?"

She nodded. "But no one's to know yet, please. He saw what I was looking at. I can't blame him."

"No," he said thoughtfully. "Nor can I. Good for him. Not that you're not a tempting bit, my dear. But if he's to remain a man, he had to, I think. But there's still our friend, the earl, isn't there?"

"Is there?" she asked sadly.

"Oho. I see. But you puzzle me. Why dream about shedding everything and starting anew? You're free now, aren't you? You ought to be excited at the chance you have now. Or is it only remorse for what you've done to the fellow you've given up that's turning you so glum?"

"I don't know. I don't understand myself anymore. That's hard for me. I don't know how much you *really* know about me," she said, turning to him at last, "but I had to fend for myself a long time before I came to live with the Sinclairs. I depend on me." She chuckled, then grew grave again. "More than most girls did, or do. I don't like being unsure. It's dangerous for someone like me."

"I see. So, you're not joking. You see me as a wise counselor? Gad! I am in my dotage unmanned. I am to assume the role of a trusted, older, wiser friend, am I? A departure for me, to be sure. And a challenge, certainly," he murmured as though to himself. "Well, why not? In spite of the obvious loss of *my* possibilities with you. But I do like you, you fascinate me. You know what I am, but you don't flirt or flutter—instead you confide in me." He grew very still. "You don't compare me with your father?" he asked with a kind of stunned horror.

"No, never." She heard the undertone in his voice and was touched and amused, and honest. "Never. As I said, I like you, and if things were different . . . who knows? But they're not, and I need advice, and you're clever, and honest—if it doesn't conflict with your plans. And since I'm being honest with you. . . ."

"You're astonishing," he said, "but I wouldn't value you so much were you not." He shrugged. "So be it. You want me as a friend. A new role, indeed. Well, I've suffered losses before. I'll try to leave you with a good memory, like any good lover. Even if I'm not to be one." He glanced at her again. She didn't move, or speak. He sighed. "Right. I'll cut line. There's nothing more pathetic than a man who can't take a resounding *no*. I'll try to give you what you want. You want advice? From someone who's made so many mistakes he'd need to go to *three* new worlds to forget them? Fine. I'll try to fulfill the role you've assigned me."

All laughter left his voice. "You say it's dangerous for someone like you not to be sure of yourself? Listen. *Life* is dangerous, my dear. You want to live safely? Find yourself a cloister and pray to God on bended knee every day that you meet Him quickly, because there's no safety in any human endeavor. Not if you put your heart in it, and it's no good—trust me—if you don't.

"The thing is, my dear Miss Giles, that you ought do nothing without all your heart, soul, brain, and body. And your love. But few of us get to do that. So if you compromise, make the best compromise you can. One thing I will say, even if you don't like it. If you really loved, you'd never be standing here with me right now. Yes, look astonished. It's true."

He let her think about that for a minute. When he spoke again the familiar curling smile was in his voice again. "No, a woman in love would never have to ask anyone what to do. Her only problem would be how to do it fastest. That gives hope for me, you see. But then, with all I know and don't know, I never give up hope. Think on, my dear. If you choose to leave the two of them to the devil, you can always come to the devil himself. I'll always take you, believe me."

He bobbed his head in a mock bow and left her to the night. He stepped back into the house through the tall doors. Once his eyes adjusted to the light, he looked for the two men she'd been avoiding all night. They were both right there, looking at him.

The Earl of Drummond was standing by the doors, staring at him, murder in his startlingly bright blue eyes. Damon Ryder stood opposite the earl on the other side of the tall windowed doors, his usually pleasant face dark, his expression intent and troubled. Both men were near enough to the window to see out to the balcony. Both had obviously been watching. Neither man stepped nearer.

He shrugged to himself. Might as well play out his role, then, Lord Wycoff thought with sardonic humor, and if he was, then to the hilt. He took out his snuff-box, tapped it, and strolled over to Drum first.

"The dog in the manger," he said pleasantly, "at least had a claim on the bone. You would do well to remember that."

Drum stared at him in surprise and growing comprehension.

Then Wycoff sauntered over to Damon. "Dignity is all very well," he said gently, "but a man ought to fight for what he wants, if indeed, he really wants it. Or needs it."

As Damon began to frown, Wycoff bowed and added, "Good evening," took a pinch of snuff, and walked to the door.

And so it was a good evening, in a strange fashion, Lord Wycoff thought as he waited for a footman to bring him his hat. It hadn't been good for him in the usual way. He had no one to go home with to help him through the rest of what he now knew would be a very long night. But even so, he was smiling as he left the party. Because though nothing had been found, all was not lost.

# 16

Gilly paced her room. She'd burned her bridges, all right. And now the smoke was choking her. It had been quiet in the Sinclairs' townhouse lately, quiet for a full two days after the party where she'd talked with Wycoff. Too quiet for her conscience and her growing anxiety. Yesterday had been strange enough; Damon hadn't come to call again. Today was odder still. A quiet morning had given way to a long silent afternoon. Damon's father had gone to his club, his mama and sisters didn't offer to take her shopping with them, and none of his numerous relatives had come around either. Gilly didn't always go out with the family, and the family didn't visit every day. But today she felt guilty and beleaguered and saw insult in every silence and felt a slight in the simplest words. It was so still in the house, she hadn't seen enough of anyone today to hear a single word spoken to her.

She paced. Neither Damon or Drum had come to call.

Damon's absence she could understand. But she regretted it. She missed him. It was more than his beautiful smile or his jokes. More than his laughter and the warmth of his company. More, even, than his kisses—though she squirmed in the night remembering them. But she was used to talking with him every morning about the previous night, sharing observations and telling him snippets of conversations, and planning the coming night. She wanted to know what he was thinking . . . and didn't. She had so many stories to tell him . . . and nothing to say at all.

Drum couldn't know what she and Damon had decided. But the man had eyes and ears. He had to have seen the distance between her and Damon the other night. *So then*, a little voice told her, *he had. And so then, so what?* Nothing had changed. Except her entire future.

Time to go back to Bridget and Ewen, then; they would be sad, but they'd understand. *Past time to go back*, she told herself, fighting tears. *A regular watering pot you've become*, she berated herself. *See what happens once you let your defenses down? Never again!* she promised herself savagely.

She wanted to go home. She missed Betsy fiercely, too, now. True, Betsy would be bitterly disappointed in her sister's loss of the fairy tale husband she thought she'd almost netted. But she could talk her around it. Betsy believed in fairy tales and happy endings. She'd tell Betsy she'd have that right enough, because she'd be happy enough with peace now. It was true. She wanted nothing more than to settle down into her old ways, the way she'd lived before she'd come to London to find a husband—and found more than she'd bargained for in every way.

She'd write the letter to Bridget and Ewen tonight. She'd ask their permission to come home straight away. When she got it, she'd tell Damon's parents, and then she'd be gone, and it would be over, and she'd never talk to Drum again—or at least not until she got over this ridiculous sense of hurt and betrayal. She was the one who'd betrayed herself, after all. All he'd done was to look at her and say a few things that were a bit warmer than he used to do. *Because he thought he could—you dunce!* she scolded herself. Because he felt safe, sure she was promised to another man. *Any dog may bark if it knows it's held on a stout leash. You were the fool, my girl, and don't you forget it.*

It was likely she'd never see, much less talk, to Damon again. Except he was a gentlemen through and through. He'd come to say good-bye at least . . .

A person could pace only so far and think black thoughts only so long until she had to get away from herself. Gilly picked up her chin, went out her door, and hurtled down the stair, looking for someone, anyone to talk with.

"Gillian!" Damon's mother cried the moment after Gilly got to the bottom of the staircase. She must have been laying in wait, Gilly thought with a start. "I haven't wanted to disturb you," Elizabeth Ryder said, "but—there's something I wanted to talk with you about. Could you come into the front parlor with me?"

Gilly hesitated, guilty and wary. But no one knew what she and Damon had decided. He said he wouldn't tell anyone yet. Whatever else in her life had changed, she'd bet her life on his absolute honesty with her. She nodded, and uneasily followed Elizabeth Ryder into the parlor by the front door.

"Now we can talk, and I think we must," Elizabeth said, closing the door behind them. She motioned Gilly to a seat beside her on a sofa. "My dear," she said as Gilly sat gingerly. "Oh, I'm not good at this . . . everyone in our family is straightforward to the point of insult, and I so do not wish to do that! The point is I want you to know you don't have to hide in your room anymore. I ought to have done something long before this, I thought things would work out—but nothing works out by itself, does it? When Damon first mentioned it, I laughed it off. I can't any longer, that's why I acted. Your happiness is more important to me than an uncomfortable moment—or two, as it happened to be."

"*Damon told you*?" Gilly gasped, appalled.

"Yes, and you mustn't be angry with him," Elizabeth said, taking Gilly's hand, "How could he not, when he saw how unhappy the situation made you? He was thinking of your happiness, which is only right. So I acted, and I want you to know you won't be having *that* problem again."

Gilly remembered to close her mouth only when she realized she had to breathe in.

"You needn't look *so* surprised," Damon's mother said. "Oh, I might as well be totally honest, I want nothing to cloud our friendship. When Damon first told me about marrying you, I'd my doubts. Well, I didn't know you or your people, and it was so sudden. We hadn't seen him in years, and then here he was with a bride-to-be, a girl we'd never heard of before, not in his letters, and not of our acquaintance."

Elizabeth patted Gilly's limp hand. "But as I came to know you I came to see no one else would do so nicely. No one. I should have trusted him," she said with a fond smile. "More than that, I saw you're perfect for him. We've grown so very fond of you . . . and Damon? I've never seen him so content. His restlessness sent him away from us, you know. Even after I heard he was coming home, I worried he'd soon be gone again, and become one of those world travelers, always roaming, never settling down. But now all he wants to do is make a home with you. So comforting.

"So!" she said with decision. "I talked it over with my husband and my daughters, and some of my sons— we're a close-knit group—and they all agreed with Damon! How sorry I hadn't seen what was right under my nose."

"The thing of it is . . ." Gilly said unhappily, trying to find the right words. She didn't understand everything, especially about how the lady could be so pleased with Damon wanting her and the fact that she'd broken off with him at the same time. That didn't matter. She had to try to explain herself now that the news was out. "I never meant to make anyone unhappy but—"

"I should say not!" Elizabeth exclaimed. "Don't bother your head about it a moment. You're more sinned against than sinning. So. It's done. She's gone! She left this morning. I made up a story about how her sister missed her, and I don't know that she didn't see through it, but it's all for everyone's good in the end."

Gilly closed her mouth.

"Yes, I sent Felicity away because, to tell the truth with no bark on it, I always knew she liked to meddle. But I vow I never saw she had such a malicious streak. Annabelle, poor dear, told me Felicity was the one who wrote to her, urging her to come to London, encouraging her to the point of making the poor thing travel all the way here to 'rescue' Damon from your clutches! She said when she saw you and Damon she was appalled at what she'd believed. Well, at least your friend Lord Dalton seems struck with Annabelle, and maybe something good will come of it, in time. And it will take time, because she was so set on Damon. . . . But if you love someone, you only want what's best for them, no matter the cost to yourself. Annabelle has a good soul, as Felicity decidedly has not. I'm glad I've seen it at last."

She pressed Gilly's hand. "And so I wanted you to know you've nothing more to fear from her. You may be comfortable again, and I'm sorry you had a moment of trouble. She's gone to Devon and we won't have to see her until the wedding. And then, only briefly. Now you don't have to hide in your room anymore, and I can send word to Damon that he can return. Because I'm sure that's why he's stayed away. He must have been *so* annoyed with me."

"Oh, I'm sure not," Gilly breathed faintly, wondering how anyone could feel so good and so bad at the same time, wishing she could hide her face—so she wouldn't have to look at herself again. And wondering how soon she could get her answer from Bridget, make a clean breast of it, and slink home.

*Two days*, Drum thought restlessly, gazing out the window of his club, his long fingers constantly tapping on the arm of the deep chair he sat in. It was the only thing about him that moved. He'd been sitting that way for hours today, and most of the day before. It was an effort. He was a man of action. But he was afraid if he stirred at all, he'd go charging off, and he wasn't ready. When would he be? he wondered. Two days of thinking and brooding, and nothing to show for it. But he had to be sure. That might take two years, he thought gloomily. But what was he to do? His heart said go to her now. His body urged him to go to her yesterday. But his mind held tight rein on both.

So he sat, and thought, and twitched, but didn't move. That was how Rafe found him an hour later.

Rafe sat down without invitation and looked at him. "Two days in the same chair," he commented. "You'll grow into it. Time to pick up and move out."

"Indeed?" Drum said. "To where? We've no more enemies but ourselves now, Rafe. We won the war, remember? And the way we won, I remind you, was by thinking before we acted. Fools rush in. If you don't want to become an angel, you don't. You know that as well as I do."

"But the war's over, you just said so."

"Yes. Now it's not my life that's at risk, only the rest of it."

"Ah," Rafe said, and nodded his fiery head. "Thought so. It's Gilly. Saw the way you've been looking at her lately, and I was shocked, I can tell you. Wasn't going to mention it if I could avoid it, but I can't, can I? I don't blame you. She's grown up to be a fine woman, and you're only a man after all. But she's promised to the lad. Nice fellow, too. Carries himself well and has a head on him. She's not your concern anymore. Let it be."

"Since you're so observant, have you seen the way she's been looking at me?"

Rafe fell still. Drum knew why. It wasn't their way to talk about their women. At last, not good women. But the redheaded ex-soldier had been his friend so long, and his ally so often when they'd worked together in life-threatening schemes for their country, that it felt as though he was talking to himself now. He had to think things through, be rational, systematic, ignore his passions and add things up like a mincing, dry-witted, bloodless clerk. Rafe could help him do that. He'd done it before, when it was their lives, the future of their country, or their countrymen at stake.

He was an intensely private man, but Rafe was like his second self. He felt he might only safely act one way or the other after talking it out with someone he trusted, trying to see all aspects of the matter. Even though he yearned to forget everything he knew about safety and prudence and fly to her now. Because shock had unsettled him, making him doubt his own wisdom. The shock of seeing Gilly come to such a radiant womanhood. The shock of realizing how much he wanted his hands on her.

"Well, I grant she has had her eyes on you," Rafe offered, "but then she always did, you know."

"I know. But then she was a girl."

"Was a woman, strictly speaking," Rafe argued.

"She wasn't a woman until Ryder got hold of her," Drum said, and winced, because it was true and the only other thing that was bothering him. He wasn't sure he'd have seen her transformation to womanhood if he hadn't seen her through the eyes of another man.

"Well, there you are. That should settle it," Rafe said, sitting back.

"Should, but doesn't. She wouldn't be looking at me that way if it did. And if you'll note, she has not been looking at Ryder—at all."

"Not with you in the room, no," Rafe said, troubled.

"Not with me in the room, no," Drum echoed with satisfaction.

"Nothing wrong with Ryder," Rafe said sadly. "Everything right, in fact. I'd be proud to own him as a friend."

"Yes, I would be, too. If matters were different. They're not."

"He's everything a female could want in a man, too," Rafe argued. "He's got money, family, and he's sound to boot."

"I know, I tested him, remember?"

"And it's clear he's mad for her."

"Who wouldn't be?" Drum said bitterly.

"But he's mad enough to *offer* for her," Rafe said quietly.

"Ah," Drum said, closing his eyes.

*Marriage*? That was the sticking point. Gilly Giles was the most unusual female he'd ever met, and he'd known many in his work and play. He was of an age to marry, but had never felt the need. The women he wanted in his bed were the only sort who could sport with him there—women of experience, who knew the game whether they were in it for amusement or pay. He didn't trifle with innocents. And though he knew Gilly's sad history—she had confided it to him long ago to show him how strong she was in the days when that meant something to her—she was an innocent in all the ways that mattered. In fact, when she gave herself, it would be a more profound thing for her than for most virgins in their marriage beds. Because she'd have to come further to give herself—and her trust—to a man. He knew that.

"Remember what a sight she was when we met?" Drum asked softly, his eyes closed, seeing her clearly again as he'd seen her then. "Scruffy—no, *filthy*, thin as a rail, swaggering, rough and ready. I never guessed she was anything but what she purported to be."

"Aye," Rafe said fondly, "she had me going to."

"Ewen knew. But she fooled me. I thought that taming such a hoyden would be impossible. But we made her into a passable girl, didn't we? And then a mannerly, literate girl. But while we were gone, she finally become a woman. And what a job of work she made of it! Who could have guessed?

"But look at her," Drum said with a quizzical smile playing on his lips at the thought. "Maybe just because of her strange experiences, she has the best of man and boy and girl and woman mingled in that delightful body now. Grace and valor, allure and honor? Where can you find that in a woman? A rollicking sense of humor and the compassion to temper it. A strong, well-informed mind and the body of a courtesan? Virtue and experience. A vixen and a boon companion. Everything a man could want in a woman, and never expect to find. The bard could have said it: 'Aye. Here was a Gilly, when comes such another?'"

Rafe looked at his friend, saw the longing in his face, and the tension in his body, even though he appeared to be at ease. But Rafe knew him too well. "You feel that way, and you're just sitting here?"

"My family," Drum said in a low voice, as though to himself. "My *name*. My father." He shuddered. "With all she has, Rafe, you know very well what she has not. A name. A family. A background, for God's sake! It's not like olden days when after a man rescued a damsel from the dragon, he simply took her to wife. Life is not a bedtime story. I have responsibilities. To my family. But by God, to myself, too! Which is stronger, I wonder? That's what keeps me pinned here as time ticks away, bringing us closer to her wedding day—to him."

He opened his eyes. They were startlingly blue, filled with anger and pain. "Did you know that rake, Wycoff, accused me of being a 'dog in the manger' the other night?" He laughed bitterly. "That was what started me thinking seriously, at last. He saw it, and God knows who else has. Well, if anyone can see how it is with us, I'd better have my ducks in a row before I see her again, hadn't I? But a dog in the manger, indeed! I have a claim on that 'bone,' thank you. She's mine, and always has been. You know it, Rafe. If I ask her to cast off Ryder, she will!"

He waved a hand at whatever his friend was going to say. "Yes, I know. Cockscomb. But I'm not. I know exactly what I see in the mirror each day. Nothing to set women's hearts aflame. But nothing to disgust them, either. Ryder may be a masterpiece of manly graces. But I do well enough for myself and have always done."

"Gilly doesn't care about looks," Rafe said, troubled. "You know her better than that."

"I know. And he's good-natured and less cynical and kind to his mother, too. But I have an advantage. I know her. And she knows me."

"Knows you? Good God! Like saying Wellington is a soldier! She's hero-worshipped you since the day you met. We all know that. It was almost a joke. Except none of us dared make it to Gilly." Rafe smiled. But then he sat forward, his expression serious. "Fish or cut line, Drum. You're not cut out to be a cad. If you want her, be damned to the world and take her. Or leave her. It's not fair otherwise. It can't go on like this. For her or you—or poor Ryder. Because the lad's got eyes in his head. And if you keep shilly-shallying, letting her know you're interested but hanging back, what about when she does wed him? What sort of marriage would it be with him knowing what she was yearning for before she wed him? Not to mention him wondering what she might be dreaming about while her head's on the same pillow as his? Not fair."

Drum raised an eyebrow. "That's the longest speech I've ever heard from you. I don't know whether to applaud or knock you down."

"Try it," Rafe said casually.

"No, you're right. Time isn't giving me an answer. But it is time for one." He uncoiled his long body and rose to his feet.

"Where are you going? Want company?"

It was astonishing how that long craggy face could light with amusement. Drum gave his friend the kind of smile that made men follow him into danger, and women gladly step into it with him. "I'm not sure where I'm off to, and thanks for the offer, but I'm best off by myself. Because I'm poor company even for myself. Thank you, old friend. I'm going to go walk until I find an answer my heart and my mind can agree on. I will, if it kills me."

He stretched his lanky body, turned, and then suddenly turned back. "Rafe? What would you do?"

"Damned if I know. I hope I never have such a question."

Drum nodded. "Good enough. Thank you."

He couldn't just *not* see her again, Damon thought as he paced his room. It had been two days. If he didn't call on her soon his family would drive themselves and Gilly mad with their speculation. She had to make a clean break, and his disappearing before it was time wouldn't help. But the damnedest thing was that his damnable pride was holding him back, he thought, and sank to a chair.

It was wrong to abandon her in the lion's den. *But she's abandoned you*, a sly voice said. Yes, the Earl of Drummond was her idol, and yes, she'd known him for years, and yes to all the rationalizations he'd made on her behalf. The truth was that he'd offered her everything he was and had, and she'd thrown him over at the mere appearance of another man. He simply hadn't measured up. It hurt like an ache in his every bone.

His hands fisted until they were white-knuckled. The sudden tension made him glance down at them. *Fight for her*, that damned Wycoff had suggested? If he 'wanted her, and needed her'? But she wasn't a bone to be growled over by two dogs. She was a person with her own needs—and they clearly didn't include Damon Ryder.

He'd never asked for a woman's hand, so he'd never been hurt like this. But he'd wanted her from the minute he'd laid eyes on her—or rather from the moment she'd laid hands on another man, he thought, smiling in spite of himself, remembering his fierce, gentle, beautiful Gilly. He couldn't forget. Not her laughter, not her tears, not the taste of her lips, or the feeling of her close to him. Not her sad past or the dreams he'd had for her happy future. But he'd lost her, and he wanted her still, and yet there was nothing he could do.

Wycoff was wrong. A man couldn't fight for a woman who didn't want him. Or shouldn't. Because who would he be fighting, after all? Only her. She was the only impediment to his having her.

It would be one thing if he thought she was doing a ruinous thing. Then he'd fight to save her, if only from herself. But in this case? What could the Earl of Drummond offer her? Damon laughed aloud. A title, a fortune, a dream fulfilled. If he offered.

Damon scowled. Drummond hadn't asked for her hand, he'd have heard about it. Damon had been getting notes from his mother for the past two days. She was fretting about why he hadn't come back. She'd even tossed Felicity back to her sister, imagining it her fault. Well, it was an ill wind that blew no good.

Damon stood and looked out the window. The sun was already setting. The days weren't as long as they used to be—autumn was coming. And with it their wedding that was not to be. And Gilly was all alone in London, despite his relatives. Which is what she'd most feared. Whatever she'd decided, she didn't deserve to be deserted. She wasn't doing it to hurt him, after all. But she'd be hurting now.

He remembered how hard it had been for her to cry. How it had wrenched her rather than refreshing her, the way tears ought to. He couldn't make her do it again. If he had to hide his hurt, it would be better for his character, he supposed. It would definitely be better for her. That decided him.

He'd force himself to dine with her tonight, and every night until she left him. Even if it made him choke. Because he'd be swallowing his pride along with his dinner. And he realized that might be more than a man like him could swallow. But he would. So be it. No one had ever said it was easy being a man. Just ask Gilly, he thought, and smiled—though it hurt.

The moon was clearing the tallest rooftops when the carriage pulled up to the Sinclairs' townhouse. A long, lean gentleman stepped out and quickly took the short flight of steps to the front door. He raised the knocker and then pulled off his high beaver hat, showing sleek dark hair black as the spaces between the moon and the stars overhead. The flickering gaslight at the side of the door made his shadow blur and leap as he stood waiting, a slight smile playing on his lips.

The smile vanished as he heard a footfall behind

him. He spun around, a silver pistol already in his gloved hand. This was night in London, and he was always prepared for it. He pointed the nose of his pistol at the wide chest of the man now poised a step below him. A man who was already crouched, the blade in his hand reflecting the dancing gaslight, his expression unreadable in the capering shadows.

Drum relaxed, lowering his pistol. "Good evening, Mr. Ryder," he said coolly, pocketing the pistol. "Good thing there's a light here, or it might have been your last evening. You startled me. Unwise. Force of habit, you see. I expect I could have got off a shot before you used your blade."

Damon shrugged and sheathed the knife. It disappeared into an inner jacket pocket. "I suppose," he drawled, "but it would have been the last shot you ever fired."

The butler's face was very white as he stood frozen in the doorway, watching. He cleared his throat when he was sure all weapons were gone, saying in almost normal tones, "My lord. Mr. Ryder. Do come in."

Drum stepped in, Damon followed. Before they could finish handing their hats to a footman, Damon's mother and father came hurrying into the hall.

"Thank heavens!" Elizabeth Ryder said.

"Good thing you got our note so soon," her husband said with relief. "I was just about to go out myself."

"*That* you would not!" his wife said angrily, "because what use would you be? That is to say, where would you look? I let Alfred and Martin go, but what they can do, I don't know, because they don't know town ways, and are hardly town beaus. At least they're younger, and together. They'll likely drive in circles until they come home as it is. I sent for Damon and here he is. What luck the earl is here, too. If *he* doesn't know London, I don't know who does. Now I can rest easier."

"What note? What's the problem?" Damon asked anxiously.

Now his mother looked uncomfortable. His father made a sour face.

"There was a note delivered. Gillian read it," his father said, avoiding Damon's eyes, "and before the cat could lick her ear, she was calling for a carriage. Or so the servants say. We were out, and she was alone here, and said she couldn't wait. She said she'd explain all later. Then she went out into the evening, and that's the last anyone's seen of her. It was well over two hours past. We sent for you when we saw it was coming on to full night. And now it is."

Damon grew rigid. He turned his head and looked at Drum. But the earl was looking as shocked as he was.

"At least she took her maid with her," Damon's mother said. "So it's not as though she's alone."

"Where?" Damon demanded.

But now both his parents seemed to be having difficulty looking at him. "She didn't say," his mother said uneasily. "She left a hasty note, but it was only two lines."

"Who, then?" Damon chorused with Drum.

"Well, there it is," Elizabeth said helplessly.

"You don't know?" Damon asked, in shock.

"Worse," she said miserably.

"*Wycoff*," his father spat. But it sounded like a curse.

Damon echoed the word as though it was one. Drum stood arrested, a muscle working in his clenched jaw.

"She said it was urgent, and that she had to see him now," his mother said apologetically, holding out the brief, much-read note.

"No," Damon said, shaking his head as if shaking off a punch. "One thing I'd swear to. She'd never run away with him. It's not in her makeup, it isn't her style. She's impetuous, yes. But no giddy fool. If she wanted to go away with him," he told Drum bitterly, "at least, be sure she'd tell *you* chapter and verse before she did. She'd go to him if he summoned her, though. If she thought he needed her. God help her, she thought he was a friend. An amusing, if eccentric, friend. Damnation!" he said angrily, his eyes wild with light. "She thinks she's invincible. I blame myself, because I let her think it. She's strong-willed and clever and fast on her feet. But no match for a man bent on mischief!"

"But he's not a villain," Drum said carefully. "A faithless lover and a adulterer, of course. A rake, a reprobate, certainly. But not a villain."

"Then why send for her?"

"Perhaps he is in difficulties," Drum said thoughtfully.

"Certainly," Damon scoffed, his hands clenching. "A man of his age, rank, and reputation would definitely ask a beautiful, fragile young woman to come out into the night in London to help him if he was in trouble. Makes perfect sense. I will kill him. It doesn't matter if it's my right anymore. I'll do it if he's even *thinking* of hurting her."

"After me," Drum said, nodding. "Right, then. We'll go to his house first."

"And then?" Damon asked.

"Then, we'll see. Oh, Mr. Ryder," Drum told Damon's father as he went out the door. "Kindly send a note to my friend Rafe—Lord Dalton—at Steven's Hotel. He *will* stay there in spite of their table. Tell him what's happened. Tell him I need him."

"No—you won't need anyone else," they heard Damon mutter, as he went back down the front steps with the earl, "not if I find Wycoff first."

# 17

It was a cramped old inn, lopsided with age, squeezed in between many others on a bustling street opposite the crowded wharves. Even with the heavy, bottle glass windows shut and the shutters closed against the night, the stench of brine, garbage, and dead fish was pungent.

"Your nose can tell you the tide is obviously out," Lord Wycoff said with a slight smile, "but it will be in soon, and then I'll be gone. And so I'm glad you came in time."

Gilly stalked the room in agitation. "To think something I said could make you do such a rash thing," she said. "I never meant . . ."

"I know," he said gently, watching her light up the dim parlor like a little roving candle, her bright head down, a dark frown on her white brow as she prowled the private dining room he'd taken. It was all he could do to force himself to sit still and not take her in his arms. But it wasn't the time or place, and the time was not yet right.

"You were talking about your dreams," he explained. "That made me remember mine. I haven't enjoyed this life I've led, did you think I did? No, I indulged myself, that's never the same as enjoying oneself. I only did what a man of fashion in my position could in my situation. Cuckolded? Why then, I'd two choices. Retire to the countryside where I wouldn't be mocked or pitied. Or pay back, so it would appear it was my own choice."

He shrugged. "I was not cut out to be a recluse or a scholar. I chose town life. Sometimes, I admit, I was amused. Sometimes, I grant, I found pleasure. But it was always tainted. Sometimes—forgive me for speaking so broad to a young woman, I'm sure you'll understand it's only for reasons of clarity—but I admit there are times that tainting sexual matters make them better. Subterfuge and a whiff of danger can do wonders for the dullest affairs. I don't understand why dirt can enhance what should be the most beautiful of human encounters, but so it is, sometimes. But only sometimes, unless you're the sort of person who can only enjoy that kind of pleasure.

"It appears I am not," he said with another shrug. "I want better. My soul—and there are legions here in London who'd guffaw at the very idea of the existence of my poor, pathetic, tattered soul—yearns for more. The other night you gave me an inkling of how I might find it. I'm acting on it before my usual cynicism poisons the one pure idea I've had in a long, long while."

She wheeled around to face him. "But your children!"

"They've funds. I'll write. I do little more than that with them now. They're both in school, and have been for years. I've never allowed them to be contaminated by their parents, my dear."

"But to throw everything over! To leave England and start anew—with all you have here? It doesn't make sense!"

He looked at her with tenderness, appreciation, and muted lust. What other respectable female would have answered his impulsive summons at all, he wondered? What other would have come out into the night now, trusting him as a friend? No, he decided, it was no dishonor to himself that she was the only friend he wanted to speak with before he left. Because she was singular, and because he couldn't quite bear to give her up yet, or to leave off trying to secure her for himself.

"What am I giving up?" he asked. "Parties, gossip, easy lovers? I'm sure they have such in the New World, too. Faithless wives and friends, and lesser men and boys, all who avoid my eyes because they've had her and don't want me to know it? Now *that* might not be there for me. Exactly my point. I might find something new."

"And so you'll give up all?" she asked incredulously.

"No," he laughed. "I'm not such a fool. I'm going, for an extended stay. But I haven't decided to extend that quite to forever—yet. I'm leaving options open, as well as my mind. But I'm leaving behind the memories, the way you said those who go to America do. I'm taking my name and my money. I may discard the first, in time. I have an heir to carry it on in better fashion, after all. I may even leave the money behind, too, if I can find a way to make more. But only a fool burns his bridges entirely, and I'm never that."

She looked away, her face growing pink. He noted that with interest. "If I find better there, who knows what I'll do in time?" he said, angling his hip off the side of the table he'd been perched on, and strolling over to where she stood.

"Time and distance do astonishing things," he said, standing next to her, looking down at her, keeping his hands at his sides with effort. "Or so I've heard. And so you said. Gilly, do you want to come with me and try it for yourself?"

She startled, looking up at him in shock.

He smiled. "You said it's what you wished. I'm here to grant that wish if you like. You don't have to share my bed, and I regret you can't share my name. *This* name, at least," he added with emphasis, trying to judge the expression in those strange beautiful golden eyes of hers. "The ship leaves on the next tide, and time and tide wait for no man or woman. I offer a ticket to a new land, my hand in friendship, and limitless possibilities."

"*Oh*," she breathed, and he watched the light go in and out of her eyes. "Huh," she finally exclaimed, "how I wish I could! I've made such a mess. . . . But I have to stay and see it through. I can't run. You can," she said, those remarkable eyes searching his, "because what's done is done. But I haven't done anything yet..That's *my* problem."

Gilly paused, tilted her head, and regarded him closely, trying to see him with new eyes. She considered him for the first time as a man and not as a possible seducer, or an arbiter of fashion, or even as a friend. He was lean, immaculate, handsome in a severe sort of way, with smooth brown hair and darker, knowing eyes. Of middle years, she supposed, though she couldn't judge a man's age after he passed his thirtieth birthday. With a wonderful sense of humor, a strange sense of honor, and, she was sure, a care for her as a person and as a woman. She spoke honestly, as she always did.

"If I had already botched things completely, I think I'd go with you," she said, thinking aloud, "though it would nigh kill me to leave my Betsy. My sister means a lot to me, but in time, I suppose if I did well there she could follow me. I could make a home for her. I'd hate to leave Bridget and Ewen and the old earl. They're my family. But if I shamed them, I'd go without looking back, lest I shame them further. And as for Drum . . . and Rafe. And Damon!"

She shook her head. "The truth is, I feel like a ball in play—like when I was young, and we tossed one back and forth over the heads of the others, never knowing where it would land or who'd catch it. I can't leave until I know where I've landed."

"Gilly," he said softly, "you're not a plaything. Your destiny is in your own hands, and no others'."

She stared at him. And then slowly nodded. "Yes. I suppose I don't want to know that, do I?"

"Take one or the other, or damn them both and come with me," he said, casting his dice for the last time.

"And what if I've already lost one and don't know if the other would ever want me?"

"Then it's simpler still." When she didn't answer, but stood looking lost, he smiled, but with difficulty. "Well, there's an answer—of a sort. Enough for me, at least. I have to get my bags and go to the ship, time's passing too fast, as always. But hear me, Gilly Giles. My offer stands. I'll write and let you know my whereabouts. I'll always have room in my house and my heart for you. It was good of you to come to say good-bye. But it's time for that, I think."

"Good-bye, my lord," she said and stood on tiptoe and kissed his smooth, shaved cheek.

"No," he said, putting his hands on her shoulders.

She braced herself. He'd been a perfect gentleman. If he kissed her now, she couldn't protest. She'd come alone, in the night, and deserved what she got. But she wished he wouldn't.

He didn't. He bent his head and kissed her forehead, and took away his hands and stood back. "I amaze myself," he said. "But that was not my objection to your farewell. I just wondered if you would call me by my Christian name, just once."

"Oh, I would," she said in surprised relief, "if I knew it."

"Hathaway," he said.

"Good-bye, then, Hathaway," she said, and blinked against the tears that prickled her eyes. "Such a lovely name. And such a nice man you are, you know? I wish. . . ."

"No!" he said in mock alarm, putting up his hands. "Your wishes are powerful stuff, my dear Gilly. Enough. I'm going half way around the world on the force of one set of your wishes. Don't complicate my life more!"

She grinned as he smiled down at her. "Remember, I'm yours for the asking. But Gilly, though it's against my best interests, I'll repeat what I've told you before. If you've difficulty making the decision, as regards me or any other man, it's not the right decision. You'll know when you find him, and there will be no questions asked or answered when you do. It will just be. You'll see."

"And if I don't ever find him?"

"For a sensible chit, you do talk nonsense. Now I'm off to further shores. Good-bye, my dear. No. Good-bye, my dearest." He looked at her one last time and then bowed, opened the door, and left her.

*Drat Damon*, she thought, as she scrabbled in her pocket for a handkerchief. He'd taught her tears, and now she couldn't turn them off! But she refused to go out to the common room weeping like a ninny. She'd left her maidservant there and could imagine the gossip that would cause if the girl saw her bawling. Bad enough she'd gone haring off into the night when she'd got Wycoff's—*Hathaway's*—note asking to see her one last time before he left England, maybe forever. She didn't need to ruin his name any further. But her name, she thought on a damp sigh, was probably entirely blackened by now, what with her broken engagement—and now this!

She sniveled one last time and marched to the door. But before she could grasp the latch, it swung open, violently.

"I just met up with him in the hall," Drum said angrily, looming in the doorway, looking like a thundercloud, "and the only reason I didn't challenge him was because he said there's time if I hurry. So tell me. Quickly. What did he do to you?"

"Him? Oh, you mean Hathaway?"

"*Hathaway*!" Drum said wrathfully.

"Yes, that's his name. And he didn't do anything but make me cry like a baby because he's leaving England, and it might be for good."

"You love him?" Drum asked, astonished.

"No! I like him very well, though. But not like *that*. And what are you doing here, might I ask?" she asked defensively.

"What am I doing here? Have you run mad? You've pulled some rare stunts in your day, my girl, but *this*! Have I taught you nothing? You go in the night by yourself to meet with a renowned rake? The Ryders suspect the worst. As did I. Bad enough you've shocked his family—what will happen to that so brilliant match of yours? Your Catch will wriggle right off the hook after this!"

"No," she said, looking down at her feet, "I let him go already, you see."

It was suddenly quiet. She glanced up and saw the shock in his face. He ducked his head all the way and stepped into the room, closing the door behind him, all the while studying her. She refused to avoid the brilliance of his stark blue gaze.

"You've broken off with him?" he asked, frowning. "Because of . . . Wycoff?"

"No. Because of me. Lord Wycoff was leaving England. He only wanted to say good-bye. And I don't give this much for custom," she said, snapping her fingers under his nose, "if it comes to my friends. Fine friend I'd be letting him go away for years without so much as a fare-thee-well from me, just because of propriety!"

"Indeed," he said, studying her face, "I see. It's typical of you. But you ought to have waited for someone to accompany you."

"Yes. I should have done. But at least I took a maid-servant. I was in a tearing hurry. Well, you know how I am, Drum."

"Yes. At least, I think I do. Gilly, just why did you leave Ryder?"

But now she glanced away. That was answer enough for him. He smiled. "Gilly," he asked softly, "had it anything to do with me?"

"I don't know," she muttered. "There it is, I don't know."

"Gilly," he said with warning, tipping up her face with one long finger, "look at me, and answer. Was it because of me? Because if it was, then that's fine."

Her eyes flew to his. She held her breath.

He saw it. "Yes. I've been thinking, you see. About things I ought to have thought about long before. But how could I? I was gone so long, looking for rainbows when they were in my own backyard. Lovely Gilly, steadfast Gilly, clever little Gilly to have grown up behind my back like that."

She stared, scarcely breathing. *Lovely, indeed,* he thought with rising delight. Because he'd questioned his decision to the last, even when he'd come to this place and seen Wycoff going up the stair. But now, looking at her, all doubt fell away. How could a man doubt his heart when he looked into those amber eyes? At that piquant little face, that fine-grained skin, full plump mouth, that little tilted nose, those shapely little breasts? He'd liked her, admired her, been amused with her spirit and verve and courage for years. And now to find desire holding as firm a grip on his body as affection for her did on his heart? He knew what he'd decided was right. Not easy. And not what anyone— least of all himself—expected of him. But right.

"Lovely Gilly," he said with a smile. "Wilt thou marry me?"

It seemed to Gilly that her heart stopped. Her blood certainly did. She felt a buzzing in her ears, she blinked and stared, and wondered if she'd heard right.

*Drum*? Asking *her* that? And not as a jest, because he wasn't laughing, not even smiling anymore, but only looking at her lips like a lover?

His own lips were close. That unique face of his, not in the least handsome, but the intimate vision of her every dream, so dearly beloved, was so close. At last. So close she could see how smooth-shaven he was, how clear his skin. The lucent blue of his long eyes was hidden by his half-closed eyelids as he drew even closer. She could feel his sweet, soft breath, and she took in her own as she leaned toward him as though compelled. . . .

And stopped. And sniffed.

"Gilly?" he asked tentatively after a second's pause. Then chuckled. "Oh, I see. No, I'd only a few glasses of cognac. Not foxed, my dear, you know I can hold more than that."

"No," she said bemusedly, her nose wrinkling, "you're not."

"Then what is it? Don't care for my scent, my dear?"

"No, not that. It's fine, woodsy, like crushed ferns, isn't it?" she murmured absently. "Very nice." It was. But it wasn't right. It was very wrong, somehow. His fragrance surrounded her and stung her nose. Apart from odors she couldn't ignore, she'd never reacted so strongly to a man's scent before. But then, she seldom got so close. Not until Damon, and that was very different. His scent was subtle, clean, delicious, the essence of the man, and she delighted in breathing it in. This was sharp and clean, too, but alien to her, almost unpleasantly so.

She disregarded it. She opened her eyes. His mouth was very near. Such a good mouth, long, mobile, with narrow lips, very masculine. Nothing like the sublime perfection of Damon's beautifully shaped mouth, but nice. And coming closer now. He brushed her lips with his, tentatively, a question and a promise, a prelude to more, she knew. So too had Damon kissed her sometimes, a fleeting tingling touch that would soon linger and grow and kindle to fire. But it didn't. She considered the feelings Drum was evoking in her, concentrating hard. *Cool,* she thought, *and firm, but somehow wrong, embarrassing even, but not—not . . .*

And then she knew.

She drew back, amazed.

He frowned. "What is it, Gilly? Am I going too fast for you?"

"No. But Drum, this isn't right. It can't be. I love you."

His head snapped back. His nostrils flared. "Now I think you're the one who's overindulged."

"No," she said, caught between astonishment and glee, "I mean it. I see. Oh, my dear Drum, but I do. Don't you? I love you and always have done. Since we met. But I don't love you *like that!*" She shook her head, because it seemed the world had tilted and was just falling back into place and she had to keep her balance. But he looked confounded. Well, why not? So was she. She tried to explain to both of them.

"I love you so much, I always wanted to be like you—That's it!" She smiled in her excitement. "See, when we met I wasn't much of a girl and didn't want to be a woman. I wanted to be a man—just like you. Yes, true. You fascinated me. I wanted to wear my cravat like you, to walk like you, to be sardonic and clever and knowing like you. But since you wanted it, I tried to be a lady for you, too, because I loved you. But now I think on it, Drum, I never actually dreamed of loving you—*like that*. Well, but I never dreamed of loving anyone like that then, did I?" she murmured to herself.

"You were too elegant and distant for me to think of you as a brother," she said as she thought it. "Ewen was that. Too aloof and superior to be like a father. The old earl was that. You were too worldly-wise to be a friend—at least then. Rafe was that for me. So I simply worshipped you. I honestly adored you. It was all I could do. I was happy to. I've worshipped and desired—no, *longed* for you all these years. I dreamed of being your wife. It was my favorite dream, did you know? Of course not. I'd rather die than tell you. But in that dream I served you tea. We sat in the evenings discussing our day together. We played with our baby.

But, you know? I only just realized that I never once pictured us doing *that*."

"One wonders how we produced that baby then," he said coolly. But then his expression cleared. It gentled. "Oh, Gilly," he said sadly, "is it because of what happened to you—before we met? Believe me, that can be overcome with time and patience, with talking and living together. I do believe we can deal with it, if you trust me, and love me as you say you do."

"No. I know I can feel that for a man," she said honestly. "But not you, Drum. It felt wrong kissing you like that. I didn't feel anything but . . . self-conscious. And you know, Drum? I don't think you really love me like that either. You were just trying to make the best of a bad situation for me."

"No," he said. "But I'll let it go, for now. It may be all too new for you."

"No," she said over a rising lump in her throat, "not new. Just not what I wanted."

He looked at her more closely. "Wanted? You're talking about desire, are you? Oh, damnation! Is it Ryder? Don't tell me you let him go because of me? And now you've got rid of him, you changed your mind again?"

She didn't answer and looked away, her golden eyes filling with tears.

"Gilly," he said gently, "it's altogether possible you're not ready for any man just yet. And that's why you've done this."

Her eyes opened as she looked inward. Then they flew to his. "You're right. I wasn't ready," she said slowly. "I couldn't be, I don't think, no matter how many years passed, not with you there in my heart, overshadowing everything. And maybe, yes, maybe the reality I found before you came home was too powerful. The sensations, the loss of myself . . . maybe I preferred the dream because it was safer. Wycoff said love isn't safe. He was so right, and so are you. I'm the only one that's wrong. How wrong, you'll never know."

Drum smiled, though it was difficult. "You're young, you're entitled to be wrong. But it may also be that you don't really know what's right. Give it time. Give it, and me, and *you* time. And Ryder, too. If it's true, he'll forgive you. He's an easygoing lad. And if not, then you can use the time to grow up some more."

But now she straightened her shoulders. She took in a breath. "Well, at least you're human, that's good to see. Because you're wrong, Drum. He's so much more than 'an easygoing lad.' And why should he forgive me? He offered me everything he had and I let him know it wasn't enough. That doesn't seem very forgivable to me. And I am grown up. If you think on, you'll realize I have been, in some ways, most of my life. But I've only been a woman since I met him."

She shook her head. Her face was ashen, her lips white. "Let's go home now, I've made enough of a fool of myself tonight."

"Agreed," he said, and was instantly sorry for it. It seemed he didn't know how to deal with rejection. He was astonished by that.

"I can send you home," he said to change the subject, "but I have to wait here for Rafe and Ryder. Rafe took one end of this street, and I the other. Ryder went directly to find the captains of the ships waiting to weight anchor here. We went to Wycoff's house, you see, and shook the news out of his valet. All we knew is that he was going to an inn near these docks and then to a ship leaving on a midnight tide. There are a few scheduled. Rafe will eventually get here and has worked long enough with me to look for a message everywhere he goes. But Ryder won't know. When he doesn't find you, he'll keep looking. He'll be searching all night if we both leave."

She nodded and swallowed hard, suddenly uneasy. But not for the reasons he imagined. "I'll wait with you," she said stoically. "No—don't argue with me. I'm brave, but I've limits. Can you imagine me facing his family alone! After all this? No thank you. We can send the maid home to tell them all's well. But let's wait for him in the common room. I won't go home without him."

"Agreed," Drum said. "It's good to know there are limits to your valor, too." Though privately he thought it boded well for him that she feared facing her ex-fiancé's family more than seeing Damon Ryder himself.

They left the cramped private parlor, and Drum told Gilly to wait while he called for a hackney for the maid-servant. But she was at his side as he told the girl to tell everyone all was well, and they'd be home soon, too. Then he led Gilly into the common room. He instantly regretted it. This was the kind of place the young bucks looking for a thrill in the slums, like the ones he'd seen at the Bent Bough, would have given a year's allowance to visit, had they dared.

The ceiling was low, and smoke from pipes and

tallow candles turned the air as blue as the various conversations did. The wooden floor tilted from age and his boots stuck to it as he led Gilly to a stained and scarred table. The patrons were sailors and merchants on their way in or out of London, and the rough scruff of the land who made their livings from them.

That was why they all stopped talking to gape at Gilly. She was a treat to see in most places in London. Here, her fair, fresh beauty was no less than miraculous.

But she watched nothing but the door.

Drum watched her. He felt foolish about having agonized so long over a decision that had been rejected. He didn't feel less of a man or a lover, though. He was very confident about possessing both those qualifications, as well as about Gilly's eventual decision. She was young, so much younger than she appeared. Given time, they would see, he thought. But she was right about one thing. He couldn't see how Ryder would ever forgive her. Indeed, he himself didn't know how long it would take him to get over the vague feeling of insult because of the way she'd rejected him—and she'd tempered it by telling him she loved him even as she'd said no. He'd bet she hadn't told Ryder that. And he knew her longer than Ryder, and much better, too.

Still, Drum decided he'd leave her for a while after this night, at least long enough for her to build up the dream again. He'd return and she'd accept him. She'd be glad to. Then he'd have his family and friends to turn up sweet about their marriage, he thought wearily. And his father. He grimaced. Just as well, he told himself, that she needed time. So did he.

A confrontation nearby, at the foot of crooked steps near the tap, the ones that led to the upstairs rooms, made him look up. It was Rafe, with his teeth bared, facing down Wycoff, who'd obviously just come down. Wycoff carried a traveling bag and wore a bemused smile. He gestured toward Drum and Gilly. Rafe turned to see them and his face cleared. But then he looked puzzled and glanced over their heads—and stared and kept staring.

Drum turned to see what he was looking at. Gilly had risen; now she stood staring at the door. Because it had banged open and Damon Ryder stood there, silhouetted against the night. His eyes were wild, his clothing and hair in disarray. He glanced around the room frantically, until he saw Gilly. Then he froze.

Drum stood, too. He looked at Gilly and saw her face clearly. His heart sank. But his expectations did not. He thought feverishly. He couldn't see how Ryder could easily forgive such an insult. There'd be so much to thrash out, so many excuses, questions, and hurts to heal. Somewhere in that lengthy emotional process, someone would make a misstatement, surely someone would say something rash, and he'd get his chance. He discovered how important that was to him now, and wished he'd known it a year ago, an hour past, a moment before the door to the inn had burst open.

Damon stared at Gilly, no expression on his handsome face, though he was very pale.

Gilly looked at Damon, her heart in her eyes.

But she was Gilly. And there was no predicting her.

She broke and ran to Damon, stopping in front of him, staring up at him. They stood that way, silent, striking in their tension, in their youth and beauty, in their obvious mutual distress. Damon looked deep into her eyes, and his own grave ones lit with sudden joy. .

He grabbed her up into his arms as she flung her arms around his neck and pulled his head down to hers. They kissed, frantically, then slowly, and it seemed they'd never stop, because it seemed they no longer knew where they were, or cared.

"Simple," Lord Wycoff sighed near Drum's ear as they watched, and the tavern's denizens began to cheer. "So very simple when it's right, isn't it?"

# 18

"**Y**ou can come with me, you know," Lord Wycoff told Drum as they stood on the dock waiting for the long-boat to fetch him and carry him to his ship, waiting at anchor mid-Thames. The wind was picking up, the tide was sliding in, and the midnight waters made small sucking sounds as they lapped at the pilings under the wharf again. "There's an extra cabin, I paid for it. Ah, well, hopes springs eternal even in an old campaigner like myself. You wouldn't be quite what I was hoping for in a traveling companion. But one makes do."

"No, thank you," Drum said. "As you say, hope springs eternal."

"There is a time when it has to be redirected, though," Wycoff commented softly. "Just look at them."

Drum didn't have to. He'd seen. They stood together

nearby, waiting for Wycoff's longboat. The wind blew Gilly's cloak out around her and ruffled Damon's hair. He stood silently at her side, she came only to his chin, but they stood as one. They might have been holding hands, his arm might have been around her waist; it was too dark, they were too close together to see, but something in their stance suggested intimacy to Drum. Nothing else did. The rousing reception their embrace had got them in the tavern had embarrassed them, when they became aware of it. It had shocked Drum. It astonished him to see Gilly throwing herself at a man that way. It might have been reaction—it could have been emotion. He wouldn't believe otherwise. After all, they hadn't spoken a word since—or now he came to think of it, Drum realized—since they'd met this evening.

But now Drum narrowed his eyes. Something fundamental *had* changed. It was like an aura around them. He saw it and denied it. "Indeed," he asked acidly, "and what makes you so sure, so wise, so knowing?"

"Because I've spent the better part of my life watching, waiting, looking for signs of opportunity, for a wedge to slip myself into places where there is the smallest gap between a man and a woman," Wycoff said calmly. "There's none there. I know. I was very good at it. That's why I'm leaving now. I'm off to look for happiness now. Which is quite another thing entirely."

"I wish you luck then. I've just returned from abroad," Drum said. "I found no such thing there."

"You weren't looking. I will be. Ah, they come, and I

must go," Wycoff said, hearing the splash of oars. He lifted his traveling bag. "Do you know? With all I've done, I haven't felt such a rising excitement about anything in a long while as I do about this."

"I do wish you luck, in fact," Drum said. "You were a friend to her. I don't know why, but you played your part well. I thank you for it."

"You're welcome. She is extraordinary, isn't she? Too bad she isn't twins, or triplets. What a daunting thought!" Wycoff laughed. "Time for farewells, I think."

He shook hands with all the men, and then took Gilly's hand at the last, just before he stepped down into the waiting boat. She started to speak, coughed, and dabbed at her eyes. He smiled. "Tears for me? And not because of me. Thank you. You surprise me again, and I'm grateful for it. I come to see this is a good ending to our association now, better than any I've known for a long while, at any rate. You needn't say a thing. I know. Fare-thee-well, Gilly Giles. You've changed my life in ways I never anticipated. I'll not forget you. Remember, if you ever need me, I'll come right away, though I be a continent or a world away. Take care of her, gentlemen," he told the others abruptly. "Or you shall answer to me for it. Adieu."

It was silent on the dock as the longboat carrying Lord Wycoff slipped into the darkness, heading for the ship that would take him further.

"Well then," Drum said, "shall we return to Sinclair's house? Or adjourn to rehearse what we're going to say before we do?"

"I want to go home," Gilly said quietly. "I'll tell the truth. He sent for me to say good-bye, I came to bid him farewell. I won't apologize for it. I'm sorry I didn't execute it better, but not because of anything else. Well, I'm sorry I worried you, too. But I will tell the truth because there's nothing wrong in it."

"I suppose there won't be if we all agree there won't be," Drum said. "So. We've a carriage waiting." He gestured to the street.

Gilly didn't move. "I'd like to talk with Damon," she said. "Can we go separately, please?"

"Of course," Drum said, with a flourishing bow. But he was frowning as Gilly and Damon drove off together.

"It's needful," Rafe said, watching them go.

"I know," Drum said softly, "but I wish I knew exactly why."

Gilly spoke the moment the carriage door closed. She'd been thinking long and hard about it. She'd tell him about Wycoff's summons, and his offer. She'd even tell him about Drum's kiss and his offer. She had to tell him everything. She said she'd tell the truth, and so she would. It all came out at once. "I know you said you wouldn't ask for me again, but the thing is I'm asking *you* now, because I finally know what I . . ."

She couldn't go on.

Not when his lips were on hers, his tongue speaking for hers in silent communion, letting her answer only in ways that made any other kind of conversation impossible. And unnecessary.

He was warm and strong, *his* mouth, *his* skin, *his* breath, this was *her* Damon, she thought in exultation. Her friend, her lover. She ran her hands over his shoulders, inhaling the scent of him, so essential, so exactly right. She clung, burrowing into him until, with a laugh and a groan, he pulled back. An inch. But his arms remained around her.

"We joked about how I always asked if you were sure, but now I am," she said against his neck, catching her breath at last. "Wycoff offered what he could for me. Because he said that if I really loved, I wouldn't have any doubts, and so it might as well be him as any other man. Of course, I refused. I wouldn't have been running to him, only away from my problems. I don't run away. But then there was Drum, and he offered, too. Marriage! Can you *imagine*? I couldn't. But Wycoff was right! It came to me all of a sudden, whole and complete and so true I could weep."

Her hand tightened on his shirt front. "Drum started to . . . court me. But I stopped it. No, don't get angry, he didn't dishonor me in any way. In fact, I hurt him. I mean, I hurt his feelings. I wouldn't hit *him*," she said. "Well, I suppose he'd never give me cause. He is a friend, you see. But only that. That's what I found out! He asked what I always thought I wanted to hear, and he thought so, too. But it turned out that wasn't what I wanted. He was shocked. Well, I couldn't believe *my* surprise. But then I knew. I'd always loved him, you see, but as a friend. Oh, Damon, of course you saw."

She went on, not letting him speak. "But the thing is, I loved him so much I couldn't see it wasn't that kind of love. *That* kind of love is either there or it's not. It doesn't make sense, but it makes all the difference in the world. Wycoff said it. But it was you who taught me that. You woke me up, and then I let you walk away, and when I opened my eyes at last you weren't there.

N*ever* let me do that again, you hear? Never. And please, please forgive me."

Damon cupped her face in his two hands. His own face, in the light of the carriage lamp, was serious and still. And so very handsome and perfect and dear, she thought, watching his mouth so closely, it took a moment for the meaning of his words to reach her ears when he finally did speak, his voice low and filled with emotion.

"There's nothing to forgive. I should've fought for you, even if I had to fight you. That's what I was going to do tonight. I knew it as I left my rooms. I was going to try to convince you any way I could. You and I are a pair, Gilly. It can't have been my imagination. It's more than convenience and expedience for you. It has to be. And it's much more than desire and novelty for me. I want no one else. I never will. Drummond's a good man, I can't say a word against him. I won't. But I was going to tell you I'd be better for you, Gilly—if only because I love you more than my pride, or myself."

"Huh," she said with a wavering smile, "I can do better. I love you more than anything else!"

"Ha!" he said, grinning. "I love you more than that!"

"Ho—" she began, but he made a better argument. He lowered his head and told her how much he loved her without saying a word.

"Let's get married," Gilly finally said, as the carriage slowed in front of the Sinclairs' house.

"We certainly had better," he agreed.

They danced. The company and the bridal couple danced the autumn afternoon away. The lawns in front of the Sinclair estate were still green, though the leaves in the trees above were plum and russet and gold and came fluttering down with every mischievous breeze, like confetti falling to help liven the festivities.

When the sun spread gold across the western sky and the younger guests began to suck their thumbs or cry and the last barrels of wine were being breeched, the bridal couple looked at each other and thought about slipping away. That was impossible.

"Here it is! Isn't it grand?" Maximilian Sinclair shouted as the flower-bedecked bridal carriage appeared in the drive. "I helped! They said daisies, but I picked mead-owsweet, too, and they let me put it on. Which is good because the horses ate most of theirs, but it still looks fine, don't it? Won't you be proud of riding in it?"

"*Doesn't* it," his cousin Drummond corrected him absently, but he looked only at the happy couple.

But who didn't? The bride wore a cream-colored gown and had camellias twined in her flaxen hair. The groom was in biscuit and brown. They were an uncommonly handsome pair. They never stopped holding hands except when they had to dance with their guests, and then their gazes never parted. It made the older guests sigh and the younger ones blush, and sometimes the other way round, but few had ever seen a happier couple. If it made some of the guests sigh with less than happiness, it was a reflection of their own lacks, and that was the way of the world, and weddings in particular.

The guests began to cheer as the carriage stopped.

"So much for privacy," Damon grinned. He took his wife's hand and they went over to where their family and closest friends were waiting to say good-bye.

Gilly went up to the Earl of Kenton first, tried to speak, and had to stop. "Will I never stop bawling?" she asked, dashing away tears. "This rogue," she prodded her new husband, "taught me to give way to my emotions and now I can't stop blubbering!"

"You've got me awash, too," the old earl said, only half joking. "Lord! Think of it! Our little Gilly a bride, and a beautiful one. I gave you away, but I still can't believe it."

"That she didn't wear breeches?" Ewen joked.

"Well, it was a possibility," Gilly said flippantly, because farewells today were a jest or else they'd be a heartbreak. "Good-bye," she said, suddenly serious. "I know it's only for a little while, and I know it's only for the form of it because I'll be close by. But I *am* leaving here a wife, and I *will* be living apart from you from now on, however close I remain. I thought of such lovely speeches. But I just want to thank you, for everything. And tell you I love you."

"Yes, thank you," Damon said, taking Ewen's hand. "However fate led you to her, I'm grateful, because I couldn't have found her without you."

"Oh, no," a slender young girl with long golden hair protested. She looked at the couple and beamed with happiness, as she had all day. "You'd have found her anyway. It's clear you two are fated. And I'm so glad of it . . . Damon." Betsy wiped away a happy tear, and stood on tiptoe to kiss Damon's cheek.

"Thank you, Betsy," Damon said. "Now make your bows, Gilly. You've got everyone weeping and it's flooding the lawns. They'll have to plant rice instead of grass if you don't stop. What I'm starting to wonder is if they're tears of relief—at least on their part."

"Wretch," Gilly said, flashing him a grin. As Damon said good-bye to his parents, she kissed Max and Rafe and Drum, all with equal intensity. And if she gave Drum a smile of apology at the last, he was gentleman enough to return it. And man enough to turn before anyone saw what happened to his smile when she looked away again.

Because then she turned and hugged her sister, and hugged Bridget, because she knew she'd cry if she said one more word. She was weeping and laughing as she waved good-bye, rice and flowers covering the carriage like manna as it went down the drive.

"Where are they off to?" the Earl of Kenton asked his son.

"They didn't want a fuss, or any country revels to mar their wedding night, so I can't say. I offered them our place off the North Road, where we spent our honeymoon," Ewen Sinclair said, giving his wife's slim waist a secret hug, "but they refused."

"Well, each couple has to make their own luck," Bridget smiled, knowing the pair were going to Damon's house, The Lindens, an hour away. "Wherever they go they'll be happy."

"Doubtless," Drum said laconically.

"It's a good time for new starts," Rafe told the Lady Annabelle with hope in his voice.

"Indeed," she answered dully, with none.

They watched the carriage leave. Then the guests thanked their hosts, wished them well, and made their way home or to houses of friends and neighbors.

"Time for bed, my boy," Ewen said tenderly, watching his son bravely trying to blink himself awake. He picked him up. Then he, Bridget, and his father made their way toward the house.

"Well," Drum said, in bored tones he had to fight to maintain, "too early for bed and too full for dinner. I'm off to the inn to raise a few pints. And you?"

"I think I'll stay a while longer," Rafe said, glancing over to where the Lady Annabelle was talking with her parents.

"Too soon, I'd say, for any luck in that direction," Drum commented. "I'd say further you'd be best off coming with me now. I thinking of touring Greece. Winter's coming."

"Winter's almost here," Rafe said, "and you're leaving for the Continent? The seas will be rough, the roads may be snowbound. Folly. You'd be best off staying here. Sticking it out. Not running off. I heard Gilly and Ryder will be visiting with your Uncle Kenton in Italy soon. Don't want to look like you're following, do you?"

"I'm following no one. And I run from nothing," Drum said with sudden haughtiness.

"Good. Nor do I. I'll wait," Rafe said, watching the sad, dark Lady Annabelle, her head bent even lower as she got into her coach. "Things change. Got to give them time. No sense running. That's all right for Wycoff, because he'd got nothing to wait for. But I do."

"Do you? And I?"

"Listen, Drum, I'll say it the once and never again. She did the right thing. Listened to her heart. She loves you, but not the way a wife ought. You loved her, too, but not too well. You'd questions, even at the end. She never did—at the end, at least. That's how it has to be."

"Ah. And how did you come to be such an expert on love?"

Rafe looked his old friend in the eye. "By finally seeing it isn't something I can do anything about. It *is*. Or is not. And if it is, then a man knows it, right off. Give it time. You'll see. And then you'll understand me."

"I can't hope to grow that wise," Drum said with irony. "So, it's likely London this season for you? Can't budge you overseas, can I? Well, why not? I tell you what—I think I'll take apartments in town, too. Hotels are too confining, and I don't want to stay at the family townhouse—one never knows when my father will take up residence. So, what did you think of the Albany? It's exclusive, but is it worth the price?"

They strolled down the lawns, talking about fashionable addresses, as though one wasn't thinking about what he'd lost and the other of what he was determined to win. But then, they were old friends and had risked their lives for each other so many times that tampering with the truth to spare a friend pain was nothing to them. And ignoring the truth to save his face was no trouble at all.

Damon and Gilly couldn't stop talking about the ceremony, the guests, what had been said and what had not, all the way to The Lindens. But as they approached the front drive, their conversation faltered and died. The huge, mellowed, old stone house was bathed in the last of the setting sunlight, all its many windows glinting, the whole of it glowing like a great golden topaz in the red and gold autumnal setting of its private park. Damon stepped down and gave Gilly his hand, and she came quiet and tentative as sunlight in early April as she ventured down the steps and up to his front door.

He swept her up in his arms and carried her over the threshold, delighted at her squeal of pleased surprise. Then they greeted the beaming staff waiting for them there. The servants, knowing the nature of honeymoons, vanished in almost magical fashion. Damon and Gilly stood alone in the front hall, with all the house silent around them.

"Well, I expect you'll want to wash, and have a rest, it's been a long day," Damon said, and was shocked at how stupid he sounded, talking to her as if she were a guest and not the wife he'd dreamed, schemed, and maneuvered to finally bring home to this place to fill it with life and light and love.

"Yes," Gilly said. As she went up the long stair with him she thought of a dozen other bits of gossip to talk about, but the thought of where they were going made the subject seem foolish and unimportant. How *did* one start? She'd been thinking about it for days. And especially nights. He'd kissed her good night each evening. Sometimes they had more time to drive themselves to distraction, but not much since they'd gotten to the countryside, what with family and friends arriving and the wedding going forward.

*When*? she wondered. After dinner? After she'd had a wash and put on her best nightshift? Just before bed? With all she knew about what was coming, that was one thing she'd never thought to ask Bridget. She couldn't wait. But she didn't know how long she'd have to. How strange that he had become her best friend and ally, and yet this was something she couldn't ask. She was *not* missish, she told herself angrily. She just didn't want to put a foot wrong.

"It's lovely," she said, as he opened their bedchamber door. The bedchamber was done in tones of shell pink and celestial blue, with gold highlights everywhere, in the Adam style he knew she liked.

"I'm glad you think so," he said. Realizing how stilted that sounded, he tried for a warmer note. "And I'm glad you decided to share your bedchamber with me."

"Well, of course. Separate rooms aren't my idea of marriage. I'm not such a fashionable creature as that!" she said, trying to make a joke.

But neither laughed. They looked at each other in the sudden silence. They gazed at each other for a long moment. Then the corners of Damon's eyes crinkled, the edges of his mouth went up in a quirky smile. Gilly grinned. He opened his arms. She came into them.

"Oh, Gilly," he said into her hair, "how long I've waited."

"Oh, Damon," she sighed with absolute relief.

That was all they said. They soon were too busy to say another word. Their kisses were almost frantic at first. They slowed, becoming long, breathless, and deep. She didn't know when the kissing became caressing, too. Or when her gown slid off her shoulder, or when his lips left her shoulder to settle on her breast, and then, with such perfect understanding of her incomprehensible needs, attended to the longing in the other breast in the same incredible way.

Her hands bunched his shirt, stroked his shoulders, she tried to touch him and not just that which covered him. It was vital to be close to him as she could. He didn't need any of the clever plans he'd thought of to get her at her ease, out of her clothing, and into their bed. It simply happened. Her clothes were eased off in a moment.

Damon wasn't thinking of clothing, at least not his own. He never remembered getting his boots off, not with the way she kept running her hands up and down his back as he did. He didn't know how he got himself out of his shirt without strangling himself, but somehow he did. He ripped his breeches away, and then stopped. He looked at her widened eyes, remembering too late that it was afternoon, and this was not the way to attract a woman who was as good as a virgin but for that terror in her childhood.

"Oh my," she said, staring. "Oh, Damon!"

He checked, awkwardly, one knee raised to get into the high bed. Their easy familiarity had made him forget she was unfamiliar with this. Passion had made him forget. His pose now fortunately hid that excitement from her. But nothing was hidden from his eyes. She sat, staring—but naked and perfect, her breasts free to his eyes, knees drawn up, showing her shapely legs in a pose too innocently tempting to be deliberate. His arousal was sharp to the point of pain.

"What?" he asked, trying to slow his breathing and temper his heartbeat, perching on the side of the bed. He angled away from her, cursing himself, fearing that in his unseemly haste he'd loosed demons, reminding her of that hideous experience in her youth.

But she never made the connection because she'd never seen anything like him. She looked at the golden skin covering the wide chest that tapered to a flat abdomen, rippling with nothing but corded ridges of muscle. He didn't have much hair on his body and the afternoon light showed that firm form all in tints of gold and dusky pearl. Even his sex, which she'd glimpsed rising high and firm almost to his navel, was fitting, handsome and shapely, old ivory with a trace of rose at the end of that fascinating length. But that wasn't all she saw. And being Gilly, not all she admired.

She shook her head. "Lud! If I'd seen you like this before, I'd have made a scandal of myself and no mistake! You're a sight to see, Damon Ryder. No wonder you could level those four by yourself that time. You're in the pink of condition." She reached out, all unknowing, to touch his chest and let her hands feel what her eyes showed her was there.

He paused, then smiled, his heart soaring in relief. "Gilly, will you never stop surprising me?"

She drew her hand back and brought it self-consciously to cover her breasts. "Was that wrong? I mean, it's only that I liked to watch a mill, now and then, in the old days, for the sport of it, and to lay an easy bet if I could," she said, slipping into boxing cant. "And I just thought you stripped to great advantage."

"Oh, but I do. Great advantage," he said silkily, going to her, taking her hand, putting it on his racing heart. "Yours and mine. Come, I'll show you."

"Oh, *that*? I saw. In fact, I never saw the like!" she said in wonder, her eyes going down his body. At his start of surprise, she added, "No, s'truth, I never did.

Blokes don't wave *that* about the streets, I can tell you, without someone takes their head off for them if they do. It isn't decent, or safe. Privacy's a rich man's right. Why, if you undress at a time like this where I grew up, you could get your clothes stolen, and there's no place to keep your knife."

She paused, looking anxious, wondering why she was blathering so much, realizing she was nervous, wanting to get back into his arms, and suddenly not knowing the way. She could only go on. "No," she said, shaking her head, "when it comes to such play, I assure you, breeches stay on, skirts get lifted, not removed. The poor keep their clothes on. Should we?"

"Gilly . . ." he said, amused and distracted, "if you want, if you wish, we can, we will, but . . ."

"But I love the feel and look of you, and if that's what you do, oh Damon, oh, so I will do, and gladly!"

He laughed, then kissed her long and deep. Then at last when her body was softly dewed with anticipation and her lips on his and those below were both telling him it was time, it was past time, and he didn't think he could bear the tension and the need a moment longer, he raised himself up over her and looked down into her face. In that second he paused to appreciate what was to come—

And saw the exact moment she remembered. It was at the exact moment he was about to enter her. Her eyes darkened, he saw panic drive out the drowsy anticipation that had been there. He stopped. Because her feverish movements had stopped. She lay still beneath him, white and silken, her head thrown back, that glorious flaxen hair splayed on the pillow, her small high breasts pink tipped, pebbled. Her body was everything that demanded his sex. But she was Gilly, everything that demanded his control. He hung back, balanced on his arms, fighting for discipline. He gained it.

"Gilly, the best thing, I think," he managed to say, "is if we change places. That way you'll be the one to decide when. That way, you won't have to remember whatever happened then."

Because she had. They both knew it. When his shoulders crested over her, when his body blocked the light, she'd remembered those helpless moments when another male had been thus, when she'd lost the fight, and darkness, pain, and fury had conquered her spirit and body. But his words woke her. She stopped seeing the nightmare of her past and saw the present, and their future.

She saw Damon. He was paused, voice and muscles strained with the effort. His eyes were pained, his face stark with longing. He was the most handsome man she'd ever seen, more so now in his extremity of need, as though nature itself was trying to ensure he continue his line by making his features irresistible at this moment before he committed his body to a woman's.

This was as far from that dark day in her youth as she was now. Because this was Damon waiting for her, her husband, yearning for her as much as she was for him. The man who'd taught her to feel, to cry, and to love a man—when she'd always believed she couldn't love anything but an idol. There was no terror of a memory that could stand up to the joy of that. She put her arms round his neck and whispered urgently, "Damon. I want you. Now. This way. And that way. Any old way you choose. But now."

He relaxed, and smiled. He came to her, blotting out memories.

This was entirely right. His skin sliding against hers, the thrill and heat and sweetness of it, though he tasted salt to her tongue as her mouth touched his shoulder. Exactly right, just what she'd never known and had always missed. He didn't lead, she didn't follow. They shared, tenderly, then greedily.

But it wasn't easy for her. His entry stung, and burned. That alone shocked her. Her eyes flew to his.

He knew. "A long time, a very long time, it's been such a long time since, that's all," he gasped, as he tried to slow himself.

She relaxed. All was explained, everything was necessary. It was almost good, because it might have been the way it would have been had she been able to come to him whole, free of defeat. And then she stopped thinking, because he was with her and purring her praises as he moved her, and it was too delicious to think about.

He exulted. Gilly, his Gilly. His. He gave himself to her as he'd given himself in marriage to her, with no hope or desire of recall. She was too awed to share such wild ecstasy. But she was thrilled. She held on tightly as he came down hard, and cradled him as his body trembled in release after release. *She* gave him that, she thought in triumph. He'd given her even more. He'd given her back herself.

She leaned over him when he lay back exhausted on

the pillow. Her hair drifted like a glowing veil, enclosing them both in its radiance. "Damon! That was wonderful!" she crowed. "I felt so much! Nothing was wrong with me. You were grand. I felt I almost . . . Let's do it again!"

He reached up and touched her grin as a heartbreaking smile grew on his own face. "Gilly, my own true love. I can't—just yet. Not right after. . . . It takes a fellow time to recover. But thank you." He chuckled and pulled her down beside him and kissed her long and well. "Well," he said, after a moment, "maybe not so long after all. . . . We'll have to see. And feel. But there's something else we can do to take up the time until then. I can finish this for you now, even so, and then we'll see whether I can measure up after, shall we?"

"What *are* you talking about?" she giggled, as his hands drifted down over her.

He showed her. He tended to the faint, unsatisfied niggling itch she felt, the need that somehow still remained, even after all their closeness. He did it so sweetly, so gently, and with such concern for her embarrassment that she had none. She felt nothing but the dazzling pleasure he brought to her with his hands and mouth, and then at last with his encouraging words, until she gasped with astonished delight.

Her response fed his. He found he could take his own pleasure again and add to hers. She was very impressed.

"Damon?" she asked, much later. The sky had gone from old gold to a violet evening. She was propped on an elbow, smoothing her palm over his chest. He'd been almost drowsing, sinking into luxurious content, but something earnest in her voice made him pay attention, and he listened closely.

She dropped a kiss on his chin, and said, her voice so low that if she hadn't been that close he mightn't have heard her, "I'm so glad you forgave me."

He grinned, as one hand made slow circles on her silken back. "I thought we'd been through that. You'll regret saying this when we have our first real argument, you know."

"Be sure, I'll forget it then," she said impishly. "But truly, Damon, I am glad."

"Then I'm glad, though I don't see it. What was there to forgive?"

"You know," she said. "Don't pretend you forgot. I never will."

"Oh. Because you weren't sure you wanted me? I could never blame you for loving too well. I hoped you'd see what kind of love it was—in time. In time for us, I mean. I was going to devote myself to making sure of it. I'm only thankful you saved me the effort. I hope you're still convinced." But his voice sounded a bit unsure at the end, and he waited, his hand paused, for her answer.

She didn't seem to notice, she wriggled even closer to him and sighed. "You know," she said, her voice filled with wondering delight, "it would have been a tragedy if I'd settled for my dreams. I never knew there was something better. I'm so glad I didn't have all my dreams come true when I wanted them to. I'm so very grateful life made me wait for the reality of you."

"Oh, Gilly," he said tenderly, drawing her down beside him, "but I never dreamed there was such a wonderful reality as you."

"Then aren't we lucky to have had so little imagination and such bad luck?" she murmured mischievously.

She hadn't known a person could make love while laughing, she told him later when they'd done and the bright and newly risen moon showed them each other's smiling faces clear.

"We will make everything while laughing, my love," he promised her. "You'll see. Everything from now on."

He was a man of his word. And she was the woman who made it impossible for him not to keep it.